A Lethal Triangle of U.S./Soviet Intrigue!

→

ED SCHILLER. His crumbling personal life earned him a one-way ticket out of Washington. He landed in Moscow, where his one friend is Alexei Barsov, the outspoken Soviet dissident. Now his loyalty to Barsov is outstripped by a secret passion to possess Barsov's wife.

→

ALEXEI BARSOV. A huge, hard-drinking bear of a man, he was a reckless genius who made enemies of his closest friends. Now—betrayed, arrested, and beaten—not even glasnost can keep him out of the gulag. But it takes more than Siberia to destroy a man like Barsov.

→

LILA BARSOV. For years she lived in her husband's shadow, ignoring his sexual indiscretions and careless abuse. Torn between two men, now Lila will make a private decision that will affect the public balance of superpower politics—and control the lives of the . . .

→

COMRADES

COMRADES

MATTHEW HUNTER

Originally published in hardcover
under the title
Schiller

WARNER BOOKS

A Warner Communications Company

1

Ed Schiller rolled out of bed in the over-heated Moscow room, stood naked at the window, and thought about last night. It had been one hell of a party. The boys of the U.S. Embassy's Commercial and Cultural Sections had really laid on the liquor, as well as inviting the hacks. The Diplomatic girls had been well spiced and for once almost on offer. The best party Schiller had been to in twenty-three months of reporting on the Soviet Union. He wondered what Darleen would be thinking of the tow-haired foreign correspondent who had taken her back to his place. A lean man with skin still reddened from the long winter, whom she had seen standing between Jubal Martin, the obese Head of Cultural, and finicky little Rolfe Hatter of the London *Times*. Hatter had been watching the women with more than a hint of desire, like a widower. They were all pretty drunk, but Darleen had seemed available for a few hours.

"I hate Moscow. The same old hardship crowd getting stoned." Hatter had waved his hand at the first-floor room above the "store," above the working deck where the Section clerks answered queries in office hours. Jim Burrell of CBS grinned back and Schiller had said, "It's OK. It's a living." The walls were lined with color shots of the American Wonderland: sea at Cape Cod, sunset on the Grand Canyon.

"My God, look at that bird," Hatter had said. "There's a pair of legs."

Schiller felt the same twinge, a man with a broken marriage that was now two years behind him.

The girl had been Darleen Simpson, who was swimming his way and looked as if she might make it from the glint in her eyes. Cooped up in the Moscow hen-house, the Western enclave, drove you to drink or fornication sooner or later. It wasn't much fun being a single girl on the Diplomatic staff.

"Hi there," Schiller had said.

She had smiled at him, glittering with a certain hardness, a Boston superiority. In the old days, wrapped up in marriage with Nikky, he would not have been tempted, but the divorce had shaken him and he told himself he was free. Fucking Moscow with its caviar and vodka parties, compromising women, lousy décor.

"Hi?" She had been half-expectant.

"Remember we met once when I came over for a briefing from Jubal here?" Both of them knew that Jubal Martin, coasting towards retirement behind the paunch and the glasses, was Head of the CIA Station as well as Cultural.

"Sure . . ." Darleen had swayed on her feet, slick legs, stilettos, hard make-up; twenty-seven, he'd guessed.

They had begun to talk, about the East Coast, and his home base in Iowa before he made a living in New York, before the marriage, and in the end he had driven her back to his own place on Kalinin.

She had said that the apartment looked a pit. Imported paperbacks scattered over the floor and the bulbous blue and white TV perched on the refrigerator. Sixteen floors below them the eight-lane boulevard of Kalinin Prospekt had been almost empty as she stared down at the lights.

"I'm not staying," she'd announced.

"One more for the road?"

She shook her bleached hair. "No way. I've got to be going."

It hadn't worked out, both of them knew it, though it might have done; Darleen was almost crying.

"OK, OK, honey. Let's move."

Another one of those pointless Moscow evenings, ending

this time in disaster, as he had delivered her back to the Embassy compound.

Shit. All too soon it was morning. This place was a dump like she said, a kind of prison. What had he done to deserve it? Put five thousand miles between himself and Nicola back in New York for a start. The Big Apple: let her screw in her own juice. Peering down in the daylight through the nylon lace to the view that Darleen had watched, he tried to come to terms again with Soviet civilization, the egg-crates of patched cement, the wishbone streetlights that only worked on one side.

Bollock-naked, he heard the outside door opening and grabbed a towel from the debris of last night's fall-out, strewn over the floor. That was old Maria Galina Rysakova marching her string bags along the passage. The peasant head appeared, trolled up in a scarf, and her pumpkin face creased into a grin as she sniffed the Chanel No. 5 still lingering in the air.

"Oh ho. Good morning, Captain—" she had always assumed he had some military rank "—I smell ladies?"

Maria was talkative as she fastened her double pinafores and winked at him. "Am I allowed to go into the bedroom?"

"Don't kid yourself, Maria. No such luck. Just fix the place while I dress." He slapped her massive rump as she wheezed by, a widow, struggling to eke out a pension somewhere in the depths of the Krasnaya Presnya tenements, or so she said. You never knew in Moscow. Her fingers were stubby as chisels and hairs grew from moles on her chin. She picked up the empty glasses and examined one of Darleen's tissues.

"You know, Captain, you ought to find a woman."

"Don't start that again."

"I'm just saying."

"Well, don't. Maria, you're not a good socialist. You believe in romance."

"If you had a woman you wouldn't live in this mess."

It was because of one, he thought savagely, that he was there. He pushed her towards the kitchen. "You old babushka. I'm not ready to start all over again."

"You should. You should. Forget these American women. Find a nice Russian girl," she giggled.

He found a shirt and trousers and shut himself in the bedroom. No returns, no going back. The past three years were a desert. American women meant Nicola. Nikky. Until that day when he had gone home early to the condo in Georgetown, in rich and steamy Washington D.C. Christ, boy, had she blown it, humping it with that bastard Carlo one sweaty afternoon. He had tipped the bed over on top of them and collected Charlie from kindergarten. Had sent Bill Packett back for some gear and the books and the typewriter. Nikky had screamed at him then that they were all washed up, but Ed always remembered Charlie's little twisted face after the divorce when he said he was really going. As far away as Sly Sylvester, the veteran Foreign Editor of the *Post*, could safely put him, which was Moscow.

Ed Schiller pumped his muscles and finished dressing. Anybody looking in would have seen a tough-looking man, good physique, middle thirties, longish brown hair and weather-beaten skin. The kind of guy back home who took over the barbecue.

There was a knock on the door.

"Captain. Come out here. I show you something."

He tucked in his shirt, and found her pointing through the living-room window, the one with the view. Down there in the street was that peculiar emptiness: toy-sized traffic, a couple of Moskvich saloons and a Volga pick-up truck which had hemmed in a pale silver bus.

"Look," she said.

The men in one of the cars were counting little black figures off the bus and lining them up on the sidewalk in the sunshine. No day in the country for them. By the gesticulations he could imagine an argument. And then one of the figures began to run, hopelessly, down the road. Two plain-clothes men in hot pursuit like a pair of linebackers grounded him at thirty meters, rolling him against a hydrant. The figure jerked wildly. One hand clutched at the yellow hydrant and crawled up it like a crab as the unknown warrior tried to pull himself upright. In the process his hat, a student's blue cap, fell off and rolled in the road. Bright hair

streamed in the wind, and it was then Schiller realized that
the runner was a girl.

"Mother of saints, preserve us," Maria muttered.

"I thought that couldn't happen now."

"Ah," the old woman sighed. "That's what they like to
say. But you can see." She sucked her ancient teeth.

"Yes. I can see." The unknown girl had shaken him,
reminded him of someone in her hopeless attempt to escape.
The figure was surrounded by policemen who carried her
thrashing and shouting into one of the cars. There were still
those around who would not be silenced, unless by force,
and some of them he knew; it was one of the reasons he
stayed. The Barsovs for instance.

Alexei Sergevich Barsov was almost a great man. The first
evening they had shared, six months after Schiller had come
to Moscow, was long before Barsov's sacking from the
editorship of *Novy Mir*. In those days Barsov and his wife
Lila held a kind of open court—their tiny apartment close to
the Vernadskova Metro. A regular Saturday thrash for which
Lila provided platters of gherkins and tomatoes, vodka,
smoked fish and Georgian wine, more fish and cheesy
things, red wine and sliced sausage with haricot beans, seed
cake and, from somewhere, a good Hungarian brandy.
Barsov would sit in the corner, patriarchal, roaring away,
while Lila moved softly among the guests and cronies.
Schiller watched her slim figure in the dark red dress, and
saw the strength in her eyes as she fed Barsov. But even in
the Gorbachev era there was no room for a dissident to run a
literary magazine, and everyone knew it. Including Alexei
Sergevich Barsov, whose comedy on the end of Brezhnev,
The Ides of March, had yet to be staged in Russia, and who
had written so movingly of greed and cowardice and survival in *The Great Patriotic Shambles*, his epic on the war
only published in the West.

That first winter meeting at Barsov's apartment had been
followed by others as their friendship deepened. The parties
went on for hours, desultory, drunken conversations that he
only half understood, songs and recitations, echoing round

the tiny flat, a bar-room of smoke and alcohol. Always the girl was there.

"My Lila," Alexei Sergevich would shout, and clap his leathery hands as he pushed across a parcel someone had just walked in with. "Another bottle to crack."

Lila had smiled at the American, and asked, "Do you find us strange?"

"Different."

She had laughed, and her throat relaxed. "Because we are under threat?"

Schiller had pretended not to know what she meant, but everyone understood. The police were in the doorway below.

"You only worry," Barsov had said, "when you can't see the uniform."

Shortly afterwards when Schiller returned for another Saturday session to meet the poet Konstantin Olenev he noticed the policemen had gone, but in their place a thin young woman was waiting, pretending to play chess in the downstairs lobby. In her wrap-over threadbare coat and thick brown boots she might have been awaiting a boyfriend, but her eyes behind the owlish glasses did not stop watching.

"Oh her, she is my minder. My little KGB sparrow," Alexei Sergevich had said. "I even know her name: Elena Amalrik. I asked her."

After that the court seemed to thin around the dispossessed king, as Barsov denounced the limitations of Gorbachev's Russia, the everlasting consumer shortages and the secret police. But some still came, including Schiller, and he noticed how Lila's eyes followed Alexei Sergevich even when she entertained. She seemed curiously lacking in self-assurance about her own goodness, disguised by a certain wry humor in the flush of her cheeks. Her dark hair and gentle eyes were not what drew the American: it was the shape of her mouth, both full and unhappy. The face came alive when she smiled, or saw her son, Yuri, but otherwise was dragged down, as if in loving the great fool that was Alexei Sergevich she carried a private burden.

Schiller remembered her, soon after they first met, leaning across that crowded room towards him, dressed in trousers and a star-patterned blue sweater, cheap patched clothes from the market in Petrovka Street, which had been washed and bleached and molded to her figure. Barsov was talking to Martina Kuskova, the television producer who would later denounce him, both of them in the corner, soused with wine, but Lila's pale face had been inquisitive as a child's.

"Do you have a wife, Mr. Schiller? Or a woman?"

"Not at present."

"Then I am sorry for you. It is good to have a companion when you are in a strange country." She had glanced at Barsov, her eyes shining with pride, signalling, "This is my man, I love him." Trying to stop him getting drunk.

Barsov had raised a heavy head, domed, enormous, bleary-eyed, swearing about censorship. Someone had smashed a glass, a red wine stained the lace cloth.

"I will see them in hell, these fleas on my back." He had focused on Schiller, somewhere across the room. "Put that in your paper, instead of your stupid anecdotes about sugar beet farmers." Martina Kuskova had giggled and blown the bear a kiss.

Schiller had written it up, the watching and the persecution, quoting Barsov in his next column. That was when the authorities had moved in, deciding they had had enough, and Alexei Sergevich Barsov had found the office locked against him.

Six months ago, Lila Barsov had telephoned Schiller and suggested they met, outside on the street. It was an odd assignment, typical of the city where few meetings went unobserved and few indoor places were safe. It had been bitterly cold as he walked down one side of the dreary road between the apartment blocks and she had emerged on the other. She waved to him gaily, her oval face almost girlish under the trim fur hat, and he crossed over.

"The pigs have wrecked our flat."

Ed Schiller had begun to apologize, fearful that she would blame him for Barsov's sacking, but Lila had cut him short, and thrust her hand through his arm.

"Don't worry," she said.

"Christ almighty. What bastards. I'm so sorry for you."

"There is no need." She had smiled, fleetingly tired.

"Alexei Sergevich expected it. They came when we were out and took his manuscripts. We want you to write about that too, in your paper."

Schiller had looked at the slim girl by his side and seen the strength of a lioness. Not the kind of sexual therapy that his ex-wife had practiced, first on him and then on Carlo, but something less fathomable.

"What will you do?"

She had smiled once more. "Alexei Sergevich has the books in his head. He will write them again: maybe we publish outside Russia."

"Like *The Ides of March* on Broadway?"

"Exactly so." Her boots were down at heel and her braided leather coat was scruffy, but she was beautiful. Women like that, he felt, did not need clothes to make them look desirable.

He had tried to comfort her: "Surely the times are changing? Sakharov is back in Moscow. Yuri Orlov is free. Irina Ratushinskaya has been allowed to leave." Then he had sown the seed. "Why not Alexei Sergevich as well?"

The way she had looked at him made him feel there was no hope. Considering the future of Alexei Sergevich always closed a door in her mind.

"Because they would not let him go. And Alexei Sergevich would not want to . . ."

"Why would they try to stop him?"

"He would speak from the heart, to the Soviet people. A voice they would understand. They will not let us go."

"How do you know?"

Almost at once he wished he had not asked.

"Because I am his wife," she said. "I understand what they fear."

She had led him to a bleak little park nearby and they had watched a few hardy skaters. Her cheeks were whipped by the cold, her nose as red as a cherry as she buried her face in the big Turkoman coat.

"Russia is too damned cold," he had said, his breath visible in the icy air.

"So healthy," she laughed.

Schiller had stamped his feet, frozen in spite of the heavy-duty boots and two layers of woollen socks.

"All right," she smiled, "I will let you go inside," and had taken him to a crowded glass café selling sad cakes and tea amid a tangle of warm pipes. As he thawed out she had removed her hat, shaken the brown hair free, and admitted she was thirty-three, and that they only planned one child.

"Don't you want any more children?"

Again she had laughed. She knew that her little Yuri amused him. Her concern for the boy was a stricture against him, contrasting with the future of his own son. "One is enough these days."

"But the Party urges larger families."

"It doesn't pay for them."

The café was crowded and dirty. Empty ice-cream dishes littered the tables even in the middle of winter. Ed Schiller had pushed the grubby plates to one side and locked on to her eyes. Over the glass of tea her face seemed to glow. Charlie at school in Newark formed a bond between them, and she twined her fingers thoughtfully round the steaming drink, shaking her head. He had told her of Nikky's letters still coming in from New York.

"Breaking up marriage is bad. I know it is common in the United States." Like abortion and spermicides, she seemed to imply.

"It happens."

"I can't imagine saying you love someone, and giving yourself to someone else."

Schiller shrugged. That was the way of it. In Moscow people romped in the snow. In New York Nikky would be in someone else's sheets. It all seemed a long way away, another life.

"We tried it again for a year before making it final."

She raised her fine, dark eyebrows. "Do you still want her?"

He had not known the answer. "She gave me a lot in one go. Maybe too much. I couldn't keep up."

Blushing slightly Lila said, "It sounds as if she was good in bed."

Schiller's laugh had been uneasy, as if they were going too deep.

"No. I mean that. It does not come so easy to everyone," Lila added.

She had surprised him again. He hadn't expected that degree of admission. A bell had rung as the music stopped and the skaters were ordered off the ice. It was nearly dark and the shadows threw an intimacy between them as they wedged round one of the tiny circular tables that stood outside in the summertime.

"I guess Nikky's getting plenty of practice," Schiller said bitterly.

"Sometimes women need an adventure with other men."

"There's always some willing bastard . . ."

She picked up her hat and wrapped herself up again, almost hurriedly. "Come on, Eddie—" he had asked her to use his first name, "—we must go. Alexei Sergevich will be awake."

The wind stunned them outside and she had gasped in pleasure, clutching his arm.

"Lila. For God's sake tell Alexei Sergevich to be careful," he had cautioned. "I'm very concerned for you . . . both."

"Yes, I know you are," she had replied, as much to herself as to Schiller.

"I hate to think that anything I've said, or written about him. . . ."

"Of course not." She had smiled. "We make our own beds to sleep on."

When they returned Alexei Sergevich had roused himself from a liquor stupor, full of apologies and charm. "Next week," he had said, "next week, Ed, you will be my special guest. Lila will stay here with Yuri and we will fart off like the wind. Listen, I will show you my dacha. A literary dacha." And he roared with laughter.

"Christ," Schiller said. "How come they wreck your apartment, sack you from the magazine, and you still have a dacha?"

Alexei Sergevich had belched and tapped his nose. "They have forgotten that I did not give back the key."

The day trip outside Moscow had blurred into one long

night. Schiller remembered the car ride, banging on worn-out springs in Barsov's borrowed jalopy down forest roads in the middle of a freezing February, the snow outside as white as the sheet on a corpse. They had careered through the fir trees and ended up at the *Novy Mir* guest-house, buried deep in the woods. Barsov and two companions, a thin young lecturer from Lomonosov University with burning, nihilistic eyes, and Ed Schiller, the U.S. divorcee, trapped and rejoicing, dangerously melancholy in the cold of winter. A Slavonic desperation seemed to creep over them, lost in the forest, as they stoked up the stove and drank in the dank, rawly furnished room. Encumbered by layers of coats they had sung and boozed, danced and hugged until the heat had built up and overwhelmed them and they had rolled under the table, drunk to the end of the world.

It was at the end of that trip that he had tried to confide in Barsov, when Alexei Sergevich had mentioned Lila.

As they raked out the fires, unplugged the percolator and prepared to leave, Schiller said, "I've told Lila that you've got to be careful. I don't want to feel I've caused you any problems. You have a wonderful wife."

"Lila, Lila," Barsov had hiccupped. "She lives for me."

"I know. I envy you." Schiller hesitated, then added, "I've never met anyone as devoted as her."

If Barsov had noticed the catch in the American's voice, he did not show it.

"Captain. Telephone." Maria came into the kitchen as he finished his breakfast—rye-bread and scrambled eggs. The bell was ringing on his desk and the old woman still seemed frightened of it.

"OK. OK." He crossed the room and picked up the receiver. "Yeah?"

It was Darleen. "Ed, I'm sorry that I took off so fast. I had the early shift."

"Sure. I understand."

"Listen," she said, "can you come over to Commercial Section tomorrow?"

"Sure. No problem." His spirits rose. She had told him

that she worked there on Kutuzovsky. Could be she was still trying. Darleen was pushing life hard. "Any time, honey."

"Don't get me wrong, Ed. Something they don't want you to write about. I guess it's a dumb story. New line."

"Don't want me to write?"

Schiller knew that meant trouble, a message somewhere. He yawned into the mouthpiece for the benefit of the MVD.

"Jesus. I don't like censors. What the hell? Can't it wait?" He glanced down into the road again. It was empty. Everybody in Moscow had a hangover Sunday morning. Why the hell should Darleen be so bushy-tailed?

"I guess it can't, or I wouldn't be ringing," she said sharply.

Every call was bugged so that was all she could say. And he would have to go. Maybe it was a peace-offering, as well as being official. Schiller gave up. Moscow was a toothache all the time, a nightmare, a sentence, full of half-hints and messages. Day by day he did the rounds then tapped out a thousand words in a concrete box on Pushkin Street, fielding the human stories for Middle America. Like a mouse on a treadmill, analyzing the press, cultivating the dissidents, watching television that made NBC look like rock video, joining the gossip in the Western press club and sending copy back home to the big, square newsroom at the *Post*. Sly Sylvester said he wanted two good stories a month: and if they couldn't find 'em, make 'em.

Maria said she was going. Sundays she only came in to clean up the kitchen mess. He told her that he had been called out, and she started clucking, nosy and concerned together.

"Weekends you ought to relax."

He nodded, soothing the old woman. "Sure, Maria."

"Look after yourself, Captain. Make more friends."

"Yeah. OK."

"Captain, where you go off today?"

"Ah, Maria. The first picnic of summer. I got to go visit Alexei Sergevich Barsov." It was no good dissembling. She followed his social life in a motherly way, and he knew that she reported it.

She pursed her lips and waved her duster at him, a note of

concern in her voice. "You be careful," she said. "Dangerous, some of these people. You know what has happened to him. He's for the treatment."

Downstairs by the elevator the concierge glared from her table and scribbled a mark in her book with a stub of indelible pencil, before resuming her knitting. She did so every time he went out and every time he came in. Schiller had filed a piece on such babushkas, the oldest profession in Russia, and he glared back.

His smart little Fiat was waiting. The sun was surprisingly warm and clear, the first hot day of June, the leaves really thickening now. The militiaman on the corner was in his blue summer gaberdine, fiddling with his two-way radio. They looked at each other blankly as Schiller sauntered past and wandered down the boulevard where the silver bus had been stopped. It was so warm, with a little sharp-edged breeze, that he decided to walk from Arbat Square down the concrete and glass runway of Kalinin Prospekt towards the river. Almost a very nice day.

2

From her post in the Institute of Culinary Arts Elena Amalrik watched the foreigner who visited the Barsovs come out of the Bulvar Building. He was casually dressed in denims that looked American and she wondered who he was, but Records would case that out from the photograph she had taken. She had tracked him back there, and now she was observing, having drawn Sunday duty. She envied him, she envied men generally, especially American ones. He had determination, muscle that showed through his clothes, and a good square face. She put him at mid-thirties, his hair too long for the military, more like a newsman. A Russian that long and thin would have had to be an actor. Snap out of it,

Elena, note the time he came out and the number of the red
Fiat.

But Schiller didn't unlock the car. The face seemed
dispossessed, troubled about something; he stuck his hands
in his pockets and mooched down the boulevard, busier with
traffic now, toward the Kalinin Bridge, past the high-rise
apartments and office blocks. Elena debated whether she
should leave her post, on the chance of a lead. Her orders
were unambiguous but at the same time confused: to see
where the stranger went, based on the Second Secretary's
office in the Culinary School. They did not require her to
stay inside there, in her reasoning, so long as she fulfilled
her job. And the American seemed unusual, on his own, not
bothering to drive off as they usually did. On an impulse she
grabbed her coat and ran to the Institute's side door, pulling
it quickly behind her. He was some seventy meters down the
road as she began to tail him. She let him walk a bit further
and then followed discreetly, the same tall girl with steel-
rimmed glasses and sensible shoes, in a navy blazer with
painted wooden buttons, whom he had seen in the Barsovs'
lobby.

Schiller did not glance back, thinking of other times when
he and Barsov and Lila had gone out for a day together.
This last spring there had been an open-air concert in
Izmailovo Park. He remembered Yuri chasing the geese and
Barsov and Lila embracing on a bench. As he came back to
them, holding a handkerchief on Yuri's hand, where he had
cut himself, Lila had disengaged.

"Thank you, Eddie, so much."

"He's OK."

"Yes. I know." And her eyes, those great tawny owl's
eyes, seemed to be embracing him too.

The Barsovs' problems were on his mind. No doubt Jubal
Martin wearing his CIA hat had other sources of information about their predicament, through access to Kremlin
watchers, spies, informers. Schiller didn't give a shit for
that: he worked on what he knew. He came to the concrete
wedding cake of the Ukraina Hotel, enormous, statuesque, a
telescoped Empire State Building. The Volgas and Chaikas

were busy ferrying guests, party big-shots out for some entertaining, Comintern VIPs.

He had once written it up, this peculiar social scene. He paused and watched them: well fed and watered predators using the system. By now the day had burst into blue sky and sunshine, summer coming, the girls in their highest heels, copied fashions from old numbers of *Vogue*. Barsov recorded all this: Alexei's unpublished story on "The Longing of Russia," which Schiller had read, said it all far more eloquently than he ever would. Unless Barsov was forced to go, thrown out like Solzhenitsyn, it seemed unlikely to Schiller that he would abandon his sources.

The girl on the sidewalk behind him went into a telephone booth and watched from there as Schiller looked at the crowds in front of the hotel.

Schiller felt an article take shape, another column for Sylvester in the Washington newsroom—plastic desks on lawns of carpet—Sly always wanting new stories, human angles. A piece on Moscow's home-made fashions, this fucking sexual desert where he had exiled himself after the break-up with Nicola, until he ended up chasing skirts like Darleen.

Barsov had once pushed a glass at him in that crammed flat and said, with Lila beside him, handling her like a beer mug, "She does what I say, eh? Good kid. You wouldn't think that her old man was a Komsomol leader in Odessa. A real swinger. He ordered the girls to shave their legs."

Lila had blushed, then put her arms around the Neanderthal frame and kissed Alexei Sergevich. That had been a real kiss, a kiss between lovers.

"Don't go, Ed."

"I got to," he said.

The girl in the telephone box lit a cigarette and waited. And Schiller, after doing nothing, just staring, suddenly darted between the cars, across the slip-road towards her. Before she realized it he was running, banging on the glass wall, wrenching the box open. His head jutted towards her, round the door.

"Comrade, are you following me?" He saw a thin girl, round-shouldered and no bust. Embarrassed, Elena shook her head, made to pick up her handbag and stubbed out her Byelomor straw-tip.

"Of course not," she muttered.

He glared at her. "Why did you come out of the building opposite, and then follow me? When I stopped, you stopped."

"Not so," she stammered, unsettled by his presence.

"Why?"

"I wanted to make a report." Flustered, she knew she had put it badly.

The foreigner grinned. "OK. You go ahead. Want to see my papers?"

"No . . . no," she muttered. He looked her up and down, the thin face, the long legs, the cheap reefer jacket with padded shoulders. A maniac, she wondered. An elderly man in carpet slippers shuffled up behind them and asked if they were using the booth. She shook her head and slammed the door, standing there awkwardly.

"I don't mind," Schiller said. "I just like to know, that's all."

He bought a bunch of summer flowers, yellow and red roses, from the stall outside the hotel, waited while they wrapped them in white paper, then sauntered back towards his car. Elena thought he had a lover, an assignation.

She followed him back, made a note in her log-book and telephoned the Section at 25 Kirova. She reported the American's walk, as if it contained a secret, but not the full conversation, and felt guilty about the deception.

Ivan Nikolaivich Bradze, her supervisor, was an old hand at the game, a survivor who would have liked to make it with her. He congratulated Elena.

"You have no idea why?"

"No, comrade," she told him. "He gave me the impression of feeling uneasy."

Bradze pondered that one deeply over two cups of sweet coffee, feet up on the desktop, before passing it on; in a way it hardly seemed worth it. But the message was received and noted at Headquarters at 2 Dzerzhinsky Square, the old insurance company building that houses the KGB. Impossible to know where it went, but someone took a decision. The American must now be followed on a regular basis.

"You must shadow him," Bradze relayed the message.

Out of the corner of her eye she saw the red car reversing from the parking bay, and turning left.

"I haven't got a car," she said.

It was to be Yuri's day "in the car with soft seats" and they were waiting for him, as arranged, by the bookstall in the Prospekt Vernadskovo Metro station, so that they could shake off the minder. Alexei Sergevich was shambling around in a cable-stitch sweater and green corduroy trousers, like an off-duty submariner, holding eight-year old Yuri by the hand. The boy, with his cropped blond hair and determined blue eyes, again reminded Schiller of Charlie, his own kid in New Jersey. But Charlie was now back with Nikky, the past was over and done with. Today there was Lila with Yuri, smiling shyly in a simply floral dress of pink and cream, and sling-back sandals. She laughed and seemed vaguely excited.

"We've given them the slip," Alexei Sergevich said, embracing Schiller. His breath smelled of ancient schnapps. "I told them we were going to visit my non-existent mother. By the time they work that out, we shall be back again. Anyway, the girl wasn't there."

"I know," Schiller said. "She decided to watch me instead."

"What, my little squeaky sparrow? Little Elena?" Barsov was roaring with laughter, hands slapping his sides so much that the bookstall attendant looked worried, in case he was an epileptic.

"That's right, Alexei Sergevich. She must have followed me home. A foreigner in the nest."

Lila looked at him, her eyes worried above the gentle, slightly flattened nose, and he noticed again how fine her eye-lashes were. She colored as she reacted.

"That is a bad omen."

"I don't think so," Schiller said. "I told her to mind her own business."

"She looks as if she's lost a lover. A lot of passion locked up there." Alexei Sergevich smirked.

Yuri was getting impatient. "Where's the car? Where's the car?"

Schiller gave Lila the roses and watched her blush as she admired them. She allowed him to kiss her cheek, smelling faintly of eau-de-Cologne. "I have a restaurant booked," he said. "Today you are my guests."

Barsov settled in the front, and Yuri and Lila climbed excitedly into the back. The Fiat was new and clean, its scarlet paintwork shining in the sun after Maria Galina had insisted on washing it. Barsov's hand roved over the switches and controls.

"One day, in the Soviet Union," Barsov said, "everyone will have cars. And one for Lila too."

'When they perform your plays," Lila chimed.

"But now I cannot even buy her colored stockings." His fist thumped on the fascia.

Schiller drove carefully across the tree-shaded parkland in front of the University buildings toward the Lenin Hills look-out plátform commanding the panorama of the Moskva River. On the granite terrace they bought lemon ice-creams and watched the barges and pleasure boats clearing the loop of the river. Moscow lay below them: the gray hangar of the Kiev station and the wedding cake of the Ukraina Hotel where Schiller and Elena had parted; on the far back the domes of the Novodevichy Convent, and in the background the golden onions of the Kremlín cathedrals wavering in the heat-haze.

Barsov watched for a minute with puzzled eyes as people climbed the steps beside them, or sat down to eat tomatoes and cheese. The kvass beer stand was under siege.

"Are all cities like this, in the United States?"

"Not so clean," Schiller said. "We have our problems too."

"Ah, but in time you solve them."

The American shrugged. "I guess so. Hopefully."

"That is what Alexei Sergevich needs," Lila mused. "A little hope." Her eyes were on his raw, peasant-philosopher face, as the wind ruffled the straggling hair that he brushed across the great domed skull. Schiller wondered again what particular sorcery had brought them together, and cemented them now: Alexei Sergevich Barsov, novelist and play-wright, a graduate of Rostov University who had lectured in Russian history, this fifty-three-year-old megalomaniac or genius, Schiller could not be sure which, and the slim girl, twenty years his junior, whom he had captured in a second marriage. Looking at her now, in Barsov's shadow, he wondered how much her life, her own intellectual interests in art and languages, even her former profession as an interpreter, had been eclipsed by Barsov. As if the same thought occurred to her she glanced across and smiled, and shook her head quickly behind Alexei Sergevich's back as he muttered darkly, "If I can't write about mother-fucking Russia, the things that I want to say, the things that are wrong with her, the lies they tell, I may as well be locked up. Locked up or dead."

"If you don't shut up you will be," she warned him swiftly, as groups of young conscripts passed by.

One of the reasons, at least, for that strange union was jumping up and down before them.

"Uncle Ed," Yuri said, "are you going back to America?"

"Sometime, I reckon," He shaded his eyes against the glare and watched the traffic flowing along the boulevards, a train on the Metro bridge. Far over to the right the modern blocks along Frunze Quay looked across the water to Gorky Recreational Park, which would be spilling over with families out to celebrate summer.

Schiller had broken his vows, or Nikky had done so for him, and it still hurt.

"Can I come with you?" Yuri asked.

The American smiled, and seemed to respond from a long way away. "That could be difficult."

"Why?"

"Well. You've got a mother and father in Moscow for a start."

"I hate Moscow," Yuri said. "I hate going to school here."

"Come on. Maybe. You would have to go to school in America."

Barsov's great head rolled round to stare at Schiller. Although he was a foot shorter the breadth of his build, the hunch of his ox-like shoulders and the wrestler's chest gave an impression of power, as if he could pick up a sapling like Lila and bend her in two. But Schiller had the feeling, an impression confirmed by their friendship, that she would never break.

"Would you like to go?" he asked her.

"Go? Go where?"

"Where Yuri suggests. America?"

She shifted her shoulder-bag from one side to another and seemed to be engrossed with the strap before replying.

"Only if Alexei Sergevich wants to. And I don't think he ever will."

Barsov found his words. "Why try and fly with the eagle when the bear has a sore head?"

Schiller grinned. "I think you just made that up."

Barsov hooted with laughter. "I'm the bear with the sore head."

"True."

"What do you mean by that?" Alexei Sergevich rounded on him angrily, but Schiller wasn't put off.

"I guess it sums you up: a bear with a sore head. It will be until the Soviet Union lets you say what you want . . ."

". . . about the lies of history, and communism, and the way to make love," Barsov growled. And then he laughed. "Come on, I'm starving. Where are we going to eat?" He could switch between ideals and venality in a way that crushed opposition, and that was one of his problems. Schiller could only hope that Lila was not crushed in the process. Barsov could write like an angel, and Schiller respected him for it, but Lila had to live with a devil.

"I've found a place," he said, "where you can reserve a table and not wait more than two hours."

They came down the steps and Schiller drove them again, happy in each other's company, round the city ring-road where the traffic snarled as usual, and out to the Kuskovo Palace on the eastern fringe of the city. This was the Russia that Barsov loved, an eighteenth-century palace standing on the banks of a lake where the trees stood like soldiers, waved across ragged grass and shut out the multistory blocks beyond. A Russia of order and civility and freedom

to move. Holy Russia. In the gardens was a newly built
restaurant, located by the Englishman Hatter of the *Times*,
where there was dazzling napery and shining glasses, one of
those surprises that Russia sometimes pulled.

Lila's eyes danced as she saw the porcelain and glassware
and read the menu.

"I can't believe it. How on earth did you find it?"

"His friends in the CIA," Barsov said loudly.

"I have no friends in the CIA."

"Every American has friends in the CIA."

They were arguing again, and Schiller put a stop to it for
Lila and Yuri's sake.

"Come on. What will you eat?"

The restaurant itself was a wooden bungalow with stip-
pled walls, displaying the latest effort at Soviet décor, and
for once the food was exciting.

"I'm told they have imported a chef from France."

Barsov's eyebrows rose. "Are ours not good enough?"

"Of course not," she chided him gently, winking at
Schiller. "Don't be so awkward, Alexei Sergevich."

"Only the Politburo could afford to come to a place like
this," Barsov muttered, peering over his glasses. "I pre-
sume all these are members?"

"Please, Alexei, you are embarrassing Ed."

"Nothing embarrasses me." But Schiller was looking at
her, and saw the tear in her heart; everything she could give
to Barsov was in those eyes: admiration, compassion, devo-
tion, companionship, concern and mothering, but was there
still love?

"We must not talk here," she said, "about America.
About politics."

"Why not?" Barsov roused himself.

"Because you won't have time to eat a good meal if you
do."

"I will," Yuri said. "I like this place."

They drank champagne with the meal: Russian champagne, sweet and heady, which complemented the steaks in
a cream garnish, and washed these down with a wine that
tasted of mulberries. Afterwards they lay in the sun in the
French Gardens and watched Yuri chase the birds. When the

boy grew tired he ran across to where Schiller and Lila were sitting. Barsov seemed to be dozing, stretched out on the grass with his hands over his eyes as if he squinted at the future. She had plaited a daisy-chain and put it round his neck.

"Will you come and play hide-and-seek?" Yuri demanded.

"No," Barsov growled.

"You should let your father rest."

"He never plays," the boy said.

"I'll play," Schiller volunteered.

"There's no need," Lila said.

"I'd like to. Come on."

The American and the boy shouted ten at each other and ran away. Yuri was smaller and quicker, and always won; he was a smart kid.

"Won't you come and play, Mama?"

"I must stay with your father."

Schiller found her close to him, sitting in the long grass, watching Alexei Sergevich on his back snoring.

"Life here is not so easy," she said. It was a cautious statement, inviting compassion and compromise, and he nodded.

"I gather that."

"Alexei Sergevich needs to create . . . to love."

He struggled with his Russian. "Some it is self-destructive, such creation."

"What do you mean?" she asked softly.

He looked sideways at her, in the faded summer dress, as young as Nikky. There was something she wanted and could not admit, and Schiller forced himself not to define it. As she met his eyes he turned away into the sun.

"It's hot."

"Yes. For me too."

Yuri came to the rescue. "Come on. Let's go home."

The sun had slipped away, down the afternoon sky. As they gathered their books and rugs and put them in plastic bags, Schiller knew it was the happiest day of his whole stay in Moscow, a day that should never end. He wanted to spin it out, to delay for ever taking her back to that cramped apartment where she shared Alexei Sergevich's bed.

But it was not her wish. He felt a sadness between them as they drove home, drunk from the sun and sticky in the small car. Nobody said much as they threaded inside the traffic lanes; this time he took them all the way, tired but elated, right to the doors of the apartment block behind the Vernadsky Prospekt where Barsov was still allowed to live, in a wasteland of concrete.

At the entrance, by the big shabby doors, Alexei Sergevich and Lila both embraced him; Yuri asked for kisses too. Just for one moment they were an extended family, and between the three adults hung a gossamer of trust.

Elena had long gone off duty, but a man with short hair in the lobby pretended to be reading a paper as he made a note of the car.

"Look at them. Look at them," Barsov shouted. "Always they want to know. No one in Russia is free."

"Then you should apply to leave," Schiller said. "Things are easier now."

"Easier! Easier! What can I write about except the country I love? I suck its blood." Barsov's eyes misted over as he stood wearily in the evening sunshine, while Lila helped Yuri to take their souvenirs from the car. They were not much, Schiller thought, to remember the day he had wanted, the day about which he had been warned: the books he had bought for Yuri at the Metro stall, the catalogue for Lila of the porcelain collection in the Kuskovo Museum, a tie he had offered Alexei Sergevich, who said, "I never wear ties, but it will do to hang myself."

Lila, tranquil with sunshine and happiness, took his hand quietly in farewell.

"Arrivederci."

"Goodbye. Till the next time."

She seemed to hesitate. "I hope so."

"You both should leave," he urged.

Barsov heard. "Ask to leave my country?" he said. "I'd have to leave in a coffin."

3

On the following day Schiller obeyed Darleen's summons. Driving down Kutuzovsky, he left the car at the entrance to the Commercial Section and pressed the bell. It was a public holiday and the buildings were shuttered and silent, like a weekend barracks, but there were crowds instead at the nearby glass drum of the Borodino Panorama. As Ed Schiller waited his sympathies were with Napoleon: Sylvester's desk back home had asked for a story on the burning of Moscow.

After a couple of minutes he heard them coming down the passage: heavy security shoes. The aluminum door was unlocked and the folding gate pulled apart as Tanner, the ex-Marine guard, stared out, his polished head cropped and shiny. Been there too long, thought Schiller, until he looked like a tortoise; the post was so hard to fill that volunteers could stay for ever.

Tanner knew him well as one of the U.S. press corps. He grunted as Schiller squeezed through the gate and doorway into the big room with the interview counter. Shiny black chairs round the walls, trade magazines on the tables, and chromium ash-bins as big as spittoons standing on pedestals. There was a faint smell of polish.

The old Marine's face cracked as he lifted the counter for Schiller to pass through. "She's waiting upstairs," he winked, the bastard.

"Who?"

"Aw, come on."

Behind the counter, post-office style, was the back room with a connecting staircase to the floor above. And there at the top was Saturday's flame, Darleen Simpson, with a man he didn't know. She gave him a sober smile as if they had only just met, a pert little East Coast blonde in a peach combat top with a T-shirt underneath.

"Hi." The co-ed greeting was flavor of the month. Darleen's eyes were dull with tiredness. "Ed. This is Taylor Sheen."

Schiller disliked him on sight. Sheen was ten years younger, gleaming, with a thick hedge of chestnut hair and orthodontic teeth that edged together when he smiled. A card-sharper, a greasy-pole man going places, and when he shook hands his voice sounded dubbed. Schiller could feel that they had been talking about him behind his back.

"Really great to know you, Ed." Sheen's hand was warm and hard, as if he'd been practicing. "Sorry to bring you in on a holiday, but you know we don't stop." *Sotto voce* he added, "Let's get along in there."

"There" was the safe room, double-lined, airless, inviting confidences, built at the end of the corridor. Schiller sensed a certain enthusiasm in Sheen to share some great secret with him as he opened the door. He saw a central table, cloth-covered, with bottles of Barzhomi mineral water and square Polish glasses. There were no windows, only a photograph of the President on one of the cork-tiled walls.

"Makes you feel kind of trapped in here," Sheen said cheerfully, "but you know the line-up, Ed. The rules."

They sat at the table, Darleen showing her knees. Sheen in his crisp blue head-hunter suit tipped his chair back as if he owned the place. Schiller tried for a smile from Darleen, something to say you nearly made it, but she was back on duty, nothing doing.

"Water, Ed?"

"No thanks."

Sheen ripped open a bottle which fizzed gently and poured himself some as if it were champagne. "Great stuff." He picked a gold pen from his pocket and opened a pad of notes.

"How are you liking Moscow, Ed?"

"It's a job."

"It's a pain in the anus." He flashed a smile. "Still, you write some good stuff. I've read it. Great stories. Keep it going."

"Thanks." Schiller found monosyllables helped.

Sheen tapped the ballpen and stared. "Langley hasn't forgotten you. No way."

"What?"

"No, sir. Watching your stuff with interest. Especially your line to the underground."

"There is no underground," Schiller said.

"Aw. Come on. You mean you don't use the subway?" Yale-smooth Sheen was enthralled at his own wit. "Come on, Ed, you know what I mean."

"No," Schiller said. "Haven't you heard of Secretary Gorbachev?"

Taylor Sheen's voice lost its reasonableness. "Cut the crap, Ed. You know damned well they are coming out of the closet with glasnost. Yakulov, that poet guy. Moisei Timobaum who led that Jewish sit-down in Red Square. And Barsov. Mister Conscience. Coming to be a friend of yours, Alexei Sergevich . . ."

A tiny white connection glowed in Schiller's brain, a warning blip. The more Sheen opened his arms, the more Schiller's trust withdrew. Sheen the Agency man, from the layered health of his haircut to the shiny tips of his shoes. Ivy League vs. Midwest they looked at each other: Schiller with his square, open face and beaten skin. The hair on Ed Schiller's head might equally sprout from an armpit, his cheeks were roughened by two years of Russian cold, but the tough skin was also a throw-back. Family origins, farmers in the Sudetenland, managers, overseers. Oberleutnants each with a strain of bull courage that had caused his father to move out in front of the Führer. Franz Schiller had impressed on his son not always to believe what other people wanted to tell him. So now Ed's features set into stone-faced refusal.

"I wouldn't say that."

"OK. Let me explain, Ed. We know your contacts. You've been building up some big story on the Barsovs."

"No way," Schiller said.

Sheen glanced at Darleen, who was running a pocket tape. He tried to rub Schiller down. "Don't get me wrong. Barsov's a great man, so they tell me. Could be in for the Nobel." Pause. "Listen, has he ever suggested bailing out?"

"He's married."

Sheen sucked his teeth, gave one of those don't-push-me-too-far smiles, a sunshine-breakfast good-morning. "Aw, cut it out. You know the set-up. They're given a warning, next thing they will knock him off. You wouldn't want them to do that, would you?" Pause. "Or maybe these days they are ready to let him light out on his own like that Solzhenitsyn guy."

"Nothing to do with me," Schiller said crisply, thinking again of the marriage and Lila's face. At times like these he regretted taking the back-hander for his Russian studies. Not under orders, paid by the *Washington Post*, but the Agency had him wired.

Then Sheen made his mistake. He flipped a subject. "By the way, Ed, how goes the personal life? Don't mind my asking: we have to check. Don't want you guys on hand-jobs." He grinned at Darleen. "Heard that Nicola still keeps in touch from New York."

"What the hell business is that of yours?" Schiller remembered Nikky's last letter. Ridiculous. Ridiculous, that was what she now argued. Ridiculous to split up, so bad for Charlie who wanted to see him. She still loved him and she was sorry. But he knew it wasn't just once. It could have been a string of stands any time he was away. He had divorced her and there was no way back for hotsy little Nikky who had resumed her career in TV production in New York.

"Everything, Ed. Everything." Sheen's pale blue eyes looked at him blandly. "Don't blow your head. We need to know where our nationals are hitting the sack." Darleen flushed under the make-up. Sheen made more strokes with the ballpen on his pad, a grid of meaningless marks, every one a straight line. "You wouldn't be playing footsie with Lila Barsov by any chance, Ed?"

Schiller lifted off, a fist of whitened knuckle, slam, on the table until the bottles rattled. Lila. Lila.

"You prick," he said. "You lousy prick. My friendship with the Barsovs is nothing to do with you. He writes like Tolstoy and she loves him. Isn't that good enough for you?" Schiller half rose to keep pace with his temper, his face darkened in anger. "I don't have to come here and listen to your dirt."

"Point taken, Ed," Sheen said coolly. "That's all I wanted to know." He poured himself out more water, gave Schiller his wolf-smile. "Have some?"

Schiller found his mouth dry. Darleen opened more bottles and they all drank the lukewarm, carbonated fizz.

"What is it you're trying to say?"

Sheen was no fool either. These days they didn't recruit them on that basis. Behind the glasses were the eyes of a seagull, predatory, as he leaned forward.

"Listen. Our scenario is that they ought to be helped out, Ed, both of them. To defect. So he can say what he wants to in the West. We got some signals already, Ed. Signs are that the Soviets may be ready to let 'em go. New emphasis on human rights. How does that strike you?"

"Crap. Barsov doesn't want to go."

"Ah. Maybe he says he doesn't, but he does. You got to read him, Ed."

In his mind Schiller saw Barsov's heavy Russian face, saying "No." Compressed as a can of corned beef, stocky, compact and Slav. Physical bigness about the head and shoulders, the weight-lifter's chest. Intellectual bigness, a kind of arrogance in his self-assurance, not a sense of importance but a creativity, as if he was adding something to the world around him, a view, a closer inspection simply by being there. One time Schiller had met him in the Detsky Mir Children's Store, quite by chance, when Barsov and Lila were looking for a birthday present for their son Yuri. Schiller had been searching for something to send back to Charlie. They had inspected the plastic baubles, made their purchases—a book for Yuri, a model kit for Charlie—and had tea together at the refreshment bar. Barsov had talked about Leningrad during the siege, in which his parents had died.

"I didn't have a childhood," he said. "They put me to work filling sandbags. Anyway, who wanted to play when your guts were starving?" And he threw up his arms like a gun recoiling. "Poom, poom." Alexei Sergevich's patriotism was an end in itself. He had no time for the system but he was in love with Russia; he wrote long letters about it, history disguised as novels. He was an oak of truth in a great decaying forest, rich in underfoot foliage, not a reed that bent with the wind. Schiller had asked him again then why he didn't leave Moscow, go to the country some place and write in peace. Perhaps leave Russia.

"Because my future is here."

Ed Schiller had looked at Lila, sitting with him, her brown hair pulled back, her brown eyes wide with some mysterious mixture of pride and fear. He remembered how their fingers touched accidentally, under the counter, with a thrill of pleasure.

"What makes you think that Barsov wants to quit? I asked him only yesterday and he said "No way." What sort of future is there for a guy like him in LA or Chicago or New York? He doesn't write the kind of crap that sells in drugstores."

"What kind of future is there for him here, Ed?"

"That's up to him."

"You ain't helped."

It touched a very raw wound, but Schiller would not let this smartarse put the needle in further. He was not the Barsovs' keeper, whatever else he felt.

"What about the boy, Ed?"

"The boy?" Yuri, aged eight.

"Yeah. Listen. We could get 'em all out together: the whole goddamn family. If he still wants her, that is." He looked at Schiller slyly. "Sometimes guys like a break, huh? A change of scene. You know that, Ed. How's your feel for the domestic situation?"

"Look," Schiller said, "don't ask me for a medical on someone else's marriage."

"Are they still making it under the sheets?"

"Sure," Schiller said. "They told me. Every night and twice on Sundays."

Taylor Sheen smiled again. "Come on. Don't piss around. This is serious. Because if they want to move, Uncle Sam opens the door. They'd look pretty good by the Statue of Liberty, dressed in furs. That would give us quite a kick. 'Great writer hounded: tells his story to Congress.' "

Meaningless. Meaningless. Barsov had given no hint. He was working on another play which he still hoped to see staged in Gorbachev's Moscow. His political views, he said, were barely relevant: it was Russia which concerned him, the soul. As for the surveillance, the police wreckers in the apartment, the letter openings, the phone taps, the pressure on family and friends, he was too big for that. He would ignore the threats, work out his art, the truth was internal. No. Schiller concluded, no way would Barsov leave Russia.

Taylor Sheen was disappointed. "So. You going to see the guy again?"

"Next weekend."

"Well, cool it, Ed. For your sake and theirs."

"Cool it? What sort of game do you think this is?"

"Listen, Ed, friendships like that go so far and no further. Especially with the wife. You get my meaning?"

Schiller's face was blank, and Sheen knew that he had scored.

"If you say so."

"Yeah. We don't say, we advise. If he ain't coming over, my advice is to cool it."

"I've told you what I know."

"Well, maybe you drop it to him one more time, if you like the lady. And then haul off."

"I'll think about it," Schiller said.

"OK, and give him Uncle Sam's love. In case he changes his mind. The wind don't stop blowing because one guy says so."

4

When he visited next time, Schiller took the subway. Every morning after Elena's report, looking down from his eyrie on the sixteenth floor, he had seen a mud-splashed Moskvich and two minders arrive. He watched them day after day, foreshortened figures who checked over his car. Sometimes one was the girl, more often there were two men. The militiaman saluted and sauntered off, then they would follow the Fiat all the way to the office and wait there until he drove back.

When Schiller came down and started walking he confused them. He could sense them pounding behind him along to the Metro station, but they only just made it, jumping the carriage behind him as it pulled out of the station. He watched their reflections in the window as they complained to each other: a fat man in his fifties and a sallow accomplice. Nero Wolfe and Archie.

Schiller gave them a run for it. He left the train at Prospekt Vernadskova, stopped for a cold pork sausage and a soft drink at a stall, bought a paper and a couple of postcards, sent one of them to Charlie, then strolled under a banner proclaiming the "Twenty-third Women's Sculpture Exhibition." It took place in an iron hall as big as an airship hangar, full of statuesque bronzes: women suckling children, pile-driving for bridges, posing with rippling muscles. Not exactly Lila. Not the sort of women he knew. Tchaikovsky's *Sleeping Beauty* crackled from amplifiers. The hall was largely empty, the air was humid, and once he saw Nero Wolfe behind the thighs of a nude.

Walking back through the hall to the strains of distorted violins Schiller realized how easily he could have junked them both, Nero and Archie, but only to his cost. Sylvester had once wired him from the security of Washington, "Give us more paranoia: foreigners distrusted."

In reply he had said, "What for: is it true?"

Maybe Sly had thought he was getting the run-around, anyway the correspondence ceased. Sly would have enjoyed the tail.

So now Schiller stood carefully in the doorway of the exhibition hall, a sad place, smelling of sand-blast, and waited until they found him. He wanted them to know he was heading for Barsov's apartment in the writers' quarter, a world of tenements on concrete pillars. Under a cloudless sky the Barsovs' block looked grubby and a KGB man was

sitting on a chair by the desk. Upstairs on the fifth, twelve
identical flats led from the central landing which fanned
from the stairwell and lift. The Barsovs had found yellow
paint and colored their door pale primrose, a cheerful
extrovert gleam in the scuffed tile corridor illuminated by a
naked bulb.

A message was pinned to the door. Schiller bent down to
read the slip of paper, which was in a round, childish hand.

"Get lost, Leo," it said.

Just like Charlie, though God knew what Charlie did now.
Somewhere in these apartments children were playing games.
Kids with two resident parents.

There was no bell so he knocked.

Alexei Sergevich Barsov came to the door. His breath
was bad, an odor like chicken droppings, his clothes thrown
over the big frame as if it was old machinery, but instant
recognition brought a grin to his face. The jutting jaw broke
into a cadenza as he shouted to Lila, "It's our Americano."

Schiller was clasped, bear-hugged, by the powerful arms.
Alexei Sergevich, smelling of vodka and sweat and cabbage, was a foot shorter than Schiller but had the strength of
a blacksmith. In his time he'd been a country boy, an army
sergeant and a short-term detainee. Leathery now, he gripped
Schiller's jacket and pulled him inside.

Two bedrooms and a living-room led off from the narrow
landing, where Lila was waiting, slightly flushed, as if they
had been arguing.

"Come in, come in," Barsov squawked, his voice surprisingly light, a high-pitched anomaly from such a chest.
Schiller looked down on the balding head as he followed
him along the corridor with Lila now behind them. Barsov's
brown coat had been neatly patched at the sleeves and his
trousers were shiny. He was clumping in Swedish-style
clogs with leather uppers and wore no socks.

Even the passage was lined with books, Russian, German, English, piled up from the floor, combed through with
reference slips. Schiller glimpsed unmade beds and Yuri's
simple toys—unlike Charlie's Walkman, his TV and his
cassettes—strewn in the smaller bedroom. Lila had stuck
cinema posters on to the discolored walls. The kitchen was

a galley no more than nine feet square, with a black pot on the stove and dishes stacked in the sink. A drying rack hung from the ceiling, festooned with her underclothes.

"Come in, come in. The prodigal returns," Barsov bellowed again, pressing him into the living-room, which was only slightly larger. "A messenger of summer. Now we can have a drink." Through one square window Schiller glimpsed the apartments opposite, but the curtains were half-drawn, as if Lila was ashamed of the view. More books and Barsov standing, grinning, his hands rocking the table in the middle, round which they would all sit. He pushed away a typewriter, perched on old magazines.

"Lila, Lila. Where's my girl?" He spoke in English, carefully, as if he was practicing for some far country. Again that monkey-faced grin, one hand brushing gray hair from a balding temple. Square and determined, he whirled round to open the cheap glass cabinet that served as a display case. Bottles appeared and small glasses, and Lila came back.

She was shy, as if she'd been hiding. Now she held out her hand, with a quick smile of welcome that touched his heart. The bones of her face were lovely, unusually small for a Russian. A sculpted, intellectual, European face, like the fine-eyed women of fashion magazines. Her hair clipped back in a pony-tail made her look seventeen. Her figure was frail, almost faun-like, poured into a sweater and Levi's. Yet as he touched her hands he felt their roughness, as if she'd been scrubbing floors. Before she had married Barsov, she told him once, she had worked eight years as an interpreter.

Barsov was beaming at them, pouring glasses of vodka. Larger than life, he called Lila his priestess, his saviour. His authoritarianism jarred on Schiller's nerves.

Schiller watched Lila sit down, a slight, still figure at the green Amur cloth, which had a fringe of bead work.

"Skol," Barsov shouted, slapping Schiller on the back.

They toasted and toasted again, the drink burning Schiller's throat but he soaked it in with a sense of relief.

"How long ago was it?" Barsov enquired, raising his eyebrows. "That night we got drunk in the forest?" He laughed. "Christ, that was a session."

Schiller said, "February. A long time back."

"Too long," Barsov muttered, wiping his forehead and subsiding into moody silence.

If Schiller had questions put into his mind by the CIA, he forgot them now. In the stuffy little room time raced to four o'clock. Lila produced a honey cake out of a round tin and cut slices for them. She brought in glasses of tea.

"Where is Yuri?"

"He has a friend on the twelfth floor," she said. "So we let him play there."

"Leo?" Schiller asked.

Her brown eyes were shining. "How did you guess?"

"I know."

Barsov loomed over the table. "You know? But what do you Americans know about our lives here? You live in a fool's paradise, isn't that the phrase?"

"It could be, but I try not to."

"You do. You do."

"Then put me right," Schiller said, "so that I can report it."

Barsov giggled and waggled a finger. "Even the perestroika of Secretary Gorbachev can be explained."

"Whatever you feel you can tell me," Schiller replied, and saw that Lila was quick to pick up the note of caution.

"Ah. Why worry that we are being recorded? Everything that I say they record, the fools." Barsov gestured good-humoredly towards the central light fitting. "So many electricians come in to check our wiring that I am expecting a fire. A short-circuit from bugging." His teeth were the color of broken biscuits.

Lila said carefully, "They can't get the wiring right."

"That's right," Barsov snorted. "Every time that we make love, the KGB count the bedsprings."

"Alex—"

"I know. I know." He refilled his glass, then Schiller's. "Now watch, Eddie, watch and I will show you what is wrong with Russia."

Two more vodkas. Barsov plucked reading glasses from one of his jacket pockets and fished out a newspaper cutting.

"Look at this." He held it between finger and thumb like

a dead fish, and Schiller could see that it was a report of speeches to the Praesidium, some of them underlined.

But he was stopped by Lila, who snatched the paper.

"You are a fool, Alexei Sergevich. There is nothing wrong with our country," she said. "Nothing. America, that is where the trouble is."

"It was in *Pravda* . . ."

"There is nothing to see," she added, and tore the cutting into pieces, then tossed them into the plastic sack that served as a waste-bin.

Barsov laughed until the room shook. "Nothing to see. Nothing to say? I shall write another book for them to ban, the Publishing Committee and the Ministry of Culture. 'The Great Patriotic Peace.' What about that, eh? A sequel." His book on the war had still not been published in Russia, where his reputation rested on underground copies and the version printed in the West. For Barsov had had the courage to open the can of worms, exposing the Red Army purges in '37-'38, the pact between Stalin and Hitler, the failures of nerve and courage in '41. Barsov's war was not the revisionist account in the *New Soviet Encyclopedia*; it was a war of collapse and murder in the desperate days as the Panzers swept up to Moscow and the party bosses packed their bags. There were no heros.

"That will be interesting."

"Ed, you must not tease him," Lila said. Barsov tugged at his hair, delighted. She suddenly switched to English. "Leave us alone."

It crossed Schiller's mind that it was not surprising, that reaction. "Shall I go?"

"Good God no," Barsov shouted. "You stay and drink with me . . ."

Lila's intensity, her looks toward Alexei Sergevich showed Schiller how much she feared. In another woman, Nikky perhaps, or one of his previous girls, it might have seemed lust.

"They will kill you—"

"They. They. No one stops me."

She sprang at him like a cat, across the table, clawing his great shoulders.

"Alexei Sergevich, you will say nothing. Nothing."

As Schiller looked again, he saw only reflected love, emotional and unnerving.

But Barsov wasn't finished.

"Don't take her seriously. She inflates everything." He blew a kiss. "However, I will stay a political eunuch for Lila's sake. Instead, maybe I read you a story."

They sat on around the table, drinking tea and eating slices of cake while Barsov refuelled on vodka. He talked endlessly, opened his heart, drank, struggled with words and expounded, novelist and dramatist. Lila was silent, a woman between two men who represented different worlds. As Schiller listened he stared at Alexei Sergevich's self-confident face, and wondered what the Russian really wanted.

Lila tried to moderate Barsov's drinking, saw him into calmer waters, and then returned to the stove. Over Barsov's monologue Schiller heard her in the kitchen through the flimsy partition. There was a thud at the door, Yuri returning, the little boy whistling, Lila talking to him. Silence. Barsov hammered on.

Schiller's mind moved tightly over the flow of talk, the monologue. He tried a couple of times to interrupt the Russian, to steer him back to politics, but Barsov waved him away. His hand clenched the clouded glass of the vodka bottle, his eyes were pouched and reddening. There was very little space to move in the small room crammed with six chairs, a music center, an East German TV and the remaining books. More quick drinks, toasts, excuses, Lila feeding the boy, and Barsov seemingly trying to get rapidly and paralytically drunk.

"Do you know the word that won't pass the Censorship Bureau?"

"No," Schiller said.

"Knickers," he roared. "In Russia. You understand?"

"No."

Barsov wrinkled his nose. "I wrote about a peasant girl and described taking off her knickers. But they said it was anti-Soviet. In a Communist society peasant girls keep their knickers on. What do you say to that?"

Barsov swayed with the vodka and, hardened though

Schiller was, the walls were beginning to move when Lila returned. Scandalized she snatched up the bottle. "The ceiling is sloping, my love," Alexei Sergevich said. Schiller saw her standing there, anger and pity and amusement in her eyes that men could be such fools.

"This is no way to treat a guest . . ." Lila scolded. "Get on with your story." Obedient as a child, Barsov gave way, opened a pack of typescript and began to read.

It was then that Schiller realized how much damage Barsov could do. An account of Soviet cosmonauts marooned in a space laboratory could not disguise the contempt in which he held authority. The dying men's voices were faded out for messages of peace and comfort programmed by Baikal Control, while the fat cats sat back: the same ones who in their time had polluted the Caspian Sea, changed the record of history, constructed the Gulag, mixed privileges and corruption throughout the system. The theme was counterpointed by the love of a cosmonaut for the girl that he would now never reach, told by a mind at its limits, mocking, tender. And wildly subversive. It could never be published as it stood, Barsov and Schiller realized that, as the evening wore on. Smiling over his half-moons Alexei Sergevich raised his glass.

"For Lila," he said. "A toast."

They drank, then toasted again. This time Barsov said, "Truth," and carefully replaced the glass like an empty egg-cup upside-down on the cloth.

Schiller wanted to leave. He had outstayed his welcome and somewhere outside Nero Wolfe and Archie would still be waiting, smoking, eating cold blinis wrapped in greaseproof paper, praying for him to return so that they could book off. Barsov's tea-party would be recorded and analyzed by the Lubianka, of that Schiller was sure. He understood only too well the roots of Lila's concern. Ignorance was safer than knowledge, silence better than words. The Bureau of Special Cases would always win; the members of the Central Committee collecting their privileged food and clothing at the licenced store in Granovskovo Street did not want the pen of Barsov to expose their backsides.

"Ed had better go now," Lila said.

But Alexei Sergevich was hugging his drinking companion as the room swayed round them.

"My advice is be careful," Schiller muttered.

"My comrade, my comrade..."

Schiller wondered how Alexei Sergevich could write so well on such a head. There were things in the cramped room that might have provided clues: technical books, a Russian edition of Dickens, foreign language paperbacks, thumbed copies of Chandler and Günter Grass, but Barsov was stoned as a crow. He spun Schiller around in a kind of peasant two-step.

"Don't worry, don't worry. Lila will look after us."

She was a shadow somewhere at the edge of the room. It was Barsov guiding him to the door, Schiller clearing his head so that he could stagger home like any good Moscow drunk. Alexei Sergevich groped for the catch on the inside of the door which opened into the empty, dark-tiled hallway.

"I'll see you down," Barsov said.

Lila was saying goodbye, a small, hurt figure, placing her hand in his. Schiller tried to find her eyes but only her mouth was smiling.

"No. No."

"Oh. But yes, my Americano. I insist, Ed."

Barsov thumbed the elevator and they bundled inside it. There was no one about. It rattled and groaned to the lobby, but no sign of the militiaman or Nero Wolfe. The concierge had left her desk.

"Where is your car?" Barsov asked with his arm round Schiller as if he were a joint of meat.

"I came by Metro."

The afternoon sun had gone and with it the day's warmth: the evening had a gloomy chill. Schiller's legs were unsteady, cool air mixed with raw fire inside his guts, but Barsov hugged him again in a show of public farewell.

"So. Good. I will accompany you to the station."

They stumbled together beneath the gray slabs, Barsov holding his arm, and walked across unkept grass turning into summer mud, under a regiment of buildings, daubed with scrawls and old posters, along the road to the Metro. There was a square green space given over to children's swings with an old woman watching nothing from a care-taker's hut, a few broken-backed cars, bicycles, two tractor tires used as sand pits. A wasteland on the way to nowhere, and as they crossed it Barsov put his hands on Schiller's lapels, heavy, final, and breathed in his face.

"Listen, my good friend, listen. I have been thinking hard about what you have said. About leaving . . . about leaving Russia."

"But I thought you had decided . . ."

"I had, but I change my mind. I am now silenced here . . . you understand?"

Schiller nodded dumbly.

"But if I come, Lila and Yuri must come too."

"Of course. Why not apply for a visa?"

"I have made inquiries. I have asked. But I have no friends in the Bureau, only enemies."

"What have they said?"

"They say they will not let me go. And if I defect they will keep Lila."

"Oh my God." Schiller's heart thumped. He did not want to be drawn in.

Barsov was lurching towards him red-faced and wild-haired, but there was nothing drunk about him now.

"But wait. Wait. Next month I visit Berlin. East Berlin, for the East–West Writers' Congress. You know Berlin?"

"A little. I've been through."

"OK. Now listen hard my friend." Barsov spoke first in Russian, then English, repeating his words quickly, as if to make sure they went home. "When I go there I want to defect. Don't look at me directly. Ha ha," he roared, clapping his hands together as if they had shared a joke. "And you, Ed, must help me."

"Help?" This was a scene from a black and white movie, Schiller thought, one that he had seen before, the sort of thing Sylvester loved.

"Hear me. While I'm there I shall receive an invitation to address a meeting across the Wall. In West Berlin. They'll let me go because of glasnost, but they will accompany me. They want me back."

"So?" This wasn't Schiller's country: he was a journalist.

"So, Ed. When I am in West Berlin, at the Charlottenburg Palace, I want you to hijack me. To arrange a kidnap."

The hammers in Schiller's head stopped. He was aware of children shouting in the distance, then of a car drawing up, the grubby Moskvich with Nero Wolfe.

"Jesus Christ," he said urgently, feeling depressed. "How the hell can I do that? I'm not the CIA. Anyway, we're being watched."

"Of course." Barsov laughed loudly again and caught hold of Schiller as if to stop himself falling. "Of course. But you've got to help me. There is nothing here for Lila and me. Nothing. Lila is going slowly mad, and my boy is far from happy. I cannot publish in Russia. You know that."

"But Gorbachev has said—?"

"Gorbachev will not change us. Things go on as they are. I ask for your help, Eddie. Eddie, for God's sake help me." He roared with laughter again, teetering like an old wino. "You follow me? You get me out, you take me out by force, and then I decide to stay. That way Lila is safe. That way Lila can come. That way they let her go."

They began walking again slowly across the playground. The car could only circle the sides.

"Will you help?" Barsov asked desperately, his eyes wild. "Eddie, for God's sake, don't let me down."

Schiller shook his head defensively, trying to clear his thoughts. "I don't know . . . I'll do what I can."

"But you will help us . . . you must."

"What if . . . what if things go wrong? Lila would still be here."

He found Barsov's arm was linked through his. "If it goes wrong I want you to give me a promise."

"What kind of promise?" They were coming out to the edge of the square, turning down the street to the Metro. Schiller hated these greasy buildings, this half derelict suburb with the queue at the vodka shop.

"About Lila," Barsov said.

"Lila?"

Barsov's voice was low and urgent. "If anything happens to me, I want you to take care of Lila."

Ed Schiller stopped. "Why do you say that?"

Barsov grinned at him. "I know, Ed, I know."

Schiller mumbled, "But I'm an American, Alexei Sergevich. And she is Russian."

"She is a woman. I've seen the look in her eyes."

Schiller's heart raced. Forgetting the place, forgetting the KGB, he swung round and faced Barsov. "Lila is your wife. I've never seen anyone more in love. What makes you think she would want me?"

"I've asked her," Barsov said.

"Now you listen to me, buddy," Schiller told him. "Just pull yourself together. If there is any fuck-up when you try and come over, how the hell can I help Lila? I would feel that I'd betrayed you."

Barsov rolled his great head; he was breathing heavily. "No, Ed. No. I would not blame you."

"And what if you don't make it, Alexei Sergevich, what then?"

A sigh from Barsov. "Ah, then I ask that you get her out. Lila and Yuri. I release her to you."

"Jesus wept. How do I get her out: somebody else's wife? A Russian wife?"

"You marry her," Barsov said.

5

There was a letter, postmarked New York, next morning in his apartment mail-box. Still shaken by Barsov's appeal he hesitated before taking it from Maria.

"Go on," she said. "It won't bite."

Screwing up her eyes as she looked at the U.S. stamp, then sniffed the paper. "A woman," she said.

For a moment he deceived himself that it was Charlie, but he knew it was Nicola's erratic hand. Schiller slit the envelope open with a pocket knife and stared at the pale blue paper. Ashamed, as he thought of her again, of the way it had all gone wrong. The break-up was three years old and he still remembered the good times, the times that she leaned against him, her washed hair on his mouth. And then that bastard Carlo who had entered the empty bits when Schiller was away. And the wretched, leaden memories of the final months with Charlie crying.

The words in the letter flowed over him and left him numbed. Maria Galina stood on her broom and watched.

"Can you put me up if I come out to Moscow? Charlie badly wants to see you. They say I can get a tourist visa without any trouble. Could you, Ed?" The words cut into the paper, black and strong.

Could you? Schiller looked round at Maria, and at his space: a depot full of equipment in a country of cold street corners, and imagined Nikky there with his son, talking, probing. Setting his teeth on edge. Asking more favors, discussing the marriage that he'd cut out and thrown away along with the holiday pics. Could you? He didn't know the answer to that one, he couldn't be expected to know, the day after Barsov's proposal. She wants to get in, and Lila to get out, he thought. In the meantime he had a job to maintain, an editor asking for feed, and the typewriter sat there reproaching him for his silence.

"I'm going out," he told the old cleaner.

She shook her head, suspecting it was a woman. "You mind how you go."

The Commercial Section on Kutuzovsky was open as if it was selling tickets. Applicants queued at the counter, the squashy black chairs were full, the air mushed with cheap cigarettes. All after information: Reagan had made some speech that had sharpened up peace prospects.

He nodded "Hello" to Tanner, whose neck looked rough and pink as he elbowed Schiller through, up the inner stairs. The strange smell still clung to the stair-rail.

"Cleaning these with fish paste?"

"No, sir. Red polish. And it's expensive."

"Caviar base," Schiller said.

They took him first to the committee room for a cup of coffee. He found both Taylor Sheen and Martin waiting,

Martin the Station Head, under cover in Cultural. That much they'd let Schiller know. A moon-faced man with granny-glasses, a complexion the color of cheese rind: Jubal Martin from Kansas City was lost in topsy-turvy land after twenty-five years of service. A bulky chief who moved his head very slowly: as he did so his eyes stayed fixed.

Martin shook hands without saying a word, while they drank from waxed paper beakers. It was always Sheen who did the talking.

"Glad you came back so soon, Ed." He flashed his executive smile. "Any developments Uncle Sam ought to know?"

"Yes." Schiller was being sucked in.

"OK," Sheen said brightly. "Let's go get the boys and have a talk."

Someone had changed the bottles and rearranged the glasses on the green baize, that was all. This time there were four of them crowding into the safe room where Sheen had met him before. A jockey-sized New Yorker from Intelligence called Harry Mirvish, and Sexton Legros, a visiting fireman from Langley HQ who had just flown in. Schiller knew trouble, looking at the newel post of Legros's face. These were the hard guys he ought to be writing about. When he sat down it was Legros who shut the door.

Sheen made a little gesture, his hair combed back as if he'd come out of a shower. "Cards on the table, Ed. What do you want to say?" He paused for effect, while scrub-haired Mirvish opened a bottle with a boy-scout tool on his key chain. "How did the Barsov visit go?"

Schiller put on his stonewall face. "Just like you imagined, Taylor."

Taylor Sheen, gray-suited today, adjusted the yellow bandana in his breast pocket, took out his notebook and began the doodling routine.

"OK. What did the old bastard say?"

"He was drunk."

"Sure he was drunk. They always are. They're a very basic people." He looked around for applause, but it was Martin's nasal voice which injected an air of reality.

"They put gooks on you, Ed, because you keep going there."

"Right," Schiller said.

"Come on, Ed. What did Barsov say?" Sheen asked impatiently.

"They know they're under threat."

"So, what's news. Does Barsov want to come over?" Sheen asked again. .

Just at that moment Ed Schiller hated Sheen more than he cared to admit, hated being other men's pawns. Barsov's vision of Lila had unnerved him.

"He wants us to get him out. Barsov."

Jubal Martin and Sheen glanced at each other; Mirvish chortled and a thin smile of gratification spread over Legros's face.

Sheen whistled in self-satisfaction. "Well. What do you know. The old bastard really wants to quit, before he gets a one-way ticket to Siberia."

Martin made clucking noises with his tongue, implying that this was now a job for him.

"How does he plan to come out?"

"Berlin. Next month. East–West Writers' Congress."

Sheen began a count down. "Three weeks. Four weeks. Shit, where did he tell you this? His whole damned place will be wired."

"In the open. He just said he wanted help." And nothing else you need to know, Schiller decided. The rest had been a private message between Barsov and himself. So far as Sheen was concerned, Schiller was a go-between, and they could leave it at that.

He explained Barsov's plea in the playground.

Little Mirvish chipped in. "Ed could take a message back. We'll work on it."

Legros took his spectacles off and sucked the ends, looking more vulnerable, as if he'd lost his shell.

"Wait a minute, boys. Hold on now. Did he say why he wants to come over? What's in it for us?"

"Not in detail. Just that he's lost his bearings. The KGB have roughed their place up. It can't be any life for the wife and kid. He wants out."

Sheen nodded delightedly. "Great. That figures. We can really use a story like that. Good material, Ed."

But then Legros cut in, pulling rank. "Hey, who says we want him out? We don't want sale offers."

Taylor Sheen flushed. "Pardon me, sir. Barsov could give us one hell of a break. Human rights. Censorship. Freedom of expression . . ."

"Just leave it," Legros said thinly.

Secrets were shut in his face, behind the recessed eyes. "Question one, why does he want to come? Question two, where do we put him?"

Sheen looked sheepish, but felt he had to say something. "Ed says he wants freedom to publish."

"That right, Ed? How many books he got suitable for Des Moines and Phoenix, Arizona?"

Schiller said, "He read me part of a story about cosmonauts stranded in space. *Challenger* in slow motion. It would sell like hot-cakes."

"Can we get that out with him?"

"Sure. But he also wants to bring out his wife and kid."

There was a sharp silence, as if he had said something obscene. Sheen poured himself water, made vigorous strokes on his pad. "Great," he announced. "We ought to make this a big one, Sexton. Hounded writer escapes. Freedom in the West. Human rights and all that crap. What d'you say, Jubal?" There was a manic enthusiasm in his eye. "As for the wife and kid, why not? Human interest story. We bring 'em out separately, reunion in . . . maybe Vienna or some place. I can see it all, tears of relief, marvelous TV stuff. Barsov hugs the little kid."

"Right," Mirvish agreed, "that's good."

But Martin was looking as if Legros had kicked him under the table and Legros's voice came from tubes in his nose.

"We don't want the wife and boy." It was a flat assertion, no way a query, and Schiller felt a cold knife blade.

"Barsov wants to bring them out." Still Sheen misjudged the message. "Listen, sir, he's shit-scared and he wants to get the hell out, with his wife. Let's hit the button for him. The media would love it."

Legros's eyes disowned him, looking only at Jubal Martin. Sheen really didn't matter.

"Just leave the politics of this one to me, Taylor. The cold war's shit. These are the Gorbie days. There's no way we bring out Barsov and family. No way. If the Reds let him go, that is another matter. But we're not working them off. No way. He gets out on his own butt, or not at all."

Schiller knew that meant never. The Soviets would not volunteer a man like Barsov, at the height of his powers, but just in case he slipped them, in East Berlin or elsewhere, Lila and Yuri were hostage.

But he tried.

"You've got it wrong, so help me. Barsov has worked it out. He wants us to lay on a kidnap in West Berlin, so that he can say he was forced to choose. There must be Krauts who would do it. That way they won't assume that it was planned. Then he lies low for a bit, agitates for his wife, and we step up the human rights campaign. Gorbachev lets her go."

"Great scenario. And Ed says that he really wants her. I asked him," Sheen burbled. "He's not screwing anyone else." With a look of amazement he added, "Ed says the woman's in love."

Legros brought his hands together, long, bony priest's hands. "She's twenty years younger, his second marriage. How do we know that she's not a KGB plant? We don't want a creeper in our back garden."

"I don't believe that," Schiller said. "It's simply not true."

"I said we don't want the wife. Even if they let him go voluntarily. Better to make 'em look bastards."

"They won't let him go," Schiller said. "He told me. There's nothing in it for them. Barsov writes stuff that would come over big in the West. He's no Solzhenitsyn that nobody really reads. It's love and blood and guts and anti-Soviet as well. He could support himself. They won't take a chance on that."

"I reckon that's right," Legros agreed. "But even if they do, we don't want her. She's worth more left behind. If she really loves the old man, and maybe he pines for her, we show up the whole lousy system.''

Schiller knew then that Legros was not there by chance, any more than he had guessed that the kid was a boy. Legros had done his homework, harbored the same suspicions that Schiller had once had on Lila, suspicions he could not accept. In the CIA tradition any story had a bum side. The safe room was inside a cat-house where none of them were quite sane: Legros with his strategic view, Jubal Martin working for a clean retirement, Sheen with his Hollywood script. They didn't want to help anyone except themselves.

"If Barsov is opting out, he's got to work his ticket," Legros intoned. "Make it worth Uncle Sam's while."

"The book . . ."

"We haven't seen the book. Only what you told us, Ed. Have you got a copy of the typescript? He talked turkey with you. Where is it, Ed?"

"The KGB took his papers."

"Well, you ask 'em. Find some of his stuff and I'll get a professional view."

Jubal Martin shifted his paunch. "Maybe we ought to keep our options open." He was overweight and perspiring: Schiller saw rivulets running inside his gold frames.

Little Mirvish took it upon himself to busybody the bottles and glasses, irritating them all. "If we don't . . . want . . . Barsov, what the hell are we all here for?"

Legros's long white face was a poisoned smile. "I didn't say we don't want him. We might, but it's on our terms. And our terms don't include the wife and kid. They stay right where they are, on the other side of the fence. A case of rights denied."

Mirvish knocked over a mineral water bottle and hastily stood it upright. "Sorry."

Schiller thought again of the letter he'd had that morning. Nicola, wanting to join him: Lila who couldn't get out, and Barsov who'd offered her to him.

"No. For Christ's sake, no. They've got to be helped as a family."

Jubal Martin leaned back on his tubular chair so hard that it creaked. "Ed, be reasonable . . ."

Depression and anger showed on Schiller's lean face. He wanted help now. Berlin, in three weeks' time. And Lila had to come too, at the end of the process.

But none of them were interested, taking their lead from Legros. Mirvish collapsed into silence, Martin sweated. Sheen said, "Go, take a rest, Ed. Forget it." Now it was Legros, precise as a surgeon, who was in control.

"Never underestimate the Reds—"

"I'm not here for the politics. I work on human stories..."

"Never underestimate them, Ed. We've got to look at Barsov as a small pawn in a big game. If we knock him off who gets the shit? We do, Ed. So let's trail the book first, then maybe in a year or two when we've got his stock going..." He cleared his throat "... that could be good, Ed. Specially with the human rights angle. We could really turn it on then: wife and child detained as author flees to freedom." He even smiled.

"In two years he'll be dead," Schiller said, "in a labor camp." He felt sick with himself and sick with them. Selfishness and self-preservation, they came from the same bottle. Sheen, Martin, Mirvish and Legros were each of them proof of that: none of them seemed aware that Barsov and Lila were human, that if you scratched them they bled.

And Taylor Sheen, Sheen who had only recently implied that he had a plan for Barsov, was now turned around by Legros, and he washed his hands and stole away.

"You look tired, Ed. Bad sign, need a vacation. Too long in Moscow."

Ice ran along Schiller's spine as Legros rubbed in the lesson.

"Don't let Barsov fool you, Ed. His inspirations are in Russia, not Mount Rushmore. Listen Ed, and don't forget. If he ever comes out it's not on his terms but ours. Uncle Sam don't set up a kidnap to play into their hands. The President's strong on terrorism. Defection like that is bad medicine, the oldest trick in the book. He'd be a thorn in our flesh. Anyway, Reds never tell the truth, you know that, Ed." He gave his wintry smile, hitched his tie forward. "Pathological liars, drunken scum by the bucketful." He

opened his arms as if concluding a sermon. "You go see
and explain."

"What do I tell him?" Schiller asked.

"Tell him the answer is no. Not now. Not yet, but maybe
some day." A chilly smile of dismissal broke through the
cavernous face. "Let's have the book first." He held out his
hand, and thrust it back in his pocket. Schiller was being
dismissed, and he took his own decision.

"No, I'm not going back to say that," he said. "Not
now. Not ever."

Walking back down the corridor, Sheen pulled him into his
office, followed by Jubal Martin.

"I'm sorry Ed . . . I didn't know about Sexton until he
arrived."

"I thought you were interested in helping Barsov . . ."

"I was . . . I am. It's as simple as that."

They looked at each other. Schiller nodded slowly,
wondering if Sheen after all might be an ally.

"You know you're already staked out by the KGB,"
Sheen volunteered.

"Is that so?"

"They are watching you, Ed. All the time. One of them
is the girl you spoke to. And those guys in the car who
follow you around."

"KGB sentries. Harmless."

Sheen shrugged. "Maybe, but you got to be careful."

He flicked the leaves of a *Playboy* calendar on the wall.
"In this God-awful town . . ." This was his cowboy style
and he turned round to confront Schiller. "You don't much
like me, Ed, but I'm trained for the game we're playing.
Better than you. Believe me, if I thought that I could get
Barsov out in one piece, I would. I thought maybe a week
or two ago that we could try. But now it's out of my hands.
Legros calls a different tune: he's National Security Agency.
NSA trumps CIA. He counts for something out here, Ed. I
guess he's got a great big stake on human rights. You read
me?"

Schiller was surprised to find his chest felt tight. Barsov's
presence came back to him: The Tolstoian head, a man who

had asked for help, for himself and his wife and child. In Schiller's pocket, Nicola's own letter was burning, promising a different reunion. He knew what that would mean; Nikky, sharp-nosed and sexy, who would not stop till she had him, because it renewed her power. And Charlie was now growing up torn between the two of them. Christ, he had messed up the kid, fucked up a marriage . . . why should he compare it with Barsov's? Because he had seen the way that Lila looked.

They were watching him hesitate, Jubal Martin and Taylor Sheen. Martin, still perspiring, eased himself into a chair, Sheen opened a drawer in his desk. He took out an automatic, black, flat-handled and heavy-looking.

"You got a gun?" he asked, cowboy again, preparing for the shoot-out.

"I'm a newspaper man, not a gun-slinger."

Sheen ignored that. "Walther P.38. Conventional handgun. Simple and straightforward. Quite a lot in circulation in Russia, from the war and since. Easy to get your ammo in from Germany. Eight-round box magazine, semi-automatic, not too big. Good killing machine." He thrust it towards Schiller. "Why don't you take it, Ed? It's disposable."

"What the hell do I want with a gun?"

"You shoot someone."

Schiller was stunned. Martin wiped his brow with a handkerchief.

"Who do you want me to shoot?"

"Barsov," Sheen said.

At first he thought Sheen was joking, but the CIA man simply elaborated, handing the gun butt first. "Check it out, Ed. You fired one of these? Offset the lock, so, one pull on the trigger cocks the hammer, full cock, strikes the bullet. Recoil then recocks for the next round. Dead simple. OK?" He demonstrated with the empty gun, and produced a packet of shells. Martin grunted.

"You're mad." Schiller said.

"No way. You've got the perfect chance. We get you back to that apartment, unmarked car, late, you see him alone, he knows you. Bang. Out. Wife and boy needn't know: we could decoy 'em outside of the house, take 'em on a trip some place. Gun disposable. Soviets glad to get rid of him . . .'' He paused for breath. ''And then we nail 'em. Accuse them of cold-blooded murder, rubbing out the protest voice. Photograph of black figure, going in with the gun. And posthumous book to prove it. Wow.'' He shone with hope. ''What do you say?''

''You're mad.''

The gun lay untouched on the table between them, an evil toy. ''Let me alone,'' Schiller said, his mind screaming inside him. Were these sane men, in a real world?

''Sure, Ed. But think about it. Know what they say? If you can't beat 'em, kill 'em. It might be the best way, Ed. Put him out of his misery. His wife'll find somebody.''

Schiller pushed the Walther away with the side of his hand. ''The first guy I shoot will be you.''

That brought the wolf grin. ''Wouldn't help Uncle Sam. No, sir, not that one. But Barsov rubbed out, leaving a widow, there's a scenario.''

Schiller was washed up with them, all of them, the hammers were in his head again. He pushed Jubal Martin aside, snatched open the door and ran.

On the opposite side of the road, KGB Grade 9 Elena Amalrik saw the American again, the one who had accosted her. This time he was in a hurry, looking mad, and because she knew he was different, possibly dangerous, she took a telephoto snapshot, for the photo files at Headquarters. She watched him jump into a car and thought he was a wild one. But the picture was of such poor quality, when developed, that her line manager tore it up.

6

Schiller couldn't go back now, without betraying them all: Barsov, Lila and Yuri. In the three weeks to Barsov's Berlin

deadline he started to run wild. In Washington, Sylvester
kept agitating, asking what he was paying for, demanding
more material; outside, the KGB sentries were always at the
door. Nero and Archie must have been on overtime. His
visits to the Press Club ceased. Apart from Jim Burrell of
CBS and Hatter of the London *Times*, two of his first
friends in Moscow, he saw none of his cronies.

Burrell took the trouble to visit.

"Come on out, Ed, the water's warm. I'll buy you a
dinner. Why are you hiding?"

In his mind he was hiding from Lila, but what he said
was, "I guess I'm feeling a bit rough." Burrell saw that he
was drinking, and counted seven empty bottles beside the
refrigerator.

Schiller could not go back because Alexei Sergevich had
changed his perspectives. The mere thought of being offered
Lila made him look over himself from somewhere high up
on the ceiling. He saw himself go through the motions: get
up, shave, dress, sit at the typewriter, write a couple of
pieces, brush up an old story on garage mechanics, correct,
dispatch over the line, buy in some basic foods, cook alone
in the apartment more like a tip than ever, drink, and hope
to fall asleep. Barsov's proposal was eating into his mind,
but he dared not return to face it, or to discuss Berlin. It had
to end here and now, that triangular friendship, he tried to
persuade himself. He saw Lila's face again, blurred as if
through soft-focus, a shadowy oval, but only remembered
her eyes, fixed on Barsov. Schiller was drowning, while
Nicola wrote to resume diplomatic relations, and Charlie
was at school in Newark, New Jersey.

There was no more from Sheen or Martin, and Legros
had gone to ground. Schiller had thought, half hoped, that
maybe Sheen would come back at him, saying that the
proposal to rub out the Russian was a kind of joke, and that
they would help after all. But no one moved, and two
women circled his mind; Nicola expecting an answer to a
letter that must have cost her, Lila the subject of Barsov's
private offer, almost as if he foretold that he might not
survive. Barsov approaching Berlin, expecting something to
happen, perhaps hoping to hear. Shut on the sixteenth floor

of the slab in Kalinin Prospekt, Schiller drank to persuade himself that fresh contact would raise false hopes.

Another frantic call from Washington. Sly Sylvester asking for better copy.

"Jesus, Ed, I went to sleep reading that last one. Get some news, Ed, bad news. What's happened to you? Crap about mending automobiles."

"Get lost."

"Say that again, Ed, and you're off the line."

"Get lost."

"You sick or something? You'd better see a doctor."

"I'm all right. Maybe a bit tired." And then it fell into place. "Listen Sly. I want to go to Berlin."

"Berlin, for Christ's sake. We got Joe Habkirk there. You stick to Moscow. That's what we hire you for."

Schiller took a risk on the unguarded call.

"My friends are going to Berlin."

Sly Sylvester had not been in the newspaper business for twenty-three years without knowing what was a lead. In the big newsroom, feet on the desk, cradling the telephone and picking his teeth. "You say Berlin?"

"A short vacation. Working holiday."

"Yeah?"

"I want to leave now," Schiller said.

There was a long pause.

"OK, so you need a vacation. Get moving, Ed."

When he replaced the phone Schiller stopped drinking. The sun in Moscow suddenly seemed brighter, slanting in through the blinds, and he had the answer to Nicola.

He rang her twice before he got through, nine hours difference, the end of her day, if he could catch her. She sounded at first as if she didn't understand him, puzzled, a little irritated.

"Ed. Where are you?"

"Where I always am. In Moscow."

The line was crackly but distinct. He imagined her in a state of undress, a slip perhaps, with another man in the room, or maybe on the bed, the curtains drawn, a sense of masquerade, watching her body.

"Is Charlie there, with you?"

"No. Charlie's asleep. Ed, did you get my letter? I posted it a week ago."

"Sure. I got it. Great to know you're OK."

"About the trip," she said hastily. "Listen, I meant it. Charlie wants to see you. He talks about you, Ed, all the time." Pulling at his heartstrings, the cat.

"I don't reckon I can do you, or Charlie, any good. I'm better out of the way."

"But I want to see you, too. Goddam it, the longer I leave it, the more . . . hell, the more I miss you."

He knew that kind of appeal, had fallen for it once, would never do so again. No way, he told her.

"But Eddie, listen. You don't have to sleep us. They've got hotels and things. Just book us in some place. We want to see you again. For Christ's sake, we miss you, Ed. The both of us."

There was no joy in that for him.

"Anyways, you can't stop me coming out. I've got the visa," she said. "The guy in the consulate couldn't have been more helpful." Maybe she was lying again, testing him, or maybe she had gone that far. He was sure there was a man there listening, sitting on her bed. It made him feel dirty.

"I won't be here," he said flatly.

"What do you mean, you won't be there?"

"I'm leaving . . . for Berlin."

"Aw shit. What the hell is that for, Ed?" He caught the disappointment in her voice. "When are you going there?"

"Following something up," he said. "In a few days. I don't know how long I'll be there."

"Where will you stay?" she demanded. "Ed, maybe we could link up there. Berlin is easy."

He yelled down the line at her. "Listen baby, I'm sorry. We aren't meeting: Have you got that? There is no mileage in it, not even for Charlie. I'm sorry, Nikky, I'm damned sorry, but I'm not unpicking the dressing I've got over the scab. And if you've got any sense, you won't either. I don't know why you pester me—".

"—Pester! I love you, Eddie," she shrieked. He could imagine her sobbing into a box of Kleenex.

"Nikky, you don't love anybody except your own sweet ass. I got to tell you that."

"I love, love, love you, Eddie, darling," Nicola was yelling. And he knew then that there was no one with her. He steeled himself to remember that she had killed the marriage, driven him out, stood there with the smoking gun.

"It's no good, Nikky. I'm sorry but I can't see you. I won't be in Moscow." He could hear her bitterness, trying to make him feel a bastard, but it had to be done. "Listen, honey. You've got to understand something. We are through. Finished. Washed up as a team. It wouldn't work again, Nikky. You must know that."

"It could, Eddie, it could. I need you."

"Listen. You're a smart girl. Plenty more fish in the sea. You don't have to rehook me."

"Charlie. Charlie needs a father."

"I've told you, Nikky. Find him one: but don't look at me."

When he put the receiver down his hands were shaking, perspiring, as if he'd been driving a car when the brakes had failed. The pit he had dug for himself, this loveless heap gave him nothing: it was a subsistence pad, loaded with survival kit, from the bank of tapes by the bed to the cans of food in the kitchen, and it meant nothing. Nowhere was permanent now. He was no better than a counter jerk, a misfit with a past, making a living from exile. No wonder that criminal Sheen had thought that he might be a killer.

The Ministry of Culture, on the other hand, couldn't have been more helpful when he paid them a visit in their factory on Pirogovskaya Street. A poster beside the door proclaimed "Artists for Peace and Freedom" and an earnest young woman sorted out a clutch of leaflets for the East–West Writers' Congress.

"You are welcome. How lucky to go to a rally in Berlin."

He smiled. A small farce to add to the Barsov problem. No doubt a few tame hacks, some left of center softnuts, would attend for the freebies and suffer a week of sermons: committed journalists, significant poets, novelists who wrote about love on collective farms. In the land of the censorship committee to publish is a political achievement.

He debated again if he should ring Barsov to find out the where and the when, and decided against it. There was always a car on his tail, a raincoat in the opposite doorway. They would be monitoring everything he said and did. West Berlin needed no visa, they couldn't stop him travelling, but any move to contact Barsov would immediately set bells ringing. He pocketed his tickets and went back alone.

The day before he was due to fly West, Schiller was pulled out to dinner at the Bucharest in Balchug Street by Jim Burrell and Hatter. The restaurant was large and steamy, with partitions dividing the tables, candles, white cloths, and a Caucasian band.

Burrell chose their table with care, well away from the music. A white-haired Russophile, doyen of the foreign press corps, he was a small, sharp man with a clipped Ronald Colman moustache, darker than his hair as if it had been glued on. He exuded *bonhomie*, while Rolfe Hatter slipped effortlessly into his act.

"We were worried about you, Ed. You seemed to have hibernated."

Schiller said no, he'd just been drinking, that's all.

"Not broody or anything?"

"Just taking it easy. A bit tired."

Burrell supped noisily, spooning a chilled soup of vegetables and meat. He was a compulsive eater; the *Times* man was more circumspect. Burrell shouted above the noise, in between trying for service.

"Not like you, Ed. You were a gregarious bastard. Got a book on the way; or some girl knocked up?"

"No," Schiller muttered darkly, shut up inside his thoughts.

Burrell had liked Schiller from their first meeting, nearly two years before when Ed had arrived in Moscow, washed out and lost, his world in two Antler bags. In a sense he had sorted him out and found him the Kalinin apartment. Now he leaned across in a paternal way, cashing his IOU.

"You need a woman, Ed. Ever hear from Nicola? Or is it really all over?"

Schiller drank his wine slowly before replying. "I hear from time to time." The telephone conversation was still fresh in his mind. "She wants . . . she wants to come to Moscow."

Jim Burrell rode that off. He ordered another bottle and tackled the roast chicken, loading Schiller's plate with a mess of mushroom and greens.

"You don't say. Doesn't she want to let go?"

Schiller shrugged. "I don't know. She says she can't. Keeps bringing up the boy."

"You've got grounds to see the boy. Maybe she'd bring him with her . . ."

"Oh sure. Cut it out, Jim."

Hatter wiped his mouth. "Women are beyond me. As human beings, I mean. Motivation impossible." He savored a slice of chicken on the end of his fork, turning it round for inspection. "Look at their eyes. You never know where you are. Like those Diplomatic girls, the handmaidens."

The last thing Schiller wanted was to be reminded of Darleen. He changed the subject. "Rolfe, I'm leaving tomorrow for Berlin. No time for diplomacy." His eyes seemed studiedly casual.

Hatter controlled his curiosity, leaving the pitch to Burrell.

"Berlin, for Chrissake. What the hell's going on there, Ed?"

"East–West Writers' Congress."

"Bullshit," Jim Burrell declared. "A garbage convention. Ideologically sterile." He rubbed his moustache. "Funny how in Moscow you come to think of that kind of jargon. But the East–West Writers' Chrissakes in Berlin. It's no go, Ed. All those dumb declarations of friendship and socialism."

Schiller gave a half-smile. "Why not? The *Post* is paying the vacation."

"You mean Sly OK'd it?"

"Sure thing."

"In that case who else is going: to make it worth your while?"

Schiller hesitated, produced a string of names. "Lermentov, Oreanda Miskhova, Surovov—you know, the guy who wrote *Night in Spring*—Vladimir Lorenz, Barsov . . ."

Hatter was less a fool than he liked to imply, which was why Burrell knew him. He pounced at once.

"Ah, Barsov. They going to let him out? Off the chain I mean?"

"So I believe."

Hatter said, "I recommend the puddings here: particularly the charlotte russe." Peering about him carefully in the smoky room, as if he expected cameras inside the potted plants, he added, "Barsov is for the chop," bringing his hand sideways down on the table.

The sickening feeling in Schiller's stomach was that he would be too late, and it would be his fault.

"What makes you think that?"

Somebody started singing, yodelling to an accordion, and the waiter was leaning over them, his shirt-front stained, pouring out still more wine until Hatter waved him away.

"It's the say-so." Hatter had his ear to the ground.

If Barsov went, Lila was left, and now Hatter was confirming his hopes and fears. Schiller set the base of his glass on the white linen, and the stain was a dark red circle.

"He's been asked to make a speech. Barsov."

Hatter nodded. "They would, wouldn't they? At the end of the rope. Enough to hang himself."

Burrell finished his dessert and produced a jar of instant coffee; beckoning the waiter he asked for a glass of hot water.

"Lemme have some decent coffee." He waited while it was brought, then, "Is that why you're going? Barsov?"

"I don't know," Schiller said. "I think I need some help."

7

At Treptow Park war memorial, East Berlin, the stands were in place and the Red Army Band played Mendelssohn as

Schiller watched the honor guard march down the avenue between the blocks of brown granite. Heroes Day preceded the East–West Congress, as soldiers in soft black boots paraded with lowered banners. Their heels crashed down on the gravel. The spectators were few but the stands were full of freeloaders: diplomats, attachés, politicians and hangers-on penned into wooden stalls together with the press contingent, and the delegates to the East–West symposium facing Schiller on the other side. They stood in the pale lemon sunshine, looking down on the burial mounds around which the red flags fluttered.

The color party finished gyrating and the band began the Dead March. Everybody stood to attention. Over the bared heads red flags whipped in the breeze. In the stands opposite, Schiller seemed to be counting the generals, but his eyes roved along the civilians grouped on the right: the delegation of writers and artists.

Across the communal graves, across the Technicolor grass, he was searching for Barsov.

There were a lot of faces, indistinguishable heads in shadow, but one of them stood out in his sights. Standing beside Schiller, Joe Habkirk, the *Post* man for the Federal Republic, watched the line of his eyes.

"That him? That your friend?" Habkirk was young and enthusiastic, still mesmerized by the glamor of being a foreign correspondent. His three-piece suit lent him an air of authority; he had taken to spectacles early.

"I think so." Schiller could not be sure, but the powerful thick-set figure even at that distance carried its integrity in the over-large, balding forehead and straggling hair.

Schiller felt a thrill of excitement, of confirmation. They had not seen each other since that last drinking session in the crowded Moscow apartment, followed by Barsov's appeal. The playground, the mud round the swings, the children shouting in the distance were as real as today. Alexei Sergevich had pressed a case, conveyed a message with a drunken twist of the arm. Schiller glanced at Habkirk, who had caught something of the excitement, and Habkirk grinned, and made a sign with his hand.

"Drinks, Ed. Coming up soon." He pointed towards the

pavilion, an elaborate blue-striped marquee erected at the far end behind the great sculpted figure on the war memorial which dominated the graves, the bas reliefs and the banners.

They waited while the band stopped and the march-past resumed, a goose step in basin-helmets. The soldiers upright as fence-posts, marching slowly, with reversed weapons. Nothing but the crunch of boots, a rattle of magazines.

The sun seemed cold as it touched the mounds in the grass. The honor guard laid red roses, the band struck up again, more cheerfully, marking the end.

"Parade, dismiss," Joe Habkirk said under his breath.

They watched the soldiers march away, first the color party then the band. Like prisoners released from detention the dignitaries scrambled down and made for the refreshment tent in order of seniority: first the ambassadors and senior political figures, next the military brass, then the writers and representatives for peace and harmony, the remaining public servants, the pressmen and camp followers, including Schiller and Habkirk.

The marquee was large and hot, lined with trestle tables laden with drink, sparkling wine, vodka and beer. There seemed to be nothing to eat.

"This won't feed the five thousand," Habkirk said gloomily as they elbowed through. He went in search of food, and at once Schiller was ambushed by a Red Army lieutenant anxious to practice his English.

"Skol, as they say." He introduced himself as Tukmanov, on the liaison staff of the garrison at Potsdam.

"Cheers."

"You are press, from West Berlin?"

"No," Schiller admitted. "Moscow."

Tukmanov's eyebrows rose. There was something goat-like about him: thin, a stubbly head of hair, inquisitive eyes, glasses, his uniform shiny and tight so that his arms stuck out. He seemed to be foraging.

"Oh. I thought that I did not recognize." He smiled grimly. "I liaise with the press. News of our maneuvers, and so on. You come a long way?"

"Yes. A bit of a vacation."

Schiller had to look for someone else, without appearing to do so. Habkirk recharged the drinks, and Lieutenant Tukmanov stuck to his victim.

"But why come to East Berlin?" He waved his arm. "Heroes Day!"

"It might give me a story."

"Ah, then you are a correspondent." His English was almost faultless. "British newspaper?"

"No way. American."

"Oh. My mistake. Which paper?"

Schiller parted with the information almost resentfully: this was a Commie Sheen. *Washington Post*.

Tukmanov's large eyes widened unblinkingly. "A good paper. You will have known Bernstein and . . . Woodward. Watergates eh?"

"That was a long time ago."

"But a great press triumph would you say? The Watergates?"

"Watergate is a hotel." Someone elbowed Schiller in the back, and he jogged forward.

"Sorry." It was Habkirk. "Ed, we'd better circulate."

Tukmanov smiled by raising his upper lip.

"Excuse me. It is busy in here. I will toast to your vacation. One more question, please."

"If you insist."

"Thank you."

Joe Habkirk had found a waitress with a tray of roll-mop herrings. "These are good, Ed."

Tukmanov swallowed a herring, his Adam's apple bobbing. "So," he said politely, "an American newsman from Moscow. Why come here to East Berlin? To a military ceremony?"

"Good ceremony."

Tukmanov considered that. "Yes. But it happens every year. You did not come last time."

Habkirk said, "I was around. I told him how great it was." Under his breath he muttered, "Arse-licking. Let's move."

But Tukmanov stuck like a limpet. "Maybe we talk more about it. I could give you good stories. You know I come from Kalinin. That is not far from Moscow: one hundred and fifty kilometers. Do you know it?''

"I've been there." Eyes still searching without appearing to do so.

"Are you looking for someone?" Tukmanov seized more vodka.

"No."

That was dangerous, for Schiller had caught sight of Barsov.

"Then why are you waiting here?"

"Enjoying the atmosphere." It was happy hour as the Russians tanked up. Over on his left there was a burst of clapping, and Barsov emerged from a scrimmage carrying four large glasses. He disappeared into more bodies.

"Why have you come to Berlin, please?" The irritating little lieutenant would not let well alone.

"Fun," Schiller said.

Cheerfully, Habkirk added, "Why don't you run off now. Leave us to cover the Writers' Congress."

"So," Tukmanov said brightly, taking off his glasses and rubbing them with a khaki handkerchief. "You will be attending those boring meetings?"

"I guess so. One or two, now I'm here."

"You write books?"

"One day I'll write a book. About Russia."

The Russian's bleak eyes weighed that one up. "Would you perhaps like a ticket for the President's reception tomorrow? In the Deutsche Staatsoper. It would be my pleasure."

It was time to back off.

"Great. No. Thank you. I've got another deal. But my friend Joe Habkirk here would be delighted . . .''

"Shit," Habkirk said.

Schiller was slipping away in the crowd through the uniformed backs. He had seen Alexei Sergevich again, moving towards the exit accompanied by another man.

They met on the grass outside, in the sunshine. Barsov's conversation never faltered as his eyes found the American. It was as if he just recalled some casual, distant meeting. A crush of people stood around in the sunshine, looking down on the war memorial.

"Hello . . . Ed Schiller," Barsov said, as Ed went over. "I remember when we last met. Last month in Moscow, wasn't it?" A good presentation, headmasterly surprise. He was dressed in a sports coat over a check shirt and tie.

"Alexei Sergevich. Delighted to find you here. I wondered if you would be coming to Berlin."

Barsov smiled, tobacco-stained teeth, as if the meeting was of no importance. Searching his face for a message, some private meaning, Schiller could only see caution, a peasant reserve. The crumpled yet statuesque figure might belong to academic. Schiller reminded himself that this was what Barsov once was, a university historian, before becoming a playwright and novelist, then the persecuted hero of *Novy Mir*. Now Alexei Sergevich had a minder, a long-headed, sardonic young man whom Schiller did not mistake for a fellow intellectual. In the background the band reassembled, playing music from the *Nutcracker* ballet. The night he had taken Nikky out, soon after they first made it, Schiller had listened to the very same music; seats at the Met, supper at Tiberio's. He drove the memory from his mind and watched for some move from the Russian.

Instead, Barsov said in the flattest tone, "So, you have come for the Congress after all? Maybe to . . . hear me?"

"No. Not really. A little vacation."

"I don't blame you. It will be boring. I long for a little excitement."

"You must come to West Berlin."

Barsov's eyes flashed, but he turned to survey the crowd behind him, noisy with free drink.

"I am coming. I hope they will let me."

"When will that be?"

"Charlottenburg. Friday. I am guest at the PEN meeting." He spoke slowly in English.

"I'm sure there will be a good reception," Schiller found himself saying. Just for a moment the sharp blue eyes stared him down, as they had done in Moscow.

"Please, we go," his shadow muttered. Schiller was

suddenly aware that Lieutenant Tukmanov had arrived there too, with Joe Habkirk in tow.

The minder was pushing Barsov away. As if to steady himself, Alexei Sergevich caught one hand against the guy ropes. His fist clawed into his coat, and he pulled out a cheap leather wallet.

"Look." A small square of paper fluttered to the ground. A photograph twisting in the sunshine.

Schiller saw it was Lila, relaxed and smiling, holding Yuri on one of the swings. A snapshot of the same playground, the same position in which Barsov had appealed, even down to the caretaker's hut. There could be no mistaking that particular message.

The minder was anxious. "We must go," he demanded in Russian.

Lieutenant Tukmanov retrieved the photograph, and handed it to Barsov.

"Ah. A pretty woman. Your wife, I assume?"

Barsov did not reply, but only nodded.

"Come on, comrade," the minder said. "I ought to be taking you back. The coach will be leaving and there are others to meet." He slipped a hand like a hook on to Barsov's elbow.

Alexei Sergevich gave one last glance as he hurried away.

"What's the matter?" Joe Habkirk asked, as they watched the Russians disappear. "You look as if you've seen a ghost."

"Maybe I have," Schiller said.

Tukmanov returned. "You have met Alexei Barsov often? You should be careful, he has a reputation."

"What for?"

"For wine and women."

"Is that all?"

"No. Not quite. He is also . . . what you call a dissident."

"I thought Mikhail Gorbachev allowed them now."

Tukmanov laughed, as if that was a good joke.

The party was breaking up and Schiller made his goodbyes. He walked away across the grass with Habkirk, down the long avenue between the bas reliefs towards the car park. They drove in Habkirk's big new Volvo across

Engelsplatz and through the Friedrichsstrasse checkpoint. It was only when they were back beyond the Wall, in West Berlin, that Habkirk said, "My advice is don't be stupid." He looked straight ahead, concentrating on the traffic.

"Why would I try?"

"Because you look hyped up, Ed. You can't bullshit him free."

Schiller smiled. "You had some kind of warning?"

Habkirk braked to avoid a van driven by a lunatic. "Jim Burrell."

"The bastard."

"Yeah. Well. Don't."

Habkirk parked to drop him off along the Kurfürstendamm, before going back to his office. As an afterthought he added, "Want me to drive you over and case out Charlottenburg?"

"I don't think so."

Suddenly serious, Habkirk leaned out of the car. "Remember what that Red lieutenant said. You take care."

"Sure. Always do."

Habkirk was hesitating, keeping the engine running. "He wants to come over, doesn't he?"

Schiller nodded. "He wants to bring out his wife and kid."

"I see that. The Agency won't help?"

"How can they with the wife in Moscow?"

"I see that too." Difficult to hear him over the grind of traffic.

Habkirk's dark eyes were not that young. "I guess it's no risks these days in Langley. Low profile. No political upsets." He seemed to be deciding something, and Schiller remembered Legros.

"What?" Schiller roared.

"Jim Burrell."

"Burrell? I've told you what I think of his interfering."

"He gave me a name," Habkirk said in his ear. "Told me to use it only if you insist."

Schiller shivered. "Yeah. I insist."

"Down in the soiled goods. The underground."

"OK."

Habkirk grinned. "There's a guy called Heusermann. He knows the Wall trade, but he's elusive." He spelled it carefully. "You could check him out."

Schiller decided. "Who gets me through to him?"

Habkirk patted the steering wheel. "There's a contact. A Brit called Andy Shawcross. A business guy. Rep for candies and chocolate bars."

"A rep for confectionery?"

"You bet. He calls 'em sweets. Mars Bars. Cadbury's. Black Magic. You go down to the KaDewe store, it's stacked with his stuff. And he goes across the wall: they've got holes in their molars on the other side."

"Is he safe?"

"Safe as a safety-pin according to Jim Burrell."

8

Schiller was not surprised when Berlin Station came for him. He had gone back to the Hotel Amsterdam and was drinking beer in the bar. He wasn't sure why he was waiting, or who would come, but he was sure they would. In the mirror behind the bottles he looked haunted by his thirty-five years. Lines of experience cut into the tanned skin; and time he found a barber. Waiting for a message from someone, the Englishman Shawcross who had his name on an answerphone, or Habkirk maybe, or the Staatspolizei.

In fact it was a guy called Flannery who said he was a PO2, as he introduced himself.

"Political Officer, Second Grade." One of those punched-in faces that seem all hair and glasses, curly gray locks, pomaded. "The Station sent me. Heard you were here. I've got transport outside."

He stood in the bar as if he owned it wearing a crumpled

fawn raincoat, his eyes flitting round like a bird in a cage. He seemed to be alone.

Getting so close to Barsov's deadline it was too big an offer for Schiller to refuse.

"Who gave you my name?"

"Moscow Station asked us to keep an eye."

"Who was that?" Schiller queried. Martin or Sheen or Legros between them wouldn't let him go.

"Don't ask me."

"Where are we going?"

"Don't worry, Ed. Everything on the firm."

"I don't work for it."

"I do," Flannery said, his face in a kind of rictus.

They walked out to the Kurfürstendamm. Parked nearly opposite, where the duty hooker in white boots was on pick-up by the display case, was one of those buff-colored Fords used to standing on trade lots. Like Flannery it melted into the streetscape.

"Come on. Get in . . ."

Schiller wondered what would have happened if he had demurred, but that was not on the cards. They threaded into the Bundes-Allee and south through the Schöneberg suburbs, driving carefully.

"We've got a house in Dahlem," was all that Flannery volunteered.

In the leafier avenues the second cars were BMWs parked on the red-tiled run-ins. Near the commuter station, just past the museum, Flannery turned into the forecourt of a house under the trees. Apart from the number of cars parked it was indistinguishable from the row, a brick-built post-war residence with a shingle roof and double glazing.

The door opened as they arrived.

"OK." Flannery said. "Let's go."

It was a sub-Station. A sitting-room on the ground floor. As they led Schiller past it he saw only cream leather chairs, the back of a large settee, a winter scene over the fireplace.

"Top deck. I'll lead the way."

As if they were climbing to bedrooms, Schiller followed him up the stairs, past the white-painted landing with fresh flowers in a vase. The landing gave on to four doors, panelled and glossy white, speaking of coverlets and chintz, but as Flannery beckoned him the bedrooms vanished.

The other side of the doors was a single room, running the length of the house. A large room with a central table and video screens at the sides, a monitoring center. And in the room he counted eight men.

"Ed, I won't introduce us all," the thin man with the cropped hair said. He might have been in his forties, could have been ten years more, a ravaged face with rimless glasses. "But you should know who I am." He held out a hand. "Vince Claymore, escape co-ordinator."

The heads were watching Schiller as if he had just crossed over. Three Americans with button-down shirts. One who might have been French, another German, while the other two had hand-tailored suits. He took them either to be Brits, or pretending to be.

"Sit down, Ed," Claymore said, as soon as the door had closed.

Fluorescent tubes above them flickered. One of the big Americans wore cowboy boots.

"Tell us about this Barsov guy."

"He's got guts."

"Leave it a minute, Harry," Flannery said. "I've only just brought Ed in."

"Yeah. Let's have some coffee."

A Cona machine was bubbling in the corner and a girl came with paper cups. They waited while she served.

Schiller said gently, "Alexei Sergevich Barsov wants to bail out, and bring over his family. It's as simple as that. He knows the Reds won't let him, so he's looking for an escape plan. Preferred option: we kidnap, and make it look real."

Claymore smiled. His pock-marked skin and complexion gave away the years in Vietnam.

"They told you not to try that, back in Red Square. Didn't you talk to Legros?"

"Yes," Schiller snapped. "Legros and Sheen and Martin, none of them prepared to help."

"Ed boy, it ain't a question of help," Texan Harry said, "It's a matter of what we want."

Schiller said grimly, "Somebody had better tell me."

One of the Brits, the pin-striped one, began to warm up. "Mr. Schiller, we might get Barsov out. We could pick him up in Charlottenburg. But not Mrs. Barsov; and I believe there's a boy. Would that really matter?"

It laid the chips down heavily with a man who had abandoned one woman, and been offered another. Schiller hesitated.

"Well? It ought to be a simple question." Pin-stripe poked a finger through his polystyrene cup.

"I can't answer that."

"Can't answer?"

"Categorically, Ed," one of the Agency staff said, cutting in, "the U.S. Government would not favor bringing Barsov out."

"Moscow end made that plain. They wanted me to shoot him."

"Don't be ridiculous, Ed."

Schiller turned his coffee cup upside-down on the table, as he remembered Barsov.

"Barsov wants his wife and child. He won't come over on his own unless you kidnap him. That way it makes it clean to his own side."

"And dirty to us," Texas said.

The little man opposite, who seemed to be French, lit a cheroot and announced, "The woman could be left."

"I didn't come here to be told that. I came because I thought you might help."

"No one has any instruction to help Alexei Sergevich Barsov," Claymore said, rolling the names on his tongue.

Schiller's bottled anger broke out. He wanted to get up and run then, just as he had run away from Iowa, from the farm as a boy, from Franz's orders, do this, do that, do as I say.

"Then fuck you," he said.

"What do you mean, Ed?" Claymore asked.

He didn't know what he meant. He was shouting at them that they couldn't expect him to abandon Barsov. Barsov had appealed to him, Barsov had stared in his face on that walk through the children's playground. They must take steps or he would.

"What do you mean, Ed?"

"You come clean with us, Ed."

"I shall do what I want," Schiller shouted.

"You'll balls it up," the big Texan growled.

But it was Claymore who mattered. "Listen, Ed. Stick to your trade. Russia's no place for amateurs. I'm warning you. Don't try things on your own. That way will end in blood."

"What makes you think that?"

"Experience."

"Why should I try anything?"

"Don't give us shit, Ed. We just get that impression. There's a lot of guys in this city think they can help jump the ditch. I've seen it all before, believe me, these private attempts to get some bastard across. All kinds of mad schemes. They end up hanging from the wire or floating face down in the Spree if we don't come in. And we ain't coming in. So jack in that scenario, Ed, for Christ's sake, jack it in."

"I hear you," Schiller said.

They sat and watched him

"Remember whose side you're on. Otherwise you'll be in big trouble."

"Just you explain that to Shawcross," Claymore added.

"Shawcross?"

"You damned know it's Shawcross. Shawcross the candy bar salesman. You ever heard of communications: Burrell to Habkirk?"

Schiller was on his feet. They sat and watched him go. After a moment Claymore came to the door. "I'll get someone to drive you back."

"No need. I'll find my way."

"Oh yes there is, Ed. We don't want you to take the wrong directions. You might go in the river too." He called into the rear lounge, poking his head round the door. "Sukie, honey, do the drop for our friend."

She came out as if she'd been waiting, a pert face and skimpy dress.

"Sure."

"Kurfürstendamm," Schiller said.

"OK. Let's go."

Claymore did not shake hands. "Just keep in mind what I said. I don't want a disaster."

Schiller followed the legs. "You had some trouble up there?" she said smiling.

"No. Just a discussion."

"Uh huh. They know the score, those boys. Crazy boys." Her skirt was riding high. "You staying in Berlin?"

"That seems the idea," he said.

"Looking for someone?"

"You could say that but not now."

Back to the hotel, where Nicola found him instead. She had managed to track him, she said, by way of the *Post*. Schiller could hardly complain, having used the Berlin card with her.

"Ed, aren't you glad to hear?"

He sat on the edge of the bed.

"Maybe." Her position in his emotions was neutral, a relationship not an affair. No real feelings, just the fact that they had cut the cable, two separate lives, Nikky on the Hudson River, Ed on Kalinin Prospekt.

She sounded strangely muted, a voice that he scarcely recognized.

"They told me you might be back sometime now. It's the crack of dawn here. But I'm so glad to be speaking to you, Ed. Bill Packett was asking about you. And Charlie. Charlie wants to come see you so bad."

"I've told you. It would be hopeless. I thought Bill was heading West. That job in L.A."

"He didn't get it."

"OK. He didn't get it. What's news?"

"Bill sends his love. The same as me."

"You don't love me."

"Darling . . . is there someone else?"

"Cut it, Nikky. You're only in love with the idea. I've got a life to remake."

"That's great after all the trouble I've taken . . ."

"What trouble? Trouble to find my number?"

"Look," she said softly. "I want to come and see you, Ed."

"How's Carlo?"

"I've hung up on that shit."

"Try me instead?"

"Eddie. Jesus. Give it a break."

"You don't want me."

"I do. I do."

In Schiller's mind she raised no image, no picture. Up there on a screen instead was the Barsov ménage, Alexei Sergevich, Lila and little Yuri, cramped into their apartment near the Vernadskova Metro. The ones who had asked him for help, a stranger passing through. It was an appeal, and an offer, which haunted him. The trouble with avoiding relationships was that they returned in dreams. He took the phone to the settee in the dimmed light of the bedroom, holding the telephone, hearing the traffic outside. Nicola was still pleading. A six-year marriage and a two-year break actually had solved nothing. But he had to listen, because of Charlie, Nicola begged, and he pictured her saying it, swaying there, crying by the side of an unmade bed.

"There are no complications with Charlie. You've got custody. It only hurts us to meet."

"There's me, darling. My feelings. I still love you."

He was silent. Remembering the high hopes both had entertained when they moved from N.Y. to Washington, and he had been offered the *Post* job and big money. At the farewell party, Charlie a babe in arms, her father had stood by proudly, for the first time really welcoming Ed, the farm boy from the Midwest, as he toasted the future.

"We love you, Ed, for joining the family."

"It works for me too," he had said.

Long time ago. Eight years. Not so long before she played him up. Once, twice, quietly, for him to try and ignore it, then round the town, then bang, that bastard Carlo with the sharp blue suits and magazine-styled hair.

Now she was sobbing.

"I want to come over to Europe, Ed. To see you. We can try. I promise you. Give it one try."

"I'm moving around."

"You're in Berlin."

"I've got no base."

"When are you coming back home? You must be due for vacation."

"Not yet. I've got a job in Moscow. I've got a place back there."

"Then why not Moscow? Darling, please. For Charlie's sake as well."

"I don't know. I don't even know my own mind."

But he knew the Barsovs. Again in front of his eyes was not a vision of Nicola but of Lila and the boy and Alexei Sergevich.

The Englishman rang next day and Schiller suggested they met. At first Shawcross's voice was suspicious, honed and distant, but when Schiller dropped Joe Habkirk's name, he seemed to thaw.

"I'm told you could give me advice, on a trade deal."

"Well, ah, Mr. Schiller, I could see you tomorrow at eleven. Is it chocolate or confectionery?"

It was neither: a business proposition.

"Understood. I'm always open to propositions."

"Fine."

"Shall we say at Fingels?"

Fingels turned out to be a brasserie on the Lietzenburger-strasse, one of those places that made its living from cakes, a coffee-house between a blue-movie theater and a shoe store. It was half-full when Schiller entered and searched for the Englishman: a place of polished brass rails and dark brown tables with shaded lamps, *ersatz* Viennese.

The man who signalled to him across the room was small

and bald and elderly, wearing a blazer with a regimental
crest, a gnome with a ruddy face, tufts of gray round the
ears. He held out a dry hand.

"Schiller? The name is Andy Shawcross. What can I
order for you?" He motioned to the table, where he was
eating a cream cake and drinking cappuccino coffee.

"Just a coffee. OK, and a strudel."

"Righty-ho. You don't look a sweet-tooth man, Mr.
Schiller, but the cakes here are excellent, I assure you. The
best in Berlin. A gregarious city."

Schiller had not been gregarious for a couple of years, not
since the break-up. He had drunk with the boys, the Moscow
press crowd, made a few passes, tried it with Darleen.
Emotionally nothing. He might have been tempted to have a
fling in Berlin but Barsov stopped him. The words of the
Russian's appeal dropped on him like a headache, and had
brought him to Shawcross now, Shawcross with his regimental blazer and old school tie.

"They look great," he said.

"They are. Now. How can I be of assistance? Are you in
retail or wholesale?"

"Neither at the moment. I just want an introduction. Joe
Habkirk says you can help."

Shawcross blew across his coffee, circulating the froth.

"Well, that depends. Who is it?"

"A German called Heusermann. I'm told he runs a line in
damaged goods. Under the counter."

He watched Shawcross hesitate. In the Englishman's
trade you picked up the crooks, conspirators, double-dealers
and idealists, as well as the few honest ones. He was wondering why this open-faced American, three days into Germany,
was freelancing like hell and seeking a line to Heusermann.
So he looked Schiller over with considerable care.

"What do you want him for?"

"I'm told he might do me a job."

Shawcross wiped his lips. Veins stood out on his nose and
he tapped strong fingers on the glass of the table-top, which
was clipped on by golden bands.

"Heusermann has a record," he said quietly. "A cub in
the Hitler Youth. Came into his own later; young man on the

make in the days of the air-lift, and the big reconstruction. Owns a building consortium, above the line. Puts his hands into a good many pies.'' Shawcross slid tortoiseshell glasses from his pocket and put them on. He seemed to be looking for some distant shore, out beyond the plate-glass windows.

"And below the line?"

There was a touch of admiration in Shawcross's voice. "I'll tell you this. Heusermann is what I call a grafter. He works, and he makes sure that his operations work too. If that means grafting on both sides of the wall..." He shrugged. "He's an efficient bastard."

"That's what I'm after."

Shawcross said, "With what credentials? Who's the firm?"

"I'm on my own," Schiller told him.

"Oh. What about money?"

"I could pay basic expenses. A few hundred dollars, that's all." He hadn't thought of the cost.

"In a funny way, that might make it easier, on a take it or leave it basis." Shawcross seemed to relax. "There are several far-Right groups here who sail close to the wind, tolerated by the authorities, covertly supported by the CIA. Groups who get people out. Most of 'em do it for money..." He placed his palms on the table, "... but not necessarily all. Including Heusermann." He leaned forward. "Now, you listen to me. It's a risky business at any time. Who do you want to get out and why?"

Schiller told him.

The spectacles slipped back into his pocket as Shawcross pondered. "Why not use the diplomatic net, for Christ's sake? Gorbachev is letting them go, one by one. Anatoly Sharansky was released. Uri Orlov got out before the Iceland summit. Solzhenitsyn, Irina Ratushinskaya. They've even let up on Sakharov. What makes you assume they wouldn't let Barsov go?"

"There's no way they'll take that risk," Schiller said, remembering the shadows in Moscow, and Tukmanov, and Barsov's minders at Treptow Park. "And Barsov doesn't want to come unless we can get his family out as well. We've got one little window of possibility when he comes across to Charlottenburg in a couple of days. That's why I need help. He's got a commitment there; they won't want to back down but afterwards they will take him home."

"Are you so sure he's dangerous to them?"

Schiller had thought about that, had discussed it with the CIA and heard Barsov's own recital.

"Yes. I'm sure. They don't want to let him go. After *The Great Patriotic Shambles* he'd be a thorn in their flesh. Alexei Sergevich knows what Joe Public wants." He finished his coffee, aware that he'd taken a risk in telling Shawcross. The little man studied him carefully, brushing a hand over his egg-shaped head.

"OK. Next, what about your own people? What do they say?"

"That's my other problem. Our people don't want to know. They'd rather let him stay inside, a humans rights cage. Just get the books out instead, is what they say."

"Ah. I get it." Shawcross did not ask him to elaborate. "And yet you want to try and spring him?"

"I want to help because he asked me. For himself and his wife and the little boy."

Ah hah. A plague on both your houses, eh?"

Schiller had the impression that Shawcross found some satisfaction in upstaging both sides.

"It will be tricky."

"So, it's tricky. That's why I want someone to give a hand," Schiller told him.

Shawcross began to play an imaginary piano.

"Why does it matter so much? One writer more, or less?"

"That's difficult for me to say."

"So Barsov won't desert his family?"

"No. That's why he suggested this way."

"Wife pretty?"

"I guess so. Yes."

"Ah," Shawcross said again. In the Englishman's mind was his own rather plain wife in East Grinstead, cozy, tucked up and safe. He stood up, checked the bill, held out a hand. "Thank you for telling me. Shall we go for a stroll?"

"Wait a minute," Schiller insisted. "Where do I find Heusermann?"

The Englishman smiled. "Don't rush your fences."

As they walked to the door of the brasserie Schiller realized how dark it had been inside. In the daylight Shawcross's face seemed almost mottled, high-complexioned and blotchy.

"Heusermann goes to ground. He's difficult to locate in a hurry. He has enemies and finds that it's not advisable, I fancy, to be too readily available. It's a shame that time is in such short supply." Shawcross paused on the pavement, sniffing the air. "The best thing I can suggest is that you find the sorcerer's apprentice: you look for the man with a monkey. He's always available to pass on a message."

"Where do I find him?"

"Oh. He's usually on the Breitscheidplatz, outside the Memorial Church. The Gedächtniskirche. Or else at the KaDeWe." He pushed his hands into his pockets. "Got to go. Nice to meet you. Good luck, old man." And turning on his heels, he added, "Put not your faith in brass or tinkling cymbals, as they say. Old Testament, I think. Put it in Heusermann."

Back at his hotel, Schiller failed to find the quotation in the bible thoughtfully left by the Gideons.

10

The Kaiser Wilhelm Memorial Church was a black stump on a traffic island. When Schiller walked there at ten o'clock on the following morning the cars were buzzing round it like bees, while office girls, executives, hausfraus and students drank coffee in the sunshine.

He stood sweating in the glare, remembering Sly Sylvester's phone call the night before.

"We going to get a story out of the Berlin trip, Ed?"

"I don't know, Sly."

"What do you mean, don't know?"

"I've got to look for some guy with a monkey."

"You don't say? Love that: send you to Berlin and all I get is a story on some goddam monkey. Jesus wept. You try my paternal instinct, Ed."

"Anyway, I'm here."

"Sure," Sly said. "You make it good."

Schiller knew he had to make it work, monkey or not, as he waited. He stopped for a beer at a pavement café, then towards midday he walked to the KaDeWe store. The shopping crowds grew much thicker, girls in smart dresses, older women with booty, jostling each other for space. And then somewhere, over the moving heads, clear and private, came the sound of a hurdy-gurdy. The melody was familiar, and after a moment he placed it: Mendelssohn's *Song Without Words*. The rippling notes were like a magnet as he pushed in closer but the music twisted and turned, even its direction uncertain, until suddenly there was a gap.

On the top of a street organ of polished and gilded wood a gray monkey danced on a chain. Someone was turning the handle: a midget in a bowler hat. And then he saw the midget was exactly half a man, a torso, a head and shoulders, sliced clean off at the hips: Shawcross's man with the monkey, who raised a brown Derby as he accepted small change. The face was firm and mature, almost handsome, but the legs were missing: from the thighs downwards only two flaps of leather on which he balanced like a ten-pin. As Schiller joined the audience the maimed man's eyes flickered over him almost as if he was waiting. The monkey jumped on his chain and the legless man raised his hat, sweeping it round the crowd.

Schiller tossed in a dollar.

"*Danke. Danke.*"

Deftly the torso flicked the note into his pocket. Without a change of expression he switched to another tune. *Deutschland, Deutschland über alles*. He did not look at the American again but after a few minutes ceased playing, shouting at the monkey to sit. The crowd filtered slowly away.

As the maimed man stroked his pet and counted the takings into a leather satchel, Schiller spoke in English.

"I was told I could find you outside the Gedächtniskirche. But you weren't there. I had to come looking for you."

The organ-grinder glared with hard blue eyes. His body seemed to end at the hips like a shooting target: he might have been standing in a hole. Otherwise the torso was full and heavy, a weather-beaten face with strong lines from nose to mouth, a powerful pair of shoulders. He nodded methodically and completed his work on the organ, shutting the carved doors and swinging the two brass candle-holders flush into the cabinet, before replying.

"I'm entitled to move my pitch. Why do you want me?"

Schiller was aware of people regrouping behind them, wondering why the half-man had stopped playing. Someone said they would like to hear him. As if to disabuse them the musician picked up his hard hat and swung it round in a gesture of thanks.

They waited while the shoppers dispersed.

"They've gone," he said. "Now what do you want?"

"Nothing very difficult. To get somebody over the Wall."

"The Wall?" The blue eyes looked at him carelessly, disinterested. "What has that to do with me?"

"My friend said you knew who could help."

"Me? What friend?" The eyes were blank and wary. The maimed man jutted his jaw and stared upwards, turning the handle soundlessly.

"An Englishman called Shawcross. He sells confectionery."

"Who are you?"

Schiller had that one ready. "An admirer of Herr Heusermann."

The doll-man shuffled quickly round the back of the organ and unhooked the monkey, which scrambled on to his shoulders.

"Heusermann?" He said the name softly, as if vaguely recalling it.

Schiller nodded, put his hands in his pockets and waited.

"Go away now," the torso said. He seemed to have

weighed Schiller up, decided he posed no threat. "When the car comes for me in an hour, Heusermann will be here. At one o'clock." He began to push the barrel organ into the side of the building. "I don't want help."

Schiller strolled inside the KaDeWe. The picture-books on the fourth-floor showed the devastation in '45. Rebuilding that wreckage was how Heusermann had started. Perhaps that was where the organ man had lost his legs. In the restaurant on the top floor he ate a steak and salad. A woman on a bar stool a couple of places away was hitching up her skirt and smiling, a young, attractive tart looking for a midday customer or just a girl on the loose. A few months ago he might well have been tempted, but this time, no. There was too much unfinished business, with Nikky in New York, with Lila in Moscow, with Alexei Sergevich in Berlin. He realized that what he was doing was as much for Lila as Barsov. In a sense it was also for Nikky, a way of avoiding her.

The dark blue Mercedes was punctual. As Schiller emerged from the crowd at the entrance of the department store he saw the big car pull up opposite the recess where the organ man was still waiting, drinking coffee from a plastic cup. The limousine window purred down and Schiller watched the torso shuffle towards it. The offside rear door opened and a dark-suited attendant with the face of a forked potato squeezed out of the back. For a moment he stood there blinking, searching to right and left, then he lifted the maimed man, his leather flaps dangling, bodily into the seat beside the driver. The monkey clung to his back.

The big man returned to his place, and Schiller could see the white-haired head in the inner rear seat. He walked across to the limousines.

"Herr Heusermann? Andy Shawcross said I might find you this way."

"*Willkommen in Berlin.*" The face was salmon-pink, the eyes uncompromisingly icy, pale blue and suspicious. He offered a well-manicured hand. "Won't you join us, Herr . . .?"

"Thank you," Schiller said in English. The attendant appeared again, opening the offside door, ushering him in.

"Vogel, sit in the front," Heusermann commanded. "Squeeze up. Poor Ernst doesn't take up much room."

The bodyguard nodded, and Schiller sank on to the rear cushions, staring at Vogel's neck. The half-man had no hips to bend from, so he stood on the arm rest between Vogel and the driver, still clasping the monkey. The Merc picked up speed and skirted the Potsdamerplatz, past the golden roof of the Philharmonic Hall, into the old East–West Axis. Schiller glimpsed the red flag over the Brandenburg Gate and the ugly face of the Wall, twelve feet of pre-cast sleepers topped by a concrete pipe.

"Look," Heusermann said, pointing. "Over there is the Reichstag. Across there, on the other side, was the Chancellery. That's where you caught it, wasn't it, Ernst?" He tapped the torso on the shoulder, but Ernst only muttered.

Heusermann, smiling, one hand resting on the interior controls, said, "You are American? Tell me why you want to see me. Why does Shawcross send you?"

"I need help."

"Help? So. What can I do for you?"

Ed Schiller picked his friends carefully, but in this case Alexei Sergevich hadn't given him much time. Short of the co-operation of Vince Claymore, Heusermann's clandestine activities were the only hope he had. Berlin Station might have helped, but Legros had warned them off. Claymore, the escape expert and a Taylor Sheen clone, had told him to keep his head down. "So jack in that scenario, Ed." Which left him with the likes of Heusermann.

"I want to get somebody out."

Heusermann studied him carefully through eyelashes that were almost bleached, like the spines of a sea urchin.

"That is what they always say," he sighed. "Tell me more."

The Mercedes sped round the Victory Column, the route that Barsov would be taking, towards Charlottenburg. There was very little time.

"It's urgent," Schiller said.

"Keep driving," Heusermann called as they zipped along Bismarckstrasse and the Kaiserdamm, bright with new buildings.

"I built those," Heusermann said, a flat statement of fact rather than a matter of pride. Schiller saw the glint of water between the trees at the end.

"Grunewald," Vogel grunted.

They were driving down to a pier tucked behind new apartments bordering the Havel Lake. The limousine stopped.

"Ernst will stay in the car," Heusermann announced. The Mercedes backed away with the torso in front as Heusermann, Vogel and Schiller took a path through the woods to the water. There was a small wooden jetty with a motor yacht moored. The boat strained quietly at its ropes, white-hulled with teak uppers and sparkling brasswork.

Vogel leading, Heusermann and Schiller walked along the jetty.

"You like my boat?"

"Very impressive."

Heusermann kicked a stick into the water.

"It belonged to Hermann Goering." The German smiled. "*Der Dicke* didn't spare any expense."

Two crewmen were already on deck and the engines thudded into life as soon as they boarded. "Blohm and Voss," Heusermann said. "Solid teak," running his hand lovingly along the panelling, "before the war."

He led the way below to an elegant cabin of laminated woods, offered drinks and invited Schiller to sit, accompanied by the silent Vogel. Outside, through the square port, Havel slid by, the pleasure cruisers and dinghies of West Berlin at play, while Schiller talked, explaining his moral commitment to someone who wanted help. Barsov must be sprung from his minders when he came across for the PEN meeting.

Heusermann asked for times and places, but not why. He ran a hand through this thick, well-groomed hair, as white as snow, exuding a late sexuality, a power to seduce, telling Vogel to take notes. Everything about Barsov: how big he was, whether he would co-operate, whether he understood German.

Schiller said, "It's not a straightforward run. He wants to be kidnapped."

Heusermann treated that as an enormous joke. He slapped his thigh and poured out more whisky all round.

"Why is that? I could get him out without any trouble. I have a—what is the phrase?—track record."

"He wants his wife released too. And their son. They are confined in Moscow."

"Ah. Hostages."

"In a way."

Heusermann considered Schiller carefully. He was young and he looked good, fresh-complexioned and honest about the eyes. That slight naïvity he often noticed about the Americans. In this case he wondered what the motive was.

"So. This Russian assumes that if he just comes over when he has the chance they will refuse the visas for his wife and child?"

"Yes. And I think he's right. He has to be taken against his will. Abducted in some way. So that he can protest, then, when the story dies, finally decide to stay. that way they'll let them out, Lila and the boy, after a while, when the spotlight is off."

"Why should they do that?"

"Because our people will put the pressure on."

"What do you think, Klaus?"

Vogel's face creased into uncertainty. "Maybe. Maybe not."

Heusermann stared from the window at the wooded islands gliding past, lovers running into the trees, their sailboats pulled up on the bank.

"But worth a try." He laughed. "Yes. Why not: it's worth a try." He sipped the whisky. "It amuses me." He saw the relief in the American's face. "How much will you pay?"

"A thousand dollars," Schiller said. "On account."

"A thousand dollars? On account? My dear sir, do you know what these things cost? Often they cost in lives."

"I'm not the CIA."

"Ha, ha, ha," Heusermann was highly amused. "I like that."

"I feared you might be a bastard. Or just plain scared," Schiller said.

Heusermann found that even funnier: his laughter sounded through the boat.

"I like it," he roared. "I like you, Schiller. You are so . . . bloody unprofessional."

"Listen, for God's sake. I'm not in this for kicks, or the CIA." Schiller's earnest face betrayed his emotions. "I want to spring a guy who has asked my help. Help. Don't you understand that? He wants my help to come over in a way that will get his wife out."

Something about that statement caused Heusermann to sober up.

"A *ménage à trois*. Not so easy to sustain."

It hit Schiller on a nerve. He hadn't even considered what would happen in the future. Where would Barsov find a living: in the States or in Europe? After Russia, what would the West be like for Lila and Yuri? They had to settle somewhere, and Schiller hadn't even begun to formulate proposals. But he knew that he would want to see her.

"You don't have to explain. We are all mad once." Heusermann stripped off his coat, looking pink and relaxed. He laughed again, enjoying himself.

"So. It is all very simple. You want me to arrange to have your Russian kidnapped because he has asked you to help him, and so that he can get his wife out. I take all the risk and for that you pay a thousand dollars." He held out a hand and rubbed forefinger and thumb together. "Rather a small *douceur*, wouldn't you say? Why should I take the chance?"

"Because you hate them," Schiller said.

The German nodded, and Vogel repeated the nod.

"OK. OK. I hate them. You saw Ernst," he added slowly. He seemed to make up his mind. "All right, I will help. For nothing. I don't want your money. For freedom if you like. How about that?" He leaned forward, a plump hand fastening on Schiller's knee.

Schiller found himself saying "thank you," his body drained of emotion. The blind bid for help had worked. He took Heusermann's plump warm hand, as soft as putty. How far could he trust him, he wondered, as the yacht hummed gently on, round the lake shore to Wannsee, where Vogel said the car would be waiting. Yet everything Heusermann asked about the man and the opportunity, the escape plan, the kidnap, convinced Schiller that he would do it.

As they came into the jetty Schiller saw the Mercedes with two heads in the front seats, and felt that he had sold his soul. Heusermann suggested that they go out on deck, and he saw their reflections join in the clear green water, trembling and confused. Heusermann put an arm round his shoulders. He smelled of after-shave, and close up his skin was dry.

"I do not generally act on impulse," he said, "but I like determined young men. Perhaps afterwards one day you do me a favor."

"That depends," Schiller said.

"You do not plan to tell your people—the CIA—anything about it?"

"They're not mine," Schiller said.

"I mean that you will not warn them, not to interfere?"

"Why should I?"

Heusermann sighed, withdrew his arm and shouted to Vogel to tie up.

"That is probably wise. They are such meddlers: the trouble with so-called professionals. If they are told anything they think that they must do something, however absurd. Leave it to me," he said.

"Do you want me to help?"

"No. You keep out of the way."

"I want to be there."

Heusermann rubbed his chin. "My recommendation is that you keep away. Leave it to us."

"No," said Schiller. "I'm not prepared to do that."

Heusermann looked him over and sighed. "I feared that you might say that. Such determination. All right. Wait at the Friedrichsstrasse checkpoint if you want to see what happens. But keep a low profile. Is that clear?"

"Perfectly."

"Good." Heusermann beamed. "Then we understand each other."

The engines beneath them died.

"When will you try?" he asked.
"When he comes over," Heusermann said.

11

It was raining as the trickle of vehicles came through Checkpoint Charlie and headed down Friedrichsstrasse. The rain hit the road like bullets out of an acid sky, sending the border police scuttling inside their huts.

Fifty yards below the checkpoint Schiller sat in a taxi, watching; knowing that they would be watching him from the platform, although he was too far distant for them to see who he was. In the no man's land between the red and white poles there were only a couple of trucks and one green tourist bus. Border guards in cheap gray gaberdine patrolled the exit to West Berlin, a square of empty concrete, frowned on by nondescript warehouses.

Schiller waited. Heusermann had telephoned once, earlier, to say it was all arranged. "Our friend" would come over that morning, and he was sending a taxi for Schiller. Something had appealed to the German, who was treating it as a good joke.

"Why the taxi?"

"To save you ordering one. I don't expect you to pay. He will know what to do."

The taxi-driver stirred in his seat. He was a middle-aged man who smoked a pipe, and knocked it out on the dash.

"Another car coming."

"OK. Just keep watching," Schiller said.

He guessed why Heusermann had supplied the cab. The German no more trusted Schiller than the other way round. Perhaps, Heusermann wanted to keep his nose clean, and the taxi would keep Schiller out of trouble.

They were waving the big double-decker out, and checking

the next car through. A bronze Audi with West Berlin registration.

The taxi-man breathed on the window, and cleared it with a paper tissue. He grumbled about the weather and the surroundings.

"Bad place, the other side."

"I guess so," Schiller grunted. Maybe something would happen after the bus had gone. "How much longer?"

"Don't be impatient." The taxi-driver produced a vacuum flask of hot, sweet coffee and they sipped it together.

Another car filtered through: the same slow process of showing papers, having the boot inspected, the little mirror on wheels pushed underneath. Heusermann had said the morning, and it was already ten-thirty. Schiller half expected to see the monkey-man appear from the café near the barrier and start up his hurdy-gurdy. Waiting gave rise to doubts, and then to inexplicable fears. Supposing it went wrong, or else Heusermann was lying, with no intention of helping?

Then suddenly he saw Vogel, in the rain. He had emerged from the café and stood with his shoulders hunched against the downpour. Under the dark fedora, unmistakably Vogel, in a prison raincoat, slouching in the doorway. Schiller froze as a flurry of activity on the Eastern side showed that another car was coming through, one that was not stopping. A black Skoda saloon with three men crammed in the back: Schiller could see the heads before he could pick out the faces.

Vogel glanced across and gave the American what amounted to a grin, his pug-face creasing under the sodden hat-brim. Schiller's heart bumped along the bottom of his ribs. The Skoda was maneuvering slowly between the pole barriers as if on a driving test, with the border guards saluting it. Schiller could see now a square white card on the windshield, giving it clearance, and he focused on the three heads inside behind the driver. The one in the middle was Barsov, certainly Barsov: that big skull and pale forehead with the receding hair. He looked round for Vogel but the German had vanished again leaving an empty street.

The Skoda came on tantalizingly slowly, as if it hoped to be stopped, but the border police waved it through without a glance at the papers. It continued across the no man's land where the rain flurries spat on the road, and was flagged down by the Staatspolizei on the Western side. Schiller could see them talking to the men inside, handing them a letter which seemed to cause some annoyance. Then the Skoda was motioned through.

He tapped the taxi-driver on the elbow. "When he goes past, we follow."

The driver muttered "I know" as if this was common practice. He was interested now, and put on a pair of dark glasses like a Chicago hood.

The Skoda wheeled slowly round the final leg of the course, its wipers moving erratically, more sinister for being unsynchronized, and chugged past the last zig-zag. As it drew abreast Schiller could clearly see Barsov wedged between a couple of musclemen, minders with KGB haircuts. It was out into the wasteland of the Friedrichsstrasse now, where the bomb-sites were full of buddleia and elderberry, as if the city had forgotten them.

"Slowly," Schiller said. "Don't make it obvious." The taxi-man turned and they followed the Skoda into the Mehringplatz. A notice read Wilhelmstrasse. The world had changed a bit since then, Schiller thought, as they followed the black car. Why was Barsov coming through like this, sandwiched between those goons? And where was the Heusermann rescue?

Nothing. Nothing except the steady, drumming rain out of a steel-gray sky. The Skoda was turning west, picking up the freeway, following the route that Heusermann had taken yesterday, close to the Brandenburg Gate and through the green, replanted trees of the Tiergarten. The taxi followed discreetly, easier now as the city traffic thickened. The Skoda turned left again, uncertainly, as if they were confused inside—Schiller nearly lost it behind a refrigerated truck—then edged along the crowded Budapesterstrasse.

"Jesus, he doesn't know where he's going—" Schiller exclaimed, craning forward. "That's not the way to Charlottenburg."

"Charlottenburg no. Hotel yes," the driver muttered.

Budapesterstrasse was busy, prosperous, lined with new

hotels and apartments. The Skoda jerked twice as if it had missed a gear and then began signalling as it pulled into the forecourt of a steel and glass building with a cantilevered *porte-cochère*.

"International," the driver said. "Best hotel in Berlin."

Someone was doing Barsov proud, maybe a luncheon party. The route had been changed. That was why he had come over in the morning. Did Heusermann know that there was some kind of reception which had brought the Russian across ahead of time? Schiller felt his stomach tighten.

"Give yourself room," Schiller said. "Pull in over there."

The taxi-man nodded and parked in a vacant bay well to the side of the entrance. The cold rain eased down. They saw the doorman come forward holding a colored umbrella as Barsov and his companions tumbled out and stood blinking under the canopy. Schiller found himself watching a scene played out in slow-motion.

There was a welcoming group just inside the glass doors. Barsov, dressed in a baggy blue suit, moved through with the heavies, one of them on either side. Introductions were taking place and the group walked across the foyer, towards the desk. No one seemed in a hurry, the minders had dropped behind, hands in their bulky raincoats. It was too slow, too careful.

"You stay in car," the taxi-man cautioned.

"Wait there!" Ignoring the warning, Schiller ran across the parking bay, following them into the lobby. The space was large and luxurious, cut-glass chandeliers sparkling over coffee-tables and nests of easy chairs. He came through the doors and saw Barsov by the reception counter, where a party of Japanese tourists were mustering bags by the check-out.

He watched from the Avis desk on the other side of the foyer. Three young men emerged, without hurrying, from the restaurant at the far end from where they would have seen the Skoda arrive. They cut into the Barsov group.

"Don't move. Put your hands up."

He heard the sharp commands in German.

One of the heavies shuffled, there was a sound like a crack, muffled by the hotel Muzak, and he slumped forward.

Then he was on his knees, face in hands, blood seeping from somewhere on the back of his head. Mugged with a pistol butt.

The second heavy looked puzzled. His arms went up to the ceiling. The group around Barsov froze. In the tourist party a woman screamed.

The injured KGB man staggered to his feet. Nobody tried to help, no one was moving. Unnatural silence made the tinny music much clearer. No one would have noticed before: a selection from *Oklahoma*. The three young men were tight-faced, unmasked, short-haired, dressed alike in anoraks and sneakers, holding flat-grip hand guns.

The young men waved their arms around. Barsov was either bemused or making a good pretense. Somebody tried the swing-doors to Schiller's right. One of the gunmen detached himself to cover the entrance but took no notice of Schiller or the Avis girl there. An information board by the doors listed a signing of books by Alexei Barsov, the Soviet Academician, at twelve noon. One of Heusermann's jokes.

The young gunmen weren't joking. Still on slow film, the Russian with the cut head put a hand to his hair and looked in astonishment at the blood. An elderly woman who tried to come across and help was waved brusquely away.

Barsov was shouting in Russian in that strangely high-pitched voice almost as if for the record. "What the hell is going on . . .?"

Very clearly and calmly the leader of the ambush, a fair-haired youngster with a khaki shirt under the anorak, said in English, "We are protecting you, Alexei Sergevich Barsov. We are taking you to free Germany. Please, you are to come with us, for your own safety."

It sounded strangely unreal. English for the benefit of witnesses, for the record.

"No," Barsov yelled back. "I am not coming."

"You must come."

"No. I am being abducted."

Schiller saw the uncertainty in the Russian's face. He had to be certain he was playing it right. He wanted witnesses.

"No. I will not move."

Sharper, this time in German, the young man said, "You come with us. Now."

The second Russian made a move. Schiller had seen it coming, signalling he had a weapon. Two of the gunmen seized him, body-searched, and a holstered revolver clattered on to the floor.

"Everybody stay calm," the leader said. "Nobody then gets hurt."

He waved his gun at the rabbits by the desk.

"Alexei Sergevich Barsov goes with us."

At that point the world cracked and seemed to dissolve in explosions which took the tops off their heads. The elevator doors slid open at the end of the foyer as smoke and flames enveloped the reception area. Schiller dived for the ground as debris swirled around him and the chandeliers shivered.

Stun grenades. Explosives. Another bomb, nearer, drove pain through his head like a nail. Choking white fumes, acrid and swirling, filled the air. Everyone down on the floor but through the pain Schiller was aware of new figures moving, hooded and lethal. Stalking through the smoke, black zombies had arrived from some far country, carrying heavy irons. Somebody firing a sub-machine-gun. For moments on which hung lives bursts of automatic fire stabbed across the lobby. Flattened against the Avis desk, Schiller found the Avis girl and whispered, "Keep down," but she clung to him like a child. Further shots seemed to be pistols: single firecrackers. One of the KGB men somehow returning fire. Another stab of flame from the automatics, the masked figures running and turning and the Russian jumped in the air like an electrified dog. Schiller saw him keel over backwards, no longer human, a red mess on the side of his face.

Figures were looming, shouting, screaming, in and out of the smoke. Another explosion smashed into the foyer, fresh white fumes, glass sliding across the floor. Shrieks from the trapped tourists, and some of the screams were of pain, louder as the firing stopped as abruptly as it had begun. An unnatural silence in which the Muzak still played: "Oh what a beautiful morning, oh what a beautiful day..."

Fifty feet away from Schiller the Russian minder was

dead, half his face sliced away. Heavy bullets at close range. The American felt something liquid under his hand. It was a piece of skin, sticky with blood and hair. Schiller was covered in plaster but, unlike the Russian, alive. He pushed the Avis girl down, and felt himself cautiously for breakages. Everything seemed in order, except for Heusermann's plan.

From somewhere inside the white blanket came a bellow of fear, high-pitched and agonized, that he recognized as Barsov. Slowly the fumes settled. Schiller could see figures around, cowering or lying prone, as the killers in ski-masks, four of them he counted, looking like spirit devils, commanded the room. They wore stocking hoods and black overalls, rubber-soled shoes and gloves, and moved with a frightening quickness. One of them was over Schiller and the girl, hiding behind the car-rental desk. He could feel the gun at his head, ready to end it. No thoughts. Just a blind anger, but the man walked away, looking for someone else. Four more single shots, a scream as somebody died, and the hooded man vanished again into the smoke.

Schiller heard shouting in German.

"No. No." Barsov again, lost in the nightmare fog, settling across the room at three or four feet high.

Schiller's mind was knifed once more as another grenade lifted the room, churning the wreckage, leaving his ears blown out. One of the chandeliers twisted on its wires and fell, flattening a coffee-table. A stench of burning, as papers and fabric caught fire: smoke and stink and choking dust. Voices moaning in pain and terror. No more firing. The black figures regrouped in the middle, and he saw that Barsov was propped up between them, the Russian's bull-like head hanging loosely between his shoulders. Barsov's eyes were screwed down, as if to shut out a nightmare.

One of the black figures fired another burst, this time through the revolving doors. The grim reaper figure was running out to find a car. Schiller twisted round and identified the Skoda which had brought the Russians in. The Skoda. Not one of Heusermann's cars. A Czechoslovakian Skoda: but one of the Russians was dead and the other had his head smashed in.

There was no time to work out the puzzle as the other gunmen moved past him, hustling Barsov, not hurrying, confident. Then he saw Heusermann's men. One of the Heusermann group was trying to get to his feet, blood pumping from a shoulder. The ski-masks did not look back, but half pushed, half carried Barsov through the doors where their companion was waiting, covering the exit. Schiller couldn't see much now, but he heard them shouting outside. The Skoda burnt its tires as it accelerated out of the parking bay.

He rolled to one side, scrambled, jumped over broken furniture, found himself at the doors. He wondered if his ear drums were ruptured but the clean air sharpened his mind. It was still raining. He realized what had seemed like an hour had only taken three minutes. The driver of the Skoda was spread-eagled on the pavement in a puddle of blood, but he was breathing. They had taken care of him too, and reused his car. That showed some nerve, or some planning. He caught a last glimpse of the car, underpowered, making smoke, and then of a second car, a black BMW with Barsov pushed into the rear. So there had been a reserve. They had to get five out.

Shouting, screaming behind him, a fire alarm going off, a stunned inactivity in the car-park. Schiller found the taxi again, white faces on the sidewalk staring at him as he raced across and flung himself inside.

"Get after those bastards."

The driver reacted automatically, swinging the taxi round, jumping the exit by crashing the plastic markers, but by the time they squeezed out the BMW had disappeared.

Halfway down Budapesterstrasse Schiller stopped the pursuit.

"Did you know what would happen?"

The driver reacted angrily. "I only do what they tell me."

"Who is they?"

"Herr Vogel," he said.

Schiller told him to turn back to the hotel.

The driver started to argue. "They won't get out of West Berlin. No way," he said in English. "We find them."

"Shut up. Go back." It was raining inside Schiller now, a pitiless private rain. He had failed to help Barsov, just as

Claymore had warned. A fuck-up that ended in killing. And where was Barsov?

As he walked back inside the foyer the police had arrived. They were clearing the lobby, heaving the wounded on to stretchers. Schiller counted three bodies. One of the KGB men gazed open-eyed at the ceiling with a chandelier across his legs. A hole had been drilled in his nose and more of his off-the-peg suit. The second Russian lay discarded like a pile of old clothes, twisted on to his side with his brains spilling out.

The young German had met death more neatly, pitched face down on the floor with two holes in his back. Someone was bending over him, a frightened man who called out that he was a doctor from Tempelhof. His professional detachment cracked as he examined the corpses.

"*Kaput*," he pronounced. "Gunshot wounds."

Schiller steadied himself as the fumes caught him again. His hair was a wet brush, plastered over his forehead.

The Staatspolizei sirens wailed. They were catching up now, sealing off the front of the hotel where the manager was crying with shock. Schiller looked for the Avis girl but she had gone.

"Identity?" A panicky policeman grabbed his arm, the safety catch off his side-arm.

Schiller flashed his press pass.

"U.S. press. *Washington Post*." It sounded too far away, too unrelated. Only Sly Sylvester would be pleased.

"Clear out."

Schiller was in no mood to argue. He wanted to walk and think, to get the assessment straight; who was Barsov, and why had he, Schiller, fucked it up? Surely they couldn't get Alexei Sergevich out of West Berlin, the killers who had come for him? And who were they? He heard again the appeal that Barsov had made to him in that shabby Moscow playground.

Schiller wouldn't bet on that one, given the ease with which the gunmen had infiltrated the hotel and made their getaway. One of the cars at least, the Skoda, as he had seen, had automatic checkpoint clearance no more than a mile away. There should be no way out of West Berlin, there was a cast iron frontier as the taxi-driver had said. And yet . . . and yet . . . he found himself doubting.

The police would know. And the Control Commission. Above all the Agency, whom he would have to face now.

"You'd better get back and tell Vogel it's all gone wrong," he said to Heusermann's man.

"You want to come?"

"No. Just tell them it destructed. Somebody loused it up."

Schiller realized that he was shaking. Fire, police and ambulance were roaring by as he walked past expensive shops selling craftware and airline tickets until he found himself by the zoo. In the glass wall of the aquarium were fish as ugly as destroyed souls. A smell of monkey and lion hung in the air but it was nothing to the smell in his mind. Schiller's worst fears were confirmed: life was hell. Nicola had once bewitched him and he had paid a price. Barsov was another magician, who had disappeared in front of his eyes leaving Lila's card. And Heusermann's people had paid in blood just as Vince Claymore had warned.

He crossed the Kurfürstendamm. How easy it was to walk away, in the rain, without a raincoat. His throat was parched and he needed to dry out. He ducked into a patisserie, like the one in which he'd met Shawcross. The waitress was young and buxom with a cheeky eye. Perhaps she thought he'd been stood up.

"A bit wet out," she said.

"That's right." Stirring the coffee, he considered the facts that he knew. Barsov had been labelled a "leaver." Even the CIA had picked that up in advance, and Schiller himself had told them. Taylor Sheen, for example, back in Moscow, had been well briefed, and so had Claymore. The KGB in their turn had put tails on Schiller. And he thought he had been clever, enlisting Heusermann. The finale in West Berlin was two dead minders, and one of Heusermann's boys, Heusermann who had offered his services without payment. Unless, that was, somebody else was paying. But that was all too pat, too easy. It didn't explain three dead men and God knew how many hurt. Claymore had repeated the line that they didn't want Barsov out, that he wasn't

much of a bargain. Suppose that they had paid someone to
bungle the abduction; but surely the CIA would not set up a
double ambush, and jeopardize Heusermann? Supposing the
KGB had a counter-terrorist group in Berlin, under the nose
of Heusermann, as one way of getting even. Jubal Martin
back in Moscow, like Claymore in the Station here, had
warned Schiller off. When it went wrong they could blame
him.

His wet clothes were drying out. The waitress returned
with more coffee, which he drank greedily.

"Who were they?" he asked himself. It was like a bad
dream.

But it wasn't a dream. He had played and lost Alexei
Sergevich basically for the sake of Lila, a disturbing thought
followed by another one. If Barsov should fail, he had been
promised Lila.

The waitress was hovering for payment, trying out her
English on him.

"You like Berlin?"

"Not at this moment," Schiller said, and went out to find
Claymore.

He returned to the safe house, and Claymore, that afternoon. They didn't come out to collect him as he expected.

Claymore's face was a frozen mask.

"You stupid bastard," he said.

Schiller was concerned for Barsov; he hadn't come to be
whipped.

"I did what I could," he said.

"You put your trust in that little shit Shawcross, and he
led you to Heusermann, and Heusermann loused it up."
Claymore was drinking brandy, and his hands were agitated.
"Just tell us what happened, Ed. Your version."

Schiller said grimly, "Somebody had better tell me." He
explained how he had followed them into the hotel lobby,
seen Heusermann's boys intercept the Russian heavies, and
then how hell broke loose from the elevator. The smoke and
the stun grenades, the jabbing fire across the lobby, and the
screaming.

In a voice that seemed to come from a run-down battery, Claymore asked, "Who in hell are we dealing with?"

Another CIA man, soft Southern vowels, almost whispered, "They weren't from Uncle Sam, and that's for sure."

"The Israelis? The Brits?"

Claymore shook his sallow features. "Barsov's not a Jew. The Brits wouldn't set that one up, or Shawcross would have known. I can tell you this, Ed, we didn't run those ski-masks. No, sir. Heusermann we knew about. We didn't approve, but we didn't try to stop him." He poured himself another drink, without offering it round. "But machine-gunning the entrance of the International. No way this firm." He put his hands on the table.

Schiller said, "The score is three dead, five wounded."

"Christ, who bought it?"

"The pair of Russian minders, KGB shadows, and one of Heusermann's boys. Another one of 'em got it in the neck and shoulder. Along with two other Krauts, one chipped Jap tourist and the Soviet driver."

"Serious?"

Schiller shrugged. "I guess the others will make it."

The escape expert Claymore swore. He had a fine gray stubble on his chin, as if he'd forgotten to shave.

"They've ruined Heusermann now. Whoever they are. One show like that and your reputation's garbage." He turned to his companion in the long room upstairs where the screens were flashing messages about the manhunt.

"Where have the bastards gone?"

They watched the girls on the monitors. Every crossing had been sealed. A house-to-house search was on in the Kreuzberg district but even the cars, the Skoda and the BMW, seemed to have gone to ground.

"There's no way they can get him out of this city," Claymore said, but he did not sound entirely convinced.

"We'll find Barsov dumped inside a plastic bag," the Southerner speculated.

Schiller screwed himself down to hope, his mind shouting inside him that this was his fault, his.

And they were a jury attacking him, as the screens

showed nothing doing, the police reports came in empty from the roadblocks.

"Ed boy, you come clean with us, or we shall kick your ass in. Who were those guys in black?"

Schiller reacted angrily. "Don't you dare accuse me."

They laughed in his face. "You brought in Heusermann."

"Heusermann was round one. I didn't lay on murder."

"But you greased it up," Claymore snarled. "What are you going to do now?"

He hadn't really cleared his mind, but somehow he knew they wouldn't find Alexei Sergevich again in Berlin. The lecture would not take place. If he was alive at all.

"I don't know. I need some time."

"Ed, boy, you'd better stick to reporting. Leave escape jobs to the firm," Claymore said bitterly.

Schiller had a future to consider: his and Lila's. Sylvester had asked for a story from Berlin; Jesus, he could give him that. Afterwards, who knew? If he returned to Moscow, Nikky could track him down. But Moscow was where Lila was too.

"You finished with me? Or are you going to lock me up?"

Claymore smiled for the first time, a tiny crack in the wall.

"You go, boy." Schiller found himself on the stairs, the room with its flickering screens shut out as if it never existed. A smell of bacon frying came from a kitchen somewhere.

Claymore said, "I'll find a girl to take you back."

"No need."

"Oh sure. It's part of the service."

It was Sukie again, the car keys in her hand.

They drove back almost in silence, and she dropped him off at the Amsterdam.

"You staying long in Berlin?" He remembered it was the question that she had asked him before, as she wound down the window and smiled. She was making herself available, any time.

"How about forgetting it tonight?"

In his mind was the image of Lila sitting on the grass by

the Kuskovo Palace, plaiting the daisy chain, while he and
Yuri had played hide-and-seek. He would play it in earnest
now: wherever they held Barsov he would seek him, in
order to see Lila too.

He shook his head.

12

Missing the Moscow high-rise, coming in at night over the
satellite townships, the ill-lit road swirl, Schiller absorbed it
like a sponge: the necklaces of lights, then grayness on the
ground, ending in a shudder of reversed engines.

He had cabled the big one from Berlin and flown straight
out, coming back empty-handed. Sheremetyevo airport was
silver and glass, the immigration control two crop-haired
guards in pressed green seersucker. Representatives of the
people crowded by: small, neat Mongolian soldiers, beefy
Muscovites, matriarchal families with Maria's string bags,
travelling salesmen from Europe, Air Force officers, a
theatrical troupe from Leningrad, women in high boots as if
winter was still coming. As Schiller picked up his baggage
and the glass panels clipped behind him the night air was
warm.

The taxi taking him in, a hiccupping Volga, was held up
by massive roadworks, then by a convoy of tank transporters
moving north. He leaned back and tried to think: what had
happened to the big Russian, whether Nicola and Charlie
would come, what he could say in the *Post*, whether he
would visit Lila, confusion of dream and reality, shadow
ground.

In Berlin the CIA had denied any knowledge of the
Barsov snatch. Claymore and the other smartasses had tried
to incriminate him. Heusermann had gone to ground before
Schiller started looking. All had gone out of their way to

wash their hands of Barsov, alive or dead. Alexei Sergevich's feelings, his wife and family, might as well not exist.

Schiller had tried to find poor Ernst, but not even the organ was there, only the top of a vacuum flask left on a window sill. He had walked the square beside the Gedächt niskirche, and down to the Wittenburgplatz. Nothing: insubstantial as air. The confectionery salesman too, Shawcross, was out of town, unobtainable on the telephone. And the crossing points reported nothing. Not even the cars had been found: all had vanished in the Kreuzberg wasteland, according to the police. Schiller was right on that: He had thought they would disappear, just as Heusermann had. That was how the German survived.

The yellow cab jerked and moved on. Schiller stared at the trolleybuses running down the busy boulevards. Moscow was a desert to him now, garish under the lights. He paid off the taxi and hauled his bags into the echoing tower on Kalinin. The road where the silver bus had been on the day it all started was humming with traffic but lifeless as Kansas on Sunday. High up in his eyrie everything looked strangely tidy, books in unaccustomed order, the television moved, his underwear in neat rows in the drawers of the tallboy, shirts folded and ironed. Old Maria had been busy, mothering him, and had left him a note, in her arthritic handwriting.

"Have done my best. It was a mess. You should find a wife."

Screw them. Life was a mess. He telephoned Sylvester and told him he was back on the patch.

"Swell, Ed. Swell. That was a great eye-witness piece from Berlin. Can you follow it up?"

"I doubt it," he said, over the open line.

"Uh huh. I understand. We loved it. Ed, are you OK?"

"Sure," he said. When Maria found him he was on the bottle again.

"You'll make yourself ill," she said.

He smiled grimly. The room stank of alcohol.

"You ought to get out in the sun. It's summer now."

"In my own time," he said. "You get on with the cleaning."

He tired to adjust the ventilation, but the window was

solidly stuck. When the old woman had gone he thought about phoning Darleen, but that wouldn't work either. He knew it was hopeless, this churning inside him about what he might have done, by going to Heusermann. Worst of all he did not know. Two days of solid drinking vomited into the sink.

The intercom buzzed.

It was Jim Burrell, crisp and laundered, wrinkling his nose at the closet air.

"Oh Christ. They told me you were back in town. This place smells like a shit-house."

Schiller groaned. He was unshaven and haggard, in the clothes in which he'd flown back.

"Fuck off," he growled.

Burrell came over and helped himself to the open bottle. "This stuff doesn't solve much."

He watched the younger man's face, which was drained of its color, as if he'd been underground. Then he went to the television, found a concert program and turned up the sound to max.

Close by the set he said quietly, "I hear Berlin was bad. I'm sorry, Ed."

Schiller's face stared back at him. "I tried to help him and lost him." Something else struggled to be said. "I've condemned them both," he added.

Burrell understood finally what was ticking inside him. "Don't say that. How do you know?"

He watched Schiller empty the glass, and then the bottle, knowing it was going to be difficult.

"There won't be a second chance," Schiller said into the glass.

Jim Burrell waited, then very softly he added, "Barsov is back."

"Back?" Ed Schiller's scalp tingled; he felt his whole body shudder.

Jim Burrell nodded. "*Pravda* report, confirmed by Reuters. Very brief. Just says he's been rescued from a kidnapping attempt in West Berlin and brought home for 'rest and treatment'."

"Who by?"

" 'Anti-capitalist forces' was the phrase."

"For Christ's sake. Two KGB men were shot dead!"

Burrell said, "Mind if I sit? Listen, Ed. Don't think the KGB is one big happy family. Maybe they got it wrong; maybe the Old Guard wanted to get its own back on some deal they thought had been cooked up with Heusermann. It wouldn't worry them to shoot a couple of softies. Anyways, they got him back. And they've announced it."

Schiller raised his head. The drinking stopped. "Or maybe the CIA fixed it."

"Don't say that, Ed."

"Where have they taken him?"

Burrell shrugged. "You ask them. That's all it says. Thought you would like to know." His blue eyes watched Schiller carefully, as if he thought he might hug him because Barsov was still alive.

Schiller's head seemed to clear. "I hadn't heard," he said.

"You were too pissed to hear. Anyway it was a *Pravda* two-liner, nothing more. You're giving him up, aren't you, Ed?"

He watched Schiller's back as the younger man crossed to the window and contemplated the cars skating along below. How could you search a city, maybe a continent, Ed seemed to be asking.

"What about . . . the apartment?" Schiller whispered, half to himself. "Their place by the Vernadskova Metro?"

Burrell stood beside him, a fatherly hand on his shoulder.

"Forget it. You've got to forget it, Ed. You're on a hiding to nothing. It can't do you any good. You've just got to quit hoping. The Barsov story is over."

"What do you mean?" Schiller spun round.

"I mean that they've all gone. The place is empty, boarded up. The gang went round to inquire."

Schiller seemed to find it difficult to understand.

"Gone?"

"Yeah. Taken away. We checked."

"When?"

"Before I came round here. As soon as I saw that

announcement. That two-liner. Knew it would be too late.
The birds have flown. They've nailed up the door. There
was a kid upstairs who used to play with Yuri. Said that Lila
and the boy were taken away three days ago. You must
know what that means.''

"Oh Jesus Christ.''

"Yeah. Well, this is Russia. Glasnost or no glasnost.''

Schiller seemed to stumble. "The wouldn't dare . . . after
Berlin . . . after the publicity.''

"No. Sure. This guy Barsov though must have some
funny friends. And who knows who gives the orders?''

He studied Schiller's face. "Don't take it so hard. You
didn't start this, Ed. They did.''

But Schiller didn't see it that way, not any more. What he
did see was frightening. He had let Barsov down, and
Barsov might never recover. Schiller knew what "treatment"
meant. And that left the fate of Lila . . . an offer, a joke, or a
pledge.

"Bastards,'' Schiller said. "The bastards!''

"Come on now, Ed. You can't fight the Soviet Union.
Sssh . . .'' On the television the concert came to an end and
they were conscious of the listening-bugs.

Burrell switched to the second channel, but it was a news
program: army parades in Warsaw. Schiller ran through the
room, brought the radio from the kitchen and turned it on
until he found movie music, loud and brash balalaikas. It
seemed that he could not wait.

"Where have they gone, for God's sake?''

"How the hell do I know, Buster?''

He watched Schiller's hands tremble, issued the same
warning as Claymore. "Don't go starting trouble on your
own, Ed.''

But Schiller was lost, remembering the cramped apartment the day that Lila had walked with him in the spring,
and how they had looked at each other that Sunday on the
Lenin Hills.

"You don't seem happy,'' he had said. Her oval face had
seemed sadder, less merry than before. Alexei Sergevich
was snoring on the grass.

"I'm happy enough.''

"Moscow's no place for someone like Alexei Sergevich now," he had ventured.

"It's not that."

"What is it, then?"

"I can't tell you." But their eyes met. Schiller had seen the young blondes with bouncy peroxide quiffs at Barsov's Saturday parties, and the way he fondled them.

"You could leave him," he whispered.

"He is my husband," she said.

"It doesn't mean you have to stay."

"Where else would I go?"

He hadn't understood then, he must have been blind.

"I don't know."

"I still love him," she said, as she touched Schiller's hand gently.

Now Schiller looked at Burrell as if he had just appeared. "Didn't you ask where she's gone?"

"Oh Christ, Ed. Who do I ring up? The KG fucking B?"

Schiller stared at him, then turned round again to watch the cars so that Burrell addressed his shoulder. He saw that Schiller was shaking.

"Come on," he cajoled, "I'll put you to bed. You're bushed. I thought I'd tell you now to get it over with. Before you started climbing the walls." Burrell stood beside him. "She's gone. They both have. It's no use pretending. Get your head down. Sleep and try to forget it. You've got to hold the job down. You're good, Ed, but Sly won't wait for ever."

A pair of bleak eyes bored through him, then Schiller walked past. The pile of mail that Maria had placed on the sideboard for his return had been there for days unread: bills, circulars, letters from the office, from home, correspondents in Denver and Boston, back issues of *Time*. He wanted something now, searching frantically, scattering them like a dog scratching leaves. Nikky must surely have written. Flooded with anger and despair, he wanted at least to know.

As Schiller stood there reading, rocking slightly to and fro, Burrell wondered again what made him run. Schiller devoured the letter and turned to face him. He waved it loosely.

"It's from Nicola."

"I guessed that. What does she say this time?"

Schiller didn't know whether to laugh or cry. "She's bringing Charlie to Moscow. To see me. She threatened it some time ago."

"Shit. When you got one problem, nothing like another one." He sucked the edge of his glass. "How old's the boy?"

"Coming nine," Schiller said.

"Do you want to see her?"

"No." He slumped into the high-backed armchair facing the TV screen and stared as if into a crystal.

Burrell yawned far more lazily than he was feeling. "You ought to get to bed, Ed. Sleep on it."

Schiller seemed not to hear.

"What about your Charlie? What about seeing him?"

Schiller thrust his fists against the chair. "How the hell do I know? I haven't seen the kid in two years. What does he remember of me?" He hammered his hands on the armrests. "For Christ's sake, what can I give to him? He's her kid now, not mine. She uses him like a shield."

"Perhaps she still wants you."

Schiller growled in despair. "For God's sake, she wants power, that's what she wants. Power over me. She'll screw me for it—"

"Don't let her get you, Ed."

"I told her not to come. Told her I didn't want her, but she won't listen."

"Guess she doesn't want to."

"She phoned me in Berlin."

"When is she coming?"

Schiller consulted the letter again.

"End of the month."

"She'd know you'd be back by then."

Schiller seemed to shrink into the chair. "I'd like to see Charlie, but not if the price is her..."

Burrell didn't trade in prices. All he said was, "Get yourself to bed, Ed. She can't stay in Moscow long. It's not much of a vacation. Look, she's told you when she's coming. OK. All you have to do is . . . disappear." He bit back the final word, and realized it was too late. He had contradicted his own advice of five minutes before. He had told Schiller to leave. He knew then from Schiller's face that he would go looking for Lila.

13

Schiller had taken trouble with the Ministry of the Interior in Gorky Street, and the Moscow Union of Writers and Artists. Jim Burrell had told him that they were worth cultivating, soon after he arrived. Try the Queen Bee, he winked, and say you like icons.

The Queen Bee was Dmitri Nevsky, head of the press department. Nevsky had a white thatch and white trim beard: Schiller had the impression he could be white all over. Underneath the surface he was a lost priest and in the evenings drew bad sketches at a class on iconography. Nevsky had taken the American back to his chic apartment, but hadn't dared to make passes. Instead he had passed on gossip, bitchy gossip about the Moscow underground. That was how Schiller had found Barsov, and kept Sly Sylvester happy with stories from the Writers' Union.

Coming back to Moscow now, with the albatross of Barsov's abduction round his neck, he needed that contact again.

He found Nevsky as usual, dapper, polite, conservatively dressed in gray, in his third-floor office at the Ministry's modern building.

The QB's eyes lit up, blending duty and pleasure as he came round the desk to meet the American.

"Eddie. A long time since I've seen you."

Schiller waited for the pleasantries to die away and

accepted the inevitable tea. Some of Dmitri's artist friends
hung on the panelled walls opposite the standard portraits of
Marx and Lenin.

"I've been to Berlin, Dmitri," Schiller said.

"Berlin?" Nevsky's eyebrows rose in polite caution.

"I was there when Barsov was kidnapped."

He watched the Russian beginning to clam up.

"I heard about that. I don't know what has happened to
Alexei Sergevich."

"What do you mean you don't know? You must know
he's back in Russia. Even *Pravda* says so." And since then,
nothing, while Schiller chewed his nails, and Sylvester
asked for more.

Nevsky shifted in his seat by the window. "Oh yes. Of
course. I seem to remember seeing it."

"For God's sake, where is he now?"

"Why are you so curious?"

"I'm not curious. I'm worried. Shit scared, Dmitri. I was
in the hotel when he was abducted. Three people were
killed: two of them Russians. Doesn't that concern you?
Who brought him back here?"

Nevsky spread his hands in a fan, locking the two thumbs
together. "How should I know? It is a matter for the police.
The security personnel. Not for me." Poker-faced.

"Christ almighty, Dmitri. I thought you knew me better
than that." Schiller half rose in anger. "Was it the KGB?"

"That is all I can say."

"You've got to tell me. Who got him back here if it
wasn't the KGB? Some special operation?"

"You should not come here asking me." Nevsky began to
look nervous: maybe he was bugged too. "Anyway there's
no such thing."

There was a tightness in the American's face that made
Nevsky more uneasy and yet impressed. He felt he was
charmed by iron.

"Don't bullshit me, Dmitri. I want to find Barsov, and
you are going to help."

Nevsky fluttered his eyes. "I don't know. How can I
know?"

Schiller's raw-looking fist hammered down on the desk.

" 'Rest and treatment,' they say. Rest and treatment for Barsov in some psychiatric bin. Holy Russia. Where the hell would that be, Dmitri? Otherwise I might tell tales, and not just in the *Washington Post*, about your hobbies.''

Nevsky went a shade paler. His fingers drummed nervously.

"Well, maybe the Union of Writers, they might help. If you follow me.''

"Yeah. I follow you. You'd better take me there fast. And if I find him outside Moscow I shall want a travel visa.''

He needed Nevsky to circumvent the Kafkaesque inquiries, Nevsky anxious, rubbing his hands, flicking names across the table.

"I will ask Comrade Dobrynin. He has the responsibility for special passes.''

"Special passes? Is that what you've done to Alexei Sergevich?'' Schiller's fuse was shortening.

"I cannot help you,'' Nevsky lamented.

"Damn you. If you won't help,'' Schiller threatened, "I'll find Alexei Sergevich myself.''

Nevsky put on his hat and took him to the Writers' Building.

Affairs at the *conservatoire* that housed the Union of Writers and Artists were, as usual, in chaos. The old baroque building seemed to burst at the seams in the new glasnost era, not, as Antoly Sherbitsky said, because they were all comrades, but because it had the best restaurant. Sherbitsky wore tight cords and studied the foreign press. He acted as a sounding board for permitted ideas pushed so far and no further: profit-sharing schemes, elections to factory boards, tourist visas to the West. Another one of Schiller's contacts, via Dmitri Nevsky, on the Moscow arts round: Schiller inquisitive, naïve, open-faced, trying to forget the past; Sherbitsky like a rangy student, long-haired and leather-zipped. The hair had already receded in those two Gorbachev years, he somehow seemed fatter and quieter, having picked up the newsdesk on one of the magazines. He grew sleek and gave parties.

Nevsky took Schiller to the door and signed him in, disappearing with a skip of relief. Schiller tracked Sherbitsky down by wandering from room to room until he heard the voice, querulous as the whine of a chain-saw. There were eight or nine round the table when he burst in, men in glasses and shirtsleeves, women with pan make-up and worry beads.

Sherbitsky broke off when he saw the American, his mouth first slack then cunning. "Ed Schiller? It is really you?"

"It's me. I'm here."

"Ed, you can see I'm busy." He flapped around. "Can you wait a little while?"

"No. I want to talk to you now." Schiller almost ignored them. "I want the answer to a single question. Barsov. Where is Alexei Sergevich?"

Sherbitsky laughed uneasily. "Alexei Sergevich? Who wants to see Barsov?" He looked for support from the editorial group. "Forgive me. We are interrupted, comrades. My friend has urgent business, as you can see." He sighed. "Well, why do you want to know? It is no business of yours."

"I saw him abducted in Berlin. I want to talk to him."

Sherbitsky sucked his lips, then decided not to prevaricate. "I think he is in hospital. Under treatment."

"I know that. Where?" Schiller was shaking his fist. "Don't you bloody well care where one of your comrades goes to? You must have the guts of a sheep."

There was an intake of breath. He felt them ganging up, closing ranks. It was hot in the sealed room, with the sun striking bars through the shutters.

"How dare you come here and say such things," one of the women muttered.

"Don't you care?"

"Care? Alexei Sergevich has rolled in dog-shit," she retorted.

"Please. Please. If we can, I will help you," Sherbitsky said smoothly, "but who am I to know what the Ministry of the Interior decides?"

"Fuck the Ministry, and the Culture Bureau, and the Union of fuck-all Writers and Artists," Schiller shouted. "I saw what happened."

They were crowding round him, curious and defensive. What did he know? What had he seen in Berlin when the West attempted a kidnap, contrary to human rights? That did not happen in Russia. No hijacks in Soviet society. Sherbitsky came across, newsman to newsman, put an arm round his shoulders and offered to buy him a drink.

"Not now," Schiller told him. "I haven't got time." The longer he delayed, the more Barsov was a non-person.

Sherbitsky took him outside and shut the door. He spoke softly in the corridor. "Surely they wouldn't dare...? Alexei Sergevich can't simply disappear..." but his voice betrayed that he was bluffing.

Schiller had no doubts within himself. Lila had gone, so had the boy. The KGB locks were on the doors, the manuscripts would be impounded, even destroyed by now. Bastards. Bastards. The Lubianka had closed in, and taken away the evidence. The Directorates of the KGB would never be open to question.

"Don't push me," he shouted at Sherbitsky, who tried to calm him, this ranting and raving foreigner. He steered Schiller through the corridors, nodding and grinning but whispering in his ear.

"I am glad Alexei Sergevich is still alive. Our boys must have been told to intercept a snatch squad." There was pride in his voice. "Our boys are very well trained. Best in the world."

"Your boys?"

"Of course. The anti-terrorist unit."

"Then where have you put him?"

Sherbitsky shook his head as if Schiller was a truculent child.

"Don't misunderstand, Ed. You must not ask for the moon. Alexei Sergevich is a remarkable man, but wild, wild as a bull. He doesn't know when to stop opening his stupid mouth. That way ends in disaster. So he has to have treatment, before he fulfills his potential."

Fulfills his potential? Which hell-hole is he in for that?"

Blandly, Sherbitsky said, "I don't know. Why should anyone know, except his wife?"

"So you know where she is too? Lila?"

Sherbitsky retrieved the stumble. "How should I know? One can only... surmise."

"Look." Schiller stopped in his tracks. "I want to see Alexei Sergevich. Here. In Russia. Now." He grabbed Sherbitsky's lapels as if he were going to throttle him, until Sherbitsky saw only a close-up, Schiller's hot breath on his face. "Don't play with me. Where do I go now?" He felt the kind of anger he had when he saw deceivers, including Carlo in bed.

Sherbitsky rocked on his heels. "Where do you go?" As if the question were unreal.

"Your mind isn't completely paralysed, is it Antoly? Don't try and give me that. What happens to sick artists? Where do they get the treatment? Don't tell me you don't know, a clever turd like you?"

"Ed, you must understand. We look after our creative minds for the benefit of the people. Alexei Sergevich is a very difficult person. He is mentally unstable."

"Then for Christ's sake where are you treating him?"

Sherbitsky had stopped protesting. He drew the American into a dusty lounge, where plants struggled in dry pots, on mahogany stands. "I'll tell you as much as I know, but you must never say your source." He looked around. "Lila was put on the train at the Yaroslavl Station along with the little boy. I saw them off."

"You what?"

"I saw them off. They were excited about it."

"You lying bastard, Antoly."

"No. No. I am not. Believe me." His eyes were shifting around.

"Where? Where?"

"She was following Alexei Sergevich. His wife is allowed to go with him while he is under treatment."

Schiller was shaking with rage, against himself, against them all.

"Where have they gone?"

"Barsov—"

"You'd better tell me before I break your neck."

"Listen," Sherbitsky said anxiously, "he has gone far to the east."

"Where? Where? Where?"

"Be sensible. Too far for you to visit."

"Where?"

"A hospital . . . in Siberia."

"Siberia is too big for me," Schiller persisted. "You make it smaller. Where have they taken him?"

Sherbitsky grew cunning. "Rest and treatment center."

"I know that, you chicken-liver."

Sherbitsky looked at Schiller's face. It frightened him. "There's a rumor that . . . he's near Novosibirsk. The science park at Akademgorodok," Sherbitsky said quickly. "There's a special hospital there for psychiatric cases." He showed gold fillings. "The latest equipment."

"Akademgorodok." Schiller relaxed his hold and whistled. "Boy, that must be some treatment." The vast technology center, constructed in the wilderness some miles beyond the city, was a restricted area, out of bounds to Western newshounds, except in shepherded parties, but that wouldn't deter him.

"Where is Lila?"

Slowly, Sherbitsky subsided, slithering away from Schiller's embrace.

"I'm not sure. A village somewhere, maybe. An exile village."

"Give me the name, you shit, before I beat you into pulp."

"In Siberia, nobody can visit her . . ."

The name, you bastard. Think."

Sherbitsky choked. "There are no means of visiting. It is incommunicado."

Doggedly, Schiller yelled, "The name."

"OK. OK." Sherbitsky's teeth jarred together. "I think it's called Madeniyet. When Alexei Sergevich gets better he'll be allowed to join her. She's there to wait for him."

"Where the hell is Madeniyet?" Schiller's hot breath was on the Russian's face.

Sherbitsky said, "Somewhere south of Novosibirsk."

"How far, scumbag?"

Sherbitsky gabbled his excuses, scared for what he had said. "I don't know. Two hundred, two hundred and fifty kilometers. Impossible to reach." A look of disbelief crept into his eyes. "You're not thinking . . . Don't be a fool, my friend."

Schiller laughed. "Shit, no, boy. Don't let that worry you."

14

What finally tipped him over was Sly Sylvester. On top of Moscow Station's inquiries, Sylvester gave him the needle, but first, Jubal Martin wanted to talk Berlin, shifting the accusations round and round.

"Why did you try to rock the boat, Ed?"

"Because I had to, Jubal."

They faced each other again in the offices in Commercial Section.

"Tell me what's on your mind."

"Nikky's coming, that's all."

"What the hell. You ain't married." Jubal didn't like domestic clouds intruding on his coming retirement, the siren call of Palm Springs.

"She'll want to go to the Bolshoi."

"So what? You got expenses."

"I need more time."

It was then that Sly pushed him from Washington. "No way you get more time. I didn't even get the Gorbachev story after the press conference. Where the hell were you?"

"I was looking for somebody else."

"For Christ's sake," Sylvester said over the line, "there were three big speeches in Moscow this week. We got nothing from you. Ed, that won't run."

"All crap."

"Ed, whose payroll you on?"

"I'm paying for Barsov, right now, Sly."

Sylvester gave him one more chance. "What is it you want, Ed?"

"A bit more time," Schiller said.

He heard the phone slam and helped himself to mineral water.

Nevsky's friend Victor Dobrynin was the next stop on the line. The Bureau of Special Passes, Ministry of the Interior, was the other side of the Gorky Street building.

Nevsky took Schiller in and they shook hands. Dobrynin was flat-faced and silver-haired, a bruiser, sitting in shirtsleeves at a big curving desk with the bottom panels kicked out. He wore a gold watch and shirt bands, exposing heavy wrists. A large clock on the wall showed the wrong time, and Lenin addressed the workers from a framed lithograph.

"I would like a pass for Akademgorodok. For a series of articles on modern Soviet science."

Dobrynin scribbled, made a telephone call, and asked him to come back tomorrow, the day that never comes.

When Schiller returned there was another man there, a sandy-haired comrade standing next to Nevsky's friend. Dobrynin picked out the visa form and said it was all in order. He showed the stamp. He smiled. "Of course you can go. No problem."

"No problem?"

"Not at all." The KGB man smiled too, a mouthful of silver teeth.

Miracles sometimes happened in the land of the Soviets.

The shapes in Schiller's mind danced, all the way out. Within seven days of his return to Moscow he had an air ticket and was wedged in a Tupolev 154, between a squat, cautious matron with tufts of hair in her armpits and a construction engineer engrossed in a history of Turkey. Below them, through broken clouds, he could see swamps, green and treeless like the froth on a pond. Empty feature-less country, north of Omsk. It reminded him of middle Canada, northern Alberta and the Winnipeg lakes, the same sense of green cloth stretched on a rock-hard land. Even in June the wing-shadows raced over wilderness. But the emptiness was almost a relief after the Moscow questions, the taste of the Berlin disaster. And Sly Sylvester would wait.

The wheels came down as the aircraft banked over a city, sprawling and anonymous, that must be Novosibirsk.

The engineer stacked his book in a canvas hold-all. "Another six months of it, comrade." He pocked a cold samosa wrapped in tinfoil that had been handed round.

But for the American, the city held a sense of beginning, a promise, an exploration as real but obscured as the oil and gas fields over which they had flown.They came in over new-cut highways, a satellite town, the high-rise towards the center, white Aeroflot freighters parked in rows lining the airport. He had the sense of getting closer with every mile, going deeper, returning.

The Tupolev shuddered to a halt and they were piling out. The matron adjusted the straps inside her semi-transparent blouse. June sun fried on the concrete as she slipped a cream linen jacket over her shoulders. Schiller asked if he could help as they exited together, blinded by the sharp blue sky. They had landed on the middle runway two hundred meters from the terminal, and there seemed to be no buses. The afternoon sun burnt the skin. Everything here was slower, far less wound-up than Moscow. She carried a travelling bag and was flattered when he picked it up.

Like a wolf with a victim, he looked her over, noting the hennaed hair and artificial pearls. The headmistress of a girls' school, or the wife of an oilman stationed in the wide open spaces.

"Glad to be back?" he asked.

She wouldn't be drawn, not sure where he was from, a foreigner with an untidy haircut. They sweated across the apron, into the glass-fronted arrival lounge. The woman put her coat on properly under the humming fans, and Schiller helped her again. She still looked at him suspiciously: what was he doing there, in his lightweight American suit?

"My first trip here," he explained.

A flicker of sympathy. She was a Muscovite.

"Yes," he said truthfully. "I've never been this far east. Visiting Akademgorodok. Do you know it?"

Galina Korochkina pursed her lips.

"Oh yes." She nodded. "My husband works there."

"Really. What does he do?"

Schiller was no more inquisitive than the average Russian.
She hesitated, liked the look of his face, and took the
plunge. "A plant geneticist." She began to be friendly.

"I write for an American paper," Schiller said. She
shook her head and smiled in disbelief. The engineer came
over and wished them luck. Security militia in dark blue
with gold flashes looked cursorily at his visa and waved
them on.

"You have no baggage?" Galina Korochkina asked,
wondering how anyone travelled without adequate equipment, a yak-load of suitcases, plastic grips, and cardboard
parcels. This man had nothing except a cabin bag.

"I am only staying for a few days," he said cheerfully, as
he helped her.

Fedor Korochkin hadn't let her down. He was waiting
behind the barrier in the passenger hall: a laboratory manager with a perspiring face. Galina threw her arms around
him and he hugged her off the ground.

"This is my friend," she said. "He's come from Moscow
to interview Academician Lassky, here in Akademgorodok.
Just think of that."

Korochkin was a mixed-race Siberiak, carved by the
weather, who looked at Galina's friend as Schiller had
looked at Carlo.

"Lassky? Which is his department?"

"Anthropology."

"Ah. I didn't know we had such distinguished men here.
What do you do yourself?"

"I'm a journalist," Schiller said.

"Is that so? The foreign press tells lies."

"Sometimes," Schiller admitted. "How about you?"

Korochkin grunted. "Fruit flies. I do research on them."

"Really."

The visit to the Academician became more necessary.

Korochkin shook hands and led the way to the four-wheel
drive, borrowed from the lab. He was a cautious man who
had taken off the wiper blades and put them inside the cab.

"Is that all?" Looking at Schiller's cabin bag.

"That's all." Grinning.

Korochkin shrugged at the foolishness of not having a margin. "You have an address? He is expecting you?"

"Of course," Schiller said.

"You do not even have a raincoat?"

"It won't rain," Schiller said, "while I am here."

Korochkin waggled his head and started the engine. This man was a puzzle. They drove into Novosibirsk while Galina explained the sights, the tower block apartments, the new Intourist hotel, the flower and fish stalls. Out by the southern exit the roads were still being built, black earth churned to the sides, the half-completed new suburbs strung out like washing. And then at last the country, a lakeland of thin birches with glimpses of water between them.

Galina chatted about the goods in Moscow as Schiller rode in the rear between a clutter of luggage. They jolted off the concrete on to temporary roads and back on to hard-top again, past struggling wooden huts that might have been there for ever. Babushkas sat by the roadside, peddling raspberries and cucumbers, children fished in a stream and outside an ancient *izba* a woman flailed clothes on a stone.

"Do you feel lost?" she called over her shoulder.

"No."

"You like Siberia?"

"I like it here," Schiller replied, with a sense of relief, light-heartedness almost, that he could not admit.

They crossed the high dam that held back the Ob Lake, and saw the orderly lines of Akademgorodok itself. The forests gave way to housing like bottle-racks, boulevards, sports grounds, departments stores, prefabricated canyons. Then the ranks of the science parks and laboratories, the institutes of physics and geophysics, Korochkin's own department of entomology.

"We try to anticipate the future," Fedor Korochkin announced grimly as they arrived at their apartment, a block fronting the lake.

"Give me Academician Lassky's apartment reference and Fedor will run you over there," Galina said.

Schiller looked over the water. Small insects with iridescent blue wings danced in the air. He had his dreams too, and he smiled at them.

"Please don't bother. This is block twelve. Academician Lassky lives over in block eight."

"Block eight," Korochkin said, scratching his head. "That's only just over there. I would have expected him to be in one of the newer ones. They are much bigger."

"He likes it there."

"I'll run you over."

"No way. Don't bother. I want to stretch my legs."

It was difficult to shake the Korochkins off, now that the ice had broken. They wanted to entertain Schiller, to hear about Hollywood.

"Are you sure?"

"Sure thing."

Korochkin shook hands and Galina touched his fingers lightly, as if he might fade away. They pulled their luggage from the wagon and then turned to watch. Schiller was walking slowly towards the block they had shown him, end-on to the lake, no more than four hundred meters. The water, the dinghies tacking to and fro, reminded him of the Havel in Berlin, and Heusermann taking him there, not so long ago. He walked unhurriedly between the trees, and into the entrance hall of the block he had pointed out. He looked back to wave once.

Korochkin turned to his wife. "Strange men you pick up on planes."

"Why?"

"He had no baggage."

"He's only staying two days."

Korochkin considered. "Why didn't he want me to drive him across? Where is he going to stay? Supposing Academician Lassky is not there? What would your friend do then?"

"Oh, come on, let's get unpacked," Galina said.

They climbed the stairs to their apartment and began to unwind. Always after that flight she felt fatigued, and wanted to open a window. Far away at the end of the road she could just see block number eight.

"I wonder what he's really up to?" Korochkin mused.

"Well, that's up to him."

But Fedor was not so sure. The directory for the Institutes at Akademgorodok, a large loose-leafed plastic folder, regularly updated, was on the shelf by the telephone, and he went through it methodically. He turned to the personal index, and then through the subject ones: nuclear physics, chemistry, hydrodynamics, thermophysics, geology, anthropology, linguistics.

"Odd," he said. "I can't find any Academician called Lassky. No one of that name at all in the Institutes of Archaeology or Anthropology."

Galina blushed, playing with the beads at her neck. She suddenly felt very foolish, almost betrayed. "What do you mean?"

"I mean that he was lying."

"Perhaps he has come for a girl," she ventured.

"Or running away from one," he grunted.

"What are you going to do?"

Korochkin thought for a while. He did not reach conclusions quickly, but when he did, he acted.

"I must let the authorities know."

But when they appeared he had gone. Hours later, by the time the militia arrived Schiller had vanished into the concrete undergrowth.

"There is no address in block eight for Academician Lassky," Korochkin kept repeating. The sun was oppressive and dry and he sat there mopping his forehead. The policemen were young and cool in their blue summer fatigues and regarded him as a clown. The idea of a stranger going to ground in Akademgorodok was mildly amusing, but they wrote it up in their books.

"I think he may be a spy."

"The Committee for State Security will check him out. What was his name?"

Korochkin became annoyed, realized he did not know. "I will report you as well for being too slow."

They calmed him down. "All right. All right. We'll take a look around: give us a full description."

It was not much good, the details laboriously written in their flip-top notebooks were already out of date. Schiller had beaten them. The best place to hide was a crowd. Inside apartment block eight he had walked straight through to the fire exit and taken off the coat of his lightweight suit. He bundled it into his cabin bag and emerged in an open-necked shirt. The path at the back of the building came out on to a side road and he carried on towards the city. The apartments gave way to workshops, then to the stores and supermarkets grouped round the main square. In the late afternoon hundreds of people passed by: technicians and secretaries, storekeepers and instrument makers, relaxing in the sunshine, shopping or sitting on benches in front of the fountains. Soldiers were queuing for ice-cream.

He went into the Passyge department store, straight to the menswear section and selected a cheap fake leather jacket, brown, hard-wearing with buttons and a belt. Plenty of pockets, anonymous, the kind of thing a mechanic would wear on his day off. No one took any notice of his accented Russian. Strangers were commonplace at the research labs, the institutes and the test-plants, collected from over the Union, even a few from the West. Ed Schiller was changing appearance, working up a new role.

"I'll take it and wear it now," he said. The sales girl hardly noticed, thinking of her free time, of a pillion ride on a motorbike.

He left his bag with the coat in it high up on a ledge behind the pipes in the toilets. By now it had no labels. He mussed his hair, and in the brown replacement jacket no one looked at him twice as he walked down to the snack bar on the ground floor. He bought himself packets of chocolate, hard-tack biscuits and a small haversack, a "camper's friend."

Behind the hot food counter a big-throated housewife in a white overall pushed across a bowl of bean soup. Schiller felt suddenly hungry and he swallowed it noisily, perched on a plastic stool.

His neighbor grinned. "Good?"

"You bet."

"Food's not bad in here."

"Right."

The place was busy, a wood and glass counter with bar

stools. There was a smell of pressed vegetables, sliced meats and coffee.

"You new to these parts?"

"Doing a job at the Language Institute," Schiller said. "Translation studies."

"Fascinating." The brown eyes regarded him crisply, then took a chance. "German? Polish? American?"

"Moscow. I work for the KGB," Schiller said. That shut him up like a closing door.

Schiller ordered more soup and a meat blini. He ate until he felt full and considered his next move. Somewhere out there was the hospital where Barsov was held, in one of those concrete forts lining the Ob Lake or stuck like stamps in the forests. Places where enemies of the state could be salted away; the question was which one. He paid for a coffee and jingled the change in his pocket, wondering how much time he had, how much time Barsov had. He couldn't stay around in town, in case the militia came looking: supposing Fedor Korochkin started checking on his story. Strangers were always suspect.

Schiller picked up his haversack and sauntered through the store, buying soap and a razor, a shirt and a change of socks. If he stayed he had to risk a hotel, or somewhere rougher. It was unwise to delay.

From the days of his first choices, back in Iowa, he had taken risks, and decided to work on his own. Now, as he wandered into the crowds in their shirtsleeves on Lenin Prospekt, celebrating the brief summer, queuing at the fruit juice stalls, the word on his mind was Madeniyet, and underneath the subtler whisper, "Lila." Lila taken away like the girl from the silver bus. At that moment, Alexei Sergevich Barsov was an illusion, simply his excuse. Schiller did not even know if he really wanted to see him: he wanted to see Lila.

A militia truck was pulling in over there by the fountain, and the blue uniforms were asking for papers.

He knew it was time to go.

15

The road out was wide and empty and heading south to Barnaul; the pick-up was loaded with pig-swill for a local farm; the body in the road looked dead until it laid out the driver as he stopped to examine it.

Schiller said "sorry" and pushed fifty rubles into the driver's pocket as he pitched him into the ditch.

Once with his father he had gone on a fishing trip in Minnesota where the forests ended and the lakes began. On the way they had picked up a drunk who had thrown an empty Jim Beam bottle at them. When Franz disappeared for stitches Ed had driven the truck on and spent the rest of the week in a tiny cabin in the woods, isolated, alone, in country much like this.

The farm truck could barely make fifty and the stinking tubs of hog-food shook and swayed in the rear: he felt almost back home in the farm-belt he knew as a boy. And nobody came looking for pig-swill. On the city outskirts where the bus had dropped him he knew that he wanted the kind of truck a farmer used. This one was almost type-cast, an ancient Zhiguli. The windshield was splattered with mud, the plastic seat had been excavated and covered with an old blanket. The police cars and the militia did not give it a spit in the bucket.

Grinding on, the dusk would soon shut down, as the pick-up rattled its big end along the pot-holed highway. The forests had been cut back on either side and plowed into communal farms, tucked away up the tracks. There was no sign of life in the fields, but battered hand-painted trucks were thundering past with feed grains and metal pipes.

He had reason for optimism. The crumpled map on his

lap, inaccurate though it was, told him that Madeniyet was now in reach: a hundred and thirty miles, off this road to the east in the great bend of the Ob. Nobody knew he had come. A couple of headscarfed women hitching home on a farm cart waved to him from the back. After that the road was empty, and he counted the telegraph poles. The thin woods were creeping back as the farming gave up.

One hundred now and getting dark. Suddenly he came across lights. A farm with a washing-line of colored sheets, and a young woman feeding chickens. A village to be negotiated, the main road through the middle blocked off for a travelling circus. As Schiller slowed someone dressed as a clown laughed and held his nose. Then he was through and picking up speed again, still on half a tank of gas, as the sun went down in a red disc behind the hills. He believed he could be there tomorrow.

There. He tried to imagine Lila, to see her face, wondering what he would say, how he would present it. Schiller was singing, putting two thousand further miles between the past and the present. The country more wooded now, birches again, then the road hit a rough. He shifted down a gear and bounced on the broken surface so that the wet pig-swill washed over the tail-gate, overpoweringly strong. He couldn't drive there with pig-feed as a present for Lila, so he pulled into the roadside and began to tip the drums of chunder one by one in the ditch. For a moment fireflies glittered, caught by some phosphorescence in the swill; then he was alone again.

A huge articulated land-train swept by in the twilight with prowling headlights, and left him a speck in the dusk.

If they were searching for him, back there in Science City, it would be too late now. One hundred or so left. He could not imagine the militia bothering to look for a needle in a Siberian haystack. What was the point, they would say, when he had nowhere to go. There was just one niggling doubt about the inscrutable Korochkin, but Schiller dismissed it. Suspicion was a Russian virtue, but not persistence. They might register that Galina's companion had not gone where he had said, because there was no such address, but inertia would leave it at that, if the police ever checked. Schiller felt he had time, all the time in the world, time coming, time now. Tiredness made him light-headed. He stretched and yawned beside the pick-up, isolated in the night.

He finished unloading the metal buckets and stood sweating by the side of the ditch on the long flat road. Headlights picked up and dropped the shape of the farm truck. Night noises echoed, rustling and creeping. He ate a bar of chocolate, and even the silver wrapper vanished into the dark.

He was down to the eighty-five mile mark when the engine began to stutter and then stopped without an apology. For a few yards the truck free-wheeled and he ran her into the side, as far off the road as he could. The fuel gauge still read half-full, but a dip into the tank, read by the single headlight, showed that the damned thing was empty, bone dry. He fumed at his own stupidity in assuming an ancient farm truck would have instruments that really worked, or gas for a long journey. He cursed, and switched off the electrics, settling down in the dark. Madeniyet receded. Nobody in the night would stop to syphon him gas, and there was no spare can. Nobody stopped by these woods, they put their feet on the pedal as if there were goblins in them. He might as well wait till first light and try hitching a lift.

Zum . . . Zum . . . hypnotizing lights roared up behind and passed. As the night air cooled Schiller wrapped himself in the blanket off the seat. The cab mirror gave a long view of the lights coming down the road.

Zum . . . Zum . . . another heavy truck, and a car, their tail lights dwindling. A fleeting moon touched the white birches which grew up the embankment where the Zhiguli had come to grief.

Zum . . . Zum . . . a blank face high up in a cabin like a command module picked him out for a moment, huddled inside the pick-up. He began to make plans for the morning, plausible plans of walking five miles from the breakdown and seeking a lift elsewhere, in case they were looking . . . in case they were looking for him. The flashing blue and yellow lights in the distance drove an alert through his brain. Two revolving blue lights, and a yellow one, increasing fast. Scouring. Schiller left the cab in a hurry, carrying his haversack, and melted into the trees. This one was noisy and big, and going to stop. A four-wheel drive militia wagon. He scrambled away up the bank, and was lost in the knee-high bracken. He watched the lights come closer, hover, circle and stop.

They were a hundred meters away from where Schiller hid, and carrying heavy-duty torches. Three uniformed highway militia and one more in the cab with a radio.

Four men looking. One of them opened the engine, trying to find what was wrong. He felt the cylinder block and said it was warm. They noted the registration and one of them signalled their base while another one urinated. In the darkness, he heard them talking, a quick murmur of voices, excited by the find, a vehicle reported stolen.

Schiller got ready to move deeper into the trees.

The militia weren't local: they had come down from Novosibirsk on call from the MVD barracks, for Akademgorodok was short-handed. Their torch beams splintered the night but none of them seemed inclined to investigate the woods beyond.

"The bastard's run out of gas," the mechanically minded one concluded. Schiller saw the flare of matches as they lit cigarettes.

Headquarters was now confirming that this was the stolen truck.

"It stinks of pig-shit."

He was a factory boy, more used to oil and noise. This country darkness was unnerving.

"Can't we just tow it back?"

"Shut up." Headquarters repeated that it had been reported stolen. Where was the thief?

"How the bloody hell do I know? You want me to search Siberia?"

"All right. All right. No clues?"

"No sign. Maybe it was a joy-ride. Some stupid bastard fancied that way to get home."

"You don't steal a pig truck for a joy-ride, comrade."

"You do if the others won't stop."

"Can you search the area?"

"How can we search the fucking area? It's nothing but trees and you break your neck in the dark. Anyway, the bugger won't be waiting around."

Headquarters sighed. ''Ok, tow the truck back. We'll dust it over in the morning.''

Schiller saw them fasten the tow-rope and stamp on their cigarettes.

There was no point in hanging around, but he waited while they backed the militia wagon and hitched up the pick-up. It groaned as they pulled it round and made an attempt to restart it. Their torches flashed over the trees, and they were gone. Schiller climbed back down to the road and began to walk in the dark.

He reckoned he had eighty-odd miles still to go, and the thought that he was so close offset his tiredness. But he knew there were police out too and his suspicions were confirmed when two more militia trucks cruised past, forcing him to run for the trees.

The plantation ended and open country began, rough tussocky grass on which he made slow progress.

Nothing moved on the road after the police cars had gone. It was now two in the morning and he was tiring. Reality and make-believe became confused, a sense of being adrift on an inland sea. The clouds were shutting in, piling over Schiller's head. He found himself crossing a gully where water splashed into the road.

Zum . . . zum . . . another car with hazard lights, another roaming militia van, the signs were looking less good. He had to hide in the gulley as a searchlight roamed idly around, then saw them flagging down one of the all-night truckers.

The country was no longer safe.

Very fatigued now, beginning to feel chilled. More chocolate gave a small boost, but he knew he was reaching his limit. He must have walked some ten miles since he abandoned the pick-up and streaks of light were beginning across the horizon, sliding lines in the dark.

If he waited till daybreak they might mount a full-scale search and out there on the scrubland he would be a sitting duck.

As the dawn broke he stared across a demoralized landscape of tussock grass and swampy creeks. Then he saw trees again, in the distance as the light came up, a faint bluish line of hills, a brush stroke where the mountains began, and a dirt road leading towards them.

Schiller picked up his bag and made for cover, away from the police on the highway. The early mist was slow to clear, and the hills almost a delusion, retreating as he came on, but he knew that he had to get there before the sunrise. Exhaustion was a bad companion, and he flogged himself to make the distance. The militia would be busy today, avenging the theft of the truck and the assault on its driver. So it was important to rest, postpone, hide. Think what he was doing, embarking on this small odyssey. Somewhere behind him they would all be wondering, friends and enemies: Burrell and the other newshounds back in Moscow, Sly Sylvester in Washington, Nicola flying east, the KGB. Only the woman whom he was going to see would be totally unaware. The sun lifted skeins of mist and he plodded beside the dirt track into the hills. Nothing moved along it except himself. The road where he had left the pick-up was far behind him now, not even its noise could be heard, and weariness climbed through his bones. Once he listened for a spotter plane, but decided it was delusion. The hills were nearer at last, a thick primeval forest, the kind of place in which to burrow.

He found a stream and followed it upwards, into a boulder-strewn forest dark with firs. The springy moss underfoot gave way to fresh bracken from which the rocks protruded, glacial debris. In the trees there was darkness, in the open air silence. The water was ice-cold and pure, and Schiller drank greedily from his hands, listening.

The noise he had heard was real. He located the choppers now, two of them glinting as they swooped down the highway and sallied from side to side. He hadn't been a moment too soon leaving the road. He realized he was on the run.

One chopper was buzzing closer, investigating the cart track that he had followed. Somewhere in this wilderness there must be a clearing, a farm, but his map was too small-scale to show where he was. And probably inaccurate. It was a military plane, with army markings. OK let them search Siberia; they'd have to check a lot of trees.

Skirting the stream he struggled inside the forest, the endless backcloth of the Altay foothills. It was much colder inside, dank and cheerless, but safer. The helicopter stuttered and hovered for several minutes over the green umbrella before taking itself off. The only noise was his breathing: there was no way they could get him, he felt as if he were charmed.

He decided it was safe to rest and wait for the search to subside. When the choppers had vanished he worked back to the rim of the forest and built himself a nest like the ones in Minnesota campsites. Then he squatted down and counted his remaining provisions from the haversack: two more bars of chocolate, a goat cheese in a plastic tub and a packet of rye-bread. Spread out on a rock they seemed a feast.

Nicola had said, "You're a loner, Ed. You always will be." That had been in one of their closer moments, lying in bed together.

He flicked a pebble into the stream and watched it settle on the bottom in the transparent water. She had not been sorry, either. He remembered coming back that afternoon to find her screwing with Carlo. Remembered what he had done then, throwing them out of his bed, her naked buttocks and Carlo's big thighs. The smell of sex in the room, his bedroom.

"You'd be better off out of town," Sly Sylvester had said. "I don't want to clean up the blood. How about going to Moscow?" And he had accepted it as a kind of penance, a hair shirt to keep him sane.

Schiller sliced the black bread and cheese which tasted sour.

So he had gone to Kalinin Prospekt and built up his reputation as an overseas journalist. Nicola got Charlie to write, trying to scramble back, and he had had to say no. Then had come Barsov and Lila.

He finished the meal and crawled out of the heat of the sun, into the nest of ferns. A hawk spiralled into the sky, but the only sounds were the stream and his own movements in the bracken.

He ate the last chocolate bar slowly, washing it down with water, watching the sky. Empty. Nothingness.

So he had gone to Berlin, enlisted Heusermann, seen the nightmare inside the hotel. Something that had been arranged, organized from outside, something beyond his control. The Soviets must have known what was happening: they had wanted a crack at Heusermann, and they took Barsov back. But how they knew, and how they could synchronize, that only made sense if his own side had tipped them off. The people who must have helped them to smuggle Barsov out of Berlin. No doubt now in Schiller's mind. If collusion had happened, maybe it was still happening, in these glasnost days. How long would it be, he wondered, before Jubal Martin, or Taylor Sheen, or Vince Claymore officially reported him missing to the Ministry of the Interior.

In spite of his tiredness and hunger, Schiller found himself grinning, then laughing aloud, before he drifted to sleep.

16

Schiller had heard them coming but they were on him like shadows, three or four shapes, in clothes smelling of horses. A knife scraped his eye and a hand twisted his throat as the heaviest one smashed on top of him. He kicked where the soft parts would be under the bundle of clothes, wrestled, tried to hit his way up. Another one was holding his legs and he grabbed at the hair, greasy and knotted. A face was glaring at him, eyeball to eyeball, carved like an old river bed, under a matted black hat.

"*Var?*" the man hissed. His black eyes were bloodshot slits, the skin smoked brown with a flat Mongolian nose and gray stubble over the face. He was sitting on Schiller's chest while the other three shackled his arms and legs. The smoked head leered, a mouthful of yellow teeth.

A suffocating, stinking cloth across his face. Schiller fought for breath like a drowning dog, thrashing, kicking, clawing, cursing. But the air supply would not come. He tried the old army trick of shamming dead, then slamming the dark; the thing sat on his chest, far away, laughing. His legs thrashed in despair, losing a shoe. Tough old fingers inside his jacket now, feeling for money, a sense of choking as, panic-stricken, he fought for air.

Then the pressure was released. The cloth was lifted, leaving Schiller gasping for breath, staring at four black heads standing with their backs to the sun. They stopped there stone-faced as he coughed and struggled, lungs bursting, holding his head in his hands.

The four men stood round him waiting.

Schiller took his own time, now that he was going to live. There was blood on his face where the knife had whipped the skin from an eyebrow, and his jacket had torn. He cleared the rictus in his throat and slowly brought his head up. Four men. All of them dressed like vagrants, gypsies, a mixture of rag-and-bone clothes, their eyes blank with unconcern. Schiller felt inside his coat where his ribs used to be. Battered but so far intact. They had taken his money and passport.

"*Var chu?*" It was not Russian, no dialect he understood, perhaps a Turkoman tongue. He shook his head slowly.

The old one, the tough one, who had leaned on his chest, turned away and spat on the grass. In his astrakhan cap and leather jacket, bagged round the middle with cord, he looked like a shepherd. Each of them wore leggings and battered boots. Two of the others were youngsters with the same flat, weathered faces and Rasta-like hair, wearing check shirts and sheepskin coats. They seemed to bulge with accessories. The ringleader, it was now clear, was the thin-faced man standing forward, lighting a cheap cigarette with a throw-away Gaz lighter. His face had blackened cheeks and a fringe of black beard; as he inhaled the *bidi* his lips pursed in inquiry, under the long nose and dark, suspicious eyes. He wore a similar cap, which he took off and waved at Schiller.

Slowly, in Russian, he said, "Army?"

They thought he must be a deserter from the war down south, a fugitive on the run from the military police. They would have seen the choppers flying low.

He shook his head.

The button eyes peered at him coldly, beginning to register that this was complicated. The old man retied the cord that seemed to hold him together. His hands were as tough as leather.

"Russian?" They realized that the stranger was not one of the wandering Kazakhs, Uzbeks or Chuvash that might have been found in those parts.

"German?" That was also a possibility: A Ukrainian exile, or a Pole perhaps, who had travelled too far east.

Schiller was standing up now, obstinate as a mule. The others were speaking the dialect he did not understand.

"No." He paused. "Amerikantsky."

There was a silence. He felt the suspicions mounting. Even these itinerant hill men owed an allegiance to Russia: anyone else intruded.

The thin-faced man drew a knife: a heavy-bladed thing with an embossed handle, and pointed it at him.

"Come with us."

"Where?"

"Abdul," he said.

They made a strange procession, following the path by the stream in the shadow of the trees. One of the youngsters first, then Schiller, with the ancient villain and the thin-faced man close at his back, and the second young man in the rear. Schiller carried the haversack, which they returned when they'd searched him.

"Is it far?"

They nudged him in the ribs and told him to keep on moving, like a prisoner. Up the rock-bed of the stream, climbing a thousand feet as the sun faded. He was eighty-five kilometers, eighty-five, he told himself, from where he wanted to be, and heading in the wrong direction. The men edged him into the wood and pushed him when he seemed unwilling. The comforting stream disappeared and the trees closed dark as murder. They were navigating by marks of their own through a trackless forest, telling him nothing. As the light waned he wondered about making a run for it, and knew that they were too dangerous.

They communicated by grunts, all of them, breathing hard, and Schiller tried to imagine their intentions. They had his money and watch. Perhaps they would kill him quietly in the dark. He stumbled and fell with a crack on a broken branch.

"Keep going," the thin man said, "if you want to stay alive."

"Where?"

"Where we can talk to you."

Schiller understood then that they had made another assumption which put his life at risk: that he was looking for them, an investigator, a KGB hound. Of course, that was it. A drug line. He had stumbled on one of the trails that led from Afghanistan, over the Oxus river and the Pamirs into the U.S.S.R., to the outlets in the big cities. A dangerous trade, and these men were hunted carriers, nomadic, moving across the deserts and mountains, unaccounted for. Moving with hard stuff now instead of the camel trains that had once come up—perhaps still did—over the high passes, in search of markets for jewelry and hand-worked stones.

They came into a clearing somewhere deep in the forest where he saw the tent. A characteristic round yurt, bound with cord like the men, thick, and felt-padded. A horse was neighing, carefully concealed by the trees, and two women in red costumes with long white caps on their heads were collecting wood.

As they staggered into the clearing one of the women pulled back the tent flap. Schiller had expected to see more people, pack mules, some form of transport, but this little camp looked forlorn, almost derelict, even in summer. He wondered how they survived.

Two of the men, the old one and one of the boys, beckoned him into the tent. Inside, as Schiller's eyes adjusted, a small man scrambled to his feet and switched off a transistor radio. This, he assumed, must be Abdul as the thin-faced man began an explanation. The face in the yurt stared back, almond-eyed and fringe-bearded, suspicious, and yet Schiller detected a flicker of curiosity, on which he built.

"*As salaam.*"

It brought the response, one hand on heart, "*As salaam.*"

They were Muslims, threatened for their religion, engaged in a suspect trade. He noticed a portable stove pushed into a corner, as if they had legitimate business too, vagabond tinkers mending village utensils on a charcoal stove. The bellows seemed to have been patented in St. Petersburg. He grinned and said slowly in Russian, "I am a friend. I am looking for someone."

That brought a stunned silence; the dirt-grained, hardened faces reflected their disbelief.

"Mustapha says you are American?" This new man, Abdul, also spoke a kind of dog-Russian, just enough to understand.

"Correct." Mustapha brought out his passport, and the billfold. The old man started pushing him again from behind and Schiller pushed back. Words were exchanged with Abdul, whose soft, sly face had the same flattened nose and almond eyes. The two young men returned, crowding into the yurt, among the tin trunks and bedrolls that packed its sides. The two women sat in a corner, silent, medieval figures. A stench compounded of dirt and unwashed flesh permeated the dwelling, which was carpeted with well-worn rugs. The faces were lined up against him, shadowy in the half-light from the opening that served as both skylight and chimney.

Abdul inspected the passport. Only he and the thin-faced Mustapha seemed to have words of Russian. He made a sign: sit down.

They squatted cross-legged on the floor, the first small token of friendship.

Amerikantsky. Amerikantsky. The word rolled around between them: a visitor from outer space. But not quite. Mustapha drew a line across his throat.

"Sarak . . . Baharak . . . Mulk Ali," he said.

Schiller understood that these were the places from which they had started, moving a thousand miles north as the high passes cleared in summer, crossing the unmanned frontiers, carrying contraband. They still thought he must be police, part of intelligence. Some kind of agent. He shook his head.

Abdul clapped his hands and one of the women moved forward: the younger one, with gold in her ears and teeth, a doll wrapped up like a parcel. She brought a flat wheel of bread, and a mess of cold fondue in a metal bowl, a yogurt with small lumps of meat. Abdul broke bread and dipped a piece into the dish, offering it to the guest. Ed Schiller ate. It tasted of rancid fat but he was hungry. The woman shuffled away and said something to her mother crouching behind in the shadows. Suddenly Schiller realized that this was a single family, the father—the old man—Abdul, now titular head, the women (his mother and wife, or his two wives), the two young men his sons, Mustapha the thin man some other relative. A small dogged group who for some reason had pushed north and like him were on the run. Migrants, travellers, gypsies who crossed over the Pamirs, the Hindu Kush and the Sinkiang deserts, in and out of the heartlands of Russia and China. That could be his way back. Whatever their line of business it was not quite Secretary Gorbachev's, any more than he could explain about Jubal Martin and Claymore, Burrell and Sylvester, Nikky and Lila.

Each of them sat there wondering about the other's trade. He could not make them understand; lack of a common tongue was a closed door through which they shouted.

Shit, Schiller thought. To have come all this way only to be picked up by a band of Turkis evading the law themselves. Like Barsov he had tried to escape, to fall head first into a trap. The idea struck him as ludicrous and he smiled, wiping his greasy hands on his jacket. As if Abdul recognized their mutual frustration, he laughed shyly too, struggling to understand. It was Mustapha who spoke, sad-faced and gray.

"All strangers are spies." He looked across for support to the old man, who was fingering his great knife.

"No," Schiller said.

Abdul opened the passport, then pointed to the American crest. Trapped in a nomad tent, in the middle of nowhere, the reasons a long way behind him, Schiller struggled to explain. Explain in simple words what had driven him from

Barsov to Lila, from Moscow to an unknown village. Madeniyet.

Somebody lit an oil lamp, making the closed company more medieval than ever.

"Madeniyet?" Abdul scratched his head.

Schiller made signs with his hands, pointing, walking his fingers. "Eighty, eighty-five kilometers."

Abdul thought he was mad: hallucinatory, staring madness. You treated madmen as holy men, touched by the hand of God. It could only be holy madness that brought a man, an enemy of the state, this far against the tide, and delivered him sleeping by the bank of a river. This was the work of Allah. He stepped into the light and examined Schiller closely, watching his eyes, his mouth, the sweat on his brow. Schiller smiled sweetly. Abdul's hands closed in greeting and he bowed to the floor.

"Welcome," he said.

The women moved forward, lighting the open fire in the middle of the yurt with sticks and dried dung, crouching, blowing until smoke curled through the central chimney. He watched as pots were suspended and a meat stew prepared, while the men smoked and drank, sat and stared, saying little, passing round a small hookah and drinking a fiery vodka from unlabelled bottles. Everyone's head was swelling. Dark ghosts in the tent, they crouched round the central warmth as night came on, and thought him mad.

The stew was warming and strong, and carried away the drink. The young men went outside, on business of their own, leaving Schiller and Abdul, the old man and Mustapha. He tried to ask if they would help, but their ignorance was a wall he could not break. Only Abdul's eyes, surveying him like a ghost, conveyed a message of hope, an enigmatic semi-worship.

Abdul poured him more vodka and offered a fresh bottle from a store in one of the metal trunks around the walls. The fire burned brighter and hotter and the old man's spittle ran in a silver rivulet down his cheek as he expectorated into the flames.

Abdul was gesturing at Schiller, returning the passport and billfold.

"You are God's fool."

At Schiller's back his shadow rose over the yurt. Was that what he had become, a fool, a madman?

He preferred not to think of it, in case Abdul was right. Anyone who roamed across Siberia to see a woman who was someone else's wife must be in that category.

The older woman, her face scraped as an etching, began to croon softly, her fingers wrapped round beads. The younger one sat wide-eyed with an unblinking stare.

"Tomorrow," Schiller said, "I go." He swayed as he said it.

"Tomorrow we shall all be gone," he thought he heard Abdul say, but he could not be sure. How quickly could they pack up and move, and where would they go? Southwards apparently, through the salt deserts of Kazakhstan, to Tashkent and the passes and wherever was home, carrying the drug-run money that was a better option than scraping a living on the mountains where they would leave their bones.

As the fire flickered, his mind went back to the farmhouse on White Ridge, as cut off as this place in winter by the snow storms from Canada. Schiller remembered his mother, dying there when he was Charlie's age. In later years he had been back only once, to find it abandoned, its fly-screens banging in the wind. Ed had escaped when he could, still looking for something.

Abdul tucked his feet under him, obdurate, crafty and private, and grinned indulgently, as more fire-water went down. "We shall be friends. Brothers."

"You bet. Tomorrow, I go."

Abdul put an arm on his thigh.

"Nowhere."

A sense of hopelessness took hold of Schiller, as the flames in the tent and the firewater in his head battered his senses. To come so far and gain so little. No: he had to succeed, otherwise his personal life was one long disaster, shifting from woman to woman, Nikky to Lila, losing them each in turn. Oh Christ, Nikky, whom he never quite forgot, threatening to fly to Moscow because of Charlie. As if she really cared. Abdul passed him more drink, a new bottle, lip to lip, and he drank to obliterate the past.

New wood smoked in the hearth; Schiller's head began to nod, Abdul's face swayed in the shadows, and Mustapha murmured beside them, sucking the hookah pipe. The women had erected straw screens behind the fire, the two young men had drunk themselves comatose, wrapped under heavy quilts. Abdul seemed to lurch forward and sideways across Schiller's lap. The fire burnt down to a dull red glow and the thin man spat in the ashes, where the saliva sizzled. Schiller now had his watch: it was only eleven-thirty but the world was dying around him, and he had miles to go.

He moved Abdul's head and set it on the floor beside him. Abdul flickered his eyes, but they were half-closed. From the other side of the circle came the low moans of the old man, dreaming his dreams. Schiller staggered to his feet, pulling himself upright, until his head hit the roof. The inside of the tent was full of the smell of bodies.

"Aya—allah—aya," the old man sang.

Schiller motioned to Mustapha that he wanted to urinate and tottered unsteadily towards the double hangings that covered the entrance. Slipping out through the door flap he found himself in a blackness, with a chill breeze sniffing the trees. A few stars, hard as diamonds, were pricked out in the dark and somewhere on his left came the rubbing of tethered horses. If there were horses, pack-animals, there would be transport for him, a way out.

He paused at the side of the yurt. The old man's low murmurings were audible inside, but no one moved. The others had drunk themselves into the night's oblivion, but Schiller was determined to run. The sharp air cleared his head, as he clawed towards the noises from the hobbled horses. It seemed a long way in the blackness, moving slowly. He could smell them before he saw them, hidden somewhere in the trees, beyond the clearing.

As he picked his way across the broken ground, one of the horses neighed, giving him a direction. He could see them now, two of them and a mule, beginning to be frightened, shifting their weigh and quivering. He felt for the tether of the nearest animal.

Then a flash of light behind him, and a great pressure somewhere on his back and neck, and the ground coming up to receive him.

17

Jubal Martin sat with Taylor Sheen in the office in the Commercial Section back in Moscow and tried to be friendly. His big hands were rubbing together, fist in open palm. Uncertainty showed in his face. He wondered why she had come.

"Mrs. Schiller, if we could help you we would." He cast his eyes behind her to the print of Grant meeting Lee at the Appomattox Courthouse.

"You know where he is," she asserted, sitting tensely in the chair, a smart woman in her thirties with blonde hair and glasses. The clear blue frames seemed to magnify her eyes. Sexy eyes, Martin thought, mentally undressing her, but there was something vulnerable in spite of the gray business costume, that made him feel protective.

As usual Taylor Sheen jumped in, doing his best to take over. He rested an arm extravagantly over the back of his head, smiled and sleeked back his hair.

"Nicola . . . No sweat. Ed's OK."

She hesitated and smiled, surprisingly sensitive. "If you say so. But he wasn't in Berlin; and now he's not here. We came to Europe to see him: the boy's his boy."

"Sure. Sure. He didn't stay long in Berlin."

"He told me he might be there for a while."

"Well, you know what it is. A change of plan."

She was quite petite, Sheen thought, no more than five-six, tight little figure, nice legs.

"So he came back here, right? Moscow."

"Right."

"I came on here to see him because Charlie wants his father."

Martin tried to defuse her. "I guess we can't take responsibility for personal matters like that, not if they don't concern Uncle Sam. I'm very sorry."

She leaned forward. "Listen. Ed and I made mistakes in the past, and a big one in splitting up. But I still love him, and Charlie needs him. For God's sake, tell me where he is."

"Mrs. Schiller," Martin explained, "I haven't seen Ed since he got back from Berlin." He was breathing heavily. "He kind of went to ground after a spot of trouble there. Some guy who tried to come over. We checked out his place on Kalinin, but he ain't home. His cleaning woman says he's disappeared."

"Tell me straight," she pleaded. "Ed was my husband: he still has shares in the boy. Now you say he's gone. He knew I was coming, and he would have stayed to see me. Something's gone wrong, hasn't it?" Her face was desperate.

Sheen gave his B-movie smile.

"I wouldn't say that. He just had to go east someplace."

"Where?" He saw her lip tremble, and reckoned she was close to despair. "And why?"

"Well . . ." he looked at Martin, who wiped his brow with a handkerchief and nodded slowly, ". . . the Ministry of the Interior cleared Ed to fly to Novosibirsk."

"Novo-what?" Where in God's name is that?"

"Siberia," Sheen said slowly.

"Jesus Christ." The news seemed to stun her. Then she added, "Charlie. Charlie's outside." They had kept the kid out of the way while they talked to her: if they stopped talking they could hear him in the next room chattering with Darleen Simpson who was showing him the photocopier. Charlie sounded wound-up.

Jubal Martin felt very old as he heaved himself round the table and put a hand on her shoulder. He could feel the collar-bone under it.

"Look honey. You shouldn't have come here. It's no place for a vacation. No place for a boy like Charlie."

"Charlie wants to see his father," she choked.

For once Sheen was embarrassed and looked at his shoes, leaving it all to Jubal, who went on.

"I don't know how to put this, Mrs. Schiller, but I guess Ed wasn't waiting."

She buried her head in her hands to hide the tears. He could feel her body trembling, trying not to admit that what had kept her going was a forlorn hope. They had both been locked into careers, journalism and television, that gave too little time for each other, and too much scope for Carlo. She had learned the hard way, too late to retrieve the marriage, but living with Ed's son she still wanted to try.

"He's got a job," Martin said weakly. "Deadlines. Copy. Maybe it was just an assignment . . ."

She was crying uncontrollably, and he was awkward in his sympathy. You forgot what love was like. Sheen made an effort, holding out a handkerchief.

"Here . . . don't take it so bad. It happens to the best of us."

Nicola clenched her fists in the effort of self-control. "How long has he been gone?"

"Ed checked out a week ago, with a visa. The Ministry of the Interior told us. Took them a while to find out. We don't normally have U.S. citizens on the loose in the middle of Siberia. Keep having calls from Sly Sylvester back in Washington." He shrugged. "But there it is, honey, he's gone."

In a strangled voice she asked, "Did he ever talk . . . about me?"

"A little," Martin said awkwardly. "He told us about the divorce . . . Maybe he didn't know that you were still serious."

"He knew. I wrote and I telephoned."

Martin said, "I sympathize."

"Why? Why run away from me?" she asked blindly.

"I guess he had to follow a story . . ."

She shook her head. "That's not like Ed, not when he knew I was coming."

Martin said, "How about coffee? Real coffee?"

She did not seem to notice him and pulled herself together. They could all hear Charlie now, agitating outside. "I guess I'd better leave you."

Gently, Martin advised, "Don't build too much on Ed..."

She dried her eyes and gave the handkerchief back to Sheen, who said, "Can I see you to the hotel?"

"No. No. I'll be OK."

"I could get the Embassy to give you something," Martin suggested.

"I'll be OK."

Glancing at the older man's face, she feared it was the end of the road.

They heard her calling outside, "Come on, Charlie. We're going home."

And Charlie's appeal. "Mum, I want to see Dad first. I got to see Dad."

When she had gone Sheen said, "Christ."

Martin thought for a bit. "I feel sorry for both of 'em, Ed and her."

"Ed found her a handful. Caught her in bed with some Italian bastard."

Martin crossed to the window, looked down to the court-yard. Moscow stared back at him. He watched a truck unload laundry; was chewed up by the small boy, Ed's son Charlie, in sneakers and T-shirt, clinging to his mother's hand outside.

"You realize Ed's on the run?"

Taylor Sheen nodded his glossy head. "That guy will end up being shot by the KGB."

Martin opened a cupboard and found a bottle of Jack Daniel's. "We got ice. You want some?"

"I could use it."

Martin organized the glasses. "That little kid was all wound up," he said. "I know."

"What the hell is Schiller up to?" Sheen mused.

"Barsov is somewhere out there too."

Their information wasn't that certain.

"You can't disappear like that in the Soviet Union."

"That's what they thought too."

Taylor Sheen nibbled peanuts. "Why don't you ask the police to pick him up?"

Martin's bloodshot eyes were troubled.

"You know what you're saying?" This was the same lunatic that had offered the gun to Schiller.

"Sure. Go over and talk to them. They're human," Sheen said soberly. "They don't want a nut-case on the hoof." He came and stood next to Martin, looking out of the window. "If we don't tell 'em first, the KGB will pull him in and squeeze his balls. That don't look too good, if he tells 'em our line on Barsov."

Martin was undecided. He didn't like smartasses. Now he had a chance to score one.

"They might learn that you were pushing to plant Barsov's murder on them."

Sheen laughed. "That too, Jubal," he said.

Viktor Suvorov was not altogether surprised when they came to see him at Moscow Central Police Headquarters on the following day. He sat at his ornate desk and looked pleased with himself. The Americans coming cap-in-hand, both old Martin, whom he despised, and one of the young bloods to whom it would be useful to watch. Suvorov made sure beforehand, as soon as he knew what they wanted, that he had the documentation from the Directorate of Special Passes. With the folder in front of him he felt primed.

The Americans were shown up and came in looking well-groomed, smelling of after-shave, sanitized. Suvorov waved them to chairs and ordered glasses of tea. He looked at them glumly over the top of his glasses. A well-preserved, thickset man with hair like an old brush, deteriorating on top, he waited for them to speak.

Jubal Martin took some time coming to the point, after pleasantries about the weather, Moscow trains, Georgian wine, and Suvorov noticed that the young man was restless. You could say uneasy. He let them go on so long and then called the meeting to order.

"Well. What do you want?" he said gruffly, as if they were under suspicion.

Jubal Martin sweated: he didn't like enlisting the police

and his voice deepened, the Southern drawl more pronounced. "I'll put my cards on the table." He swallowed. "One of our U.S. newsmen—I assure you he's nothing more—one of our guys has gone missing. We think he may have gone looking for Alexei Barsov."

Suvorov pushed up his glasses, consulted the file, taking his time.

"Edwin Schiller. On the Moscow bureau of your Washington paper?"

"Yes." Martin nodded.

"Why do you tell me?"

"Because—"

"Because we don't want you to think we wound him up," Sheen interjected.

"Interesting." Suvorov tapped his pen on the file. The carriage clock behind him chimed the quarter hour.

"He's not one of ours," Martin said flatly, "any more than that kidnap business in Berlin. We think he's gone off his head. His ex-wife is here in Moscow, trying for a reconciliation, dragging their kid around with her."

Suvorov made disapproving noises in his throat. "I'm afraid the matrimonial problems of your fellow citizens are not our concern," he said primly, sipping his tea. "How do we know that this is not a cover story?"

"Cover story? What do you mean?" Martin asked.

"He asked for a visa for Novosibirsk and Akademgorodok," Suvorov announced, consulting his notes. "Sensitive places. He flew to Novosibirsk on the 15th and apparently was given a lift to Akademgorodok. Once he was there he gave false information and disappeared. Now you come here to tell me he's not one of your men. It doesn't sound entirely likely," Suvorov announced, folding his fingers together over the file.

"We want him back," Sheen said. "He's not fit to be loose. He's out of his mind about this Barsov guy after what happened in Berlin."

Suvorov allowed his face to express a pained surprise.

"What happened in Berlin?"

Martin hesitated before speaking. "You should know that Ed Schiller had some crazy personal idea about helping

Barsov and his family to . . . er . . . leave. Personal, you understand. He may be sweet on the wife. Your guys fucked that one up, and now he feels . . . guilty. Bad vibes about it. So he wants to see Barsov.''

"You mean that is why he has gone to Akademgorodok, to try and interview Alexei Sergevich Barsov? Comrade Barsov is a sick man. He is in hospital.''

"We're aware of that,'' Martin muttered. "Just don't want any harm to come to anyone. Through misunderstandings.''

"I do not follow you.''

"That's OK,'' Sheen said. "We just wanted to register we'd like you to find him . . . Schiller. And bring him back. So he can see Mrs. Schiller and his boy. Family ties, blood thicker than water, right?'' He smiled like an open piano. "He don't work for us. No way. But equally we don't want to cause trouble.''

There was a pause.

"More tea?'' Suvorov asked.

"No, thank you. We got to be going.''

Suvorov rose, and held out his hand. "I appreciate what you have said. I assure you if he is still at large we will uncover him.'' He smiled thoughtfully, showing his silver fillings. "It is not so easy to run away in Siberia . . .''

"Quite,'' Martin said. "We would reciprocate your help.''

"Of course. Of course. Do not worry. You say he has gone to find Barsov. In that case it should not be difficult for us to locate him.''

"Before there's any trouble . . .''

"Before there's any trouble, I agree.''

Martin would have loved to ask Suvorov's version of what had happened in Berlin, but he knew the request would be met with that same wall of indifference.

Suvorov came to the door, making sure the secretary would escort them from the building. His thickset figure exuded confidence: he knew that the KGB wouldn't let a loner slip past them. When they had gone he gave orders.

"I want all crime reports, sightings, registration queries, Novosibirsk area, over the last week.''

It took some days for the information to come in, includ-

ing the report by a geneticist called Fedor Korochkin, and
the account of a pig-man who woke up with a lump on his
head on the road outside Akademgorodok. The truck had
been abandoned some way south. Suvorov began to wonder.

Schiller pushed his thumbs into Abdul's throat.

He had come round in the forest consumed by thirst and
an icy fury, to find that they had left him nothing. The
Turkomans had robbed him and left him half-naked without
water or money or food, after he went to the horses. His
possessions gone and the campsite cleared as if it had never
existed. Only the smoldering embers and the fresh dung of
the horses marked their passage: warm enough to show they
couldn't be far ahead.

Schiller had wasted no time. He cleared his head in a
stream then followed a track through the trees where the
animals had broken the ground, and found them moving
slowly through a defile, climbing to a fresh path. They were
not attempting concealment, one man against seven. The
bastards had misjudged him. A little group of seven, with
two horses and three pack-mules. He picked up the signs
then heard the jingle of harness and worked his way round
the caravan so that he could intercept it.

The two sons had come through first leading two of the
mules, next the old woman riding, with the old man by the
third mule, looking even more villainous with another
night's smoking. Schiller waited until they had passed, then
he jumped on Abdul, Abdul in front of the big horse and
talking to Mustapha, the three of them knocked to the
ground by the weight of Schiller's attack. He burst out of
the trees and pulled back Abdul's head, clawing Abdul's
knife from his belt and holding it at his throat. For a
moment Abdul lay stunned, looking at this apparition in a
ripped shirt and trousers. Someone who should have run.

"You dog-shits," Schiller roared. Abdul's eyes rolled in
agony, as he flailed with his hands. The young woman
leading the second horse, which was loaded with boxes and
bedrolls, looked on impassively.

Abdul was screeching, as far as his windpipe would let
him. Mustapha, winded, squatted on his haunches, aware of

the knife hovering by Abdul's throat. The others had formed
a ring.

"Tell him I want my money back. And my coat,"
Schiller screamed. The words echoed down the glade,
startling wood-pigeons.

The thin man spoke rapidly as Schiller relaxed his grip.
The old man and the two boys circling Schiller did nothing.

Abdul nodded, straining to breathe. Just to make sure,
Schiller kicked him in the ribs until he howled in pain.
Abdul gasped, "You are truly mad."

Then Schiller knew he had won, and let him go.

Abdul collapsed. Mustapha threatened to move and Schiller waved the knife at him. Resistance had crumbled as
quickly as it began. The women rallied round Abdul,
producing a bottle of firewater which Schiller drank too.

Suddenly the old man laughed, a thin, cawing laugh like
a nesting rook which the two youths took up. Next moment
they were all laughing, Schiller included, as Abdul recovered
himself and repeated the greeting he had given when they
first met.

"*As salaam*."

"*As salaam*," Schiller responded, and once again Abdul
folded his hands in greeting.

"Money back," Schiller said.

The young woman understood. She unlatched one of the
saddle-bags and brought out Schiller's possessions: the haversack, his coat, the passport, his wallet with the money
intact and his wristwatch.

Schiller retrieved them, then put the knife in the haversack just in case. As his anger cooled he turned to Mustapha,
whose Russian was better than Abdul's. "Right. Now. I
want your help."

It never occurred to him that they would deceive him
once the surprise was over. He had only to look at the
strangeness in Abdul's eyes, the awe with which they
received him. A holy madman. Only his attempt to flee had
broken that illusion, making him mortal again, and they had
pursued him for it, Mustapha and Abdul. Now that he had
reappeared, jumping out of the trees, he was a god once

more. The old man's laugh confirmed it. Abdul's astonished face and slanting eyes fawned upon him like a dog.

Schiller threw him a bone. He waved the wallet with its roubles intact. "You help me. I pay you."

Abdul said something that Schiller could not understand. Schiller smiled. Mustapha said in Russian, "He will not expect money. We will help."

Abdul clutched at Schiller's coat. All of them watched Schiller's eyes. Where the madman had come from, where he was going, were not important to them.

"What do you want us to do?" Abdul asked, and Mustapha slowly translated. The old man had sat down and begun more of his singing, a quiet, childish wail; the pack-mules shifted their feet, looking for grasses.

"Madeniyet. Take me there," Schiller said.

"Nothing there," Mustapha said. "No trade. No food. Bad place." He patted his stomach, under the ancient trousers. His pancake cap was shiny with grease.

"Take me there," Schiller blazed, as if he would shake Abdul to jelly.

Abdul understood. He rolled his eyes up and down.

"Yes," Mustapha said. "Yes. We will take you there. Long time, but we take you."

18

It took them two weeks, moving through the foothills and along the goat tracks of the Altay mountains. He found himself becoming confused about both time and place. Unable to go back, he knew he had to go on.

Somewhere behind him were the remnants of his past. Nicola in Moscow by now, if she came. And Charlie. He tried to cut them from his mind. Above all there was Lila, and his guilt about Barsov who had asked for his help.

Lila's eyes were full of sorrow, and he wanted to see her laugh again, and smile, and indicate that she understood.

Pacing beside the slow caravan he seemed a philosopher, as the nomads watched him brooding, thinking, wondering what he would be able to say to her. In this lonely world of the mountains he felt himself suspended between his past and his future, so much so that reminders were an intrusion.

Abdul was suddenly there by his shoulder one morning after they had struck camp and resumed the trail.

"You got job?" he asked, patting the mule.

"Probably not any more." Sly wouldn't wait for ever.

Abdul grinned lecherously. "Wife? Jig-jig?" The younger woman giggled. "Sons?"

Schiller shook his head. If she had arrived in Russia, Nikky would be agitating. He hoped that she wouldn't bring Charlie after all.

"One day they catch you," Abdul said cheerfully, and drew a finger across his throat.

From a crest in the hills they saw the road snaking south to Biysk and the high passes of Mongolia. Schiller traced it on his tattered map. There was a highway all right, and a railway; once he saw a thirty-five box-car train. But there was little else, just land, and the empty rivers reminding him again of Canada. Choppers came over in pairs, skimming the trees in a hopeless patrol, big aircraft headed east with vapor trails. They moved slowly south, a few miles a day, making up camp and striking it, feeding and watering the animals, eating a diet of fondue boiled from dried yogurt and scraps of meat.

He learned that the nomads were Kirghiz, not Turkoman. Mustapha's thin face twisted in pain as he explained. They had lived far to the south-west in the Wakhan valley in the north-eastern tip of Afghanistan. Mustapha pointed it out on Schiller's map, showing that he could read: a thin sliver of land between the Soviet Union and Pakistan.

Mustapha spat in disgust, looking across at Abdul and the old man one night in the yurt. They had helped the Mujahedin. He waved his hands above his head: a gunship. They had fled across the border with saddle-bags full of hash, thinking it safer in Russia, moving back to old pastures, bartering drugs for food. Abdul made signs to show the work they had done: picking cotton, planting sunflower strips along the wheatfields, forced to move on for fear of being rounded up.

Now they had had enough. "Finish," Abdul declared. "Afghanistan peace." So someone had said. He switched on the transistor radio and held it close to his ear.

"We go home now."

It was Mustapha who emerged as the strong one. He showed Schiller the pictures of his family, dog-eared black and white snapshots of two boys and a girl. The war planes had swept up the valley in a frenzy of killing, scatter-bombing the farms. Everything he cared for had gone: his parents, his wife, his children, the homestead, the barns and the cattle. Only Mustapha survived, working alone in the fields, machine-gunned and left with a bullet in his lung. He showed Schiller the scar.

"I hate Russians," he said. "If you Russian, I kill you."

Having a U.S. passport, he implied, allowed them to spare his life.

Abdul listened with his head cocked on one side.

"Anyway. You are mad."

Schiller agreed. It would have been far simpler to walk down to the road and give himself up. Maybe they were still looking. But Moscow was now in the past, along with Nikky and his other life. Madeniyet was an end in itself. He watched Abdul's black eyes, closed in the heat, and wondered what he really thought, whether he had any conception of worlds outside his own.

Abdul roused and scratched himself. "Madeniyet. Jig-jig," he said.

On the fourteenth day, in the afternoon, Abdul followed a path high on the mountains. The sun was hidden in cloud and mist clung to the slopes. The air was thin and cold and only the steady jangling of the loaded animals gave any sense of comfort.

Abdul came back along the line. He pointed to a pile of stones marking another track which spiralled downwards, and the American knew that they had arrived.

Abdul nodded and laughed. "Down there."

Madeniyet. Schiller had finished one part of a journey. Madeniyet. The caravan was far above, and moving on. They would continue southwards, hugging the mountains, and now that the parting had come Abdul's eyes flooded with tears. The women cried and the old man broke into his dirge.

Schiller found himself wondering at his own hopes.

Abdul was pointing to where the path plunged through the mist, but they could see nothing. Schiller gave them back the horse blanket, which had protected him from the night cold. They would not accept money.

"You go now," Abdul said.

Schiller embraced, each one in turn, the old man smelling of unwashed linen, the two weeping women, Abdul and Abdul's two sons, Mustapha, the lonely one with whom a bond had been forged. He patted the horses and picked up his haversack, into which they had packed a hard-tack of bread and biscuits and some parting sweetmeats. A gift for the journey, the women explained.

"Allah be with you," Abdul said, as if he made similar partings every day. He pointed on Schiller's map at the passes for which they were heading, offering to take him with them if he wanted to follow. "Long time. Very slow."

"You bet," Schiller said.

Then the mist swallowed them and they were gone.

Schiller wasn't sure about Allah as he began the descent, sliding down the goat-track towards the settlement. Below him might be the answers to Berlin, he persuaded himself. Perhaps Lila could explain what had happened to Alexei Sergevich, but the outcome he craved, he knew in his heart, was that she would explain herself.

Then there were footsteps behind him, only a few yards away, a figure out of the mist. He waited, and saw that it was Mustapha, sliding after him.

Mustapha's face told him nothing. With two weeks' growth on his chin and his caved-in mouth, still wearing the pancake cap and sheepskin jerkin that seemed his permanent clothing, he looked a scarecrow.

"I come down . . . with you."

Schiller shook his head. "You go back. My business. I shall be OK."

"I come with you," Mustapha said grimly.

Something about his eyes caused Schiller not to argue.

One behind the other they slithered down the goat-track, which soon followed a stream, pouring out of the rocks. It was precipitous going, but Mustapha picked his way with ease from outcrop to outcrop. As they came lower the cloud-cap broke, sending a shaft of light across the landscape.

Far down below them Schiller saw the settlement. A jumble of clapboard houses lined a single street, power and telegraph poles criss-crossing the roofs of thirty or forty buildings, all that there was of Madeniyet. Wooden fences leaned drunkenly. The broad road up the middle, unsurfaced and pot-holed, was a sea of dark mud. A bleak place, impoverished and so remote that it was hard to accept that Moscow remembered it. Schiller dropped down towards it but a cry from Mustapha stopped him.

Tiny figures were moving between the houses in the sunshine.

"Wait," Mustapha cautioned, pointing.

At the end of the road, where it turned off to the highway, an armored personnel carrier was parked. Three tiny figures in dark green uniforms were lounging beside it, probably smoking and talking. The tracks from its wheels led from one of the houses in the middle of the settlement, where, they could now make out, another soldier stood guard.

Mustapha caught Schiller's sleeve. "Police. Dangerous. Don't go."

"I must."

But Mustapha pulled him back. "Woman waits. You wait till dark."

Mustapha was cautious, a sense of self-preservation born out of experience. That was why he had come, Schiller realized. He offered help. They sat together in the shadow of the trees beside the tumbling stream. Mustapha rolled one of his *bidis* and Schiller accepted gratefully, his heart hammering. The urge to go tearing down, ignoring the militia, was suicidal.

"After dark," Mustapha said. "We go tonight." He grinned, his sallow face alive. "Now we eat."

They unpacked the haversack, ate the bread and biscuits. The mountain water was cold as ice. A thousand feet below them the village lay like a map. Schiller imagined it in winter, the mud turned into ice, a blanket of snow on the houses, the steam from their stove pipes hanging in the bitter air. Today it seemed strung together by its electricity cables. No sounds climbed up the hill, but they could identify people; tiny figures going to privies, collecting wood, two children running. It was an eerie place, an open prison. "I don't like it," Schiller said, half to himself. He wondered if one of the children was Lila's son.

Mustapha stretched out on his back and closed his eyes. "No problem." He smiled. "You sleep."

Too far away to be seen, Schiller watched the soldiers drive off in the a.p.c., lurching across the tracks. Madeniyet lay becalmed in the long wheatfields of the valley, a settlement surrounded by birch trees that had not changed in a century apart from the power lines. At the same time, an empty landscape, buildings abandoned with age, a dead place.

It was hard waiting, having come so close, but Mustapha was in no hurry. He scratched and smoked, then rolled over on his side and dozed, his chest rasping. Schiller watched the remaining militiaman, who patrolled the muddy road aimlessly, once or twice talking to women, black widows shaped like sacks.

"I wait. I sleep. I help," Mustapha said, grinning. "I find jig-jig girl."

"What about finding Abdul?"

"Abdul wait."

At nine o'clock they moved lower, waiting for the dusk, near enough to pick out faces, to separate old and young. They had noticed only two children and he wondered if there were others, maybe a school. Schiller could see nothing he liked. Madeniyet had gone to seed, the lots stood empty, bindweed and convolvulus grew across abandoned yards. Smoke rose from cooking fires and he counted the live chimneys: no more than twenty in all. A tiny dot on the map, a community lost to the world. If there were more children they must be bussed away: perhaps they were exiles too. Perhaps it was a place of exiles.

Lila was in one of those houses, not in the cramped apartment where they last met. A tractor returned from the fields, then a horse with a solid-tire trailer, driven by an old man. At the end nearest the highway, the opposite end to Schiller, an old woman grubbed for herbs. They were in earshot now, hearing the bells on the horse-collar, the sound of sawing wood. Nothing else.

At last Mustapha said, "OK. Go."

They kept to the edge of the little stream, through the wood, moving carefully down the path, and came out at a picket fence. It was now nearly dark and they were at the first of the houses, but Mustapha was taking no chances. He watched both sides of the settlement as the straggling street in front of them shut itself down for the night. Somewhere a dog was disturbed.

Mustapha leaned against the paling and felt for loose boards. The militiaman was still around. "Soldier boy somewhere," he whispered.

Schiller said, "You leave it to me now."

"Not yet."

Mustapha pushed Schiller against the fence in the darkness.

"I find militiaman first. Then your girl."

And he was gone.

There was nothing that Schiller could do. Mustapha had pre-empted him. The nomad had made up his mind: he was to be a friend, and friends were sworn to each other. Neutralizing the policeman was to be Mustapha's work, then he would disappear as suddenly as he had come in time to pick up Abdul's caravan.

"You bastard, Mustapha," the American muttered. As he crouched there, every noise was a nightmare, and he knew that there was no escape.

No escape from Nikky, who would be pursuing him somewhere. No escape from Sylvester, who would want his pound of flesh. Above all, no escape from the trap that Barsov had set him that day by the playground in Moscow where he had been given an offer: if anything goes wrong, take Lila.

"Coo . . . coo . . . ree," a night creature, an owl or night-jar, brought him to his senses. Mustapha was a long time gone, but if he began to move now they would miss each other. There was a sound of a door, and someone shouting far away up the street. A zinging in the telephone wires, the damned dog barking again.

Where had Mustapha gone? Had he got the right house? Waiting. Eleven o'clock.

Blue-black night. Not a sound or a light. The militia boy must be indoors somewhere; perhaps at Lila's. Why didn't Mustapha come back? Mustapha, the go-between, the wounded man.

Schiller picked up his sounds along the ground long before he could see him. He shifted his feet, ready.

Then Mustapha was there beside him, breathing heavily: Schiller could see the outline of his head.

"Well?"

"Amerikantsky?"

"Damn you, where've you been?" Schiller whispered. "What kept you so long?"

"A little business."

"What about the militiaman?"

He could sense Mustapha smiling. "It is all right. I talked to him. He is no problem."

"Where is he?"

"Soldier boy sleeps by the house. So as to cover the place . . ."

"Did you see her?"

"I saw the soldier boy. He came to the door. I asked him outside. I said I wanted him to meet a friend." He paused. "An American." He laughed. "Of course he did not believe me."

Schiller's blood ran cold. "You told him I was here?"

"Of course."

"And he came out?"

"Yes. He came outside, and I killed him."

"Killed?" Schiller croaked.

He was sure Mustapha was grinning; he knew now why

the Kirghiz had come. The knife that Mustapha might have driven into Schiller's back had eliminated some young conscript, a simple act of revenge.

Schiller felt sick. Betrayed. He flew at Mustapha's throat. "You stupid bloody bastard. Why? Why?" There was nobody to help him now. He had failed Alexei Sergevich, and now Lila. Lila loving, Lila trapped and now condemned.

Mustapha, who stank of tobacco and sweat, chuckled and pushed him away. "Russki not helpful."

"Bastard. Jackass. What happened?"

"OK. OK. I tell you, Amerikantsky brother." Mustapha sniffed, and wiped his hands on the grass. Schiller saw the dull green of the knife blade.

"I go down street . . . so. I find the jig-jig house, so. Ten houses down. "OK?"

"Go on."

"I go across the yard. All quiet, like a ghost. I creep up to the door. I listen, no lights, no noise. As black as hell. So I knock on the door . . . and . . . I hear shouting, then nothing."

"What do you mean, shouting?"

"I wait. I knock again. Then . . ." Mustapha caught his breath. "The door opens, and I see this soldier boy. Buttoning up his trousers . . ."

Schiller's arms tightened around the other man's neck, as if nothing would stop him. "What did you see?"

"I tell you. I tell you. There is the soldier boy, in his shirt and trousers, and the woman . . . let me finish."

Shuddering, Schiller released his grip. "Tell me the truth or I'll break you in two."

"I see her in the room behind, with her hair all down and dress ripped open . . ."

"Impossible . . ."

"No. I swear. He had been attacking her, the soldier boy. He was inside, on his own, and when he came to the door he was having to do up his pants."

"Go on." Schiller, dry-mouthed. He could feel Mustapha beginning to wiggle, as if he would slip away into the night. "Go on."

"OK. I'm telling you. This soldier boy all damp and limp, he came to the door. No gun, just puzzled. And the woman half-dressed. I could see her on the bed behind him."

"Lila . . ." who was to have imposed her gentleness on Schiller's troubled mind. Savagely, he pushed Mustapha to the ground, locking his arms, in case of the knife.

"You let me go now. You promised."

"I promised nothing, you turd. Tell me what happened."

"OK. OK. Well, when he opens the door I stand there, looking. And he is red as a turkey, pushing his cock in his pants. He give big laugh. 'Well?' he says. 'I'm told this is where the widow is,' I say. 'What widow?' 'The Amerikantsky's widow, of course.' He stops and rolls his head. He is dim country boy, after fuck. 'What do you want?' he says. 'I have Amerikantsky outside.' He had pale eyes like a pig, a fat porker, and he doesn't think so good, being disturbed on the job."

Schiller forced himself to wait, numbed by a sense of foreboding, a sickening, impotent fury.

"Did she hear you?"

"She was buttoning her dress. On the bed." Mustapha's hot breath was on Schiller's face, spraying him with flecks of spittle. "Of course she heard me. She cries out. She sobs."

"Listen," Schiller whispered, his hands pressing Mustapha's windpipe. "If you play me false I'll twist your skull from your neck . . . like a chicken."

"No, Amerikantsky," Mustapha gasped. "I tell you what I said. No more, no less. And this soldier boy, he is very stupid. He stands there in his shirt and trousers and bare feet. Your militia boy, on duty, on guard. All he wants is to fuck the woman, and she is terrified. So I explain to him, he must meet my Amerikantsky. And the woman rushed to me. 'What has happened?' She cries. 'Where is Alexei Sergevich? What has happened?' 'I don't know,' I say. 'My friend is waiting at the end of the street.' 'I don't believe you,' she cries. But the soldier boy pushes her back and grabs his boots and his rifle. 'Stay there,' he says. 'I go.' The fool thinks there is some Kamaz truck which cannot come up the street because of the mud. Or maybe I am senior KGB man. How do you like that, eh?"

Schiller hit him. Slowly and deliberately, knocking
Mustapha's jaw from side to side until he yelped, blood
running from his lip. Schiller saw the future crumble, his
and Lila's, if there was a murdered policeman.

"What happened, shit-bag?"

"Stop. Stop. I tell you. Please, Amerikantsky. Don't kill
me," He shook his head free, springy as a jack-in-the-box.
"I'm telling you. This soldier boy he puts on his boots and
picks up a big army torch, and I say, 'Follow me.'"

"Lila . . . ?"

"She is on the bed, crying. I told you. She comforts the
little boy." Schiller could feel the other man's face, pleading, bloody, pushed back on the ground, head resting
against the fence where they had grappled. "Soldier boy
mutters 'OK' and comes with me, big, bold militiaman."

"You bastard."

"So, we shut the door and I say my friend is real
Amerikantsky, and I knock the torch from his hand and he
stands there in the yard like a bull in the slaughterhouse. So
slow he does not understand. Then I get this knife . . ."
Mustapha wrestled his right hand free and Schiller could
feel it moving inside his coat, searching for the thing. "I get
the big knife and . . . slip, slip . . . it is so easy with the thin
blade, under the ribs, right through. He doesn't even shout,
just a little sigh, like a butchered calf, you have heard it,
eh?"

Schiller let go his grip. Mustapha sat upright, his breath
rattling.

"The knife went in and soldier boy rolls forward . . . and
very soon he is still. He just rolls over and dies in the
yard."

"Oh, Jesus Christ."

"So. I check him over, but he bleeds a lot and is soon
dead. Still. No noises. Nothing. And I come back here."

"What about the house? The woman?"

"The *izba*? Ha. Nothing. She shuts the door on the
soldier boy. She does not open it." He cleared his throat and
spat into the night. "Why should she want him back to have
her again?"

Schiller rose unsteadily, grasping the rough palings of the fence. His body was trembling.

"What are you going to do?"

It was very simple now in Schiller's mind. Mustapha did not matter.

"See her."

Another whisper in the dark. "And me?" It was almost as if he feared being left, like a dog tied to a post. "Shall I come? Do you want me?"

"Go to hell," Schiller said. "Go to hell."

19

Somehow he found his way, groping, stumbling, down the sidewalk, over unidentified obstacles, planking, discarded oil drums, trying to count the houses. The power poles loomed up like sentries, the sloping roofs were hard black against the night. Nothing moved. He could hear the sound of his footsteps, and his own breath. Even the dogs had stopped.

Six. Seven. Eight. Nine. Ten. He had counted them slowly, carefully, because there must be no mistakes. Here was an open gate, and he felt his way cautiously forward, up the muddy path, lined by indeterminate bushes. Some where . . . somewhere in the blackness was the militiaman, if Mustapha told the truth. He found him almost at once, just as Mustapha had said, a bundle pitched on its face. As he blundered over it he put out a hand to steady himself, and it came away sticky. He could feel but not see the blood, warm and oozing. The thing had been a country youth on his conscription period. Schiller lugged it on to its back, could feel the outlines of the face, a bony forehead, deep-set eyes, open and staring, a thick nose, open mouth. Some mother's son. It was lying across the path at the foot of the

wooden steps to the front door; bigger, heavier than he
expected. Very human in death. He steadied himself, catching it by the boots, pulling it into the bushes at the side,
where it would be less obvious for four or five hours until
dawn broke. Hours were a long time, and the hairs on his
neck were wet with sweat. The house loomed blank in front
of him: he could just see the silhouette of its gable roof. A
square peasant's house with a central door and windows like
eyelids: two rooms at ground level with an outhouse beyond.
And the feeling running over his spine that Lila was inside,
waiting.

He began to walk cautiously the last few yards, not
knowing what to expect, fumbling his way up the four
rickety planks that constituted front steps. His heart was
thumping as he pressed against the door. What if there was
a second militiaman, now, inside?

It was a risk he accepted, his nerves frayed by waiting.
With his fist, Schiller knocked gently on the rough wood of
the door, half-planed planks, unpainted.

Nothing. Only the rustle of night noises out there behind
him, beyond the dead militiaman. Not even a light.

He knocked again.

A small moan, a muffled cry, he could not be sure,
somewhere inside. Someone moving at last, in that dark
place. Footsteps. The sound of a bolt being pulled, where
they had shut themselves in.

Then the door swung open a fraction, and he peered into
darkness, trying to make out shapes.

"Lila?"

If they opened the door, they were expecting a visitor.

He called into the deep recesses of the front room,
catching the smells of bedclothes, dirt and cooking, poverty.

"Lila . . ."

"Stay where you are!"

The light snapped on and he was dazzled. Confronting
him stood a small boy he hardly recognized, clad in a great
blue jersey, several sizes too big, his cropped head emerging
tortoise-like from the top. But the features, the clear blue
eyes were unmistakable; so was the AK47 assault rifle

pointing at his chest, gripped tight in the boy's hands, and
tucked underneath one arm.

"Yuri . . ."

Schiller was unrecognizable too in the child's eyes, with
his torn and bloodstained clothing, in which he had slept for
two weeks, unshaven, dog tired, his face alight with a
mission. Yuri's memory was short: Schiller was another
world.

"Yuri," he called again. "Where is she?"

The carbine came up with the safety catch off, the
militiaman's carbine that Mustapha had said the soldier boy
had taken outside with him. Yuri must have known what
happened, found the body and collected the gun.

Schiller said, "You know me, Yuri. Amerikantsky friend."

"Shut up," the boy said shrilly, "and keep your hands
up."

As Schiller's eyes adjusted, he measured the distance to
Yuri on the other side of the table. He thought better of it.
One slug from that automatic would tear through at twelve
feet like a circular saw. He raised his hands and tried again.

"Where is your mother . . . ?"

The room was a lived-in tip. An impression of debris,
packing cases and broken furniture. A single large room
with the table in the middle, behind which Yuri was standing, and a passage—no more—to the big bed in the corner
pushed against the great iron stove that in the winter would
warm the living-room and the kitchen beyond. The door to
the kitchen was shut. A rack of clothes hung from the
ceiling, drying; anonymous, much-patched clothes.

The boy's mouth opened as he half-recognized Schiller.
He backed away behind the table, the barrel of the gun
wavering. In the dim light of the naked bulb the room
looked like a stage set, cluttered and half abandoned, a
sloping room where none of the lines converged, floor and
ceiling uneven, the table itself crooked, rocking on a patched-
up leg.

The door to the rear room opened. There was Lila,
wild-eyed, in a peasant's black dress, bare-legged, her
coppery hair dishevelled. She came through the door like a
fury, snatching the automatic out of her son's arms.

She held the gun at him. It was then that she knew it was
Schiller, a ghost from the past, and shrieked. Her finger
seemed to tighten on the trigger.

"Don't . . ." Schiller said.

She was as white as flour, dark rings in the skin under her
red-rimmed eyes. She had been weeping.

After the shock of recognition, he was numb. His arms
came down and a wave of exhaustion ran through his body.
This was a different Lila; only the face was the same and
that face was tense with fear. He did not even know what he
wanted to say, and his voice was hoarse with effort.

"Alexei Sergevich . . ." he croaked. "I came to tell you
that I was not responsible—"

Lila put her hand on Yuri's shoulder as if she needed his
support. Her eyes swept furiously over this specter who had
returned to haunt her.

"Don't move," she shouted, swaying, the automatic rifle
levelled at Schiller's heart.

Words came slowly to him.

"Lila—"

"You bastard."

"Listen, for God's sake . . ."

"You bastard," she bawled. "Do you want to kill us
too?"

He stood there undecided, confused. This was the scene
played a hundred times in his mind, and it was wrong.
Seeing her so distraught was the end of a dream.

Lila was screaming at him, her face gaunt and ashen, her
hair wild on her shoulders, and in the plain black dress she
seemed already a widow. Her hands trembled as she pressed
the steel butt of the automatic against her body. The little
boy clutched her skirt. She was shuddering with fright.

"You . . . you . . . you Judas. What have you done to Alexei
Sergevich?"

"Lila. Lila. I came to ask you."

He stood rock-still in the doorway. Stretching across the
table, he might have been able to reach her. His eyes never
left her face, yet he was aware of the room, the loaf of black
bread on the table, the empty storage bins, the box-bed in

the corner against the unlit stove. A fearsome place, dirty and neglected, a human kennel. It stank.

"What do you want with me?" Her voice shook but she kept her hand on the trigger. She was at a frontier of pain and misery: he could not cross to touch her, the barrier was a gun.

"Want?" He leaned against the table wearily.

"Stay there. Put your hands up. Don't move." She seemed to remember the boy. "Yuri. Go to the shed, and find some rope."

"Lila . . . listen."

"Don't move. You started all this, and I can end it."

"Lila. I came because . . ." he hesitated.

"Why did you dare come here?"

Within himself, he wondered how well he knew.

"Because . . . because I saw Alexei betrayed in Berlin." Those were the simplest words. "He asked me to look after you . . . if anything went wrong."

She threw back her head and cried out. He saw the veins throb in her throat.

"Wrong! My God. You entered our lives. You gave Alexei away, you destroyed our happiness. Do you understand? What do you want to do now? Destroy me too: say that I killed the soldier boy? Is that it, now?"

She swayed, and he seemed to move.

"Oh no you don't. Keep your hands up, pig."

"I'm tired," he said.

"Tired? Tired? Don't you think I'm tired, don't you think Alexei Sergevich is tired?" She laughed hysterically, her hand still tucked behind the U-curve of the magazine clip.

"Lila. Please . . . Listen to me."

Yuri came running back with a coil of rope. She did not waver.

"Put it on the table, and leave us. Go to the kitchen, Yuri." The boy looked like a frightened rabbit.

"I want to explain."

"Why did you bother to come? Who brought you here?"

"Lila, put the gun down first. Then we can talk."

She shook her head. "And let you kill me too? Like the militia boy?"

"For Christ's sake, Lila. I didn't kill that guard."

"No. But your crazy friend did. Where is he now? Waiting to stab my back?"

Schiller's arms were lead weights. She called out behind her to the child waiting outside.

"Yuri."

The startled head reappeared. "Yes, Mama?"

"Yuri. You must help me. I am relying on you."

The boy nodded.

"Go out to where the soldier is. Do not be frightened, Yuri. Unbuckle his belt and bring it to me. He cannot hurt you now." And to Schiller, "Keep your hands up."

The boy shot outside, brushing past Schiller.

"Can we talk?"

"When Yuri is finished," she said.

"For God's sake listen, Lila. I didn't know what the Kirghiz would do. He told me . . . he told me that the militiaman was raping you. That he saw it."

"You lying, cheating, American bastard." She choked with anger, then began to calm down. "Do I look as if I've just been raped? That's one more of your foreign ideas, isn't it? Is that what you want, too?"

"No." Mustapha had lied to him, invented a reason for killing, revenge on the uniform.

"Stay where you are! Keep your hands up." A sharp silence between them.

"I came to help you."

She scoffed. "Like you helped Alexei Sergevich." Schiller stood by the table, Lila on the other side.

The door creaked open behind him and Yuri returned, wide-eyed with anxiety.

"I got it," he whispered.

"Good. Give it over to me." She waited while he pushed past the American, and left the belt at her side, a black leather belt with a revolver holster, pouches, a key-ring and handcuffs.

"Lila . . ." He tried again to break through.

"Shut up. Yuri, take out the pistol, put it here by my hand."

The boy did as he was told.

Still commanding Schiller with the automatic, she said, "Now you can put your hands down. On the table. Go on. One false move and I shoot. Yuri, hold the rifle."

Schiller did not argue. He pulled his hands down and watched Yuri handle the big gun that could punch a hole right through him.

"That's better," she said.

They stared at each other, made strangers by coming together.

"Can I sit down?"

She nodded vaguely.

"I came to help you," he said again, unclear about the end of the journey.

Lila's face was bone-white, the strength seemed to drain from her legs. He saw her pick up the pistol, flick back the safety catch. Schiller sat on a stool, hands on the stained oil-cloth. "I risked my life to get here."

"Go now, Yuri," she said. "Leave us alone." When the boy had disappeared behind her into the kitchen, she put the Kalashnikov within reach, and steadied the revolver; a shudder, as if she were cold in the thin black dress.

"You took Alexei Sergevich away."

"No. No. For God's sake believe me, Lila, I tried to help. Alexei Sergevich asked me to."

She shook her head. "He tried to cross over in Berlin. They told me you were involved. That he had confided in you. Now they have taken him." But her tone was softer. "How did you know where I was? How did you get a visa?"

The thought had been troubling Schiller too. The visit to Nevsky's friend in the Bureau of Special Passes had been too easy. Someone was setting him up; it could even be his own people.

"Give me a chance. I can explain."

"How do I know I can . . . trust you?"

"Why do you think I came two thousand miles?"

She ignored that. "Who killed the guard?"

Schiller shifted uncomfortably on the wooden seat. "The guy who picked me up when my truck broke down. An Afghan. A Kirghiz who lost his family in the invasion."

"The Soviet Union did not invade Afghanistan. We were invited."

"Oh, for Christ's sake, Lila. Come off it. I don't want to talk politics. Other things are more important."

"Why did you let him kill?"

"I didn't know. It was dark. He went into the village ahead of me to find the house. He lied to me that you were being raped. He wanted an excuse for killing."

She bowed her head, then put her finger back on the black pistol. "Killing is murder." But the tone of reproach was gentler. "Now I have a militia boy, dead, outside. He will be missed soon."

Schiller's throat was dry, his body ached. "Lila. Don't you understand why I've come?"

"No." A lonely, frightened woman. "Why have you?"

It could have come out then, the tangled wires of his past, short-circuiting, but, sitting there like a fool, he was unable to find the words. He was scarcely coherent.

"I wanted to see you. And to talk about Alexei Sergevich."

"You have been responsible for the death of a soldier. A country boy," she said.

"Don't you understand? I had to come."

"I cannot think. You confuse me."

Lila was shivering. It was cold in the night, but the big stove was not alight, and there seemed to be no other heating. They were both exhausted.

"I must get Yuri to sleep."

"You do that."

She seemed to remember. "Swear not to touch me?"

"Yes. Yes. Yes." Confused by fatigue, she might have been his mother—he was the son who could not help her, in the farmhouse at White Ridge.

She fiddled with the militiaman's belt and extracted keys and money from the pouches. Still holding the gun, she said, "Stand up. Turn around. Don't try to be clever."

He felt her hands touch him quickly, searching his arms and legs.

"I'm clean," he said.

Lila returned with the weapon to the opposite side of the table, and called to Yuri to climb into the bed by the stove.

She piled the blankets around him, while his eyes stared at Schiller.

"Mama . . ."

"Hush. I want to talk, and you must go to sleep. It will be all right."

It will be all right. Yuri gave a tired grin, and rubbed his eyes with dirty knuckles. He put his thumb in his mouth and disappeared beneath the bedclothes.

When the boy slept, they stared at each other, almost afraid to speak. He saw a little color begin to return to her face, as she calmed down, but also a recognition of the enormity of that death.

She went to the window and peered out between the shutters.

"Where is the body?"

"Out there, in the bushes."

"I don't understand. Why? Why?"

He said, "I didn't give away Alexei Sergevich."

"How can I believe you?"

"Have you got a drink? Some vodka?"

She cleared the rifle out of the way, stacked it on the wall beside her, still in reach, and found a bottle and two glasses. She pushed them across to him. He gulped the raw spirit down. It burned inside him, and he felt better.

"I want to explain . . ." he argued.

"You explain nothing. I hate you," she said quietly.

"Hate me?"

"Yes, damn you, hate you. Hate you for what you have done. For everything that has happened." Her bitterness and resentment cut into him. "You have brought nothing but trouble." She pointed a finger. "You betrayed us."

"No, Lila, no. I wanted to help you both." He found himself defending an impossible position, based on his own obsession.

"Why should I forgive you? In a few hours' time you will be under arrest."

"I want you to know—"

"Is there anything to know—except this hell-hole?"

"Yes, there is," he said angrily in return. "In God's

name why do you think I got involved? Because Alexei Sergevich asked me to help him. He asked me to get him out. To get you all out. Right?"

She put her head in her hands and he saw that she was crying, but he made no move. "We thought you were our friend," she whispered.

He poured himself more vodka. She had not touched her glass.

"For God's sake, Lila. What has happened between us?" It was as if they had become bewitched.

Her fine eyes stared at him.

"Alexei Sergevich wanted freedom. And he had enemies. You were a way out. And you destroyed us," she said.

"No."

"Yes. Yes. Yes."

The boy in the bed stirred. Instinctively they both waited until he slept again.

Schiller said, "He begged me to help."

"So you told your people. The CIA rats," she spat.

Schiller remembered Legros's carved totem of a face suddenly appearing that second day in Moscow. "I asked them to arrange things. First they said yes, then no. Something happened to make them change their tune. A new guy arrived with different ideas, and an official escape for Alexei Sergevich was no longer on."

"So you betrayed him?" Her voice was low, almost inaudible.

Schiller placed his hands on the table, shuffling between bottle and glass.

"I tried with a man called Heusermann, and someone gave us away. Your people grabbed him back. I did not arrange that: why should I?" he said bitterly.

"Why should I believe you?"

"Because I came here."

"But the Americans knew Alexei was coming out . . ."

"And the KGB knew when it would happen . . ."

"Are you suggesting . . ."

". . . that they planned it between them? Yes, I am."

She sprang to her feet, standing beside the butt of the assault rifle, stacked by the wall.

"We would not contaminate ourselves." A spark of the old fire.

"OK. You're wonderful people. Then why isn't Alexei here, after you got him back?"

Tears flooded her face. "He was ill."

"He wasn't when I last saw him in Berlin. He looked great. And you weren't in Siberia. We know about the Gulag places."

"It is not like that," she said, but he saw the uncertainty in her eyes.

"All right. So what do you propose to do about it?"

She drew herself upright, staring at him, round-eyed. "Have you arrested," she said, "for killing the guard."

Schiller looked at Lila, then at the rickety room under the single bulb. The table, the scraps of food, the wooden chair and the stools, the iron stove, the great box-bed where Yuri slept, the misery of it all. He sensed the despair in her voice, and longed to comfort her.

"While you wait here alone?"

She wavered, toying with a piece of stale bread, as if her mind was elsewhere. "He will be back soon, Alexei Sergevich."

"Some chance. Have you been allowed to see him?"

She hesitated. "Not yet." He seemed so confident that she wondered how much he knew about Alexei's imprisonment.

"Not yet?"

"It is not possible. I am in exile."

"For exile read shit-house," Schiller said.

"Exile is part of Russia. It is a purging."

"Let's go and see." The plan came into his mind fully formed. They would rescue Alexei Sergevich. If Schiller could vanish inside the U.S.S.R., the Barsovs could use the same route as the Kirghiz nomads.

"Go and see what?" Her hands went white at the knuckles.

"Alexei Sergevich, Lila. Let's go and find him."

Incredulous, she laughed at him. "You're mad."

"That's what they all tell me. It got me here."

"You? Go to visit Alexei? Without a visa? With a dead soldier in the yard? Before I hand you over?"

"Right. On the button," he said.

She stroked her hair. "You are really crazy."

"Only where you are concerned. How long have we got?"

"How long for what?"

"Before someone comes to find out about the militiaman?"

That brought her to her senses. "They will come back in three days, with the relief. But there will be people who notice before then, in the village. And they will see the body."

"Three days is a lifetime. We must get rid of the evidence before daybreak."

The thought seemed to stun her, but for the first time he saw a gleam of hope in Lila's eyes.

Time had already slipped by. "It will be light in a few hours," he said. "What can we do?"

"Bury him." This was the American she understood, but she seemed unable to move. A tremor ran through her, as she came to terms with what he was suggesting, and seemed to decide.

"All right. Let's get it over. Before Yuri wakes up."

She was compromising, and he saw the mixture of fear and despair in the shadows of her face.

In the corner, Yuri was snoring peacefully.

"I wanted to kill you," she whispered.

"Lila."

"Now you want me to find Alexei?"

"I want to find him with you," Schiller corrected. "After we bury the guard." He was determined, braced by his self-confidence, and she found herself following against her will.

"Listen," he told her. "After Berlin I went straight back to Moscow. I talked to Antoly Sherbitsky. You know him?"

She twisted in displeasure. "That peddler of other people's ideas. That liar."

"Well. He told me you were here. I have to thank him for that." Schiller grinned. "Not that he expected me to take it up."

"He hated Alexei Sergevich."

"Sure. Alexei had genius, and that's always hard to stomach. But Sherbitsky made me realize that some of the guys in the Writers' Union wouldn't exactly be sorry to see him put away. The State has sent him for treatment, not me."

Lila pulled herself together, catching her breath.

"Perhaps..." she said. "I don't know any more."

She might accept him now, believe his side of the truth. A huge sense of relief came into Schiller's mind. Bobbing on the sea behind him, somewhere far away, were the other players in his life, but this for him was the future.

"Wonderful. Marvelous. The first thing for us to do is to dispose of the body, before day breaks."

20

She lit a stub of candle in a lantern and prepared to lead him into the backyard, still carrying the pistol.

"There is no need for guns," he said.

She hesitated at the kitchen door. He could not discern her features in the outside dark. "I have your... word?"

"Oh Lila. Trust me."

"All right. But there must be no tricks."

She put the gun down carefully on the kitchen table. Beyond the door was a shed next to the earth closet. Lila held the lantern to show a collection of tools: primitive wooden rakes, two forks with broken prongs, a heavy spade. He picked out the best of the forks and the spade and they made their way round the side of the house. The moon was a faint crescent between the clouds, and wind rustled through the birch trees.

They found the militiaman where Schiller had dragged him into the brambles. Already as cold as meat, but not yet rigid. There was a lot of mess, as if he had bled for some time after Mustapha had knifed him.

Schiller pulled him on to his back and they stared for a moment at the blank young face.

"Would he have felt much pain?"

"I don't know," Schiller said.

She touched the body gently with her foot, as if to make sure it was real. There was sticky blood on the chest, as well as the back. Mustapha had knifed him from both sides, giving him no chance.

"Let's get on with it," Schiller said. "Bury him in the forest." He was suddenly unable to respond with any feeling of remorse, cold with fatigue. Lila took the tools from him as he picked up the man's legs and hauled him out from the bushes. They were joint conspirators now and she followed him as he dragged the body, feet first, across the ground.

Behind their picket fences the wooden houses on either side were black daubs in the night. Once there was a noise, a dog disturbed, that made them freeze. But no one came.

"They sleep like pigs round her," she said.

She directed him up a track towards the trees. The path was pot-holed and overgrown bushes tore at their clothing. The corpse was plastered with mud. He could see Lila shivering as a steady drizzle began to soak her thin dress.

"This is madness," she said.

"It's a way out," he replied.

This was the path that he and Mustapha had used, coming down from the hill. The houses were impossible shapes on either side of the road. The dog whined again, but no one stirred.

They reached the fence at the end of the street, the grounds of the empty building that blocked off the top of the settlement. Schiller and Mustapha had emerged there from the hills. It must once have been of some importance, commanding the road, the overseer's *izba*, but in the moonlight they could see it was abandoned, its woodwork plundered for fuel. Schiller half expected to find Mustapha still there, crouching and fingering his knife, but of course he had gone. Mustapha had made his contribution, he thought grimly.

He dragged the body through the rotting palings and hauled it up the path and round the side of the old house, into the trees. The thin birches closed together like giant match-sticks, with more dry sticks underfoot. They made a lot of noise.

"I can't go much further," she said, chilled and frightened.

"Not long now." They had reached a small clearing which would serve.

"I don't care. This can't help us."

"It gives us time," he said. "Hand me the tools."

Schiller began to dig, pulling the dead branches aside, forking the layer of bracken to get at the loamy soil. The lantern cast chiaroscuro shadows.

It was hard, heavy work, as he marked out a shallow pit. Lila made no attempt to assist, but stood holding the light, bedraggled in the rain.

The grave was not very deep, but it was all he could manage. He gave the militiaman one final heave and rolled him into the earth, then turned him over and brushed the mud away. The rain had washed the blood from the boy's face and his open eyes reproved them mercilessly.

Lila started to vomit, but pushed him away when he tried to comfort her.

"I'm all right. Don't touch me. Just hurry," she said.

He closed the boy's eyes before shovelling the earth on top and stamping it down, replacing the fronds of bracken as best he could. It would be hard to tell the soil had been disturbed.

He rested, panting, on the spade. "It's done. Let's go."

She held the lantern closer, as if inspecting him for the first time: the open face she had known in Moscow was thinner and darker, with a two-week beard and cavernous eyes. He was haunted, a spirit come to plague her, and this, the earth they were standing on, was a Russian boy's grave.

"In three days," he said, "we can be far away."

He could not see her eyes behind the light.

"What do you mean?"

"I mean before the relief comes, I shall have taken you to find Alexei."

She laughed uneasily. He was insane. Did he really think, she wondered, that he was rescuing her?

"Don't be absurd. You're mad."

"Listen. I want to take you away. You and Yuri."

She laughed again, softly as if to herself. "You killed that boy."

"Don't say that." His heart stalled. "I had no part in it." It began to rain more heavily, and they were chilled. "Let's get back," he said.

He trailed her this time, back down the track to the house. The rain was forming in pools, making the road impassable; even the militia truck had stopped at the end of the hard-top. It was a terrible place.

"I'm going to find Alexei Sergevich, and take you out of Russia with him, you and Yuri," he whispered. "If that's what you really want."

In the darkness she froze. He knew he had touched a nerve, the emptiness she strove to conceal. However much she waited for Barsov, did Barsov need her?

"Don't be stupid. Absurd. You're on the run."

"I found a way in. We can find a way out."

"You are an American spy."

"No way. I want to help you. Can't you see?"

"You are a lunatic."

They were inside the house now, out of the rain. She put her finger to her lips, warning him not to wake Yuri. The tip of the little boy's head was just visible, where he had burrowed into the pile of blankets. She kissed it gently.

"I am not coming with you."

He was too tired to argue and drank the remaining vodka in the bottle on the table. She had not switched on the light and the shadows from the candle made them both look grotesque, her face as white as parchment, his hollow-eyed, like some devil from the forest.

"We must get some rest now," he said. He tried to fight off sleep.

But she had reserves beyond him and seemed to gather her resentment.

"You brought a man who killed that boy. Now you have condemned us all. You have no hiding-place."

Exhaustion was sweeping over him, but he held on.

"You've got to leave here, Lila. You and Yuri. You know where they are holding Alexei Sergevich. We're going to get him out."

"No. I wait here for Alexei."

"Then what about the militia? Why let me bury the guard?"

She stared at him fatalistically. "They will come back. I shall have to denounce you."

"You won't, Lila. You can't. Because it implicates you. They would take Yuri away."

He saw her tears begin, lowering her head.

"Don't give up, Lila, don't. Let's talk in the morning."

It was a long time before she looked up.

"All right. If you give me your word . . ."

"I don't give words," he said. "I write them. And this will be some story."

Still she did not understand, but she pulled a blanket from the pile on the bed and threw it towards him. He sat on the chair trying to steady his head. The table was coming towards him, his elbows were sliding across it.

Lila steadied herself, made sure he was asleep, and cautiously switched on the light, a bulb swinging from the ceiling, but it disturbed Yuri, who sat up in the bed like a jack-in-the-box.

"Mama . . . what's happening?"

He saw the American sleeping with his head on his arms, sprawled out across the table. The cloth had been pushed to the side, the tin plates had rolled to the floor, along with the half-eaten loaf.

"Hush. Nothing. He's exhausted."

"Why did he come?" Yuri brushed sleep from his eyes, rubbing them red.

"We shall find out, Yuri, darling. You must go back to sleep."

"What are you holding that gun for? The policeman's pistol. We must tell someone he's dead. They'll find him here." His eyes were wide with alarm.

She smiled, a small figure in a black dress.

"He will not be found here. We have taken him to the forest. Now you sleep soundly, Yuri. There's nothing to worry about."

He gave her a fleeting smile, and pulled the bedclothes tighter.

"Are you coming to bed?"

"Yes, yes." She tucked him up and kissed him.

Inside herself, when Yuri was settled, she seemed to find new strength. She stood and looked down at the unconscious Schiller, remembering the parties in Moscow and the time when he had taken them to the Kuskovo Palace. He was a tough one, this American, someone she had admired. Could it be true now, this story he'd told her, and the impossible suggestion that they should somehow free Alexei Sergevich? What did she really know about Schiller? And what kind of life would there be for her and Alexei, as exiles in the West, if he ever succeeded? For her and Alexei and Ed Schiller.

She pulled the chair away and slipped him on to the floor. Waited, in case Yuri was disturbed again, but he was sound asleep. Schiller roused but did not awaken, lying on his side on the wooden planking, knees drawn up, one arm crushed underneath him, the other across his legs, in a coma of exhaustion.

His body was a dead weight and she had trouble moving it, but she made him comfortable as best she could, tucking the blanket round him and finding a pillow for his head.

"I don't understand you," she whispered.

She picked up the militiaman's rifle and concealed it in the kitchen. She too was tired, but she was also triumphant, as if she had been in a tunnel, and seen a glimmer of light. Schiller had bothered to find her, had risked his own freedom to come, and that excited her. She found that she was smiling.

She turned out the light at last and undressed by Yuri's bed. In her cotton underclothes, a cheap set of knickers and vest, she climbed into the box beside him, and hugged the boy to her.

"My darling," she whispered, in the dark.
The pistol was under her pillow.

21

Two thousand miles away in Moscow, in the U.S. Embassy,
Jubal Martin, sweating in spite of the air conditioning,
picked up the telephone and asked for the direct line to
KGB Headquarters at 2 Dzerzhinsky Square. Sexton Legros
sat with him, listening, his long face shrouded in tobacco
smoke. It was a line that Martin knew existed, but never
expected to use.

In slow, careful Russian he asked to speak to Special
Commissar Mayakovsky, head of the Main Directorate for
Internal Counter-Intelligence. In that labyrinthine organiza-
tion a man of substance, who knew who Martin was.

"He is not available."

Legros gave a sour grin, stuck two fingers in the air.

"Tell him it's Counsellor Martin, Jubal Martin, CAO,
U.S. Embassy." He spelled it out. "Chief Administrative
Officer. A friend of his," he added with unself-conscious irony.

"Who? Please repeat."

Martin repeated. Waited. Did they expect him to add that
he was Chief of Station?

"He is still not here."

Martin sighed. He pushed his shirtsleeves further up
hambone arms.

"Tell him it's urgent," he said. "Go find him."

It was a conversation he had never imagined having, but
times were changing. Contacts were now encouraged. He
numbered the points in his mind as they waited. First there
were the *Washington Post* boys, downtown D.C., complaining
about no material from their Moscow desk. Then there was
Burrell, belly-aching that Ed Schiller's flat was empty and

the bird had flown. The third joker in the pack was Schiller's ex-wife, who had dragged his little boy to Moscow and threatened hell if they did not find him. Nicola had given them trouble right up to her day of leaving, and he had watched her plane take off from Sheremetyevo with a sigh of relief.

"If you don't tell me what's happened, I'll spread the Barsov cock-up and Ed's disappearance all over network prime-time back in the States," she had threatened.

Martin had tried to smooth her down.

"There's no connection. Of course we'll find him. He's just gone on a story . . ."

"A story? And the paper doesn't know?" Her big eyes stared at him through the glasses. "You find him," she said. "I'm scared. You find him, please."

What was it made her still want Ed, Martin wondered. What kind of invisible tie, in spite of the divorce? Was it simply the boy, or was there something deeper, some rope she couldn't let go? Martin had lost his future when his own wife died. The last sight of Nicola's face as she went through the departure lounge was of a face underwater, slowly drowning.

On top of which there was Suvorov, Viktor Suvorov, Commissioner of the Moscow City Police, whom he had contacted in the first place over a week before. Suvorov had recently come back to him in an outburst of glasnost and said, "You know you asked me about your newspaper man?"

"Ed Schiller? Yes."

Suvorov relished the moment. "And you advised us that he had gone looking for Alexei Sergevich Barsov?"

"Yup."

"Well, I have to inform you of something," Suvorov explained politely. "We have cross-checked with the Novosibirsk District, and I am happy to say—but sorry to have to tell you, you will appreciate—that he had not attempted to see Comrade Barsov. Which is just as well, for we would not have wished to have his treatment disturbed."

Martin could well imagine the thin smile on the policeman's face.

"Well, that's interesting . . ."

"However," Suvorov had continued, "we have recently had a report from there which sheds a different light on the matter." The smoker's voice seemed to be enjoying itself. "I'm afraid that it has been a few days coming through, but . . . you know what it is with these places in Siberia . . ."

"Well?" Martin had muttered.

"I have to inform you that a man answering to Schiller's description stole a vehicle after assaulting the driver on the southern highway. The truck was later found abandoned. The matter is now being investigated by the Committee for State Security."

The KGB. "Anybody hurt?" Martin put his hand over the telephone and grimaced at Legros.

"I suggest you use the appropriate channels," Suvorov said dryly. "Special Commissar Mayakovsky."

So Martin had gone round the labyrinth, and waited for Mayakovsky to reply, because Mayakovsky knew something. Nearly two hours later the unknown secretary returned the call.

"The Commissar is leaving. He would be obliged if you could meet him for a few minutes at the Novodyevichy Convent, the entrance off Pirogovskaya Street."

"Where does he mean? Which part of the Convent?"

"The Gate-Church of the Transfiguration. In half an hour."

"Fucking Commies," Sheen said, "all monks under the skin."

Legros nodded. "Take Taylor Sheen with you," he added, "and be careful."

The golden cupolas of the ochre and white building dazzled in the sunshine as they arrived. It was crowded with visitors but there were still cool walks among the trees, and the big black Zis of the Commissar, curtains drawn, parked outside the walls was already an object of speculation. Martin noted that the Secret Service still refused to invite him inside the Lubianka.

A militiaman shooed back the curious.

Martin and Sheen found Mayakovsky smiling, waiting inside the grounds, under the shadow of the five-domed church. He seemed to be admiring the architecture of scalloped windows and baroque excesses, then turned at a sign from his two colleagues and held out his hand.

"So good of you to come. I am on my way home, but I like to take the air on days like this. So much of our history has been preserved, don't you think . . .?"

"Sure," Martin said, introducing Sheen. Neither was in the mood for a historical tour.

They waited for a few minutes, circling each other like boxers, then Martin said, "Commissioner Suvorov tells us you may have information about a missing U.S. national, newsman Edwin Schiller. His wife has been in Moscow recently making inquiries, and we find he has disappeared."

"Disappeared?" Mayakovsky frowned. He was a thickset man in his fifties, balding and battle-scarred by a three-inch gash in his cheek. Jubal Martin wondered how he'd come by that. By contrast his younger companions, tough men in plain clothes, looked positively modern. Martin could see Sheen photographing them in his mind for the incident report. Direct contacts with the KGB still had a certain glamor, on which Sheen would dine out.

"You know the story," Martin said curtly, his top-heavy figure brushing against the branches as they walked up a tunnel of plane trees. "This guy Schiller's gone a bit cracked in the head. Marriage break-up, isolation, you know the sort of thing . . ."

"No?"

"Yup. His ex-wife said she was coming to Moscow to try and see him and I guess it drove him over the top. He goes out east on a visa to try and interview Barsov. Then he disappears. Suvorov tells me your people in Novosibirsk are handling it." Martin rubbed his paws together. "We want him back. We don't want trouble," he added.

"That's right," said Sheen.

Mayakovsky dusted his light blue suit. "I am advised the visa was to see our scientific city at Akademgorodok."

"Yeah. Well. I understand that. But we guess it was Barsov."

"I am grateful for the information."

"Any time."

The Commissar ignored the jibe.

"The fact is that Akademgorodok, where Mr. Schiller may have . . . ah . . . disappeared, is a sensitive area. And there is evidence that he may have committed a serious assault, which is a criminal offense. I can assure you that he had made no effort to see the dissident Barsov . . . my, my, look at that bird."

They watched a black and white magpie hop between the trees, then the Russian continued. "He had made no attempt to see comrade Barsov, because our writer friend has had no visitors. But your Mr. Schiller appears to have been on the run for a couple of weeks after injuring a Soviet citizen going about his lawful affairs, and he has committed a theft."

"You'd better find him."

Mayakovsky picked up a stone and hurled it through the trees.

"We are looking for him. What are we to do with him when we catch up?"

"Give him back," Martin said. "Forget the offense. We'll pack him out of Russia. Neither of us wants an incident about a newsman in custody. His wife's in television. She is threatening coverage."

Mayakovsky scratched his bald spot and ruffled the silver side-hair. "How do we know he is not on a more secret mission?"

"Because he's not," Martin said.

The Commissar paused in their walk round the grounds to enthuse over the onion domes. He sighed. "Well. We shall see if we find him."

"Are you looking in the right place?" Taylor Sheen interjected.

The Commissar stared at him. Sheen, the young American with the leading-man profile and swept-back hair whom he had not seen before. His watery eyes beckoned. "What do you mean?"

"I mean you don't worry about Barsov. You think about his wife."

In Mayakovsky's mind the processes of counter-intelligence

were beginning to click again, and though he did not
disclose it, he cursed himself for a fool.

"Ah. Thank you," he said, smiling at the golden domes.

22

For one fragmentary moment it was Charlie, speaking in
Russian. Then Schiller saw the round face peering down at
him: Yuri's baby-blue eyes and spiky hair.

"Amerikantsky?" Yuri said, prodding him with a sandal.

Schiller's head began to clear; he found himself on the
floor and his body ached.

"Are you all right, Uncle?" Yuri asked.

Lila had gone. Daylight streamed through the narrow
window looking over the yard at the rear, from which the
shutters had been folded back. Those in the front were still
closed. He struggled up from the blanket as Yuri returned
with water in a plastic cup.

"Mama is frightened," he said. "You killed the man."

Schiller drank the water gratefully: it was cold and
refreshing. He stared at the miserable yard, with its earth
closet next to the tool shed, and the broken-backed fence.
Long grasses grew against it, and here and there a few
poppies. A large cast-iron roller from some ancient imple-
ment was embedded in the ground. Through the fence was a
wheatfield, and then trees.

Yuri's curiosity overcame his alarm. He saw the American rubbing the iron filings on his chin. After the night of
the killing, the burial and the vodka, Schiller felt bruised,
but then as he gathered himself every muscle was tense.

"Need shave," Yuri said.

Lila came in from the kitchen, wearing patched trousers
and a gray-blue sweater. She stared at him, saying nothing.

He saw her face with its hurt eyes, and longed to talk, beginning to explain the Kirghiz and the journey.

"Lila. It's not safe to stay here. You've got to leave."

"You killed the boy."

"I told you. I did not want it."

"Why have you done this to me?"

"I had to see you." He realized how frightened she was, of him, of the KGB, of what would happen to Yuri.

"I have to tell the police. I was half-mad last night when we buried the militia boy." She seemed to be addressing her conscience, rather than Schiller.

"Go on. Tell them. I'll wait."

"What guarantee have I got?"

"Let's get this straight," he said abruptly. "You are coming with me. Not the other way round."

"With you?"

"That's right, Lila." His eyes had the certainty of an obsession. "To find Alexei Sergevich. I made a promise to help you if things went wrong. Why do you think I came? I came for you."

She shook her head in disbelief. "You came to Siberia for me?" She thought again of those confidences shared in Moscow when they had left Alexei working in the cluttered apartment and taken Yuri for walks, or skating in the park.

"Alexei said—"

She cut him short. "I think you're from another planet." But there was almost a chivalry in his hopeless mission that contrasted with Alexei Sergevich's roughness and womanizing. She thought of Barsov taking liquor like fuel, and Schiller in Moscow grieving for the marriage he'd once told her about.

He misinterpreted her hesitation.

"You are frightened because if they find the body you will lose Yuri."

"That too," she said. "Oh Mother of God, I'm scared. This is an awful place. Why do you laugh?"

"Things could be worse,' he said. "At least I found you."

He wondered where the others were, including the rest of Madeniyet. There was an army out there looking for him, some of them on his own side. Sylvester in Washington,

Burrell and the press boys, old Martin the Station Chief, and his ex-wife Nikky, all of them. And he did not care; he was where he wanted to be.

"I don't need you." She put her hand on her breast.

"But you want Yuri to be safe."

He knew that she was weakening.

"You'd better have breakfast," she said. "There is not much but I can make tea." She found it much easier to think in such terms, as she groped to adjust.

"I still don't know how I can ever trust you," she said later that morning.

Schiller sat on the bed by the window. Lila fed him on eggs and potatoes, stirred into a kind of omelette on a wooden platter. Then she came and sat with him, staring at the hills and listening. Outside in the sunlight the long flanks of the mountains over which he had journeyed shut off the end of the valley. The palisading between the houses was as high as a man and only their roofs were visible.

Schiller pointed up to the sky where birds were spiralling on the air currents. "They migrate. So can we. Out of this hole."

She shook her head. He knew she was still thinking of Alexei Sergevich and the future of Yuri.

He put his arm gently on hers and risked the question that had slowly been forming in her mind. "Do you really want to go back to Alexei?"

She inhaled sharply. "Do I want? He is my husband."

"That's not the same thing."

She turned away from him and pushed the shutters wide open, leaning out as if for air. The day was hot and sticky, promising more rain.

"I don't know what you mean." But she knew all right the implications of his question. If Barsov did come back, would things be the same between them, after Ed Schiller?

"Listen," he said. "You don't fool me. That guy dominates you. And he hasn't been faithful for years. Don't kid yourself, Lila."

She was silent, trying to define her loyalty to the absent Barsov.

"Do you love him, Lila?"

"Love? I have Yuri to think about."

"Sure. Sure. We all do." And Charlie too, he thought grimly, but that hadn't stopped him breaking up with Nikky.

She retreated from the window and stood by his side, her manner calm.

"Don't worry," he said. "We'll find him. I know a way south, out through the mountains. It's not impossible. The Kirghiz have told me where they will be waiting."

"Don't be ridiculous." She was breathing deeply.

"I'm being serious."

"What about Yuri and Alexei?"

"All of us. We'll go together."

"All of us? You are mad."

"Well. You can choose. Just come with me instead."

In spite of the sunshine, she seemed to feel cold, and put a wrap around her shoulders, an old woollen shawl.

"Alexei will never leave the Soviet Union."

"Maybe. But he tried in Berlin. Did he confide in you?"

She shook her head and seemed to contemplate some distant vision.

"What would I do in the West?"

He shrugged. "There's always America."

"America? Don't talk to me of America. How could I live there?"

He searched her eyes. "With or without Alexei?"

She looked at him like a schoolgirl. "I don't know."

"Well," he said slowly. "I guess from my point of view you'd have two options. You could live with me, or you could marry me."

It did not seem so strange to her now, that unbelievable solution, after what had happened since they first met, but of course it was impossible. Alexei Sergevich would come home, and she was the mother of Yuri. She glanced around to make sure the boy was not there.

"Marry you?" A question, not a denial.

"You heard," he said. He sat straight-backed on the chair, as tough in his way as Barsov, and she felt the choice was dangerous. The fact that Alexei Sergevich had taken all she had to give, had used her without return, was not a reason for adultery, but his absence had been almost relief, after the tensions in Moscow, his drinking and fornication, right under her eyes.

"I'm still married to Alexei Sergevich."

"I know that. But Alexei once suggested it."

She jerked as if hit by an electric shock, and then stood still, her pulse racing. How could she break her vows in the Wedding Palace, vows she had insisted on having confirmed in the old church in Kropotkin Street? No way. No way.

"What do you mean?" she whispered.

He told her then what Barsov had said to him on that encounter in the playground, when he had extracted the promise about Lila. And Lila now, two thousand miles from Moscow, surveyed her tattered rescuer as if for the first time.

The impossible took shape in her mind, against her own judgment. "You really want me to give up Alexei Sergevich?" she said slowly.

"I can't act for you. I only know you're not happy, and haven't been since we first met."

Her eyes, were calm. She looked at him steadily and her small hands, rough from work, were clasped together. "I will go and see him," she said.

Yuri had been sent to the village. Schiller had almost forgotten, in the warmth of the day, that other people were working in and around the houses of the little settlement. It was as if Lila felt the boy was safer, making inquiries.

"Are there any more militia?" Schiller asked.

"No. Only the one you silenced. The KGB leave a militiaman wherever they place the family of a dissident in exile. Just to make sure."

"Billeted on the family?"

She shook her head. "He was staying with the widow who lives in the next house. Old Masha Leloubskya, who said she wanted a man."

Schiller said, "She will know that the boy hasn't returned."

Lila was unperturbed. "That's not unusual, with a few daughters around. There are fifty families here. It takes them a time to notice someone isn't eating his supper."

"But the widow will ask about him? Report him missing?"

"Yuri will find out," she said.

"Won't they be wondering why you don't go out?"

Lila considered. "Most of us are exiles for one crime or another. This is a correction settlement. Few people know each other."

"Do they know who you are?"

"You ask too many questions." But she smiled. "They know I come from Moscow. That means they must know why. It does not pay to inquire why the militiaman stays."

His mind jumped on. "How do we find Alexei? We shall have to move from here, you and Yuri..."

She had just begun to explain how difficult it all was when she stopped him, hand on lips.

"Somebody coming."

They could hear heavy footsteps up the path, and Lila glanced through the shutters.

"Quickly. It's the widow. Into the kitchen." She reacted without nerves, once she was resolved. "I will deal with her."

Schiller responded. He bundled up the blanket, found his coat and disappeared. There were feet on the wooden steps. A child's voice. Through the crack in the shutters he had glimpsed an elderly woman, trailing a child of two, arriving at the door.

"Hurry up," Lila whispered.

He heard them talking, first on the porch, then in the living-room, Lila and the widow Leloubskya, a gargoyle face enveloped in a floral overall with her hair pinned back in a scarf.

"Your boy says the soldier's gone. He didn't come back last night."

Schiller could hear every word, through the wooden partitions.

"What do you mean?"

"Did he stay here?" the widow Leloubskya queried. "Come here, child, and sit down." She placed her grand-daughter on the great built-in bed.

"No." Lila said. "Why should he stay here?"

"I just wondered," the old woman sniffed, rubbing her dry gums.

"Did you hear noises? In the night?"

"No. I was asleep with Yuri."

Lila came into the kitchen, saying, "I've got an orange for Shiska," to pretend that there was no one there.

The old woman took it for the child with a grunt.

"Anyway, he's gone."

"Gone?"

"He didn't come in last night. I had a breakfast for him. He didn't come back this morning. His stuff's still there on the bed."

"You mean he's left?"

The widow Leloubskya picked at her moustache. "What do you think?" she asked. "Good riddance, I say."

"I don't know. I haven't seen him since yesterday evening."

The widow rebuttoned her overall. "Well. I think he's gone. Done a bunk. Pushed off."

"What?" Lila seemed puzzled.

"That's right. Gone home. Deserted. Probably scared to death they would post him to Afghanistan."

Lila tidied her hair, tried to be objective. "But that is a serious offense, comrade."

"Don't comrade me. I'm not one of the Party. Nor are you, sister." The old lady's eyes were shrewd. "What did they send you here for, with a militia boy?"

Lila ran her hands through her hair. "My husband is Alexei Sergevich Barsov."

There was silence as the other woman chewed that over and her granddaughter sucked the orange.

"Who?"

Lila told her again.

"I can't say I've heard of him."

The small girl bit her tongue and cried.

Lila held her hand, which was very sticky. It seemed to please the grandmother, who said, "Did he try anything on, the soldier boy?"

Lila laughed. "I'm old enough to be his mother."

"No you're not."

"Well, anyway. He didn't."

"Are you sure?" the widow asked suspiciously.

"Quite sure."

"Why was he posted here? Don't they trust you?"

Schiller heard Lila say, "It's a standard precaution if anybody is sent from Moscow. It stops unwelcome visitors."

"Humph. Are you one of those . . . dissidents?"

Lila sighed. "I have my views. So did Alexei Sergevich." She used the past tense already.

"Well. Anyway. Good luck, sister. You've got a fine boy in that son of yours."

A pause as the widow straightened up and collected the grandchild.

"Where do you think he's gone?"

"Who?"

"The militiaman."

"How should I know?" Lila said. "Maybe he'll turn up again."

The widow looked at her thoughtfully. "Somehow I doubt it. I think he's gone home." The tone of voice made clear that there was no love lost between Madeniyet and the police.

When she left the American came out of the kitchen.

"Well done."

"I did not do that for you. I don't want Yuri hurt."

"We've got to work that one through," Schiller said, "after we've seen Alexei Sergevich."

She stood amazed. "You still talk like a lunatic."

"I'm going to get him out."

"No. You can't take on the State."

He put his hands in his pockets. "You have said you will go. That woman could help us."

It was his boldness that attracted her.

"The widow Leloubskya?"

"The same. She's got no love for the cops."

"How can she . . . help us?"

"By arranging some transport."

Lila clapped her hands, amazed and irritated. "Just like that?"

"Sure. If you ask her right. Tell her you want a wagon out of here, to visit Alexei Sergevich. For Yuri's sake."

"You're still crazy. Do you think the world stops for you?"

"Sometimes it helps," he said.

She shrugged, impressed in spite of her doubts. It was as if he brought hope. He beckoned her out to the yard to look at the mountains as the sun went down, and Yuri came home to tell them no one suspected they had a stranger there.

Nothing moved, but they could hear far-off tractors. Bees abounded, and midges milled in the air.

"Yuri," Lila said, "we're going to find your father."

Yuri's face fell. "Why? Do you know where he is?"

"I have an address," she said.

"What are we going to see him for? He doesn't want us."

Lila was pale as she looked at Schiller, who was holding the boy's hand as if the conspiracy about the militiaman had become a game between then.

"He is not well," she said, "but there are things that I have to find out."

23

Everything was plain to him now except her position on Barsov, which she refused to discuss. That night she disappeared to see the widow, and then began to pack. He watched her put the boy's clothes, and a few of her own, into a cardboard suitcase. There was very little to take, and he had nothing.

"I travel light," he said. "How about Alexei?"

"I do not know what they are doing to him. What state he will be in."

"But you won't give him up?"

"No," she said.

"OK. Then we'll find out. But don't let him ever again walk on you."

She hesitated. "What do you mean?"

Schiller said, "He treats you like a servant."

She looked at him across the table as they finished a thin meal of cabbage soup with canned meat. This madman.

"Who are you? What do I really know about you . . . Ed? Your past? Your childhood, when you were Yuri's age?"

Schiller dredged his memories as the boy and Lila listened.

"My folks tried to farm in Iowa, coming out of Europe. Cold as hell in winter. Big summer skies. Just like here."

Yuri's eyes sparkled. "Was it good for fishing?"

"Sure. It was pretty good. Old Franz, my old man, would take me up north for the fish, to the Lakes."

Yuri looked at him suspiciously. "You catch fish without paying?"

"Well. Sometimes you had to pay. Boy, those barbecues . . ."

"I would not want to go there," Lila said.

"Why not?"

"It is not a good society. It exploits the workers. It has depressions. It is wasteful. And I am a Russian."

"Hey. Wait a minute."

"I have told you. I do not want to go."

Nevertheless she had thought of it, that much was clear. Yuri, half-understanding, became excited.

"Are we going away? Are we leaving the Soviet Union?"

"No. Only to see your father."

The boy was disappointed. "He doesn't even like me—"

"Of course he likes you. It's just that . . . he's not well."

"That's crap," Yuri said. "He's been arrested."

"No, it's not."

They settled the boy for the night. She gave her son a long kiss, intense with concern.

"Don't you want to see your father?"

The boy shook his head, before dropping off to sleep.

As for Schiller, if she had shown affection his happiness would have been absolute, sitting there alone with her, in that improbable place to which no one came. But she reserved her feelings as he explained the past. Once, when he mentioned the newspaper, she asked him with a flash of interest, "Have you still got a job?"

"I don't know. Maybe." Even Sly Sylvester, he thought,

must have written him off. He wondered what was happening in Moscow: Maria Galina fussing like an old hen in his apartment, and Jubal Martin, Sheen, Burrell and the rest of them. Even Nikky.

"Ah!" She saw the look of pain. "But you have your own family. Friends. It is a different world. How do you explain me to them?" She paused, looking out at the dark. "Perhaps you are escaping from yourself."

"Perhaps we all are."

As the night deepened, she baked potatoes which they ate with a little milk, almost in silence. He knew she would come to decisions that he could not press.

Again she asked, "Why did you decide to come?"

"I told you. To find Alexei Sergevich, and to see you."

"Well. You are seeing me." She crossed her hands in her lap and stared at him, wondering at this juxtaposition of two human beings. The chemistry that drew him to her, against all the barriers of culture and language and convictions, puzzled her as he sat there waiting.

"How long have you known Alexei Sergevich?" Schiller inquired.

"Since I was twenty-four." She spoke without emotion. "He is my only man."

"But you are not his only woman?"

"No. There have been others." She was completely honest. "Before and since."

"How did you meet?"

"When I first came to Moscow to work as an interpreter." She placed her elbows on the table, frowning slightly. "He asked for a translator to work on some stories. From the French."

"He had left his first wife then?"

"Later. He divorced her," she said. She began to close the shutters at the back of the room. The moon rose over the trees as they looked at Yuri sleeping. They were quiet together.

"That was before he wrote *The Great Patriotic Shambles*?"

"He was writing it. That was when his troubles started."

"I wonder. What about the other affairs?"

She flared up and counter-attacked. "Have you had only one woman?"

"When I was married."

"So. What happened to your wife and child to make you so self-righteous?"

"I told you that we parted."

"Leaving the child?"

"I know." Charlie being dragged around, his fault and Nikky's. He could not be chained to her just for the sake of Charlie. In any case she had custody. How could he do anything else?

"You are defensive," she said, sitting there watching him.

"Too right. I couldn't handle it."

"I handle Alexei Sergevich."

"You reckon?"

"Sure."

"In spite of the other women?"

Lila flushed. "In spite of everything." She bent to touch the brush-top of Yuri's head.

"You still really want him? Alexei?"

"I tell you, you are mad. You cannot get in there."

The American grinned. "You can. Look. I'll do a deal. You come with me and choose."

"Choose?"

"I want to talk to him; and so do you. Then you can decide between us."

She laughed. "You will be inside by then."

"You have to bury the past sometimes," he said.

"The past is never buried. It comes back to haunt us."

"But will you try?"

She hesitated, looked at him and the filthy room and the gray light outside. "I said I will go. I do not change my mind."

"Eddie. Eddie." It was Lila shaking him awake a few hours later in his pit on the floor. Lila, alert as a new leaf, having jumped from the bed in the corner, fully dressed.

"Get up. Get out quickly."

Her face was a white blur of anxiety in the dark. He was there, not dreaming.

"What is it?" He scrambled up.

"I heard something." She whispered to him to hurry.

"I can't hear anything. What about Yuri?"

"Yuri's still asleep. But I heard them. Listen again. Get your shoes on."

"A car. A truck," he said. "That's all."

"That's all?" It was grinding somewhere in low gear. "At one o'clock at night?"

Schiller was ready to move. He too slept in his clothes.

"Out in the yard, quickly. Use the back fence, across the field. Wait in the woods," she urged.

As he opened the door and slipped out into the night she was tidying away the blankets as if he had never existed. Heavy-duty headlights reflected back from the sky and Schiller could hear the grind of the four-wheel drive.

He found the wicket-gate in the yard which opened on to ploughed land. A dog was scavenging as he went through and both of them ran for the trees. He could hear the militia jumping down from the truck and banging on Lila's door.

Noises from three or four pairs of boots on the wooden steps; some fool kicking over the bench outside. The dog began to howl somewhere. As he slipped into the trees Schiller saw a light, a crack in the kitchen shutters, and then another in the widow's house next door.

Inside, Lila had moved quickly, hauling up Schiller's blankets, tucking them away, some in the drawers of the bunk, the others on top of Yuri, who scarcely moved in his sleep. She straightened up, looking around carefully, put away an extra plate and glass, and was ready.

They hammered on the door, and she gave them a moment tousling her hair, pulling one hand from the sleeve of her sweater as if she were only just waking.

"What is it?"

"Open up. Police."

She edged the door open timidly, and they brushed her aside. Four young men in gray-blue uniforms with red stars on their caps, one more in plain clothes. The uniformed men, she thought, would not be difficult, ordinary militia from the Ministry of Internal Affairs, the MVD. She concentrated on the middle-aged one in the raincoat, whose eyes were too close to his nose.

"Who are you? What do you want?"

At first he ignored the question, pushing into the room and sniffing.

"Don't wake the child," she said, pointing to the big bed.

"Where is the security guard?"

Her blood pounded. "He left . . . two days ago."

Lieutenant Grosny stopped in the middle of the room, feeling big, hands on hips, the gun in his pocket as his men filed past, out of the kitchen, and Yuri woke up frightened. She shook in spite of herself.

"He what?"

"He left . . . two days ago."

"He left?"

"Yes."

"Didn't you ask him why?"

"When? After he'd gone?" she said.

His pale eyes lingered suspiciously. He was looking for an extra man, as detailed from Novosibirsk, and not one less. It was very confusing. As he leaned closer she smelt alcohol on his breath.

Yuri began to whimper.

"Now you've woken him, you fools," Lila snapped. "Yuri, go back to sleep."

They confronted each other, much as Schiller had done, separated by the boxing ring of the table, the pale woman in a sweater and the tired lieutenant, ordered out suddenly from headquarters. He had come two hundred kilometers to this Godforsaken place and his face showed that he resented it.

"You had a guard detail, as required for a detainee."

"Is that what you call me?"

He ignored her, swayed, pressed on. "You had a guard detail . . ." He consulted a red plastic notebook. "A corporal, Boris Lozovsky. Is that right?"

Her lips were tight as she agreed.

"What happened to him?"

"I told you. He left. Two days ago. I don't know why: he didn't tell me."

The lieutenant wiped his face. "Have you got a drink?"

She nodded and produced a half-bottle of cheap vodka and half-a-dozen glasses, also some hard biscuits. In a moment they were sitting drinking and the atmosphere had relaxed.

The lieutenant licked his pencil and began to make notes. He reminded her of the apparatus, the cities from which she'd come.

"Corporal Lozovsky absconded on the night of the second?"

"Yes."

"Anybody see him go?"

"I expect so. You can ask in the village."

Lieutenant Grosny began to perspire. He leaned over the table and winked, while running chipped fingernails across his scalp.

"Did he try and grab you?"

"What?" Face blank and white.

"You know. Did he try it on?" His finger moved obscenely, in and out of a circle. "Been having it off, have we?"

Perhaps he hoped she would react, or give herself away. Instead she poured more drink.

"He didn't try anything. What makes you think that?"

Lieutenant Grosny seemed disappointed. The militia boys sat awkwardly.

"Oh come on. We won't hold it against him when we pick him up. It stands to reason—an attractive widow with a randy young lad, he's bound to make a pass. I wouldn't blame him or you."

"I'm not a widow, you idiot."

Lieutenant Grosny flared up. "No need to—"

"You are a clown," she said.

He growled. "You watch your step." He lurched towards her.

"You watch your conduct."

Bully-boy, he shook his fist. "Don't you try and be funny."

"I could report you," she said.

Baffled, the lieutenant retired to the vodka bottle, then peered round the room. "This is a dump."

She did not reply.

"A bloody dump. How do we know you're not concealing your loverboy? Or anyone else?"

Conscious of Yuri, half-asleep behind them, she said, "You mind what you say." That seemed to stir the lieutenant, who began to probe in the corners, pulling aside the curtain that concealed the few books Lila had salvaged from Moscow.

"Hullo. What's this."

A few hard-won paperbacks in German and English, Mann, Grass, Graham Greene, which he could not begin to understand.

"Subversive rubbish. Not fit to be printed."

"You ought to know," she retorted.

The lieutenant subsided, glowering darkly. "Search the house and yard, boys."

They rose reluctantly, almost sheepishly, not knowing what they were looking for. When one of them asked, Grosny snapped, "I don't know. A deserter. Or a body. An escaped lunatic, maybe."

He turned to Lila. "We have a report that there may be an American criminal in this area. He came to Akademgorodok on a visa. A spy. He has attacked a member of the proletariat and stolen a vehicle. Have you seen him?"

She laughed in his face. "What are you talking about?"

"Have you seen a stranger? Anyone calling here?"

She shrugged. "In this place, the only person who came was a gypsy. Selling pegs."

"Did you buy anything?"

"Of course not. I sent him packing."

In the end there was nothing, though Grosny overturned the room, pushing his hands inside the blankets underneath the box-bed, blankets that Schiller had been sleeping in; pulling the kitchen to pieces; stamping into the yard to inspect the toolhouse and privy. One of them went to the gate and shone a torch across the field.

"Maybe the corporal is in the forest?"

"Yeah. Playing with the fairies. He's pissed off home. I don't blame the poor bastard, stuck out here."

The search found nothing except Yuri's penknife: the one-dollar scout knife that Schiller had given him. Lieutenant Grosny turned the little knife over in his hand, admiring the stainless steel. He opened up the three blades.

"Nice. Where did he get this?"

"My husband bought it in Moscow."

He looked at her disbelievingly. "When? I have never seen knives like these."

"I can't remember. Maybe a year ago."

The vodka bottle was empty, and he had a sore head after all that riding in the draughty truck.

"Are you sure you haven't seen anyone else? Someone who gave the boy this, for example? It is an American knife. Look, it says so."

She sounded annoyed. "Don't be so stupid."

"All right, I'm stupid. I'll ask the boy." And he shook him awake, thrusting the knife in front of Yuri's sleepy face.

Yuri looked frightened, seeing the uniforms. With a hand on his shoulder, Lieutenant Grosny asked, "Where did you get this knife?"

Yuri saw his mother's face, groped towards what was happening.

"Who gave it to you?" Grosny roared.

"Leave the boy alone, I've told you," she shouted. "It was my husband."

A signal passed between mother and son as she pushed Grosny away. Yuri understood. "My father," he said.

"Are you lying to me?"

"No."

Baffled, the lieutenant put away his book, cursed and looked around the room. The five men crowded it out, and Yuri had begun to whimper.

"Where do we sleep then?" Grosny asked.

"Where do you what?"

"Sleep. Here."

She was a wildcat, with cub, spitting into the wind; not to be denied. Threateningly, she pointed toward the door.

"Out there."

Lieutenant Grosny recoiled. "What do you mean, out there?"

"Get out. Out. Out," she shouted.

"Do you know who I am?" He puffed himself up, throwing out his chest.

"Yes, Pig-shit. Now get out."

He blustered.

"You are talking to an officer of—"

"Get out of my house, and take your boyfriends with you."

For one moment his fingers played with the revolver in his pocket, and then he thought better of it. In his eyes he loathed her. But he retreated. "I will report this treatment."

"You do that. And explain why it happened, comrade."

"I shall report it in Novosibirsk."

"Good. Go back where you came from," she said. "Here . . ." And reaching behind the curtain she found another vodka bottle. "Drink yourself sick *en route*."

He stood there grinning weakly, unable to refuse the booty, at the same time wanting revenge. The bloody fools at headquarters had no idea what they were looking for, sending him to interview this bitch.

"Alexei Sergevich Barsov—"

"What about him?"

"Alexei Sergevich Barsov is your husband? Under treatment for criticisms of the State?"

That caught her on the chin. She wavered, put a hand on Yuri's head. "Yuri, hush." Then to Grosny, "What about him?"

"I warn you," Grosny said, "his recovery could be delayed by my report on your attitude. Seriously delayed."

And with that he turned on his heel.

She stood immobile as the door slammed behind them, listening to their footsteps receding.

Schiller waited for what seemed an hour after the noise of the truck had died away, just in case they were clever; waited until the kitchen door opened again and he saw her silhouetted there against the light.

When he emerged, she hugged him. Not fiercely, but
briefly, all that he could have wished, a sign of her concern.

"Are you all right?"

"Of course," she said. "They were fools, who didn't
know what they wanted."

But he found that they had asked about the soldier, and
both knew that they would return and that next time they
would be more thorough.

"We've got to shift fast," he said. "Those pigs will
come back." He began to sketch out wild plans. "Let's go
find Alexei Sergevich, then move into the mountains. I can
get you out, before the heat is on. They will come looking
for the soldier boy. You can't stay here."

She smiled. "Of course not. It is all arranged. I said that
we shall go."

"When?"

"Tomorrow."

She had that capacity to surprise him, putting her plans
together even when she seemed to be passive, neither
accepting nor rejecting.

"I will go to Alexei Sergevich," she said, "just as you
have suggested. The MVD will make no difference."

"How?"

"You forgot," she said, "to ask me where."

"All right. Where?"

"He is in State Hospital Number Three. Akademgorodok,"
she said.

Her determination was absolute, in the line of her mouth
and the firmness of her bones.

24

At five o'clock in the morning, one day later, the widow
Leloubskya came. A farm cart, iron-wheeled, drawn by an

old black horse, had been edged up to the gate. Its platform
was covered with gunny sacks and a few boxes; it had no
sides and no seats. The driver stood upright, holding the
reins, his breath steaming. There was a gray mist and a
dawn chorus, promising heat.

The widow came bustling in, red-faced, her working
clothes spattered with mud.

Lila turned to Schiller with an air of quiet pride. "You
see, I took your advice."

"Hurry up," the widow said, stamping her feet in her
overshoes. Her small eyes gleamed in the walnut face as she
saw Schiller.

Lila was dressed in black again, with a white headscarf.
Yuri was wrapped in an overcoat, carrying his school pack.
They breakfasted hurriedly on cold pancakes.

"Into the cart quickly, and lie down flat," the widow
ordered, "like a sack of potatoes. Or you'll get nowhere.
Pavlovich will cover you up until you are outside the
village. There are eyes and tongues about."

Lila embraced the old woman.

"Trust Masha," the widow said. "I was young once."
Her cheeks creased. "You will be safe enough. No one
wakes early here: except me when I want to."

Yuri ran ahead through the yard and clambered on to the
cart, clutching a small wooden truck. The moon-faced youth
with the reins adjusted the U-collar of the horse and looked
at Schiller blankly as he sat down between the boxes, then
pulled the gunny sacks over him.

Lila came, and sat on one side of the cart with her legs
dangling. Yuri, excited, balanced on the other. The driver
stood in the middle, feet braced against the frame, and
whacked the horse with a stick.

Schiller heard the widow wish them good luck as the old
horse pulled and the cart lurched across the ruts, turned and
swayed down the road. Lila began to talk quietly as he lay
under the sacking.

"There is no one about. In the third field we will change
to the tractor, which will take us up to the highway. After
that there will be a bus, and we will be all right."

The swaying stopped and Lila and Yuri jumped down.

They were under a clump of trees growing on a drainage ditch. The youth tied up the horse and press-started a Zilosi tractor. Lila helped Schiller to transfer the baggage.

"He won't talk," Lila said in English. "All of them hate the police."

Madeniyet was now behind them, a blur in the mist, a lost world under the mountains; the dusty road stretched ahead, straight as a ruler between the wheatfields, until it met the main highway. They rocked and pitched in the trailer for half an hour before they reached the crossroads: a concrete ribbon running south to the passes at the border. Schiller wondered how far by now Abdul, Mustapha and the Kirghiz would have moved along that route, but he and Lila were heading in the opposite direction.

The youth on the tractor nodded. Then he turned and was gone, leaving what looked like a family grouped there on the road. They sat on the trailer and waited, where the track from Madeniyet intercepted the highway. Telegraph poles leaned drunkenly into the distance.

"He is the widow's son," Lila said. "Not quite right in the head. But he says nothing."

To Yuri it was all excitement. "Where are we going?"

"I've told you," she said, "to see your father."

"I don't want to see him," the boy replied, looking at Schiller. "I want to go to America."

"The bus comes from Gorno Altaysk," Lila said. "It doesn't quite go that far." She gave Schiller a tiny smile, and asked Yuri not to complain.

Schiller read through the clutch of papers that she had prepared. Barsov's ID card, some Writers' Union letters, a card from the *Literary Gazette*.

The ID card had a black and white photograph of Alexei Sergevich's big domed head and Neanderthal jaw.

"I've changed a bit," Schiller said, "and added twenty years."

She shrugged. "It's good enough to get by. They won't be looking at papers. No checkpoints out here."

"How do you know?"

"Who would they be looking for: a peasant like you?"

"An honorary Soviet citizen."

"A fool," she said.

The bus was an ancient Kamaz which had long given up being smart, repaired and repainted so often that it could be forgiven for not remembering its youth. It was full of families and packages, the treads on the steps were ragged and the windows rattled with age. The seats had been replaced by boards, on which now sat or slept a mixture of incurious faces: families travelling to Barnaul, servicemen returning from leave, babushkas with granddaughters" children, taciturn, wiry men clutching parcels and cardboard cases. There was a smell of sliced sausage; soft drinks could be bought from the driver, who had a crate by his feet.

Crushed against Lila on one of the benches, with Yuri wedged in between them, Schiller felt light-headed. Whether she liked it or not they were now a family together, a unit at last, and nobody stared at them. He stole sideways glances as the bus crossed the plain. Time and place were relative: a week ago the journey had seemed so difficult, another life, across the mountains, across the tree-line, ending up in murder, a soldier buried in the forest. Lila's profile, etched against the window, framed by her headscarf, was a woman composed, while his own thoughts were in turmoil.

Yuri wanted attention, stories about cowboys. Schiller was tolerant with him, but the child was excited, inquisitive, and there was always a chance that they would be overheard.

"Keep quiet," Lila warned him. "America is a myth."

By midday they reached Barnaul, a straggling city that the nomads had bypassed. Its suburbs were smoky with open fires, pots hung over naked flames, tribal women shouted at tiny children. Many of the overnight passengers disappeared. The old bus refuelled, then ploughed on northwards in a cloud of diesel fumes, on the same road that he had used absconding with the pig truck. He tried to tell Lila, and share the story with Yuri, who stared at the fields, the rows of sunflowers, with endless curiosity.

"You must have come this way before," Schiller said to them.

"In an army truck with canvas sides, so you couldn't see

out," Lila replied, and left him wondering how much she wanted to see, her face fatalistically calm.

Schiller nudged Lila's arm. Somewhere here was the ditch and the bank where he had abandoned the pick-up in the dark.

"I reckon I left the trail about there."

She looked at the passing landscape without emotion, thinking of what she would say to Alexei Sergevich, of whether they could even begin to escape from the fates in store.

"Don't worry," Schiller said. "They aren't looking for us yet. And when they do it is a damn big haystack."

Twice they saw traffic patrols, idling by the side of the highway, making entries in their log books, but none of them stopped the bus.

He whispered to Lila. "They're not busy."

She traced a finger along the window. "For your sake that's just as well."

"What about that gook, the lieutenant and his boys?" Again it seemed a long time ago. "What will they be reporting?"

"They will say they found nothing. Except an American penknife," she said crisply.

They came to Akademgorodok after two hundred miles, in the evening, tired and bruised from the long day on hard seats. To Schiller it was almost familiar as he saw the point on the outskirts where he had dropped off the city bus and waited to ambush the farm truck. Then they were into the center, the last few kilometers along the clean, wide boulevards, deposited in Lenin Square, where the supermarkets and department stores fronted the fountains. Downtown USA, without advertisements.

Yuri was fractious and hungry, and Lila led them away from the plaza to dull streets at the rear where the sun heated acres of concrete. In a cardboard town of apartments supplied for technicians, construction workers and store clerks, she found what she wanted, a shabby rooming-house mistakenly called the Harvest Hotel. Its main entrance in an alley was almost ashamed of itself, with a broken electric sign and a plywood repair to the door.

"We are poor," Lila said.

The tired woman in a headscarf behind the desk smiled at the grubby-faced boy and asked no questions. Three flights of concrete stairs brought them to a box room where two beds divided the space, with a gangway in the middle disguised by a slip of brown carpet. They undressed Yuri and settled him in the smaller bed, where he slept to the sounds of pile-drivers hammering the banks of the river.

Then they sat on the big bed and looked at each other.

"Well?"

A double bed with springs that creaked, and a dusty patchwork coverlet.

She smiled. "Not here," she said.

"I know—because you're married. Don't be so stupid, Lila. But understand what I say—"

She hushed him, aware of the sleeping child.

"I don't care," he said, more softly, "whether he hears or not. Yuri should know. When you've seen Alexei Sergevich, you make your choice of beds. I'll get him out if you say so. I'll get all of you out—"

"It's madness."

"Shut up and listen. Hear me, Lila, and think hard whether you want him now after all this. Really want, I mean, as much as I want you."

Very quietly, she said, glancing at Yuri, "And if I don't?"

"Then I'm going to take you. On my own."

Lila did not reply. She did not undress, but climbed into the bed and lay there under the coverlet. The thump of the pile-driver was a backing to her thoughts. They rested side by side, scarcely touching, as moths fluttered round the lamp.

"Why do you want me?"

"Because I love you."

Lila was silent for a moment. Then she said, "Is that why you offered to help Alexei Sergevich?"

He turned his head. "No. I did not understand it then. I offered because he asked me."

She said, "Turn out the light."

In the darkness he could hear her weeping, but when he put out a hand she pushed him away.

"Lila. I'm sorry."

"How did it happen?"

"I don't know. Meeting you, I suppose. Thinking about you."

"Is that all? Is that what made you come?"

"It was enough. I rationalized it by hoping that Alexei could tell me what went wrong, what happened in Berlin."

"I can't abandon Alexei Sergevich!"

"Do you still love him?"

"He needs me," she whispered, as if Yuri were listening.

"How do you know?"

"You will see," she said.

"But I asked whether you loved him."

"I don't want to talk about it."

He waited for a long time, thinking of what would happen the next day, and then added, "You reminded me once that women need other men."

"Did I?"

"Yes. It surprised me."

Lila sighed. "There can be no future in it. Not between us, I mean. I am a Russian, you are from another world."

"The same world," he said. "A hick from the Midwest who wants to go back to his roots."

She laughed. "Nonsense. You left them long ago. You talk of New York and Washington. What do I know of them?"

"More than I do."

"What do you mean?"

"I mean you understand more. About men." He tried to imagine her past as she had explained it: a schoolgirl in Kiev, the daughter of a Party man.

"That makes me sound like a whore."

"What we have in common," Schiller said, "is a search for someone, an interest in the truth, and a need. Isn't that enough?"

For a moment he took the initiative. Suddenly she was closer, her body touching his, her hands feeling his face, her lips on his mouth.

"I'm sorry," she whispered, and as quickly drew away.

Miles away to the West, Commissar Mayakovsky reread the pedestrian report of an obscure lieutenant called Grosny,

despatched to Madeniyet by the KGB in Novosibirsk. It had
been telexed overnight and was awaiting him in the morning. He read it with his feet on the desk, sitting alone in his
office drinking coffee. A colored photograph of wife and
family smiled from the filing cabinet.

"The militia guard having decamped, on suspicion of
desertion," Grosny wrote, "and having had an unsatisfacto-
ry interview with the wife of A. S. Barsov, I requested an
immediate replacement. This was arranged on an interim
basis from the police barracks at Barnaul, pending an
enquiry into the disappearance of Corporal Boris Lozovsky,
whose town of recruitment was Gorno Altaysk. I am indebt-
ed to Lieutenant P. V. Yukabovich of the 23rd Militia
battalion stationed there, for his co-operation . . ."

Cut the cackle, Mayakovsky thought, you pompus bastard. It was the next paragraph that interested him.

"Further officials visited the Barsov house later from
Gorno Altaysk to discuss the arrangements for billeting and
to establish the circumstances of Corporal Lozovsky's disappearance. They have reported by telephone that the place is
no longer occupied. Mrs. Barsov and her child appear to
have left in the night or early morning. According to reports
from the settlement they were seen riding out on a horse-
drawn cart early on the previous day but the destination has
not been established. Enquiries are continuing."

Enquiries are continuing. Mayakovsky swallowed his coffee hurriedly and cursed the local MVD, which didn't know
arse from elbow. Any sane man would have seen something
was up, something had caused her to panic. He tried to get
through on the telephone to Akademgorodok but there were
no lines available. Kick the fools into action, something was
bloody well up. You didn't up sticks and leave with an
eight-year-old child unless you had a strong reason, not
when under surveillance. But of course there had to be a
reason, and that must be connected with the sudden disappearance of Corporal Lozovsky. A lifetime in security had
bred in Special Commissar Mayakovsky a very suspicious
mind. His nose twitched at the possibilities, among them the
thought that the militiaman might not simply have disappeared:
on one scenario he might be dead. Rape, or attempted rape;

homicide in self-defence; or just plain murder. Why had the woman left, and what had happened to make her? His thoughts zoomed on as he sketched out the options on his yellow police pad, at the top of which he wrote the world Schiller.

It was good of them to have told him about Ed Schiller, the two Yank comedians he had met at the Novodyevichy Convent at Surovov's request. He remembered Jubal Mar tin, the Chief of the CIA Station, sweating like an over-ripe cheese, while the young man, Sheen, with the slicked-back hair, had dropped the vital hint. Don't worry about Barsov, just check up on his wife.

Mayakovsky banged on his desk until the wire trays rattled, and shouted for more coffee.

He put the pieces together. Schiller had gone to Akademgorodok and disappeared. So had the guard on Lila Barsova's house, a couple of hundred kilometers further south. And then so had Lila Barsova.

He got through to Novosibirsk, angrily, at last, and blew up a startled receptionist at MVD headquarters.

"Where is Alexei Sergevich Barsov? Hurry up."

A long pause while they checked.

An apologetic voice eventually said, "He is receiving treatment at the Psychiatric Wing of State Hospital Number Three, in Akademgorodok."

Mayakovsky recognized the code for a security establishment where the treatments would be classified, but he was not satisfied.

"I want an immediate doubling of the security guard. A close check on Comrade Barsov. Special treatment increased, and a report of anything unusual. And a check on any visitors. We are looking for a man and a woman possibly with a child. I also want checks on all roads into and out of Akademgorodok. Is that understood?"

"Yes, sir," the local commander, suitably chastened, assured him. He hesitated over the word "treatment."

"Would you care to specify the increased treatment required?"

Mayakovsky said, "Jesus Christ. Have you all lost your balls? Just make certain that you keep him there in accordance with the prescription."

25

The Psychiatric Wing of State Hospital Number Three, Akademgorodok, was a walled-off compound at the end of the city. They walked there the following morning under a boiling sun which had melted the road joins into puddles of asphalt. Lila, Yuri and Schiller, finding their way across the street grid. The forests which formed a backcloth were still being smashed to box-wood, and they could see the bulldozers carving away at the hillside. A prefabricated concrete wall with strands of barbed wire on top surrounded the hospital, making it into a prison, a great square box with only the top story of the two nursing slabs peeping over the rim.

At the end of Ninth Avenue, Vassilovsky Prospekt, where the metalled road ended in mud scoops, they came to the entrance. Schiller saw a small gate, with a wooden hut inside it, and three militia on guard, who stared at them as they approached.

When she saw them Lila said quickly, "Don't go any nearer."

They took a side turning along the block where the apartments stopped, and found themselves on a building site: dumps of brick and cement, discarded steel props and plastic drums, and an old man looking for firewood. The sun burnt down and they rested in the shade of a half-completed apartment.

"There's something wrong," she said.

"What?"

"Too many guards. Too alert."

"What do you mean?"

"Look at the way they jumped when we appeared."

"Something new to see. Nothing else for them to do."

She shook her head. "You can't go in."

He blew his fuse. "Nobody, nothing, stops me now. I want to talk to Alexei Sergevich as much as you do. To find out what the hell went wrong. And to see if the old bastard still wants you."

Her voice was calm. "Now, listen to me. You have no proper papers. I wasn't expecting them to check us here. Someone has warned them. They are on the alert."

He saw, at the end of the road, that he could not reach Barsov like that. He had to concede.

"Three guards, with automatics. You wouldn't stand a chance," she said.

"I could get over the wall. Tonight, in the dark . . ."

"Don't be a fool, Ed. You would end up as cat's meat."

Still he would not give in. He kicked a broken bottle into the rubble. The old man was stacking his wood on a trolley made from a perambulator, without even glancing at them. A sackload of cabbages was rotting in a corner.

"We'll hijack a vehicle," he said. "They are just boys in uniform. They'll wave us through. Cars always look official."

"Without papers you're not even going to try. You go back to the hotel and wait."

"No."

She fixed him with her eyes, her mouth determined. "I shall talk to Alexei alone."

"No way. I helped to put him there. I must know how it happened."

"No."

He scrambled to his feet, grim and angry, more like a peasant than ever, unshaven, tousled, in the grubby brown jacket that he had lived in for weeks, bought in the men's store. She dragged him back.

"No. You stay away. I want you safe."

I want you safe. The words stopped him in his tracks as the tug of war between two men began again. Yuri looked on alarmed, watching her clutch Schiller's arm.

She pushed him out of sight. "I will go in with Yuri. On our own we are permitted." Her hands were in his, he could feel the pressure in her fingers. "This is my risk now. You tell me your questions, and I will ask them for you. You must go back and wait."

Standing there, in the shadow of the half-completed tenement, its scaffolding still in place, heat rippling the dust, Schiller blazed with impotent, unconsumed anger.

"I'll kill those bastards on the gate—"

"Calm down."

She stopped and drew in breath, her face tense, then directed Yuri to a pile of road markers, dumped further down the street.

"Yuri. Run along and look at those. Tell me what they are for. Leave us alone a minute."

Obediently the boy ran off, and she turned her full attention to Schiller.

"Leave Alexei to me," she said.

"Don't keep telling me that. Lila, we are in this together. A militia boy's been killed. Sooner or later they will find him, just as they will find you. You must get out of Russia . . . before that happens."

"Out of Russia . . ." She seemed to be considering it for the first time, seriously, conscientiously.

"Yes. Across the southern border."

She smiled wanly, and pointed down the road towards the hospital.

"My husband is here."

"Damn your husband," he said. She could feel the heat of his breath, six inches away, eyeball to eyeball, as he held her to him in the shadows of the empty building. "Damn him."

"What do you mean?" she replied. "What do you know about us?"

"You're going through the motions of a marriage for the sake of the kid. I thought about doing that once, but it doesn't work, Lila. It doesn't work. Not when he plays you false."

She pondered for a moment, watching Yuri jump on the road cones.

"You think I should leave Alexei?" She sighed, and just for a moment rubbed her eyes, a gesture which told him not that he was winning, but that there was inner doubt. Then she shook herself free, and brushed down her dress. The look between them was a form of embrace.

"Don't be a fool," he said.

"You must wait," she commanded. "I can't bear to think of the future. Go back to the room, and stay there. I must talk to him alone."

Trailing the boy behind her, in her widow's black, she showed her papers at the gate.

"You can't see him now," they said, three bored conscript boys.

She laughed at them, a woman in fury. "Are you going to stop me?"

They looked at her awkwardly, and then gave in. She found herself in a courtyard, a place of gravel and earth which ran like a dry moat around the two hospital slabs, each seven stories high. A central tunnel led through them to the other side, with more militiamen there.

When she asked for Alexei Sergevich Barsov there was a sudden chill at the reception center inside the fortress. A shaven-headed orderly in blue fatigues leered at her, and jerked his thumb through the tunnel.

"He's in with the lunatics in the second block."

"Lunatics?" Dry-mouth, her fears started. "What do you mean?"

"Wait and see. I'll phone through for you to look, but be prepared."

Ashen-faced, she hurried through the passage to the second building, where the rows of small windows and wire-mesh balconies reminded her of a bottle-crate. More guards there, who looked at her papers again, and a police truck with a machine-gun parked in the far corner.

A doctor in a soiled white coat was sitting at a desk in the vestibule, reading *Pravada*. He had sunken eyes, as if medicine had become too much, and nothing mattered.

"Where is Alexei Sergevich Barsov?" she demanded.

He put down the newspaper and stared at Lila, who was still clutching Yuri. "What do you want him for?" His teeth glinted with silver.

"I am his wife. This is his son."

He gave a long sigh, as if he had swallowed hot coffee. "Show me."

Again she offered her papers. He sucked on the end of a ball-pen and made a mark in his house-book.

"You can't visit him. He's a special case patient."

Furiously, she leaned across the desk until she breathed in his face. "Don't give me that shit. I've come three hundred kilometers to see him."

He laughed. "What for?"

"I want to talk to him. To find out how you are treating him."

Again that braying laugh, the narrow eyes swivelling from Lila to the boy and back.

"Well, maybe, for you. If you say so. But you won't get much out of him."

"Why not?"

"He's in the mental ward."

It all went wrong with Lila Ivanova Barsova then: her lingering belief that Alexei could beat the system. From her schooldays she had followed the code, seen her father rise in the system, been all the things she should have been at school in Kiev, at university in Moscow. Heavy with aspiration, studying, believing in the Party's infallibility, and then in Moscow, away from home, as a young and earnest translator, she had met Alexei Sergevich. Alexei, who knew women and seemed to her to know most things as he took her to bed. She remembered the strength of his body, and the way she had moved to it. She had wanted to stop the world then, freeze it in time, but it had gone on, Alexei Sergevich had gone on, and she had clung to him against the odds. In the end she had won back something, and Alexei had taken her again and moved to the flat provided by Party connections at Vernadskova Prospekt, enough to give them a home.

She put her hand on Yuri's head, to make sure he was still there. The boy was shivering. "I don't want to go," he cried.

But the doctor was already telephoning.

"Come down and take up this one. It's his wife."

Dumbly she followed the nurse with calves made from storm drains, mounting three flights of stairs which gave on to sealed wards. Looking through the portholes in the plywood firedoors, she caught a glimpse of beds, long rows of iron beds slipping on concrete floors.

And then floor number three, which had another militiaman sitting on a chair outside, smoking and reading a
magazine. The nurse nodded and led Lila through. Yuri's
hand tightened in hers as he whispered, "Do we have to
come here . . .?"

"I must see your father."

"I don't want to," he said. "I'm scared. This place
smells sick, and it's dirty."

They were marching down a long corridor, partitioned on
either side, more like a prison than a hospital. Each box was
a tiny cell, bolted outside, with a grill for a window looking
in. The place smelt of urine and feces coming through the
open grills, and the barn-door nurse in front turned and
wrinkled her nose.

"They can't control themselves."

Lila was swaying on her feet, and Yuri began to cry.

And then the nurse was stopping, unbolting door number
nine, which swung back on heavy hinges.

She saw a board on the floor, on which stained blankets
were thrown, heaped and dishevelled. The stench of feces
hit her from the open pail in the corner. No furniture, not
even a chair. A glass window high up on the outside offered
a view of the sky and for that she was grateful.

The wardress came in and stood with them. She picked
up an aluminum plate that had been thrown in a corner.
"You won't want to stay long," she said. "He's out of his
mind. Dangerous."

"Dangerous?"

"Of course."

Fighting back her own panic, Lila bent over the figure
huddled under the rags, which were pulled up to cover the
head. She saw the scabs first, as she eased the blankets
down.

"Wait outside, Yuri," she said, but the boy was frightened and tearful.

"He must stay here with you," the wardress told her
abruptly.

The big domed head seemed to have shrunk to a skull,
pitted with small red gashes where he had clawed his skin.
Waxy, sweating, filthy with the silver beard of an old man.

Only the eyes were recognizable, as he came awake at her screaming. But they were clouded and empty, like blue tissue paper. Not quite sane.

Lila shrieked. "What have you done? What have you done?"

Barsov levered himself with difficulty on to one elbow and scratched the scabs on his head as if they were biting. His hands and arms were bandaged with loose, dirty flaps of linen. There was no expression in the half-familiar face. He could not recognize her. He was a skeleton who terrified Yuri.

In spite of the stench from the bedclothes, wet with his own urine, she tried to hold him but he pushed her away.

Lila turned to find Yuri, knuckles pressed into his eyes, unabled to accept his wreck.

"Is he going to die? What has happened?" the boy whispered.

It seemed to her too that Barsov was dying.

"Murderers." Lila struggled to her feet, choking back nausea, shouting, "Who is responsible?" Her clenched fists pummelled the air.

The wardress looked on grimly. "He's under corrective treatment."

Lila pushed her against the wall where she stayed like a plank. "Corrective treatment. You're killing him. Get a doctor."

"I am a doctor."

"Lies, all lies." Lila's hands clawed at the woman's stained housecoat.

"How dare you. The patient is under correction."

"Correction? You call this medical treatment?" Lila spat. "Where is the bed, the records? He had been here a month, and you have made him a monster." She ran back to Barsov, trying to catch his arm, looking for the needle marks, but the wardress pulled her away. The arm smelt of festering flesh.

Barsov's head was lolling from side to side, and he seemed to have lost his legs, collapsed under the blanket. A thin trickle of urine seeped on to the concrete floor.

Lila shook him again. "Alexei Sergevich. Listen to me."

The dumb ox-eyes would not focus: instead he rolled on to his side, facing the wall.

Lila went down on her knees, but Barsov would not turn his head. He was no longer a man, lived with and slept with, but an injected cabbage, existing on a diet of drugs. She had believed in his genius, supported him against the State, sure that he would win in the end, borne up by hopes of his greatness which would be her reward too. All smashed now, in this obscenity.

Yuri said, "Please. Let's go." He wanted to hide. "He is very ill," he said. "I'm scared."

"Wait. I know. I know." She tried again to rally Alexei and failed, then straightened up, gathering the boy to her. The wardress smiled, ruthless, uncompromising.

In a brittle voice Lila said, "I want him in intensive care. He is my husband."

The wardress laughed. "He can't be moved. You must see that." She stood jangling her keys as if Barsov, rolled up against the wall, did not exist.

"Who is responsible?"

"Responsible?" The woman shrugged. "He has to be treated."

"He came in here sane. Under duress, but sane. Someone has made him mad."

The wardress unlocked the door and forced them out, their time completed. Other stone boxes no doubt held similar stories but the emptiness of Barsov's eyes was stamped in Lila's mind as she struggled down the filthy corridor. She was crying blindly, and raging within herself that she had not understood before, when they took him away. The illusion of their marriage seemed shattered, but she swore to bring them to book.

"Who is responsible?" she shouted.

"Doctor Grigory Rakovsky is the superintendent of this wing."

"He's going to die, Mama." Between his sobs, Yuri was sure of that. He tried to run away, but she caught him and held him close.

"Let's go home, Mama—"

"I know, I know," she murmured to comfort him, knowing that there was no home, no future any more. Impotent, exhausted, they clung to each other while the stone wardress stood by. It was beyond her reasoning that it should come to this: not just that Barsov should lose, but that the State, the system, should turn on him with such fury.

"Where is this Rakovsky?" Lila shrieked.

"He is away."

"Who is in charge then?"

"There is no one in charge."

The corridors seemed endless, her legs like rubber. A bureaucratic nightmare as she tried to consider how she could begin to help Alexei and bring to justice the criminals who had done this.

"What in hell do you mean? No one in charge?"

"There is no need. The treatment has been prescribed."

"Who in God's name prescribed it?"

"The appropriate authorities."

The wardress was opening more doors out of the third floor cage. A shuffle of other prisoners, thin and ill, emerged from another stairwell. This was the evil landscape of the Gulag that she had heard rumored, and turned away from and denied. Schiller had been right after all. And not in some frozen camp, but there, in Akademgorodok.

"There was nothing wrong with him when he was taken away."

The wardress stopped, hands on her ample hips. She was big enough to use force, and ready to try, gripping Lila by the arm.

"You'd better go."

"I want my husband," Lila shouted. Her voice was thin with despair, as if she did not believe in miracles any longer.

"That is impossible."

It was the end of a road for Lila too, the end of belief. If she shouted at them now it was only the motions of protest.

"I will appeal . . . I will appeal to Moscow, to the Party, to General Secretary Gorbachev. You will not get away with this."

"The treatment was prescribed by Moscow," the wardress said.

* * *

Soon afterwards, in Dzerzhinsky Square, the telephone rang in Mayakovsky's office. He was busy, always busy, but not too busy to listen to the priority call. A name he did not recognize, but the source was important. A Doctor Rakovsky, State Hospital Number Three, Akademgorodok.

"I have been asked to report—"

"Yes. Yes."

"A woman has been to see special patient number nine. Her papers were in order. We let her through. Lila Ivanova Barsova and their son."

"Was there a man as well?"

Rakovsky hesitated. "No, but one of the guards reported that he saw a man with her earlier."

"Bloody fools," Mayakovsky snapped. "Where is she now? Did your people detain her?"

"Detain?"

The emptiness in the answer infuriated the Commissar. He roared into the telephone, "Yes, you fool. She is wanted for questioning. Good God Almighty, are you all pissed to the eyeballs? I wanted her picked up. What the hell are the militia doing?"

At the other end Superintendent Rakovsky stumbled on. It was nothing to do with him: he was only a medical man, he hadn't known about the order. Nobody had instructed the guards to arrest Mrs. Barsova. When she came with the child it had been treated as a compassionate visit. But . . . But . . .

"What is it, man?" Mayakovsky shouted.

"I have to say that I am concerned . . . concerned about the treatment being effected on the patient."

"Oh you are, are you?" Piss-pot, thought Mayakovsky.

"Yes. It is very . . . old-fashioned. It is not in the interests of rehabilitation. I request that the drugs be stopped."

"Stopped? Stopped? Do you know who ordered them? I ordered them," Mayakovsky thundered. "This process of harboring the enemies of the State, vipers within the nest, has gone far enough, comrade."

"Orders on whose medical authority?" Rakovsky asked weakly.

"Medical authority? How dare you." Mayakovsky wiped his head. One did not ask that sort of question of the KGB, but times were changing, so he had secured his cover, others within the system who for whatever reason wanted to silence Barsov. He calmed down. "I'll tell you something, comrade, that treatment was ordered by the Ministry of the Interior, after extensive consultations."

Mayakovsky believed that the right to violent solutions must be protected. He thought smugly of the vested interests of his associates, Suvorov of the City Police, and the turncoat Secretary of the Union of Artists, Antoly Sherbitsky, both of whom had warned the Lubianka, both wanting Barsov culled.

"Listen, my friend," he hissed, safeguarding his flank, "this is a big country. The biggest in the world. A lot of things go on in Moscow that we don't expect you to understand. But let me tell you this. The release of a few tamed tigers from prison and labor camps doesn't mean the system has changed."

"This is a medical matter, not a political one."

"Medicine is a part of politics."

"But there is talk of openness of expression. A new freedom."

Mayakovsky's fist hit the desk. "Go back to your patients, laddie. Leave the crap to me. Barsov stays where he is. Now get off the line."

He swung into action at once, calling Novosibirsk.

"I want them arrested. All of them. They are in Akademgorodok. Schiller the American, the woman and the boy. Do you understand me? Move."

They jumped so slowly in the sticks.

"We'll do our best."

"Move. Do you understand? The woman, the boy, and, if you can find him when you've got out of bed, the American lunatic."

26

Schiller knew from the expression in her eyes as she returned to the shabby room in the hotel that it had gone horribly wrong. Her black dress was stained with sweat and grey with dust from walking back in the heat. She looked exhausted, and he watched appalled as she collapsed on the bed, clasping Yuri to her. Yuri himself screamed at him, "He's going to die, isn't he?" over and over, as if it would expunge the thought.

Schiller tried to calm them both, to comfort the boy.

"Don't touch him," she said.

He poured her a glass of water, all there was to offer. "Tell me about it, Lila."

"We can't stay here." Her face was grimy with tears.

"Why? What happened? What did he say?"

She closed her eyes, unable even to begin. He knew that the boy would tell him, sooner or later, but he waited for Lila. She shook her head and sipped the lukewarm tapwater that tasted of rust.

"I'm terrified. Terrified of the future. For Alexei Sergevich. You, me, Yuri. They are turning him into a cabbage, mindless." She broke down in despair.

Yuri said, "I saw him in the corner, like an animal."

"What about Berlin?" Schiller said doggedly. "Did you ask?"

She gave a harsh laugh. "He is beyond questions." Lila's options were narrowing. "This is the middle of the Soviet Union, don't you understand? I have seen what they can do. Alexei Sergevich is dying. My Alexei."

"Dying?"

"Kept in a wire cage, just like some animal." Slowly she

admitted, as much to herself as to Schiller, "I cannot help him any more. And you will be next as soon as they catch you." The Barsov in her past seemed destroyed, a warning of what would happen.

Schiller did not accept that kind of defeat. "No way. They don't even know where we are."

"The militia will have reported. They noted my name. The KGB will start searching. We are on the run." She spoke in tones of exhaustion, almost automatically.

He asked about Barsov then, and whether she would still want him. She looked from his new phenomenon, this confident stranger, to the small boy in the corner. She wavered. "I don't know. How can I know? But you must go away."

"No way," he said again. "I'm going to take you with me. Where the hell do you go otherwise? Back with Alexei to that God-awful dump at Madeniyet?"

She looked at him and did not deny it.

"There has been enough damage," she whispered. "Among us all." She was gathering their packages together as if she had made up her mind: the boy's case and her own, and Schiller's bag. "Yuri and I will make our own way."

"Where to, for Christ's sake? I've got a plan," he said, aware of the long march that he had contemplated with the Kirghiz.

She shook her head. "I have a friend in Novosibirsk. Someone who will hide us while we work things out."

"For God's sake, Lila, I'm not leaving you. Get that into your head."

His own mind was equally firm, and she hesitated, her eyes puzzled. His certainly alarmed her.

"It can't be, Ed. It won't work."

"Don't give me that. How long have we got, before the shit starts to fly, when they discover we've been here?"

"A day or two. Maybe a little more." She looked at him dumbly. "But we must separate. There is no other way."

He would have refused to believe her as she rose wearily and stood with him in the room, between the beds with Yuri sitting by his pack, already a refugee, if they had not heard the wail of sirens in the streets below. A banshee howl.

"Jesus. Not us already?" he said.

"Don't be so sure." They ran to the window on the landing and saw a police van shoot by flashing its lights. Something made them realize that the militia were already searching, the streets first, then the rooming-houses. He had a choice now, a crude choice, to break away on his own, or force her to come with him. But there was also the boy, Yuri, his eyes open with fright, looking to Schiller to lead them, to take Barsov's place.

"It will be OK, son," he said, and Yuri clutched his hand.

"Lila. You must choose." His eyes were on her. It was a decision only Lila could take, and she felt Yuri take it for her.

"Don't let Ed go," the boy cried, the bitter tears starting again.

While Yuri sat and watched them both with those terrible eyes she made one last desperate attempt to rationalize her own life. She had been taken by Barsov, one of his many conquests, and loved him and stuck by him, in spite of all the agonies, the triumphs and humiliations of that degrading little Moscow flat. She had borne Yuri for him, and he was all that she had, until the fatal conjunction with this streetwise American who did not seem to understand that Russia was another place, a different way of life. Now the Moscow existence was gone, destroyed, and Barsov himself reduced to a heap of pus-stained clothes, dead to her own emotions when she tried to revive him. She knew she could never go back, any more than she could return to Madeniyet, and face the inquiries, the inevitable charges, about the militia-boy's death.

But this man, the American, seemed to be offering something in which he believed, and which not even Barsov had been able to achieve: an individual who could buck the system, take on the Soviet State. Looking at Schiller now, alert and ready to move, not even tense any more, she ran through a scale of emotions from fear to uncertainty and disbelief, but he stood beside her in the passage, simply watching the police van cruise down the street below.

"Well?"

"Listen, Ed. Leave me alone. Save yourself."

But Schiller was not open to argument. He came and put his arms round her. He kissed her. She forced herself to draw back. "We'll get up to the mountains. The way that I came in."

This was the last absurdity, that he thought he could pick up a trail like some Red Indian and follow the Kirghiz band over into Afghanistan. She stared and stared at the wall, the empty stairwell opposite where a blowfly was trapped, buzzing hopelessly. It was no good, and yet his courage took hold, inspired her to believe in herself. She turned to him.

"You'll never make it that way. But my friend in Novosibirsk works for Aeroflot. I've know her since Kiev days. We were at school together. I know I can rely on her. She may be able to help, to get us on a plane going south, closer to the border."

A smile came into his face, a tremendous sense of relief. She would. She would. He felt like shouting, but his mind was pacing out facts, requirements, reporting the necessary details.

"Name?"

She told him. Katarina Zasulicha, 419 Semilov Cut, off Krasny Prospekt in the nearby city, an address that he was to memorize. They would split up to get there as a way to elude the police checks, but he no longer doubted that she had given up Barsov, and that she was with him now.

The sirens were heard again, echoing around the streets.

He asked how far south, whether this Katarina could fly them outside the country, how far she could be trusted, and Lila smiled in return, as if they had made a bargain. Each of them needed the other in their mutual attempt to strike a line through the past.

He watched another police van. "Maybe we just sit tight?"

It showed that he needed her judgement as much as she needed him. The system was slow but sure. She knew the way their minds worked. When Moscow told them to jump, they jumped. The best way was to leave now, separately, because they would be looking for the three people reported. A mother and child on their own had a better chance of slipping through whatever net they would now be throwing around Akademgorodok. Schiller was the one without satisfactory papers, the American they would want. He was the one she must save. There was a bus into Novosibirsk—that would be a chance for her and Yuri. She must find another route for him.

The bags were ready, and Yuri said, "I want to go. I don't like that noise." She turned towards Schiller, and pointed to the forests still encircling the outskirts of the science park. There was food in the bags, and he would be able to hide until the panic died down, just as he had done before.

Carrying the three bags that constituted their possessions they left the room. The concierge did not look up as they walked down to the entrance: the afternoon heat was too trying.

Out in the grim Marx-Engels Prospekt at three o'clock the pavements were empty although they could hear the sirens wavering across the buildings. They were standing by the yellow sunblind of a pharmacy window, which offered reliefs for chilblains and hemorrhoids. The few cars were official, the traffic thin: anyone not at work was sweltering behind awnings. The light dazzled their eyes as they stared at the faded cut-outs and cardboard figures.

"Lila. Let's take a chance together." Schiller made one last plea. "They may not be looking for us."

She shook her head. "They are."

Another police van, silent this time, came nosing down the street. Schiller had a sudden memory of the girl being beaten in Moscow, on Kalinin Prospekt, her hair streaming in the wind. That could happen to Lila.

"Quick. Get inside," Lila said.

The pharmacist was buffing her nails, resentful of the intrusion. The girl took her time to find them some ointment and when they emerged the street was quiet again.

They reached a corner where the apartments stopped. From there the boulevard began, heading towards the train station and the Square of the Revolution. A few dusty benches and a statue to Peace. She told him there was sour bread and apples wrapped in paper inside the bag she passed over.

"Make for the forest and wait there two or three days before you try to join us. For God's sake take care of yourself. Don't try and slip through until the heat is off."

Yuri was sobbing, "Don't go. Don't go." Schiller was the father-figure that he still desperately needed, and Lila knew it. He felt something pressed into his hand. Looking down Schiller saw the scout knife. Yuri's treasured two-dollar penknife, the one that the boy had lied about when the police had searched.

27

Jubal Martin called the conference in the Embassy's Commercial Section at much the same time. Taylor Sheen was there, and crew-cut little Harry Mirvish, with Darleen, freshly blonde-streaked, to take the record. Only Legros was absent, having gone back to Langley as silently as he'd arrived, and Martin was thankful for that. Schiller's embarrassing wife was safely back home as well, but the Schiller problem remained, and was item one on the agenda. He had photocopied the telex from Sylvester in Washington.

"Why no contact now four weeks our Moscow correspondent?" Sylvester was asking. "All enquiries thru official channels, and correspondents' group blank. Has he seconded for special duties? Is this possibility? If so why no clearance with me? Regular dispatch Moscow needed. Information needed. Have you contacted Soviets? Explanation required."

Martin didn't much like the tone, *en clair*, accusatory and expecting him to do something. Sylvester had threatened for weeks on the telephone and then sent the message as a form of writ. Martin was also aware that he had friends in high places in the State Department.

"Christ, Taylor," he said, "where the hell is the bastard?"

Sheen put his hands in his pockets and his chair back on its heels, tipping his head against the safe room wall.

"Mind the glasses," Mirvish squeaked.

"Search me," he said slowly. "The guy can't just disappear. Unless he's dead."

"Unless he's dead? How the fuck can he be dead—if you'll pardon my language," Martin cursed, with a show of courtesy towards the girl, who smiled.

"He can be dead because they've screwed him up some place along the line," Sheen suggested.

"Aw, come on, Taylor. This ain't the cold war. They want to talk turkey with us: they don't help that by jumping on one of our boys."

"He's not one of our boys," Sheen retorted. "Doesn't do to forget that. He's not a pro, he's an amateur. That's more dangerous."

"He's got to be certified."

"He's got a guilty conscience if you ask me." Sheen put his gold pencil neatly inside the breast pocket of his button-down shirt. "About that cock-up in Berlin. He also fancies Barsov's wife."

Martin looked at the summons from the *Washington Post*.

"Aw, Christ. Then what's he doing now?" His spectacles slipped down his nose, a fleshly, ageing professor.

"If you go it alone you either fish or cut bait," Sheen responded.

"What the hell d'you mean by that?"

"I mean if he's alive he's either with the woman, or sitting on a riverbank some place watching the world go by."

"Taylor, you're too smart for me."

"No, sir. Just speculating."

"I'll tell you this..." Martin's midriff rolled over his belt-line, "the Reds don't know either, so if you've got an idea you'd better tell us. Because something has got them worried."

Sheen just grinned. "What they say?"

"That police bastard Suvorov. I spoke to him yesterday. Said they were doing all they can but after knocking off some truck Schiller's gone to ground. In Novosibirsk District, can you beat it?"

"Suvorov is only one of the Moscow metropolitan boys. You want the KGB version."

Martin did not like being told his own business, and it showed. "What the hell did we suck up to Mayakovsky for? They've been combing Siberia like you suggested, Taylor, in your wisdom—as well as sticking pins in Barsov, I guess. They found a body in the woods."

"Jesus," Sheen said. For once Martin had scored.

"Your friends the Lubianka boys sent tracker dogs into the forest round Madeniyet, looking for Lila Barsova. They got a body, shallow grave, freshly dug."

"Identified?"

"Sure. The militia squaddie who was keeping an eye on the Barsov ménage. Young conscript corporal. Knifed in the back." He watched the faces with a hint of satisfaction. "As for Lila and son, they've hot-footed it."

Everyone talked at once with Sheen as usual pushing through the ruck. "Could be that lets us out."

"How come?"

"Schiller must have been tupping her when the militia guy came in. They had a fight. It stands to reason why he has gone on the run."

"Hold on a minute," Martin cautioned. "I didn't say they knew who'd killed him. That's pure speculation."

"You got a better explanation?" Sheen was leering at him.

"Nope. Suvorov tells me they're still looking. There's no proof that Ed Schiller ever got to the God-forsaken dump where she'd been exiled."

"Aw hell, Jubal. Come on—"

Martin's lightly boiled eyes glared over his glasses. "The question is, what do I tell Sly Sylvester?"

"Tell him it'll make one hell of a story. *Post* man slays Red Guard in Siberia, how about that?"

Jubal Martin was angry. "Don't try and monkey, Taylor. We got a credibility problem if one of our accredited reporters is nailed as a psychopath."

"Exactly," little Mirvish agreed, feeling he had to contribute. The goddam Embassy, Martin reflected bitterly, was full of too many yes-men, the tired old gang of over-familiar faces.

"Don't record this, Darleen..." Martin lowered his

voice to make it sound more confidential " . . . but the fact is I've told both Suvorov and Mayakovsky that if they do find Schiller, alive that is, we want an early warning."

"What the hell for?" Sheen asked.

"There could be some kind of deal. We get him out without a scandal, and no big story about the Barsov exile, and why Ed went there to see him."

"Her." Sheen was his old confident self, staking out a new theory at the drop of a hot. "We could say they tried to pin a murder rap on an innocent guy after we got him out. Take the credit and nail them . . ."

Martin looked old, as if he saw his retirement slipping away for ever. "Look," he said, "the war's over. If they get him, they get him. You told 'em where to look."

Sheen grinned. "Meanwhile what do you tell the . . . *Post* . . . ?"

"Meanwhile I tell Sylvester that he's on a story in Siberia, but not to make too much of it in case it goes sour."

"And Barsov?"

"Barsov's in treatment. Forget him."

For Schiller in Siberia, the odds had lengthened. In winter he would have been dead, but the summer gave him a chance as he made his way through the streets. Suddenly there where police around, spilling from trucks on corners, beginning to thumb through papers. Slow enough for him to avoid them, they signalled their presence by sirens, disgorging eight or ten at a time into the groups of shoppers. They were checking papers now outside the stores and cinemas, under the classical portico of the Opera and Ballet Theater, even questioning the flower-sellers by the soft drinks stall.

He caught a trolley-bus down to the camp sites along the Ob Sea. From the window a glimpse of oil drums being pulled across the main road north at the end of the buildings. He wondered if Lila had made it before the road block closed.

The trolley dropped him off at the lakeshore, where sailboats were skimming the water in the afternoon breeze. Schiller watched them closely. With a two-bit dinghy like that he could get clean away, but the only way out by water was to the south. At the end of the lake were the sluices and the concrete drum of the high dam, where the militia were stationed. The sea was bordered by forest, primeval forest of high, tapering spruce trees under which the vacation tents were pricked out like canvas mushrooms. And in front of the forest a meadow bordering the lake on which a tent-town had sprung up.

Carrying his plastic grip he left the trolley-bus and walked towards the campsite, tired and stained, a steel-worker, perhaps, on a three-day break. No one paid him attention.

There were hundreds of tents, numbered and ready for hire: from one-man pups to three-roomed family apartments, igloos and pentagrams with star-shaped ridge-poles, most of them close to the water with rubber boats and dinghies moored nearby. Inside the forest were others, less popular, darker under the trees, and these were the ones he favored. In the middle of the working week most of them were zipped up, empty.

He chose a big one, well away from most of the rest, and slipped Yuri's scout knife through the tough nylon coating to make an entry from the rear.

Inside there were two large rooms, fitted with camping basics: tables and chairs and camp-beds. There was even a food box full of tins, and four bottles of mineral water. By manipulating strings he could open louvers in the roof which circulated some air. He pulled the torn flap shut and thankfully took off his coat to rest, listening to the shrieks of campers down by the river. Using one of the bottles of water he began a slow and painful toilet in the shadows of the tent. Three weeks of beard came off like iron filings, but when it was over he felt better. He was no longer a peasant.

In the evening sun he walked back down to the water. The heat was bearable now, and long shadows slanted over the grass where families were sunbathing; bare-chested young men in caps, well-fleshed girls in bikinis, mothers with squawking children, lap-dogs running wild. No one took any notice as he filled a bucket from a standpipe and stopped to chat in his precise Russian.

"Busy in town today."

A man in a floral shirt, sleeves rolled up, was laying a picnic table on one of the barbecue sites. Sandy-haired, barrel-chested, wearing sandals, preoccupied with his preparations, he hardly glanced at Schiller.

"Didn't notice."

"Lot of police activity. Road blocks, asking for papers."

The other man shrugged. "Another exercise to keep the militia happy. Where you from?"

"Finland." Akademgorodok was one of those places, one of the few in Siberia, where strangers were not uncommon in the academic community.

"Uh huh. Rich country, I believe."

"So so. How long do the exercises keep going on?"

The other man opened a couple of stubbies of Ob beer and offered him one, a frothy brew which they drank from the bottle.

"The bloody militia," he said. "Too many of 'em and sod all to do. When they have an exercise they're pissed after day one."

"Skol," Schiller said.

Walking back with his bucket, amazed he had survived so far against the odds, he felt the real test was still to come. And there were unanswered questions. What had they done to Barsov? Why was he treated that way, in spite of Secretary Gorbachev and human rights? Russia was too big to fathom, big and inefficient. Maybe they did not know. He wondered what they were doing about his own disappearance, three weeks old now. A sudden image of Sylvester in Washington sending an ultimatum about coming off the payroll. Like a gambler, he didn't care. The risks he was taking were brazen, but they became a challenge to succeed where Barsov had failed, now that the reward was Lila.

The shadows lengthened and the sun dipped below the trees; only a few lights remained, shining along the bank. He decided to risk his own. Setting up a paraffin lamp, working the little gas stove, the tent was surprisingly cozy...

It was the lights that woke him, different patterns around the top of the tent, wavering and flickering. The patterns were made by moving beams, and the voices had begun again. Protest shouts by the lakeshore.

Instantly he moved to get out. Self-protection made him run, carrying the grip, but leaving the overturned evidence.

There were four or five of them, shadows crossing between the tents, with hand-held flashlights. He could hear someone bellowing. "Shut up, do what you're told."

Schiller melted into the trees and kept on running.

Behind him a voice shouted, "Police."

28

"Papers."

"Papers, in my bloody pajamas?" Awoken at midnight by the MVD, Grigoriev looked a big bear in the shadows, booming at them, bare-chested and tousled. His wife squawked inside the tent.

"Who's in there with you?" the lieutenant demanded.

"Who do you bloody well think?"

The policeman began to be apologetic. These days you had to be careful, or you got some complaining in the press, and naming the District involved.

"OK. Seen anyone strange?"

"Strange? Who are you chasing?" Grigoriev remembered the young man who had come through the trees and shared a beer.

"A woman with an eight-year-old boy. And a tall fellow with brown hair. May by now have a beard. An American called Schiller."

"An Amerikantsky?" Grigoriev the lab technician had heard of such people in the land of two heads but never expected to see one. He savored the word.

"May be on his own. Had a visa to come here, then disappeared. Anyone answer that description?"

Grigoriev thought for a moment of the clean-shaven

young man who had appeared that afternoon. "No. Only a young guy from Finland."

The policeman stared at him blankly. "Where'd you meet him?"

Grigoriev jerked his thumb behind him. "One of the tents in there."

The uniformed militiaman, smart in his gray-blue jacket with the red and gold shoulder tabs, eased his thumb in his belt. "When was this?"

"Earlier tonight. We had a drink together. Anything wrong in that?"

"Get your coat," the lieutenant, a professional from police headquarters, told Grigoriev tersely. "Show me his tent."

Grigoriev grabbed a raincoat, feeling rather pleased with himself as other heads emerged from their quarters and enquired about the disturbance. A team of police a dozen strong was combing through the campsite. He plunged through the pine-needles with them in a pair of flip-flops.

It took them some time to find the tent Schiller had used, for most of those in the forest, as he had noted, were closed up, awaiting the weekend. The lieutenant was the first to see that one of them had been ripped at the back.

Grigoriev crawled in with him. The inside was a mess, blankets pushed on the floor, a camp-stool overturned, the remains of a meatloaf on the little picnic table.

"Somebody's left in a hurry."

"I can manage to deduce that," the lieutenant growled. "You can go now—"

"Oh, but—"

"I advise you to go, before you become an accessory." He called his men together.

"Suspected break-in and theft. Caucasian, said to be Finnish alleged to be using tent." He dictated the proficient note. "Suspect has left in a hurry, after recent occupation. Intensive search required."

He told his men that they might be on the point of a historic arrest; an American agent was on the loose in Siberia, implicated in the murder of a militiaman from the Barnaul District, two hundred kilometers to the south.

Enemies of the State were at large and must be brought to justice. The solution was in their hands. The man they were looking for could not be far away: the bedclothes were still warm. Immediate reinforcements would be called upon to seal off the forest, but in the meantime they had a task and a duty: to comb through the trees in line, and see if they could flush him out. Whoever managed to do so would be a candidate for a medal. It was not a bad little speech, at one o'clock in the morning.

Schiller had stopped. The black trees were endless as he stumbled between them, his only orientation the lights by the shore where the searchers were. For a time he lay listening, watching them come slowly nearer, looking at each tent in turn. As if they'd had a tip-off, no doubt from the bastard he had talked to. They had found his tent now, judging by the shouting. That was a dangerous development, and he moved back further, seeking an escape route. More shouting, then the lights seemed to disperse, fanning out in a chain, moving slowly towards him, so that he would be caught in the middle. He started to run. Noisily, between the trees, avoiding them in the dark as best he could, tripping and cursing. They heard him and were excited. Running, blundering, he began to put distance between himself and the pursuers; they dared not come on very fast, even with flashlights, and he was confusing the line.

"Get the bastard," somebody said, then went the other way.

Schiller flattened and waited. One of them was coming in his direction. The trees were very close together, thick enough to hide a man. The policeman was breathing heavily, nervous at the shadows swinging in and out of the dark. Within fifteen yards now, so close that Schiller could have jumped him. Lying prone in the undergrowth he even considered it, but one dead policeman was enough. The man swung his torch round the trees and noticed nothing.

Somebody called to him, "We're leaving it."

"Great."

Schiller shared the relief in the other man's voice. He waited until they had gone, listening for a long time, beginning to realize his luck. The nervous reaction came slowly. He dug his fingers into the rotting bracken and gave thanks.

The police would come back in the morning, if they so decided. They had plenty of men: the State was not short of militia, and hunting a running dog would make a useful exercise. No point in waiting until the light broke. If he was to get away he needed to move fast: they could put a ring round the city and five hundred men in by breakfast.

He could smell the water through the trees, and made his way towards it. It was further than he had thought and he was surprised at how far he had run into the endless forest, but he managed to find a fire-break and worked back towards the campsite, where two lights swinging on poles marked out a slipway.

Down by the lake were the boats. It was slippery underfoot now, as he approached the water. The bank sloped slightly, a little cliff, six or seven feet above the level of the lake, which had fallen from the spring floods. The water lapped cold and shiny as he crouched, listening. Someone snored in their sleep. Unknown night sounds, movements of birds and animals, magnified by the dark. The police had gone. No one was there to challenge him.

He slithered the remaining few yards, past the tents where they would be sunbathing behind their screens in the morning, then an eight-foot drop to a shingle beach. He landed in mud, faintly luminous mud, littered with broken branches and tidal flotsam. The boats had been hauled up on it, pegged to loops on the bank.

He needed one with oars, and they were less easy to find. The mud came over his shoes as he waded from one to another, searching. Perhaps as a precaution, all the oars had been removed. The fiberglass flat-bottomed fishing punts were not maneuverable, the sailing dinghies were too clumsy, and he dared not risk an outboard motor, even if he could find one.

Then he saw the canoe. A two-seater plastic canoe with the paddles left in the bottom, pulled up and waiting.

He waded across and untied the mooring rope. The canoe had not been used for some time and rainwater stank in the bottom. He felt with his hand round the hull to make sure it had no patches that might sink it under him.

The canoe rode the dark ripples of the Ob Sea, and he nosed it out from the shore, the chalky blur of the bank a distant guideline. Beyond it the tents glimmered under the lights of the campsite. It was utterly silent as he paddled quietly out on the water; in his mind he was also paddling away from Barsov.

Mayakovsky's mistress was sitting on the edge of the bed repainting her toenails when the news came through. The Commissar was in the bathroom and she had to fetch him out so that he stood there steaming, pot-bellied and belligerent, draped in a towel like a Roman, while they told him.

It was the KGB desk officer in Novosibirsk obeying orders after the lieutenant's report of the events at the campsite a few hours before. Mayakovsky was at least gratified that communications were improving.

"Sorry to trouble you."

"I gave instructions to be troubled."

Grishkina was smiling at him, rubbing his hands to her legs, which was disconcertingly erotic. Mayakovsky looked forward to his weekly assignation on the far side of Moscow, safely away from his wife, but duty came first. Duty and the damned Americans—that fool Jubal Martin who kept enquiring from the Embassy. In the old days conversations like that would have sent Mayakovsky himself behind the wire, but now it was all changing. He looked at the white hairs on his chest. "What's the news?"

Sitting on the bed beside Grishkina the towel fell off his loins and she pulled it away, leaving him naked.

"Give it to me."

"Sorry, sir?"

"Not you." He managed to retrieve his dignity as she giggled. "Hurry up with your report." The fools out there were too slow to catch snails.

The desk officer read over the terse prose of the MVD lieutenant.

"Is there any evidence that the man hiding in the forest is the American Schiller?"

"Circumstantial evidence, sir. It is unlikely that a local vagrant would choose to break into the campsite. And we have a description of a man of similar build to the accused."

"He's not accused. I just want you fools to find him."

"Yes, sir. I was to ask if you had further orders."

Mayakovsky glowed pink from his recent bath. He enjoyed bathing there because Grishkina came in and soaped with him. It relaxed the cares of the week, and he liked big women. Big women with red hair.

"Yes. Yes. How many men can you muster, with the militia?"

The desk officer thought for a moment. "We have seven hundred militia on immediate call, and can mobilize five thousand if required."

"Get the whole of 'em out," Mayakovsky snorted. "Get them off their backsides and go through those woods with a toothcomb at first light. I want tracker dogs as well. A manhunt, you understand?"

They jumped to take down his orders because the Head of the First Internal Counter-Intelligence Directorate was now closely involved.

Grishkina put her arms round him; he smelt her perfume and tried to enthuse. Normally he had no problems, felt as strong as a bull. She always said he took her like a twenty-five-year-old just out of a labor camp.

"What's the matter?"

He disengaged, sitting up on the bed, suddenly disliking the boudoir with its brocade and chintz which had given him so much pleasure over the years. Now he looked fat and worried. She wondered for a moment if his heart was all right.

"Barsov," he said.

"Barsov? That rebel?" Normally she never discussed his business, as discreet as a doctor.

He stared at her as if she were not there, hearing instead the American's whining in his ear. And all this because of Alexei Sergevich Barsov, trying to write his guts out on behalf of free Russia. They would want pornography next.

Barsov went round in his mind, and frightened him, although the man couldn't write now. Sherbitsky and the

other phonies propping up the Union of Writers had wanted
him silenced. Did they fear his ability, or hate him for
screwing their women, Rasputin-like, Mayakovsky wondered.
Poison the bastard, they had said, addle his brainpan. Yet
something was going wrong. It worried and niggled in
Mayakovsky's fertile mind. Even the deal with the Americans had come unstuck. The KGB had got Barsov back, and
now if they weren't careful he would become a martyr.

Grishkina cupped her breasts in her hands and tried to
tempt him, but he shook her away. He suddenly looked an
old man.

This American Schiller was more dangerous than he
seemed. If he was really intending to get Barsov out of
Russia, and if Lila Barsova had told him what she had seen,
that would be one hell of a story. What if the news broke,
and Schiller got away to tell the great U.S. public? It would
show the KGB as incompetent. And if that story got
publicity, Commissar Mayakovsky might soon not control
much of it.

"Vodka," he said, and drank it greedily.

He lifted the phone and gave another series of orders. "I
want an iron ring round Akademgorodok. Lila Barsova and
the American must be found. Schiller must not come out
alive."

With that his power seemed to return. He jumped back on
the bed, breathing vodka fumes.

"Take off your slip," he said.

In the apartment in Semilov Cut, Lila considered her future,
lying against the wall with Yuri in Katarina's tiny living-
room. Katarina was one of those women that nothing
surprised, least of all Lila's reappearance two years after
she'd last seen her. Her cheerful snub-nosed face had
beamed a smile of welcome as she hugged and kidded her
old friend.

"Lila, Lila! Come to see the exile? This place is the pits.
I wondered if you would visit me when I read the papers
about Alexei Sergevich's treatment. At least they report it
now. My dear, how are you? And it's so good to see Yuri."

Then Lila had told her that she had seen Alexei Sergevich

brainwashed. And whispered about the mad American, and the death of a militiaman.

"I know," Katarina said. "That was in *Selskaya Zhizn* only yesterday." She had delved in a box of newsprint and fished out the Novosibirsk edition. "There."

Lila had read the account. "The body of militia corporal Boris Lozovsky has been uncovered by dogs in a shallow grave in the woods outside the settlement of Madeniyet. He had been killed by stab wounds in the front and back. Corporal Lozovsky, from the 11th Division, stationed at Barnaul, was one of a detail assigned to the Altay region for internal dissident Alexei Sergevich Barsov, who recently attempted to flee to West Berlin. It is believed that a CIA agent, Edwin Schiller, contacted the dissident's wife, and was involved in the murder. A full police and security forces search is being mounted, following the disappearance of Lila Barsova and her child."

Katarina had looked at her old friend calmly, hands on hips. A report like that was certainly a sign of the times.

"Let's put the boy to bed. Then you can tell me. Somehow it doesn't surprise me to have you calling."

They ate a meal of fish and mushrooms in sour cream, washed down with glasses of kvass. The spare bed was in the living-room, and they pulled it out from the wall, making Yuri cozy.

"The kid's exhausted," Katarina said. She was a good aunt, a stewardess on the internal flights, who had tried marriage once and forgotten it. Her blue eyes and chubby cheeks gave an impression of humor, but nobody pushed her around.

She waited till Lila had eaten at the round table in the center of the room.

"Now," she said. "You're lucky I'm on my rest break. You'd better tell me all about it." Removing the used dishes, she parked her elbows on the plastic tablecloth and put her hands under her chin. Her enquiring eyes stared at Lila. "What has happened to your marriage?"

And Lila found she was beginning to explain: Barsov needed women as bears need honey, enough to keep him searching for others, whatever she could give. And she had borne it out of love, because he had greatness in him. But, in turn, Alexei Sergevich had given the authorities more and more cause for concern, so they had stamped on his books, destroyed his post on *Novy Mir* and tried to silence him. That had been the Moscow position, and then the American appeared. Alexei Sergevich had asked him to help them get out of the Soviet Union.

"Did you want to go?" Katarina asked.

"No. Not then. Why should I leave my country?"

Lila told the rest of her story: the Berlin abduction that the KGB had forestalled, and the price they had paid. Exile to Madeniyet, and "treatment" for Barsov. At first she had thought the new era meant that such treatments were genuine. The condition of Barsov in State Hospital Number Three showed that she had been mistaken, and now she was trapped by the death of the militia boy. Unless she escaped with Schiller.

Katarina inspected her carefully. Lila's old friend was no fool, and she sensed the sexual tension between Lila and the American.

"Do you love him, this Amerikantsky?"

Lila had looked at the floor, "How do I know? How can I tell?" She was embarrassed by Yuri's presence in the bed, even though he was sleeping.

Katarina had given a long sigh. "That means you love him."

Such talk made Lila uneasy. There was a case for Schiller in her mind, but she saw him as an escape route, a way out. Could it be more than that: could it be permanent in any sense?

Katarina laughed. "What would you do in the West? Where would you go? Where would he take you?"

"I don't know. It terrifies me. I daren't think about it." She pulled the blankets round Yuri, aware of the boy's faith in Ed.

"Then you should. If you've got a man like that, willing to risk his neck by coming two thousand miles into the middle of nowhere, just to see you." She sighed. "Is he married?"

"No. But he has a boy, about Yuri's age, by a previous marriage."

"Ah," Katarina said. "Perhaps you're a replacement."

Lila played with her fingers. "I don't think so. He told me about his wife, and she was very different."

"In that case," Katarina said, "hang on to him. Because you are an alternative."

Late that night, lying with Yuri's body pressed against her, and the sound of Katarina snoring through the flimsy partition of the bedroom wall, she thought of that conversation. If she did anything now, with Alexei gone, it would be done for her son, and she felt that between him and Schiller the bonds were growing steadily closer.

29

Hard to tell how far he was paddling, but Schiller kept the gleam of the bank parallel with his right shoulder. A faint cream line if waves rippled against the shore. There must be a road near for occasionally he saw lights flickering round the headland against a backcloth of trees.

He stopped the canoe and listened. The night was black as bitumen, quiet as the grave, and cold. Only the slap of water on the side of the canoe. If he lost that distant phosphorescent line he would have no sense of direction, and he resumed paddling, trying to get closer inshore. He had seen no more moving lights now for some time: the road must have turned inland, as he recalled on the map. He remembered being lost once on a lake like this: a midnight fishing trip when he was fifteen. It had scared the hell out of him then, the sense of being lost on the water, and it scared him now. Franz had told him not to go, and that had made him disobey. A rainstorm had swept across the water and he clung to the sides of the rowboat. When it was gone he smelt land. He had rowed back with the dawn, and his father had thrashed him.

Now there were lights ahead, round a bend in the lake, distant, powerful lights shining on a grey wall. The hydro-electric plant on the top of the dam. Red lights on the sluices, picked out miles away. He swung the canoe in quickly towards the bank, thankful to have got his bearings. He was further off than he thought and he found himself sweating, but the white line of the surf grew slowly bigger. The canoe hit something in the water, then grounded with a bump. He pushed it off with the paddle and felt a submerged stump. A few more yards and it was grinding on shingle. He took off his shoes and walked on pebbles. The water was up to his calves, and bitterly cold. He scooped up handfuls of gravel and weighted the bottom of the canoe, then tipped it on to its side. It sank without trace and he let the paddle float away.

The top of the bank was four or five feet above him. In the early morning he was shaking with cold.

He clambered up to find a slope of grass, similar to the one on which the tents had been pitched, and wondered how far he had come. The trees were there again, at the end of the grass, and he moved into them thankfully. But whereas he had expected another thick belt of forest, these were a thin screen through which the noise of vehicles could be heard.

He began to walk up the road in the first light. It ran straight as an arrow on the far side of the trees towards the curve of the dam with its guard-posts at the entrance, part of the same metalled highway that he had driven down in the pick-up. The morning traffic was light and he was just another worker, trudging from nowhere to somewhere. Or so it seemed when the big gas tanker pulled up.

"Want a lift, comrade?" A grinning, sympathetic head leaned out of the cab, an oil-stained torso in a string vest.

"Thanks a lot."

Schiller climbed into the cab, which reeked of onions and hair oil and had small plastic charms fixed to the side windows.

"Ride is better than walk," the trucker said, mistaking him for a serviceman. "Where are you stationed?"

"Novokuznetsk. General duties. Absent without leave."

"Ah. Bit off course."

"Not for Novosibirsk. That's where my girl is."

The driver nodded, scratched his chest and yawned. "How did you get dumped back there?"

"Local farmer. Took me as far as he could."

The driver winked at him, licking his lips. "You'll cop it when they catch you."

"If they do." Schiller grinned back.

He watched the line of traffic queuing up over the dam, a metal stream of trucks and cars, showing their papers. "Do me a favor," he said. "Keep me out of the way. I don't want those comedians asking for my leave pass. It would spoil my romance."

There was a conspiracy between them now, as the tanker crawled to the barrier. "OK. Leave it to me." The driver pulled back the sheepskin that covered the passenger seat and motioned Schiller on to the floor. He spread it over him and tipped on top his coat, a towel from the side of the cab, a radio and magazines.

"Keep still," he said.

The militia were calling them forward and the string vest said, "Hurry up. I've got a morning delivery."

"Papers?"

Schiller could hear the log-book being passed from the cab as the guard put his hand to the door still three feet above him. He held his breath.

"OK."

A handslap on the door of the cab and the engine restarted.

The tires were rumbling over the concrete arches of the road on top of the dam. As soon as they were across the cover was drawn back and the trucker said, 'There you are. They've got about as much idea as the police looking for that Amerikantsky."

"What American?" Schiller's head re-emerged. They roared over cobbles now, towards Kiev Street with the dome of the Academy of Science gleaming from a recent respray.

"Some poor devil on the run near Akademgorodok. A CIA agent, according to the radio."

"That's crazy," Schiller said.

"I agree. How could he live out here?"

Close to Krasny Prospekt, Schiller said, "Drop me off now."

"Bet you can't wait. You going to marry her?" The trucker laughed and waved him good luck.

Schiller gave him thumbs up. He walked along the uneven footpaths of the half-awake center in the early morning with the sun on his back. It was eight o'clock, the cream buses were on the move, pedestrians waiting at corners. He found himself by a bread shop and went in to buy a roll and ask the way. A woman in a white turban told him he wasn't far off. Another park with gravel paths and children on their way to school. Across the main artery of Krasny Prospekt, two blocks further and there were the narrow apartments of Semilov Cut, with bedding airing on the balconies: two sets of buildings which stared across a canyon.

He circled the address once, making certain there was no surveillance, then sat down on a seat close by some children's swings, remembering the windswept playground where Barsov had made the appeal that started all this. Would he have ever known Lila if Barsov hadn't wanted his help? Now he was almost a substitute for Yuri's father, as well as Lila's lover. He tore the bread roll to pieces and threw the bits to the sparrows. His own relationship with a wife and child had been shattered to pieces over three years ago; it must not happen again.

The woman he took to be Katarina opened the door cautiously. She was an apple-cheeked blonde with wide blue eyes and a fringe, and still something of the schoolgirl.

"I'm Ed Schiller."

He glimpsed Lila behind her in the passage, seeming tiny beside her. Katarina drew back the door chain which hung like a rosary.

Lila was in his arms. He kissed her brow, feeling her tense against him. She was still in the old dark dress, an involuntary widow, barefoot and anxious.

Katarina bolted the door, and left them standing for a

moment. Then she bustled back and said, "You'd better come in and sit down."

The living-room had the trappings of Katarina's mobile career: good quality curtains, a varnished table, bookcases and record-player. Airline souvenirs were scattered on polished surfaces: a silver Tupolev, photographs of flightcrews, a *mannikin pis* from Brussels. Icons of affluence which showed Katarina's success. The lace net over the windows sealed off the space from outside.

"Where's Yuri?"

Lila released him, put a finger to her lips, a gesture he had come to love. "He sleeps a lot."

They sat on a settee with large loose cushions. The flat had only two rooms and Yuri was still in bed: he could see the top of his head just as he'd seen him tucked up in the box-bed at Madeniyet. From the start Katarina made him welcome, as Lila's friend. She gave him a cheerful grin, then closed the door and took herself off to the kitchen. Schiller and Lila were together on safe ground at last.

"Well?" he said, defeated for words.

Lila sat almost immobile on one side of the settee, hands folded in her lap. She smiled wanly. "Thank God, whoever he is."

She held up a copy of the Novosibirsk paper. "Ring of steel round Science City. The city of Akademgorodok is the center of a manhunt for an American agent believed to be at large in the district. Edwin Schiller, posing as a reporter, is wanted for questioning in respect of the murder of a militia corporal at the community of Madeniyet close to the Biya mountains, and in connection with the disappearance from the same place of the wife of the dissident and turncoat, Alexei Sergevich Barsov."

"They haven't been very successful."

"No. But who gave the orders?" she asked. Schiller said, "Does it matter?"

"Eddie, you still don't understand this country, do you? They have been smart, even if they haven't found you."

"What do you read into that?"

She turned to look at him and he saw a silver strand in her

hair. He wanted to touch and stroke it: she must not lose her youth.

"The same hard truth that I learned from visiting Alexei. Top people must be involved. People in Moscow."

"Tell me," he said.

"Alexei is being dehumanized. Reprogrammed. Treated like an animal to break his spirit. He is sleeping in rags, and fed on dope. He may not even survive. And that is not simply because of what he has written."

"You've got to forget him," he said. "It's over for you now."

She looked at Yuri, beginning to stir awake.

"I may have lost Alexei," she said doggedly, "but I have to secure my son."

Katarina's head reappeared like a maiden aunt who expected them to be kissing.

"Would you both like to eat? Some tea and wheat cakes?"

"I'm not hungry," Lila said.

"But you are both too thin."

Katarina brought a tray to the table and watched while they ate: Schiller content with the present, but Lila always facing the future. She knew that they could not stay there, putting Katarina at risk, always fearing the midnight knock.

As if she were sleepwalking, Lila said, "We must go."

"Go? Go where?" Katarina asked. She came and sat by Lila, and put an arm round her shoulder. "Do you really want to leave Russia?"

Very quietly, Lila said, "I have to now...for Yuri's sake."

Katarina looked at the man who had come for her. "Yes. OK. For Yuri. For yourself." She smiled at Schiller. "And for him."

"I doubt if it is even possible," Lila said.

She counted the odds, without knowing where to run.

"Of course it is," Katarina said firmly. "I will provide the tickets."

"Forget it," Sheen said across the table. "Write if off. He's either dead or native; it don't much matter which."

Schiller was now AOB on the weekly agenda of the Management Meeting chaired by Jubal Martin in the safe room, but Martin still felt the need to justify what had happened, if only because Legros, back home in Virginia, had asked for a progress report.

"The KGB have admitted they've drawn a blank. He's vanished into thin air." He couldn't resist a dig at smartass. "Maybe you got it wrong, Taylor, in sending them to that Godforsaken hole where Lila Barsova was out to grass . . ."

Sheen gave his TV soap smile. "Then why has she gone too?"

Martin consulted notes. "Our friends say they're still looking. Barsov is under wraps."

"You bet." Sheen was doodling again with his fancy gold pencil. A pained look down the table at his Station Chief suggested it was time he took that one-way ticket to Palm Springs. The old boy was really past it, wanting a quiet life. Jubal had never been in favor of the double-cross on Alexei Sergevich in the first place.

"Who is leading for them?" he asked Martin. "Mayakovsky?"

Jubal Martin shuffled his papers, looked at the wall clock. "As far as we know. The last report was from his department. Or so they said."

"Mayakovsky can't be so secure these days. Heavy-handed old bastard."

"May need to re-establish himself," Martin suggested.

"He won't do it this way. Ordering half the police force to find a needle in a haystack," Sheen retorted.

"You know something we don't?"

"Nope. Just common sense."

"OK." Martin concluded with a touch of annoyance. "No more news. The Reds say they can't find him. We write him off. OK. I'll tell Sylvester he could be dead and buried. They can find another Moscow hack."

Sheen threw back his head, touched his fingers in prayer. "Any more from the wife? Schiller's ex?"

"I guess she's given up: let's hope she stays home."

"Keep her around at the end of a telephone."

"She's back in New York City."

"OK. Just keep her on a line."

"I don't want more pain over Schiller's domestic problems. The guy's a freak."

Sheen said, "When he comes over—if he comes over—we may be able to use her."

Martin stared at him, glasses slipping from his nose, which had ginger hairs on the end. "What makes you think he'll manage to get himself out?"

"Because," Sheen said, "my hunch is he's still got Lila Barsova in tow. If he gets through that'll be quite a news piece, one way or the other, pro-Barsov or against him, and we ought to milk it. We'll make the Reds look sick."

"I don't figure about Ed's ex-wife," Martin said. "Unless you want to make Ed look sick."

Sheen only grinned. "Maybe that too."

Martin wanted the last word. "If he makes it."

30

They waited in the cramped apartment for two more days, while Katarina worked out their escape. Days to try and settle their minds, days to explore each other, but Lila only worried and brooded about the best course for Yuri. She watched Schiller amuse the boy with a half-serious smile as the plans took shape. Yuri's future was at stake and she had no means of controlling it.

Katarina now served on the domestic runs, internal flights from Novosibirsk that could take them further south to Tashkent or Samarkand, where they would be relatively safe. They could worm their way over the borders, east through the Pamirs into Kashmir or China, west into Iran or Turkey. Papers could be supplied. There was even Afghanistan, now that the war was ending. She laughed and said, "No problems. But the sooner you leave here, the better."

"Tickets?"

"I can fix that. I have flight concessions on Aeroflot, when seats are available. The Samarkand plane is always half-empty these days now the Afghan border is closed. So you will be my guests."

"How can we repay you?" Schiller asked.

She looked at Lila. "By being happy," she said.

As Schiller and Lila edged closer in the process of understanding, it was Yuri who led the way, overjoyed to see him, jumping up and down with excitement.

"How did you manage to get here, Uncle?"

"Thanks to your knife," he said, returning it.

"Why are you back so soon?"

"I was lucky. I want to take you to America."

"Do they have schools there?"

"Sure. That's usually arranged."

The boy asked his endless questions, while Lila looked on in silence, appalled by her own indecision. Jumpy and nervous, she withdrew inside her defences.

"Is it really possible to leave the Soviet Union? I have never even seen another country," she said, fingers playing with a tiny necklace of painted beads that Katarina had given her.

"Of course it is. Once we get away from here, everything is possible." Schiller's old optimism seemed to encourage her.

"Internal flights are no problem," Katarina explained. "It is getting outside."

"But we are taking your passes?"

Katarina beamed. "I wouldn't use them. I have no family. I see enough of the air. Besides . . ." she wrinkled her nose, "I want to help you. Send me a card from America." Her sense of fun and generosity caused her to burst into song, light, surprising notes from her thick throat. In the crowded little room she reminded Schiller of a canary in a cage.

They slipped out on the following day, picked up a taxi at the corner of Krasny Prospekt and rode through the town like escaping prisoners. His reunion with Lila had not been an easy one, but Yuri was full of enchantment. Lila sat with him quietly, her mind elsewhere.

He remembered the airport from what seemed a previous lifetime, when he had arrived from Moscow and picked up Mrs. Korochkina. It was less busy today, stylized and shabby. Airports were the same from Cedar Rapids to China: only the people changed. They even bought popcorn for Yuri from a machine.

Lila's head was pressed so tightly to the window of the department lounge as they waited for clearance that there were marks on her forehead.

"Are you OK, honey?"

"Yes. I think so."

They watched the hot concrete outside, stained with tire marks. An insidious stink of kerosene infiltrated the building which shuddered as the jets took off. The chairs were uncomfortable.

"You know something," Schiller said. "Your country and mine, they're not so different."

They were talking quietly.

"But we are two different people," she said, so softly that he could hardly hear over the whine of engines warming up. "You have a history, a love affair, a child. And so do I. They do not meet."

"I put it behind me," he said.

"I wonder."

They stopped, aware of a mountain neither knew how to climb. Two soldiers came in, with paratroop shoulder-flashes. Then Lila added, "It takes a lifetime to change a life."

"The General Secretary has it in mind..."

"One man does not change the Soviet Union. That's why Alexei has suffered...there are many bad people."

"There are shits in any system."

"All the time. Everywhere."

Running off with another man's wife, he reflected as Yuri clambered over the seats, did not put him in the best position in her eyes.

They were called to Gate 9. An airline steward with a chest of lapel badges checked them in without comment and they walked with their hand baggage across the apron to a big old Ilyushin, a battered white cigar.

"In the States," Schiller whispered, "you'd have to be checked through security. But there would be a bus."

The plane was full of engineers from Sverdlovsk, on their way to a conference. Someone leaned over the aisle, picking at the padding of the arm-rest and breathing fumes as the aircraft took off.

"Why are you going to Samarkand?" Fyodov Belinsky introduced himself and winked. He sat in the adjacent seat.

"Why not?"

The deceptions began again as they would continue to do, Schiller realized, until they were married or caught.

"Please. Where are you from?"

"Kiev," Lila said.

"Ah. I am Byelorussian. My family moved to the East during the war." His narrow face and curly hair seemed out of place among the engineers, more the eyes of a teacher or an off-duty official. Schiller was uneasy about him. Belinsky had a peasant's curiosity about other people's lives—how old were they, where were they from—and a temperamental insecurity. He had musician's fingers.

The Ilyushin flew in and out of cauliflower clouds, over the southern end of the Ob Sea and the forests of Kazakhstan. Their unwanted friend opened a bottle of lemon vodka and would not let them alone, his nose twitching like a rabbit.

"Are you sure you're not in the Army?" He grinned at Schiller.

"Do I look as if I am?"

"Business, then?"

"No."

Belinsky sucked at his teeth and belched. "Otherwise why travel?" Schiller watched the land slide by; a pattern of finger lakes among the forests, the mountains to the east.

"I'd rather not say, comrade."

"Ah. Mysteries." Belinsky tapped his nose. "Do you know who I am?" A great slug of drink went down.

"A secret agent?"

The joke flushed through Belinsky's system and he rattled

like a delighted child. "Yes. You have guessed. I am on a mission."

Alarm bells sounded in Schiller's mind. Lila was alert beside him, but the other faces were incurious, dozing in the narrow seats.

The stewardess warned Belinsky not to be noisy. They would be there in two hours, she announced, and he should sleep it off.

They tried to ignore him, but Belinsky suddenly asked, "How long have you two been married?"

"Ten years," Lila said.

Belinsky spoke to the boy, shouting above the engine noise. "Is that so, sonny?"

But Yuri was too smart for him. "I'm only eight," he said.

Belinsky clapped. "Do you know where I am going?"

"No, comrade, why should we?"

"Afghanistan. That is my mission." Belinsky wiped his forehead, and bought a pair of socks from the trolley to keep the stewardess happy.

"Yes. Listen. A long war during which many of our heroic soldiers have, shall we say, taken the local women."

"Is that so?"

"Which worries the authorities. Especially when the soldier boys have become fathers. Fathers of Soviet children, you understand."

The plane was headed south-west now over the dry deserts which showed they were getting closer.

"What are you trying to say?" Schiller asked.

Belinsky eased the collar of his shirt, rolled in his seat like a porpoise and winked again.

"Ah. You see, someone has to save the children."

Schiller's hand tightened on Lila's as they came in to Samarkand.

There was not much doubt now that they had lost them, Mayakovsky told Jubal Martin in a corner of the reception for visiting U.S. senators. It was a sign of the times that Mayakovsky could meet him there. Perhaps, Martin thought, swallowing caviar, we are both on the way out, the Ameri-

can on his way to retirement, Ivan Mayakovsky because the
KGB was feeling the wind of change. Looking at the
Commissar's squat, balding figure, he speculated on whether the ruthlessness that had taken him to the top would be
able to keep him there.

Mayakovsky had signalled to him across the mirrored
hall, and glided across the parquet like a tug-boat. The
chandeliers blazed with light and the diplomatic corps was
drinking. He had pulled Martin's arm and nudged him
behind a pillar. Interesting, the CIA man thought, that you
were safe in the Kremlin to spill a story: they couldn't bug
St. George's Hall.

"Well, my friend, we have put a ring around Akademgorodok, but no sign of your Schiller."

"Perhaps he got past too soon?"

"Unlikely," Mayakovsky said, beaming at someone else.
"We had it sealed within twelve hours."

"Twelve hours is a long time."

The Russian considered. "A woman and a small boy can't
disappear into air, any more than an American."

"Are you checking the airports?"

"Air, road and rail. Even the boats on the Ob Sea."

A waiter with a tray of drinks intervened. Martin was
drinking more than was good for him and was sweating
badly.

"You know," Mayakovsky muttered, "I must be getting
soft in my old age. I think we have a romance. How did this
man Schiller turn up nearly three hundred kilometers to the
south? We don't know, but he must have slept rough. A man
of the *taiga*. Is he that kind of person? A Rambo?"

The room was beginning to circle round in Martin's
brain. "No."

"Very interesting. Then maybe we have a phenomenon, a
love affair, east and west. A runaway team."

Martin seized his chance.

"OK. So if you find 'em, and it's really like that, why
not let 'em get out? That would be a good gesture."

The KGB man smiled. "A story you could manipulate,
eh? You forget we have to solve a murder." He drew closer.
"You forget too, that I now have a problem with the

husband, Alexei Sergevich Barsov, our new Dostoevsky. My difficulty is this. I had instructions that he was in need of treatment. Instructions from the top of the tree, you understand?''

Martin had never heard a KGB man being so open before. Something must have gone haywire. He saw small beads of perspiration running from Mayakovsky's temples. He nodded.

''I followed instructions. Psychiatric treatment in the security wing of State Hospital Number Three. His wife has been there to see him. He was in a bad way: maybe why she ran off. Yes?''

''Well?''

Mayakovsky's alcoholic breath came even closer.

''Now those instructions, those orders have been changed. Do I make myself clear? Barsov is to be rehabilitated. A national treasure.''

Martin tried working that one out, but thought came slowly.

''What I am saying to you,'' Mayakovsky whispered, the enamelled Party badge in his lapel glinting like a third eye, ''is that if by any chance—by any chance—they turn up outside Russia together, your Schiller and my Lila Barsova, that situation will have to be closely controlled. We could not have a bad story, could we now?''

Martin became very correct. ''Why not, if it's the truth?''

''There is no such thing as the truth, only a set of variants.''

''I couldn't stop Schiller writing about his experiences.''

''No? But then we might have to spoil a beautiful romance. Wherever they are. The price of rehabilitating a national hero will be finding a villain.''

''Or the price of your job, Commissar.''

''Exactly. Now here come the senators. Be pleased to introduce me.''

31

Fyodov Belinsky by now was very drunk. He rolled his ferrety face as if looking for the sun as they sat in a *chaikana* where ancient men played chess. After the landing at Samarkand Schiller had taken care to go with him while Lila found a cheap room. They had hired a taxi together into the old city, where arches of blue glazed tile opened on to stable yards and the domes of repaired mosques.

"I really must be going," Belinsky muttered, cradling his head in his arms.

Schiller ate with his fingers. The garlic-seasoned meat pancake helped to dull the new bottle of vodka, bitter with ash berries, that the investigator had ordered.

"No hurry. Lila has fixed your room."

A red eye from a fresh herring winked at him.

"OK?"

"OK."

In the street-market outside the tea-house the fruit was piled in blocks of color: green and yellow melons, strawberries, oranges, lemons, red apples, black and green bunches of grapes, bananas, pawpaws, in shrieking confusion. There were chickens trussed by the legs, geese crammed into cages, rabbits with bolting eyes, sheep with obscene, fat rumps. Water running down the gutters washed round the piles of debris; an old man was having his head shaved.

In a slurred voice, Belinsky complained, "I have to report to the barracks: the military. The fucking Army, about those little bastards. I am a social historian, not a psychiatrist."

"What bastards?" Schiller asked.

Drinks all round. He paid for a bottle for the old men too, who grinned and scratched.

"Half-castes," Belinsky said.

Plenty of time. Plenty of time. Belinsky belched, his sandy hair flattened with sweat. A Byelorussian, a White Russian from a long way away, ill at ease in the pawn shops of Asia. Even more ill at ease about Afghanistan, where he was detailed to go. Belinsky spat on the floor.

"A shitty country. They hate us." He ran a finger round the collar of his shirt.

"Why bother?"

The puffy eyes looked at him. "What?"

"You're not in the Army. Why do you have to go?"

That was enough to cause a shaky claw on the bottle, refuelling again. The finger came out of his collar and wagged at Schiller. "Orders."

"Ah. The mission." Schiller leaned closer. "My friend, tell me something. What are you going there for?"

Through the open shop front they watched a flock of goats whacked by a boy with a stick, who shouted in high-pitched dialect at Muslim women in trousers and patterned headscarves. He might have been seven or eight. Charlie's and Yuri's age.

Belinsky became idiot-cunning. He seemed to be looking at an eclipse of the sun as he shielded his eyes from the glare.

"Why should I tell you?"

Schiller paid for some nuts, roasted peanuts with salt on the outside shell. They cracked them with their teeth and sucked the salt. It helped the vodka.

"Maybe I could help?"

Belinsky was almost crying, a mother's boy, lost. "Impossible. I have to go."

"Why do you have to go? The war is almost over."

The Russian's eyes were moist now. "I am not in the Army."

"Then what is the problem, comrade? What takes you there?"

In a voice little more than a whisper Belinsky said, "I am a school inspector."

Schiller remembered the man had been drinking since they first met. Drinking because he was afraid.

"A school inspector? In Afghanistan?"

Belinsky nodded sadly. "It is my socialist duty. The Ministry have ordered me to inspect the educational facilities in the refugee camps. And find the boys by Russian fathers."

"But are there any school facilities?"

"No. Of course not. The fact that they do not exist does not mean I do not inspect them. You follow me?"

Small wonder Belinsky drank. Schiller put his hand over the pianist fingers and felt them tremble. Belinsky was out on his feet.

"You need not go."

"Ha ha ha ha ha. I have to suggest arrangements before the war ends."

"Listen. Relax. Drink." Schiller knew his way through now. He could see Belinsky's face white with fright beneath the freckles. "I will make you an offer. I will go in your place."

"You?"

"Why not? I am a journalist," He showed him Barsov's old card.

"*Novy Mir*?" Belinsky's eyes dilated.

"Comrade, let me investigate. On behalf of the Soviet people. The people must know the story, then they will help. Listen." He pressed on the back of Belinsky's hand. "Let me take your place, so that I see these things. The times are changing. We can talk of them now. What are we doing to the children in the name of international socialism? Comrade, let me go for you."

Belinsky stared at Schiller as if he had risen again.

"What would I do?" he worried drunkenly.

"You? You would stay here. Safe in Samarkand, until I return. Then I shall write your report."

A look of wonder flooded the pink of Benlinsky's eyes. "Is that possible?"

"Don't be a fool. I am offering."

"But my report?"

"For God's sake, the report is easy. Tell me what you have to do. You can tell the authorities that you have become unwell. Is that a problem?"

Belinsky was too drunk to think, and his head vibrated from side to side.

"No," he sighed slowly. "I suppose not, my dear friend."
An immense sense of release seemed to blanket his face.

Belinsky was shuddering, petrified with funk: he had
been drinking solidly for at least six hours. Even the ancient
chess players had stopped in mid-game, wondering when he
would collapse. But Belinsky did not fall; some clip in his
rib-cage managed to hold him together, rigidly upright.
Schiller pulled him to his feet and they reeled into the dusty
street. Belinsky began to retch, leaning against a wall. The
street-market did not pause and the sound of his sickness
was lost as the last deals were struck. Two mangy pye-dogs
looked on, one of them with three legs, ready to eat his vomit.

The Russian shook and rolled. A stream of bile ran down
his shirt, yellowish, evil-smelling, and Belinsky made no
attempt to brush it away, sitting collapsed and gasping on a
pile of mud-bricks.

Schiller waited.

In the sun, Belinsky was now the pallor of a dead frog.
The stream from his mouth subsided, the pye-dogs moved
in, and Schiller tried to wipe him down with a piece of
wind-blown paper.

"Better?"

Belinsky looked at him blankly, his eyes refusing to
focus. He would not make Afghanistan.

Somehow Schiller walked him back. Lila had taken two
rooms in an Islamic flop-house in the old city, the Hotel
Tehran, a rabbit hutch propped up by its neighbors where
the communal toilet was a brown floor with a hole. Belinsky
fell on to a charpoy and they left him there, in an alcoholic
coma. He lay on his side with his arms outstretched like a
drowned sailor, his slack mouth open, a monumental drunk.

"He'll be OK. In a couple of days."

Lila showed more compassion. "Are you sure?"

"You must have seen them like this before."

She felt his pulse. "Sometimes they die. In their own sick."

"Not this one. I've cleaned him out."

They went through Belinsky's papers. Letters to a girlfriend
in Moscow Frunze District, two letters from his mother in a
single envelope, his ID card, his Ministry of Education
credentials, his authorization in Afghanistan. In his brief-

case they found the pass to the airbase outside the city, and the ticket to Kabul.

The airbase was south of the city, as Belinsky had explained. A military compound. The wire cage was packed with hardware: aircraft, choppers, rockets, stores, crated, uncrated, stacked, unstacked, camouflaged and in the open. The distant line of the mountains glowed pale in the sunrise. A transport was tipping out conscripts who lined up along the apron, next to an Antonov 32, a flying freighter.

They watched the flights take off while the guardroom examined their papers.

"Orphan run," Schiller said.

The lieutenant in charge nodded. He had seen them come through, bewildered and round-eyed, clutching their cardboard boxes.

"Check in at main reception," he saluted.

Schiller and Lila, the American and the Russian woman who was still Barsov's wife, walked down a stone corridor and entered an ante-room where a sergeant and five signals girls were decoding. The sergeant ran his eyes over Lila, and appreciative grin on his lips.

"Colonel Dorokhov will see you."

A staff room where another lieutenant in a well-pressed grey jacket nodded quickly. No one had asked for their papers once they were through the gates.

"He's in a bit of a mood."

Dorokhov stared at them icily, then smiled at Lila. A busy little man, plump, balding, with a splash of ribbons on his chest. His office showed signs of pressure, a large desk littered with maps, telephones, cipher books.

He flicked through Belinsky's letters. "You say that the school inspector is sick?"

"That's right. I am taking his place. I have come with my wife, who is to make a special report."

Lila smiled at the colonel. "The Central Committee is becoming increasingly concerned at the way that these flights are handled. There is a feeling they may bring discredit . . ."

The colonel was standing up. "There are no grounds for

criticizing the Army. The airlift is one among many military operations, carried out with precision. We are working to orders."

"That is what I hope to say," Lila said smoothly. Schiller had the impression that the colonel's heart wasn't in it, already a smell of defeat about Afghanistan. Noticeably no one had queried their proposal to fly in: there were plenty of seats on the transports.

Colonel Dorokhov stared at them silently, then marched across to a wall displaying the large GRU map of three operational areas: Kabul to the Salang Pass, Qandahar, and Herat. The windows rattled as a jet roared towards take-off. He still held Belinsky's papers.

"What a shambles," he said softly. "So many dead. So many orphans all in the name of the people."

There was a knock at the door: an adjutant and a major entered. They could hear telephones ringing.

"Loading completed," the adjutant said. "Are they to be included?" pointing at Schiller and Lila.

The colonel hadn't finished thinking, but he worried about the boy. "Do you know what you are doing? The Central Committee's interest is commendable, but seeing it on the ground . . . it can be very . . . distressing. You should not take the child."

There was no sign of doubt in Lila's face. Her golden eyes looked at Dorokhov, and she held Yuri's hand.

Airbase to airbase all they needed was clearance.

And Dorokhov hesitated. "I really don't know. The Kabul situation is dangerous. We are not in full control."

"I have to see the children, Colonel."

The adjutant was standing waiting, an obsequious fair-haired young hopeful.

"Most of them have already been taken out." Dorokhov fingered their papers again, trying to articulate the doubt somewhere in his mind.

Schiller said, "I have full authority."

"Yes, yes. But your child?"

Lila stood very still, a slender, intense figure. "We are going to find his father."

The colonel wanted to give in. He sighed, complained

about the war, was conscious of the major fretting, anxious to settle other business.

"I am only human," he said.

"Seats are available?"

The adjutant confirmed. "But hurry up," he said, "or you wait four days for a plane."

Lila's eyes were locked on the colonel, who finally nodded.

32

Jubal Martin sat in a bright saffron room in Moscow—he hated the Embassy décor in Tchaikovsky Street—and yelled down the telephone, "I tell you he's gone. Gone."

At the other end in Washington, DC, Sly Sylvester, foreign editor, looked over his staff list and crossed off a name.

"You reckon so? How come?"

That was ironical, and it hurt. Over the open line, hot-faced, Martin shouted, "All right. All I know is what I say. The stupid prick disappeared. Even our friends say so." Jesus, calling them that, in daytime. "They've been combing Siberia. Take my advice and find another hack."

"Don't worry yourself. I'm sending in Habkirk to fill up the desk. Joe Habkirk from Bonn. Knew Ed in Berlin. Maybe he'll find something that you guys have missed."

Martin nearly threw the telephone at the opposite wall. "Christ. Who do you think I am? Sherlock Holmes?"

"I guess the evidence doesn't point that way."

Away in Washington, Sylvester counted his losses. A temporary interruption of the Moscow copy, a good reporter gone. Irritating little phone calls from Schiller's ex, who was as obsessed as he was. A story somewhere for digging, and Habkirk had been told to dig.

And Martin, on the defensive, relayed all that he knew: the things Mayakovsky had told him in their curiously furtive meetings, the last one "by chance" at the Bolshoi, for which the Russian sent tickets. They had stood under the portico, awaiting their respective cars after *The Rite of Spring*.

"I've called it off," Mayakovsky said. "I can't spend half the summer looking for a lunatic. Think of the expense."

"I didn't think that worried you."

"Well, it does, these days."

So Gorbachev was cutting down on the cost of the KGB. Martin would report that, but what he said was, "How hard did they look?"

The squat KGB chief had glared at him. "We don't do things by halves."

"I appreciate that."

Relenting, Mayakovsky added, "I had a police ring around Akademgorodok, and somehow they got through it. Schiller, the woman, the boy. I think they are together. I warn you that if we find them . . ."

"Good luck to them," Martin said. But he was not as confident as he let Mayakovsky assume.

Now he listened to Washington, Schiller's boss on the *Post* preparing to write him off, and felt a surprising affection for the pig-headed fool who was mad enough to go into Siberia. Maybe he was getting too soft, soft or old. Through the louvered blinds at the window he could see shapes outside, vague, color-washed, across the Embassy courtyard. Bright-eyed young women in the opposite offices unobtainable to sixty-year-olds going home. He felt a pinch of desire, and understood Schiller better, divorced, alone, carrying on with Lila. Let the poor bastard go.

"What did you say?" Sylvester was asking.

"Nothing."

"Nothing? That all you can do?"

"Look. Ed Schiller's not on the Government payroll, he's your baby," Martin said in exasperation. "You want him, you find him. Got that?"

"If I find out what's happened," Sylvester thundered, "I shall make it a hell of a report."

"You do that," Martin retorted. "The State Department would welcome your in-depth views." He slammed the telephone into its yellow cradle, and found himself trembling. To cool his nerves he picked a cheroot and lit it. Then sent for Taylor Sheen, who came in like a tailor's model.

"The KGB tell me that Ed is away. They reckon he's clean through the ring. Probably with Lila as well."

Sheen flashed a grin and whistled. "Jeepers creepers. If that boy makes it . . ."

"How the hell can he?" Martin muttered wearily. "Getting out of Russia without papers is impossible."

Sheen thought for a while. "Sometimes the hard bit's easy; it's the easy bit's hard."

"What the hell does that mean?"

"Well. If he's got the woman with him, and the kid, posing as a family, they could be sold a dummy. Looking for the wrong people. Schiller's problem may be different: not getting out, getting laid."

"Oh for Christ's sake," Martin said, feeling not for the first time that the tiresome Sheen could be right. Then, relenting, "What do you suggest we do?"

"Keep an eye on the crossings," Sheen suggested. "Finland, Turkey, Pakistan. I'm going to alert our stations."

But they hadn't made it yet, Schiller thought, as the Ilyushin touched down on the skid marks of Kabul airstrip. He looked at Lila, sitting tight-lipped. The plane disgorged its passengers: a mixture of Army men, support staff in casual clothes, a few obscure civilians, all of them depressed. The airbase itself was huge, another sprawling collection of war material, replicating Samarkand. Through the kerosene haze they saw the size of the effort. An enormous compound, treble-wired, which seemed to fill the plain with runways, depots, temporary buildings of every shape, among which transport was moving, camouflaged Army trucks, buses, motor-cycles. They lined up outside the aircraft, with Yuri jumping excitedly, the center of attention.

One of the majors who had been on the plane gave him a bar of chocolate, half-melted inside its wrapping. "Why do you bring the boy? This is still bandit country, unless you stay all the time in barracks.''

"We shall stay in the barracks," Lila said sweetly. It seemed to Schiller that she was now an automaton, not wanting to think or talk. Nikky had been like that before they broke up.

They were bussed to a transit lounge, part of the reception building, where the military separated. Once they were inside the base, the American noted, security was relaxed, almost non-existent. Slogans chalked up by squaddies showed that they hoped to go home soon now that the fighting was ending. That meant it should be easier to get away to the frontier.

Schiller retrieved their baggage, two cheap cardboard cases that were more for show than necessity, and they sat by them in a corner, eating tomato rolls.

The airbase direction finder showed that the civilian quarters were on the edge of the wire, prefabricated apartments, inward facing. The blank wall towards the outside was reinforced against attack, the only view was the airfield.

"No place for a boy," the major said again. He had reappeared, brushing his service cap, which had a red and gold staff tab: a polite, unassuming man attached to the artillery. "I have a car outside. Can I give you a lift?"

They accepted the offer, and the major dropped them off at the entrance to one of the apartment blocks. He said goodbye to Yuri, and shook their hands. They stood in the echoing foyer, travel-stained and abandoned, but no one asked why.

"Thank God for the Red Army," Schiller said.

Lila smiled wanly, looking weary. "Why are we here? Where are you taking me?"

We. He hesitated, wanting so much to kiss, not knowing how to break through. "Away from all this," he said, indicating the lounge with its plastic chairs, pot-plants and picture of Lenin. "Any second thoughts?"

Perhaps it was the thought of Alexei Sergevich, or the antiseptic pictures, or something else inside her that made her shudder. She clutched at Yuri's hand as if he were supporting her.

"I have come too far to go back," she whispered.

But did she want to leave with him, and live with him? Schiller had no means of knowing. Russia was still all around them, and someone would ask their business. People were coming through the doors even as they hesitated: off-duty Army personnel, girls who seemed to be nurses, a soldier in a flak jacket and bush hat carrying a roll of cloth. Schiller crossed to the wire-meshed windows and stared out. A helicopter whirred away, carrying rocket pads, circled and moved off crab-wise towards the pall of pollution that lay over Kabul itself. Above and beyond it he could see the tips of the hills through which the road would be heading east into Pakistan. They needed to be on that road.

The soldier removed his hat to wipe his face, tired from the exertion of carrying the heavy brocade. It was shot-silk, a bolt of material looted from some bazaar. A Kamaz jeep was ticking over on the path outside, with two other rolls in the back. Schiller glanced at Lila and saw the same thought in her mind.

The soldier was sweating in his body jacket, and carrying an assault rifle like the one they had concealed at Madeniyet. The gear had made unloading difficult, and he sat down to recover.

It was then that Lila went across and talked.

The boy was uncommunicative, a bullet-headed Ukrainian, but he perked up a little when she said she came from Kiev. Yes, he had been there; Chernobyl had been bad. His family were further south, near Odessa on the Black Sea. Ah, that was country. Orchards and farms and water, not this shit-hole where as soon as you went outside the wire some bastard with a stolen rocket tried to blast your a.p.c.

Yuri stood wide-eyed, looking at the bush knife in the soldier's belt. The flashes on his khaki shirt showed that he was bomb disposal, not easily scared but not imaginative either.

"Was that what happened?"

"No. Not to me. We were just clearing up. They are such lousy shots. Missed the patrol completely: set fire to part of the bazaar."

"Ah." Schiller watched Lila sympathize as she admired the cloth. They knew now where it had come from.

"Plenty more where that was," the disposal man said defensively.

"Is there a market for it?"

He showed the gaps in his teeth, and jerked his thumb up to the ceiling. "You bet. Upstairs."

Somebody up there was a dealer, trading in illicit supplies. The path was clearly well trodden.

Schiller said, "You take that one up. I'll help bring the others in."

The soldier hesitated, but the offer was too good to refuse. He didn't want to be hanging around: he probably wasn't off duty, just sneaking in.

"Why not?" Lila exerted her charm, looking at once ten years younger, managing somehow to say that it would be all right.

"Are you sure, comrade?"

"Of course. You take it up, and we'll get the others in."

He picked up his sun-hat again and shouldered the cloth roll. "Just dump them down there."

They dumped them in the road outside as soon as the soldier had gone. Two more rolls of artificial silk, tipped from the back of the jeep into the dirt.

Schiller moved, and Lila was ready with Yuri. The ignition keys were still in place. He jerked the gears and was off, fast without being crazy, round the airfield perimeter, towards the gate. There was a zig-zag checkpoint. Soldiers in sandy uniforms and bush hats lounging in the sun. A camouflaged truck was coming through, and an ambulance, but no one seemed in a hurry. On the other side of the airfield the civilian quarters were already lost in the haze. A heavy stench of diesel hung in the air and Yuri, tucked down beside them, complained that it hurt his throat.

Schiller said, "We're rolling."

Lila held the boy's hand.

Schiller had no time to explain: the next minutes were crucial. He dared not look behind, fearful of hot pursuit. On the other hand, purloined goods brought in on a duty jeep were asking for trouble: the soldier boy's first job would be to hide the evidence. When he reported the jeep, he would need a better story, and he'd be tempted to wait, in case it turned up again.

"With luck we've got an hour," Schiller said. "Time to get through Kabul."

The duty guard was in no hurry, beckoning them on slowly. Schiller told Yuri to sit up so that he was seen more clearly.

A sunburnt face peered at them. "You taking him out?"

"Any objection?" Lila retorted.

The face became puzzled, then worried. "Where to? It's not safe outside. Rocket attack on the bazaar earlier today." He wasn't stopping, just warning. Anyone going outside was obviously a bloody fool.

"I know. Official visit to the orphanage at the Chaman-i-Houzouri, the place by the race track."

The guard recognized the name, although he still looked doubtful.

"You involved with those war kids?" Still looking at Yuri.

"I'm responsible," Schiller said icily. "Hurry up."

"All right. All right. Keep your hair on. What's the rush?"

"The next flight home. That's what."

The guard scratched his head and was inclined to argue. Beyond the remaining pole barrier Schiller could see the Kabul road, tree-lined, littered with debris.

"Why take the kid with you? Better leave him behind."

It was Lila who rescued them. "Look, soldier, are you in charge of this war?"

"No, ma'am. But I don't think it's wise to take out one of our kids."

She rounded on him. "Oh you don't, do you, comrade? You think we just come here for the good of our health. Is that it? He's going to find his real father. One of your friends maybe."

Schiller understood then that he was still not accepted: in her way she was using him.

The soldier looked embarrassed. A second man was

sauntering across, wondering what the trouble was. Horns began sounding behind them.

"Sorry."

"Come on comrade, hurry up."

There was a commotion now, with Lila standing in the jeep, a trim figure in black.

"I haven't got all day."

"All right." The guard stood up his rifle, glanced perfunctorily at Belinsky's letter-headings and the purple stamps from the Samarkand colonel. It all looked extremely official, including the jeep.

"All right. It's on your head, but you take care of the kid."

He gave them a half-salute, the black and yellow poles lifted and they were through into Afghanistan.

Schiller sighed with relief, but Lila gave nothing away. Afghanistan, an occupied country, was only half-way home.

"Hold your head," he shouted to Lila, as he stepped on the gas. Lila looked nervous, but Yuri laughed with excitement.

"We'll make it," Schiller said, as if nothing could go wrong.

"Perhaps," she answered.

There was a lot of traffic, slow-moving, hauling trailers. Market gardens, then irrigated fields, where urchins tried to sell oranges underneath the shade trees. No sign of fresh fighting as the war drew to its close, leaving its ugly reminders: a rusting troop carrier, the skeletal ribs of a bus, rotors from a crashed chopper, mangled and thrown by the roadside. More abandoned vehicles, old Tata trucks, one of them marked with red crosses. Still there was no pursuit.

Downtown Kabul was in their sights now, mud and concrete slums and feudal faces. Here there were fresh patrols, Afghans in Soviet a.p.c's, even a traffic queue.

They drove unchallenged through the center, along the frothing Kabul river, under the shadow of the Bala Hissar. Afghans in striped chapans and flowing turbans rubbed shoulders with women in purdah. A gunship wheeled overhead and sentries stood on the corners, but no one stopped them.

"I need a drink," Yuri said.

"OK, young man." At the far side of the town Schiller bought oranges and grapes. "How far to the border?"

The Afghan stared sourly out of an unwashed face. "Two hours. Maybe four. Or six. Or eight." He shrugged. "Why bother? It is closed."

"That's my boy," Schiller said.

There was a second road-stall selling dusty kebabs, and he bought them too. They were hungry as wolves, and Lila's face gained a color that Schiller had not seen before as she caught Yuri's excitement. The boy began to sing as they roared along with the canvas sides of the jeep flapping in the slip-stream.

The ramshackle highway headed north-east, along a fertile valley that at first seemed untouched by fighting: apple and citrus orchards and long-needled tamarisk trees. Mulberries and pomegranates grew unattended, the farms had been shattered, the mud buildings punched by gunfire. Mustapha's twisted smile had started somewhere like this, the bitterness that drove a knife into the militiaman's ribs.

He muttered, "Mustapha . . ." and pointed.

"I know."

The valley led into a skeleton country, raked by war, a rock-strewn, dust-grey landscape between the mountains. A burnt-out landscape, where the fields had been ploughed by half-tracks and the minefields were marked by roadsigns.

"Eddie I'm scared," she said suddenly.

"Don't worry, honey. We're almost home."

"I don't like it." The sun went behind the cloud. "I smell trouble," she said. Vultures picked at a carcass outside a shuttered stall.

He grinned. "You don't want to go back?"

"I can't," she said.

An Army truck roared down the other side with its hatches battened, heading back to Kabul.

What should have been a gas station was now a heap of rubble from which a Coca-Cola sign swayed.

"America here we come."

"I'm not sure," she said.

The road narrowed again, a gorge through outcrops of ferrous rock, stained red with rust. A pillbox at the entrance was empty, and next to it a fire-blackened tank with its cannon blown off.

The sun shut down as they entered the defile, and Lila shuddered. The helicopters had gone, the mountains darkened the skyline.

33

That evening they abandoned the jeep and made for the hills in case the Army came looking, and began to pass by the farms which the fighting had wrecked. There was no food to buy, but the people seemed indifferent to whether or not they were Russians, conditioned by years of war to the strangeness of refugees. Lila looked drained, as if she moved through a nightmare, but it was Yuri who saved them by scrounging scraps of chapatis somewhere in the mud-walled settlements, half-tenanted, that remained.

They climbed for hours in the valley, a desolate place thick with dust and covered with struggling goat-thorn. The road through to Jalalabad was dangerous bandit country, littered with the signs of violence, pock-marked with old explosions and broken hardware.

"I need you both," Schiller said as they huddled together, sharing the last of their rations. "Can you manage?"

He saw the bones of her face as she turned it away, and knew how she had been bruised.

Lila smiled. "I'll manage. Always." She glanced around for Yuri, who was waiting to be comforted, as the sun went down and they faced a night of cold.

"I want water," he pleaded. His tongue was swollen, but the plastic drum they carried was almost empty.

"As soon as I can," Schiller promised. He could see Lila's eyes, wondering why the boy should suffer as they dragged him with them.

"I need water."

"Please wait, Yuri," she begged.

They had reached the top of a fold of rocks which looked across a series of gullies and ravines, through which the road was threaded. And still there was no sign of life, as if refugees themselves were an act of nature, so commonplace that no one bothered.

"Mama. I can't swallow."

His face was black against the setting sun. It seemed to Schiller like the edge of the world.

And then there were men beside them, rising out of the rock, two men festooned with hardware, grenades, ammunition, knives. Turbaned medieval bandits, offering the boy a goatskin of brackish water.

Yuri drank greedily and they pulled it away. "Too much," the leader said in English. "Bad."

Schiller understood they were friends, at least to the boy, who once again had saved them. Two men, crowding round, lean and dark-skinned, with bearded faces. He could not understand their Afghani but the leader, Hafizullah, spoke English as he led them away, a bird-like man cross-belted with pistols and knives beneath his stolen combat jacket.

"You sturdy boy. Good," he said to Yuri, and flashed his golden teeth.

They were moving higher into the hills, reminding Schiller again of Mustapha and his party on the other side of the mountains. Each person made his own bed, the American thought, and these men could cut their throats as easily as butchering a goat. But they did not; they merely asked them to follow.

"Russsky?" Hafizullah said when they stopped for breath. He seemed to be limping badly

"*Nyet*. No." Schiller's lungs were gasping from the near vertical climb as he tried Russian and English.

Hafizullah shook his head. "Yes. Russsky."

Schiller ignored him, talking to Lila and Yuri as they collapsed beside him. He wanted her, he wanted Yuri, the rest did not matter. It was getting cold and dark, and the little boy squeezed beside them, seeking warmth.

"Not Russian," Schiller announced, and pulled out the

tattered passport that he had kept with him. "Uncle Sam. American."

They seemed to understand. Hafizullah embraced him, then Lila and the boy. Yuri began to sniff, trying to stop himself crying. His body felt cold, and he was hungry again.

"Boy needs blanket," Schiller said.

"There soon," Hafizullah replied as the daylight faded. He pointed to a cleft in the rocks, and began to remove the thorn bush pulled over to conceal it. The cave was a kind of base, lined with ammunition boxes, constructed high up on the hillside, impossible to see from the air. Thirty yards along in the cliff, a half-opening covered by scrub. Even when they were on top of it Schiller could not be sure.

He held the boy's hand as he and Lila followed Hafizullah along a narrow ledge and into the recess, which was no more than two meters high. They found Yuri a sheepskin, rancid and freshly scraped, which they laid on the floor, inviting him to sleep. There was no fire, no food, but the little boy curled up at once. The Mujahedin sat by themselves, talking softly, while Schiller and Lila waited, by the light of a candle wedged into the rocks.

He put his arm round her, but she was very still, almost rigid.

"I love you."

"I no longer know what that means." She moved her head away. "I should not have let you lead me, me and Yuri. Now what have we come to: refugees at these men's mercy?"

"We'll be OK. We're on our way. Where would you rather be? With Alexei Sergevich?" He was still confident, and she saw Yuri's faith in him.

She was silent for a long time, sitting with him in the cave where the shadows made them all illusions, Schiller the American lunatic, the bat-figures of the two Afghanis, even the boy.

"What would I do in your country, if we ever reach it?"

"Let's get there first," he said.

The Mujahedin handed them scraps of bread and a few dried dates, then began a game with sticks and dice. They seemed both uncaring and tireless, as if the strangers were incidental, but Lila roused herself.

"You must help us," she said to Hafizullah, in English.

"Help?" He smiled. Perhaps there was a price.

Needing a future for Yuri, she had made up her mind. "We go to Pakistan. You take us there."

Hafizullah shook his head, and his eyes rolled. "Too far. Too long. You safe here. War kaput. We kill more Russkys now."

Schiller heard Lila cry, and moved to comfort her. There was no divide. At that moment they were as close as at any time since Madeniyet. He put his hand out to her, searching for physical contact, touching her dirty hair. By turns grieving and passionate, now she seemed to flow to him, oblivious to them all, the watching guerrillas, the sleeping child. They met in a long kiss, and this time she did not pull back.

"Hold me," she said, shivering.

Schiller held her tightly, never wanting to let go.

And Hafizullah stared in silence. Then broke the spell. "Woman. Son," he said, pointing. "No good here."

Lila addressed him slowly, in halting English. "You must help us." She scrambled to her feet. Schiller saw Hafizullah eyeing her. "Please." It was almost an offer.

A chuckle started somewhere inside Hafizullah's hollow chest as he and his companion closed round her and she disappeared from view. Schiller tensed, aware of their eyes and hands, pawing as close as they dared. Russky. Amerikantsky. They knew now, they understood that the strangers were lovers. He heard her talking softly, then a silence as the figures parted. In the half-light water dripped from the limestone.

Hafizullah clasped his arms round Lila and then released her. He pushed the other man away and steered her across to Schiller. Yuri began to stir as Hafizullah laughed, laughed more at himself than anyone, some private and bitter joke.

"You lucky man. OK woman." He slapped his ribs.

"Pakistan," Schiller repeated doggedly.

"Money? You give us money? American dollars?"

Schiller had nothing to give. "Maybe."

Hafizullah waited to see if there was a better bargain, more guns to fight with, and it was Lila who answered. She nodded. "Yes. American money."

Schiller's ability to deliver that promise put her in his debt. Hafizullah's face split into sly humor.

"OK, memsahib. My comrade."

They stayed in the cave two days and made the border in seven, travelling mainly by night, hiding up in the day. The Mújahedin supply route ran through a series of passes where each stopping place was a depot like the one they had been taken to. Existence was a diet of gruel and cold chapatis, washed down by water, and their clothes were in rags. Lila maintained her silence, intent on survival; they communicated by signs, body language; squatting, primitive, in a country of rocks.

Hafizullah asked no questions and made no demands, a scarred man directing his hatred against the sky, cursing the MIGs which howled across the valleys. Hawks wheeled in the silence after the planes had gone. They dared not move until dusk, when they would scramble lower and trek along the goat-tracks. At dawn they would seek the high ground again, eat a handful of raisins, drink brackish water from plastic bottles, and try to sleep before the first planes skimmed the hills. Lila grew fragile and her skin was blistered, while Yuri cried with fatigue.

"How long?" he whispered.

"Soon. Soon," was all Schiller could say as the days wore on, trying to give the boy comfort. "Keep going, kid."

At noon the planes would patrol again, and then once more in the evening. A false move on the hillside, any mistaken sign, would bring a flurry of gunfire rattling the stones of the wilderness.

Hafizullah shook his fist at the departing aircraft, drew a line again across his throat and grimaced. On the fourth day his composure cracked: they saw the pain in his face as he stretched out his leg, pulled back his striped robe and rolled up the loose pyjamas. Underneath was a mass of bandages, yellow and blood-soaked, which he slowly peeled off. A festering, dark blue wound where a bullet had passed through the calf, tearing the muscle. Damage maybe three weeks old, treated with a herbal poultice that had kept gangrene at bay but left a dark knuckle of meat. Yet he had walked and climbed on it for a week since they first met, and Schiller had never suspected such a suppuration. Hafizullah had seemed impervious to pain or tiredness. Lila gasped as she saw the raw flesh, shielding it from her son's eyes.

"Bad. Hospital," Schiller said.

Hafizullah revealed the stumps beneath the gold caps on his teeth.

"You pay?"

Schiller knew then why Hafizullah was taking them across the passes. American money for treatment. The Afghani re-bound the leg with the same pus-stained bandages, nodded, slid into sleep.

In spite of the wound, Hafizullah urged them on, night by night, heading towards the frontier. On the eighth morning they reached it and lay up on the hills examining the ribbon of road that weaved through to Landi Kotal. They reconnoitered the barbed wire, the barriers across the road, the tanks and gun emplacements. A chopper was up in the sky, and the Government troops were dug in as if they expected attack. They could see the glitter of windscreens on the far side of the border beyond the poles and the minefields.

Schiller pointed to the damaged leg, and promised, "Pakistan. Hospital. Soon."

The bony shoulders shrugged. Once he had decided to walk, the Afghan would carry on. Either he died from the leg, or it got better: they lay in a hole in the earth, alive or dead. But Schiller and Yuri now shared a desperate impatience as they saw the border, tantalizingly close. Lila was more fatalistic, malnourished and exhausted, and he feared for her strength. Vehicles puffed up dust around the frontier but the real hazard was foot mines, which made the last mile dangerous. Hafizullah picked out tiny movements camouflaged into the pass, and held up his fingers like aerials. "Listening post. One, two, three."

That night they moved crab-wise, north then east over two ranges of hills, a five-hour scramble around the outposts, and emerged through the minefields. On the following morning they were in another defile, precipitous, empty and waterless, under the same burnt-metal sun, but his time they stood in the open.

"Pakistan," Hafizullah said. Lila sat down and wept with Yuri in her arms. They waited for the Army.

The first jeep appeared at midday, a patrol directed by a spotter plane which circled like a bee. Schiller wanted to shout, "We made it. We made it," but Lila was too tired to respond.

The soldiers picked them up without comment, as if that too was commonplace, and they began the drive to Landi Kotal, where the cooking fires were being lit as they arrived. The town seemed a huddle of refugee shacks, the debris of the war: cripples and children, undefined bundles in rags, smoky paraffin lamps and scavenging dogs. But they had come out.

The Army moved through at speed, hooting and cursing. They were driven through a gate in a high wall, beyond which a tin-roofed building fronted a defunct fountain. Chickens scratched in the courtyard, but the house still retained some pride, tessellated stairs to the verandah, broken urns on the steps, and inside were high cool rooms.

It was there they found at last someone willing to listen. The political agent from Peshawar, Aslam Khan, a Brevet Major, made no bones about his feelings, hating the Russians almost as much as Hafizullah, and Mustapha before him. A fierce, traditional Muslim, the presence of Lila unnerved him.

"Why did she come?" he demanded.

"She came with me."

Their eyes met, Aslam Khan's as dark as used oil. His cropped hair was streaked with gray, sticking up from his forehead, a porcupine.

"And the boy?"

Yuri was happy now. A lukewarm bottle of Fanta was a new and unnerving taste.

"He is my son," Lila said.

"Where is your husband?"

Schiller tried to explain, but explanations were banal. They were dog-tired. They were there: that was enough. And he had a debt to pay as Hafizullah squatted in the corner.

"Hospital," Schiller said fiercely. "The U.S. Government pays." They owed him that, at least.

"You very lucky fellows. Lucky fellows," Aslam Khan murmured, with his uneasy charm. "Nobody gets out of Soviet Union unless the Reds want it."

Hafizullah's gums grinned.

With a new ten-day beard, in the jacket from Akademgorodok, Schiller looked like an old pillar, a tree-trunk, a phenomenon rivalling Barsov now.

"We need plane tickets West."

The brown hands waved, offering sympathy. "In good time. In time."

Lila was a weight on his arm, her tiredness pulling him down.

"No. Now. Tomorrow."

The major's Adam's apple was like a piece of cork in his throat. He put out a restraining hand. Black hairs grew on the back. "I must ask explanations."

Schiller was adamant. "I will talk to the CIA."

The major smiled with relief. "In that case—" the hand waved"—is no problem. CIA ready and waiting."

34

"They got by," Jubal Martin screamed down the corridor in the Commercial building. "They made it. The son-of-a-bitch made it." He was running and sweating, belly flopping over his belt, his puffy face creased in pleasure. He hugged himself by the armpits, yelped in excitement, and ran into Sheen.

"Made what?"

Martin pushed him into the safe room, slamming the door. "Ed Schiller's in Peshawar, Pakistan."

Sheen punched the air. "Jesus fucking Christ."

"Holy Bible. Linaker just got a message. The bastard turned up with the woman and boy."

"How did he make it?"

"We don't know yet. Just a message that he got out."

Sheen gave a clenched fist salute, slowly grinning. "Told you, man. Wow."

Now they were slapping each other. Sheen thought Martin would kiss him. "Jesus," Martin said, "what a story. I had the feeling that guy was a winner."

The realization stopped Sheen in his tracks. "What story?"

"The way they pulled back Barsov. Ed Schiller visits the wife. Little kid too. The big lie about human rights," Martin burbled, seeing his retirement vindicated, going out on a high. "Rescue mission."

Sheen took off his coat. "Hey, wait a minute." He sat down with a frown, elbows lining the table. "Who we going to glamorize? Us or them?"

Martin stopped bouncing, recalling Mayakovsky's chilling remarks inside the Kremlin. Barsov rehabilitated, the KGB heads starting to roll, Mayakovsky saving his skin. If Barsov was going to be reinstated post-glasnost, the Reds could still get back at Schiller, one way or the other. One way would be to discredit him, the other a poisoned umbrella.

"So . . . ?" he asked more soberly.

"Remember something Jubal . . . what about us? What if Schiller suggests we let 'em take Barsov back? That business in Berlin."

Martin paled; the perspiration now looked unhealthy. "He wouldn't do that?"

Sheen gave the old, superficial superman smile. "No? Maybe his memory's failing?"

Martin's good humor faded, remembering the offer of the handgun, Sheen's mesmeric suggestion that they rubbed out Barsov and pinned that one on the Russians. "Aw, Christ . . ."

"Getting out is no big deal, no story these days. No hype for Ed." There was a hint of self-defence.

Martin sucked the end of his glasses; underneath his eyes were pouched, a tortoise head.

"Anyways, he's survived."

"Yeah. Like I feared."

They contemplated uncertainly, and Martin picked absent-mindedly at the cork wall tiles, straightened the picture of the President.

"Langley will want to know why. Sexton Legros didn't want Barsov at all; how will he take to Schiller's running off with the wife?" Martin mused.

"Fuck Legros. All we got to do is to work this one into the ground. It's just a routine little story, nothing more. Rogue reporter screws Barsov's wife. Reds let 'em go. Interesting: nothing orgasmic," Sheen declared.

"But the *Washington Post* will want to spread it," Martin said cautiously. "Bradlee likes a crusade."

Sheen shook his head.

"Not if we work on Sylvester. He's pissed off with Schiller; he's dropped him off the payroll."

"Meaning?"

"Meaning we have to persuade him not to take Ed up, in the interests of Uncle Sam."

"How come?"

"Do we really want Schiller to lay the CIA connection on the line, and report our position on Barsov?" Sheen could be more careful than his appearance suggested. He wanted a career.

"Supposing Ed takes the story elsewhere? Like that guy Wright in Australia?"

"Well. I guess we'll have to forestall that when we know what he's up to with this hooker."

"Is that so?" Martin felt his age again, trapped in a game he should have left.

Sheen tipped back his chair, the old style, running his hands over the slicked-back hair.

"We got one more option."

Martin wondered. "Yeah?"

"Yup. Ed's ex-wife is hanging on. Remember that neurotic little pussycat, waiting some place in New York? That sort don't give up. She's got Ed's boy too.''

Not for the first time, Martin wondered what kind of crazy logic went on in Sheen's mind.

''Hanging on? What the hell for?''

Sheen smiled silkily. ''Always keep a few marked cards. I reckon Ed's uxorious—ain't that the word?—so he needs women, and she needs men. The fact that he's got another one don't make her less interested. Otherwise what the hell did she come out here for?''

Gloom descended, as Martin's euphoria evaporated. Taylor Sheen complicated things. If he hadn't alerted the station in Pakistan they wouldn't even have known. Schiller might not be a hero, after all.

''But Ed will go back home and spill the beans . . .''

Sheen wagged a finger. ''Oh no. First we find him a safe house, and do a debriefing job. I need your authority.''

Martin had to accept that; it was in the book.

''OK by me.''

''Great.'' Sheen smiled.

The rusty lines of flat-wagons outside the window seemed to go on for ever. Schiller woke to the noise of the railway, scarcely remembering the drive to this white-walled bungalow in Peshawar. He was in his underclothes, covered by a sheet on a charpoy. It was already hot, the flies were moving over the stained plaster, and he was on his own.

Lila. His clothes were on a chair beside the bed, washed and neatly arranged.

It came back now. He had slept for twelve hours, utterly exhausted, taken to the guest-house overlooking the Cantonment Station. Lila and Yuri would be next door: she had picked separate beds. He slipped on his trousers and tiptoed across the room. A dozing soldier was cradling a snub automatic on a chair outside and jerked awake as he emerged.

Schiller put a finger to his lips and the man nodded.

In the room next door two heads were on the pillow, and his heart beat a little quicker to see them there. Her hair lay loose on the covers, while Yuri's head was turned towards her, on her shoulder. They had come through so much that Schiller felt they were his own.

He returned and finished dressing. There was a basin and washstand and he made a cold water toilet. Outside through the shuttered window the trains clanked past. A cover guard lounged in the sun. He pulled back the shutters and saw a scarf of bougainvillaea wrapped round the outer walls.

He felt refreshed, rested, as he let Lila sleep on. There would be time for plans, for readjustments. He had three lives to sort out, not just one, and Asia was not the place. Russia was closed to him now; all that he had to do was fly back home, see if he had a job, explain what he meant by America, and write a book on the past. It seemed so easy that he was worried.

There was a scratch at the door and an Indian in a linen suit, off-white and creased, accompanied a tray of food: pawpaw, fruit juice and scrambled eggs. With him came the political major Aslam Khan, who perched on the end of the charpoy, and said politely, "This is Mr. Mendoza. You will know him, I think. Do you mind if I wait?"

Schiller had never heard of him, so Mendoza showed him a card, as if he was selling computers, to prove he was on the payroll, one of the firm. A middling man with an ivory skin, dressed in an open-necked shirt, blue-chinned, Anglo-Indian, half-way accent.

They shook hands. Mendoza's eyes were brown seaweed polyps, his features carved from soft wood.

"You have amazed us."

Schiller's hand rasped his beard, he picked at it like a bird searching for crumbs. Beside Mendoza's tailoring he looked a freak from Skid Row.

"You amaze me too," he said. "Getting to know so quickly."

Mendoza accepted the compliment. "No problem, Mr. Schiller. We were told to watch out. All posts had a description over a week ago. I find you fitted."

"What did it say?"

Mendoza shrugged. "You, and maybe the lady. And the little boy."

The mood of optimism with which Schiller had awoken

was dwindling now, replaced by unexpected doubt. If they had known he was coming, known or assumed, only Jubal Martin's outfit on Kutuzovsky Prospekt could have issued that identikit. That coon-dog Sheen, running about after smells. A sour taste in Schiller's mouth. He watched Mendoza watching him. They were the sort of eyes that you walked on in rock-pools, and the Indian was wheezing asthmatically, nervous of close inspection. Schiller began to wonder if their exit from Russia could have been assisted.

"Clap your hands if you want more *char*," the major suggested. "Even coffee."

All Schiller wanted was information, but the main question was in his mind: whether the Agency had linked with the KGB, back in Berlin, and were in league with it now. Somehow the rules were changing.

"Listen, old boy. . ." Mendoza squelched into a chair and introduced a note-book. The ring-binder flashed in the sun. "I need your story, from the start."

Schiller struggled with indifference. Nothing mattered to him now, except to live with Lila, when she could understand. Nothing, he said.

"What was that?"

"Nothing. My thought. What do you want to know?"

It took a long time, retelling, replaying the agonies, interrupted by trains. They all had a cup of tea, milky and sweet, which the major sucked through his moustache. Schiller took it stage by stage, from the first meetings in Moscow to the Berlin hijack, and the flight through Russia into Afghanistan. Exhausting to recall.

There was a long silence when he ended. Finally, Mendoza said, "What do you plan to do?"

Schiller listened for sounds next door. "Go home. Live with Lila, if she'll have me. Find myself another job." ·

Mendoza waggled his head. "That should not be too difficult." He paused. "But an awkward story to publish, eh? What do you say—collusion?"

Schiller had not yet decided. Suddenly they were vulnerable, the whole nest of intelligence ants into which he had stumbled . . . he realized what was in his powers; and Mendoza was there for a reason. Before they could move further, Lila came in. Ignoring the others, Schiller held her to him, feeling the heat of her body. She was dressed in loose cotton pyjamas and an Indian blouse that someone had found for her, washed green muslin against the once-pale skin, now darkened by exposure. He realized how thin she had grown, her features stretched to the bone as if she'd survived a disease, her hair still sticky with dust. He brushed it back from her forehead.

"You must come home with me," he whispered. "You are safe now."

Her eyes reflected love and fear and uncertainty, as she stared at Mendoza. Another train shattered the peace, flickering by the windows.

It was Mendoza who spoke. "I would like a written statement in your own words. A deposition."

"In time," Schiller retorted. "I'll write it up in Washington."

It broke the spell. Major Khan was on his feet, reaching for his swagger stick. Mendoza consulted his notebook.

"I have another thing to tell you, sir."

"What?"

"It's not yet a question of going to the United States. You have to report in person some place. I have to ensure debriefing."

A dull pain in Lila's eyes, a kind of despair.

"Report where?"

Mendoza shook his head like a dog shaking water. "I have to arrange. Take you to special place."

"Where?"

"Oh, not to worry. Just for check-up."

"Look. It says here. My orders. No choice. Sorry. Geneva, Switzerland."

"Europe? Ridiculous."

"No. It says so."

"Tell them to fuck off, whoever they are. We're heading back to the States. I have a U.S. passport." Schiller had carried it with him all that time, along with the remaining dollars. It was there in his jacket.

Major Khan was smiling again. "I'm so sorry. It is confiscation. For the moment only."

"And Mrs. Barsov," Mendoza added, "has no passport at all. Sorry."

Angrily, Schiller stood facing them, with Lila beside him. "What kind of firm is this?"

"Please, very sorry." Mendoza seemed embarrassed. "But one more thing to say." He hesitated. "I'm not sure whether it helps."

Schiller waited, but Mendoza was looking at Lila.

"I regret to tell you. I'm very sorry. We have another report. It says that Mr. Barsov is dead."

35

"How can I live with you?" she said to Schiller. "I failed Alexei Sergevich. Abandoned him in that place."

The sense of loss was pervasive. As they flew out of Pakistan, escorted by Mendoza, the knowledge of Barsov's death sat in Lila's face as she stared at the clouds.

"You saved yourself, and Yuri."

"I saved your skin."

In Istanbul they changed planes, Mendoza said goodbye, and the USAF took over. They boarded a Douglas transport bound for Frankfurt that had been diverted to make an unscheduled stop. "Backyard exit: U.S. newsman leaps the Curtain" he read in the *Herald Tribune*. He could not find a *Post*.

A U.S. medic was with them now, monitoring Lila's state of mind. In a nightmare of grief she seemed to be hovering between myth and reality, and Schiller knew he could not touch her, so fierce was her profile. In their separate ways neither Ed nor Yuri understood the hell she was living through. Yuri was the one who held on, curious and unafraid, and the bond between them grew stronger. Yuri in red pants and sneakers, a little boy on an adventure with the tall

American who had come to the rescue; but his Lila, in the
gray skirt and jacket that someone had given her in Lahore,
what did he know of her?

As they flew over the Alps the sun turned the tips of the
mountains a strange pearly blue and flashed on the lakes like
a mirror, but Lila seemed frozen in space.

"All that time . . . those deaths . . ." she muttered once.

"Tell me, Lila. Try and get it out of your mind."

But what was she really thinking? As he looked at her
beauty he told himself she would recover when time stopped
being suspended, in their new life.

The medic was whispering in his ear. "Let her sleep, let
her rest. Post-traumatic conditions take a long time."

"OK," he said. "OK. Don't push me."

"You take over the boy. She'd like that," the medic said.

"Why are we going to Switzerland, and not America?"
Yuri was asking. "You said America."

"Sure. It's on the way." But the doubts in Schiller's
mind were niggling. Those same bastards who had let him
down in Moscow and Berlin still would not let him go. The
debriefing was to be in Europe, where Solzhenitsyn and the
others had gone when they first came out. Perhaps Lila
would mend better there, Schiller hoped, in the sanatorium
air, while he gave his account to Martin and the Agency.

"Why is it always so busy?" Yuri asked as they touched
down.

His nose was pressed to the window of the big Citröen
whisking them from the airport in Geneva along the Quai du
Mont Blanc, up into the classy suburbs on the road to
Lausanne, where leafy villas hid in the trees.

"It's like that, I guess, over here," Schiller said,
remembering the emptiness of Siberia. "All the time."

Yuri wriggled with excitement. His whole world had
changed. From Siberia to Switzerland was a journey into
magic, and he pressed Schiller's hand while his mother sat
silent, looking at them both. Schiller felt he knew the boy
better, had lived with him more intensively, than his own child.

A lieutenant-colonel and a civilian doctor, Mike Helman
and Gus MacPherson on their name tags, were waiting
inside the rest house. Helman, a tall thin paramedic on

detachment from the Airborne in Bavaria; MacPherson from Vermont, who said that he was on contract. Almost before Schiller knew it they were shut up inside, surrounded by psychoanalysts. The villa Panama: a neutral country. Lila saw the white coats and shuddered, and he knew that she was remembering State Hospital Number Three. The rest house was lost in a woodland behind a wall, with closed-circuit cameras on the corners. It might just as well be a nut-house. The medical checks began.

Schiller was separated from Lila and the boy. "Just for a while," they said, "while we assess the problems."

"I've got no problems," he answered, and MacPherson smiled, a neat man with gold-rimmed spectacles, a freckled face, fortyish.

They tested his blood and urine, heart and lungs, checked over the scabs on his body, pronounced him physically fit. Then they turned to his mind, stretched him on a day-bed while Helman made notes as MacPherson asked the questions, and young nurses brought fruit drinks.

"I want to see Lila," he said.

"OK. OK."

"Now."

"OK. Just let's finish it off. We got to get the background."

"There is no goddam background. Only a God-awful balls-up with Barsov dead."

MacPherson smiled. "Relax. No one is going to blame you. You came through the hard way."

"Relax!" Schiller was sitting up, as heavy as iron. "All I want to do is go home."

"And where is that, Ed?" MacPherson wondered. "New York, or Washington, or Iowa?" Silkily, he added, "Nicola is still in New York. With your boy, in case you wondered. We checked her out."

It was intended to be a blow, and it hurt, but Schiller was not deflected.

"Wherever Lila decides."

"That's a little bit obsessional, Ed. Who says she wants you?"

"That's not your business."

"No. I guess not." MacPherson sighed.

He went for a walk round the grounds, MacPherson trailing, watching the windows in case Lila appeared. But she had vanished under a separate inspection. "After all," MacPherson said, "she's still a Soviet citizen. A displaced person."

Displaced? Schiller felt the same himself, walking down paths where laurel bushes had been clipped into order. A gardener raked the gravel, and did not look up. The air had a softness, a warmth that slowly mended his mind as the days lingered, but he was still in a no man's land, living on hand-outs. Where was he, who was he now, he asked himself. A man who had started with Barsov and ended up taking his wife. If she would have him.

MacPherson seemed to read his mind. He stopped and polished his glasses. "Take your time, pal," he said. "There's no rush, Ed."

What did they want, he wondered, now that they had the story? There was no miracle disclosure, no revelation: why not just let him go, release him to Lila?

"All in good time," MacPherson responded. "I know what hell is like. I've wintered in Vermont." In the lily pond, goldfish swam round and round.

On the fourth day Lila returned. "She's joining us for the meal tonight," MacPherson said, "and then I'll leave you, so's you can get back together. Mike has taken little Yuri into town. The kid wants to visit the movies. Can't keep the boy holed up while we straighten things out."

"Straighten what?"

MacPherson looked dogged. "You, Ed, of course. You must know that. Your conduct ain't been exactly normal."

"No I don't," Schiller growled.

But Lila came in just then in a dark dress with her hair washed, drawn back with a red ribbon, paler, younger than he imagined. As she entered, bewildered after so long and so much, MacPherson rose from his chair in the panelled room at the side of the villa where the reading lights cast pools of brightness.

Schiller's feelings could not wait. He hurried across. "Oh Lila, Lila."

She hesitated, a slight resistance, a sense of wanting churned into a single gesture as she held his hands.

"Eddie," was all she said.

MacPherson cleared his throat. "Come on now. How about drinks?" Unlocking an elaborate cabinet he displayed many bottles, but she shook her head.

The meal was an anticlimax, mostly in silence, the three of them sitting together, MacPherson a father-confessor watching them politely. Lila seemed to be floating, disengaged, and Schiller found the small talk died. The stained pine of the room enfolded them; outside through the French windows the woodland stretched to the wall. It was another prison.

Schiller accused them.

"No. No. Don't say that." MacPherson smiled, his spectacles glittering. "Think of this as a guest-house. While you both get straightened out."

"Keeping us under surveillance?" Barsov too had gone for rest and treatment.

"Aw, come on, Ed. You got a future to go to, when you're ready." He put down his coffee-cup as if relieved it was over. "Look. I'll leave you two exiles alone."

Exiled and alone? With the recorders on somewhere, that was for sure, Schiller mused, and did not care. Two figures in light and shadow, in the warm air, undisturbed. He leaned across and touched her arm. The room was a dark bubble, old furniture from some Swiss burgher, inherited with the house, blue Delft plates on the walls, shining primly. He found it hard to engage her, to jump across the gap.

Lila turned, looked across the empty dishes.

"We have to start somewhere," he said. "How about now?"

A slow, sad smile overtook her. "A death is not something you can forget." Her hands folded in her lap.

"I know." Schiller felt confused and awkward. "But it was really over a long time ago. You know that. Yuri understands it."

Deftly the local maid removed their cups, asked if he wanted brandy. Schiller drank with relief, finding the closed room oppressive. He pointed to the garden beyond.

"How about walking some place?"

"Not now. I'm tired, Eddie. When will Yuri be back?"

"Soon, I guess."

"I must talk to him," she said. He noticed how small her fingers were. Not at all relaxed.

"Let him alone."

"He's Alexei Sergevich's son."

What future for the dispossessed, Schiller wondered, whether Lila or Yuri, or for that matter himself. Could he ever convince her?

As if she divined his thoughts, she said, "What can I do now? I am stateless."

Schiller was standing, walking around the table, putting his arms on her neck, whispering, "Live with me. Lila. Lila."

He touched the line of her collar-bone and felt her tremble.

"Alexei . . ."

"Alexei Sergevich is dead. We have to find a new tune."

The maid was returning again to refill his glass, and he did not care.

"I am lost without Russia."

"Listen, Lila. You do not understand. Now we have come together, I can never let go."

She did not move. Yes and no were both impossible. He had a sense that she pitied him, felt he was seeking a replacement for his own wife and son, even that he had used her.

"You can. You must . . . I cannot think . . . in this prison."

Freedom too was a lock-up, the room shadowy with an ill-defined menace. Her throat arched as she tilted her head, questioning.

"How will you live? Are these people paying you?" There was concern and disbelief in her voice.

"No," he said fiercely. He would not live on hand-outs. He had a book to complete, a skill that he would trade. "Lila, darling, listen. Back in the States, everything will be different . . ."

"I cannot forget my past."

"Of course not, but you will build layers over it."

"Impossible."

"No. Just take your time."

He thought she might snap at him, row with him, and would have welcomed it, but she was silent. He wanted to help and could not; instead he walked to the doors leading into the garden and opened them. The evening air was sultry and at the end of the gravel drive a skein of mist lurked in the pine trees. It was not yet dark, but the early stars were in the sky and someone was burning a bonfire. He glanced back to Lila and saw her staring at him. What was he to her, except a problem? And yet they had come this far against the odds, and Yuri was relying on him.

Schiller began to reinvent the wheel. His own job needed securing; he wondered what Sly Sylvester would be saying now they found he had made it. Had they forgiven him for five weeks' silence, and continued to pay him? Another query for the morning, but above all how could he help Lila to find a life, a kind of future? Lila sitting like a statue.

Unable to break through her thoughts, he closed the door behind him and stepped outside. He could feel her watching, but he made no gesture. The air enmeshed him: somewhere far off there was a sound of dance music, someone playing a radio, otherwise nothing. Yet there were shadows, in the walk and the trees, and as he stood there one of them moved towards him.

It was Helman, the military man, incognito in a dark jacket and soft shoes. His long, raw face loomed in the twilight, not unpleasant but intruding. Schiller could see the square-cut Army hair-style.

"You OK?" Helman said.

"Sure. Do I have to have a bloody nursemaid?"

Helman shuffled closer. "My apologies."

Schiller waited as if expecting him to disappear, but he did not.

"We've got to take care of you," Helman stated.

"For Christ's sake it's like a prison. All I want to do is go home."

"Sure. We know. You will." Helman was only vaguely reassuring as he fell into step on the path. Turning, Schiller glanced back to the yellow light in the room. It shone on the

central table and slanted across the floor. The maid was
clearing the dishes but Lila had vanished. Schiller almost
began to wonder if she had ever been there, but Helman
interrupted his thoughts.

"She needs time," he said. "That girl's at the end of her
tether."

"The sooner you stop this charade, the sooner she'll get
things straight."

Helman said, "I'll walk you down to the gate."

They strode together in the tightening half-light and the
villa dwindled behind them to the size of a doll's house.
The wall around the estate was further off than Schiller
thought, but through the tunnel of trees they could see a
small lodge at the end, with the guard there. As Helman
came up he emerged from the box, a U.S. marine in mufti,
carrying a side-arm.

"All quiet?" Helman challenged.

"Sir!"

Outside, through the padlocked gates, Schiller could see
the road to Lausanne, shining like wet coal. The urge was to
run and run: he wanted to be on it, going someplace with
Lila that he had not yet worked out. He felt angry. Baffled.
All this for a woman who would not, could not . . . unattainable
as a picture. A smell of burnt leaves; the guard saluting
Helman and disappearing. And Helman himself nudging his
arm.

"Let's go back."

Schiller said, "How long must this go on?"

The Army man smiled. "Until I'm told you can go."

That night, and the following days, Schiller had to recognize Lila's mind was in turmoil. A sense of something
hanging over them, though he could not understand it. In
the dark house in the woods they were thrown into each
other's company without relief. What could they say to each
other? He found it hard to relate their shared past, those
dangerous weeks together, to this subdued house where the
analysts gathered.

When he asked to go outside the grounds MacPherson or
Helman shook their heads, then one of them said OK,

they'd bring the car round. The gates were opened and
Schiller and Lila drove out in a black limousine that he
guessed was bullet-proof and ran round the lakeshore drive
to Nyon, into the Juras. In the fields they were cutting hay;
bells tinkled at sleepy crossings and cats dozed in the
sunshine on porches, but, seen through the tinted windows
of the Plymouth, none of it looked quite real. Schiller had
the impression he was living in a story-book where the curse
of some ogre still hovered over the land.

It took him three days to get through to Sly Sylvester, and
ask his help. "I'm ready to get back to some work," he
said.

There was an awkward pause. "Look, Ed," Sylvester
blustered, "don't think we didn't want you. Hell, no, man.
But we also got a newspaper to run and that don't stop.
Remember, Ed, I let you go to Berlin, but that wasn't on the
basis that you fouled up with the Russians."

"All I want," Schiller said, "is somebody to get me out
of this goddam dump."

"Sure. Sure. But you got to do what they say. You are an
international incident."

"What's wrong with that?"

The line went dead, as if they had cut him off. He turned
in flat hard fury to Gus MacPherson, who was listening.

"I'm not on your damned payroll. Let me go."

MacPherson lit a cheroot, his small eyes twinkling. They
sat in the lounge, knee deep in newsprint—Ed had asked for
all the papers but there was nothing in them, nothing which
he understood.

"Who's paying you, Ed?"

It was a shrewd dig. Sylvester had not reinstated him. His
life savings amounted to $20,000 in a Washington account.
His effects, the notes for his book on Russia, were all
locked up in Moscow.

"I'll get work," he said. "As soon as I get home."

"Where's home now, Ed?"

The bastard was still probing, but Schiller's mind was
clear. "Where I can get a job."

Lila was somewhere outside talking to Yuri. The boy
should have had the biggest problems, jumping between two

cultures, two identities, and yet he seemed the most collected because the future held more. The bond between him and
Schiller when they talked sport and fishing, camping and
back-packing, grew steadily. Yuri wanted America, much as
Schiller wanted Lila. It was as if they were waiting all the
time for higher clearance, while Lila edged slowly towards
him.

On the sixth day she admitted that the past was over. "It
was no good," she said.

The television showed pictures of the French President in
Moscow, reviewing a guard of honor. Lila sat low in her
chair, small and delicate, her hair washed, her skin sunburnt.
He knew that she was thinking of Alexei Sergevich, and
stretched out for her hand. Her fingers curled in his,
small-boned as a bird's wing, and yet he felt the wires.

That night they kissed.

"I love you."

"I know."

Her bedroom was next to his, then Yuri, then MacPherson
as a kind of duty nurse.

"We can't go on like this," Schiller said, as they parted.
Again she said, "I know."

He waited until the house was dark, the maids had gone,
and then went to her room. The corridor smelt of dusty
carpets, the house seemed to wrap around him, disapproving.

She was awake in bed as he slipped in beside her. The
softness and warmth of her body overcame him and she did
not resist. At first she was silent, her arms about him and
they huddled together scarcely daring to move, in case the
fates should change. He traced the line of her neck and
breast and thigh.

"Lila."

"Eddie."

She had to hold on to someone, and he was there. The
bed was as big as a field in which they rolled; her body was
running warm. Afterwards they slept like children.

In the morning they had no secrets, as if a wall had broken.
He kissed her nakedness and watched her dress. He heard
her singing before they woke Yuri and walked together

down the staircase to the breakfast room which opened into a conservatory at the back of the house. There, as usual, MacPherson and Helman were waiting, poised over bowls of cornflakes. There was a smell of hot coffee and crisp rolls, and Lila and Schiller were hungry.

MacPherson for once seemed awkward, as if he had seen or guessed. His small head cocked on one side reminded them of a parrot, someone used to cages. But it was soon apparent that there were other causes: he had a dossier at his elbow against the toast.

Helman helped them to coffee, ambiguously polite. "Had a good night?"

"Great," Schiller said. "When do we get to go home?"

"Well . . ." MacPherson poised over his toast and honey. "I have some news for you."

Lila stopped smiling. The color had drained from her face as if she had been hit on the heart.

Schiller waited. "What kind of news?"

"I don't know how to put this . . ." tapping the packet beside him. "It's news about Alexei Sergevich."

They heard the clock ticking, the soft bubble of the percolator, something rustling the ferns in the glass porch beyond.

In a slow, small-girl voice Lila asked, "What about Alexei Sergevich?"

MacPherson sighed, adjusted his glasses, pretended to glance at his notes, but he knew what he had to say.

"I have to tell you our information was wrong."

"Wrong?"

He nodded. Schiller found Lila's hand but not her eyes.

"Yes. Our boys in Moscow picked up a false account."

"What do you mean?"

"I mean that Alexei Sergevich Barsov is very much alive."

Schiller looked, but Lila's emotions were frozen.

"Where?"

"We got the news from Moscow Station. KGB source, authentic. Relayed through Jubal Martin, who has his contacts there."

"Tell me," she said.

"Oh Christ almighty, no," Schiller said.

"I'm sorry," MacPherson stuttered, "but I don't make events. In fact we were told to hold you because there was a threat hanging over you: somebody swore to make sure that you wouldn't spread the dirt. But now it appears all that is changed. This guy Gorbachev moves the posts: he wants Barsov back onside. So Barsov is picked up and dusted down. The treatment has been reversed. I guess it was just in time."

They looked at Lila. Her hands were folded in her lap. Yuri's big eyes were on her, and she signalled to him, just as she had in Akademgorodok, before the final visit to Barsov.

"Leave us a moment, Yuri."

Obediently, the boy walked out through the ferns and into the garden. They heard him running on the drive, shouting to himself.

"Have some more coffee?"

"How is he?"

"Well . . ." MacPherson hesitated. "The fact is we hear he's much better. A kind of miraculous recovery. Everything seems to be changing . . ."

"Go on."

"I hate to say this but our source is authentic. Jubal Martin," he said again, as if that was a commendation, "Jubal says he's been told that there's been . . . ah . . . a reversal of policy. Barsov had a lot of enemies; it seems that all of a sudden he's got a lot of friends. The guys that locked him up have been put away themselves . . ."

"Well?" she asked in a whisper.

"And we're told he's been granted permission to leave the Soviet Union."

Only the plants were breathing, it seemed to Schiller.

"When?"

"As soon as he likes," MacPherson added quietly. "It appears that any day now he is expected in London."

36

Then Lila cried. A howl of betrayal, stunning, sad. Her world seemed to dissolve as she remembered, eyes on some distant mountain. Schiller knew that he could not join her: she climbed in her own grief. Instead he walked through the conservatory into the garden, where Yuri was kicking a tennis ball along the gravel.

"Hi," the boy said.

"Hi there." Ed, the surrogate father, beckoned him over, holding the return catch. Yuri trotted across, his face dark with concern.

Schiller threw the ball up and caught it, higher and higher. "You heard that? Your father's alive. That's big news, Yuri."

Yuri could not believe it. His mind had written him out, that creature in the cell. He stared at Schiller. "What does it mean?"

"It means he's alive and well, and coming out of Russia."

The boy turned, his eyes flooded. "He's dead."

"Apparently not."

That obdurate barrel-chested parent, ranting, womanizing and creating, had come back from the dead. Had he played with the child, talking and joking in that crowded room full of his books and papers? Or was Yuri just an embarrassment, a piece of the furniture? Ed had never asked and Yuri could never explain. The sight of his father's carcass on the soaked floor—Yuri could only believe what he had seen with his eyes.

"He's dead," Yuri asserted. "I saw him there."

He took the ball back from Schiller and threw it into the pines. Schiller watched him run away.

MacPherson was waiting, joined by a stocky woman, raven-haired and white-coated like a pharmacist, a duty doctor. The sun infiltrated the tree-ferns in the conservatory, creating an underwater greenness, a tropical steaminess, as they walked through.

In the breakfast room the table was empty, Lila's plate and cup cleared as if she had not been there.

"I've given her sedation," the woman said. "She'd best rest up for a while. News like that is one hell of a shock." Her eyes were on Schiller and he knew his visit to Lila had been monitored and recorded. It made him angry to stand before their tribunal, his old resentments, calmed and displaced by Lila, heading to the surface again. It was as if they damned him, under the guise of protection, making the shadowy, shuttered villa a sinister place.

"If Barsov really appears, you may as well go home," the woman said.

A deep sense of despair. If Lila went back to Alexei, Schiller was lost, there was no way he could recover. The blank faces in front of him, Helman and MacPherson behind his gold-rimmed glasses, the white-coated woman, seemed to be taunting him.

"What are you bastards looking at?"

"Just trying to help you, Ed," Helman murmured.

"Nobody helps except Lila."

The woman doctor said, "Easy, now. She's got a lot on her plate."

"Easy?" Schiller's mouth was a dry line. Then he began to fight. For Christ's sake why should he take second place to Barsov creeping out of Russia, half-crazy Barsov on some dispensation? Lila was her own woman, no more Barsov's than Schiller's: that very night they had made love, symbolizing her change and his possession. He had fucked her; fucked her. The soft body in her bed, his bed, their bed, that had opened to him.

They were staring at him; Helman, MacPherson, black-haired Dr. Carlisle.

"Don't do anything rash, Ed," MacPherson was saying.

They had no hold on him now, no undercover motive. If Barsov wanted, Barsov could tell it all, the whole shitty subworld of collusion, arrest and treatment condoned by both sides. The sands were shifting under the CIA's feet, just like the KGB's. He gritted his teeth and went to find Lila.

She was sitting on the edge of the unmade bed, her shoes off, her brown legs dangling. Last night when he had come to her it had been in the dark, but now he saw with different eyes. The coverlet was pink and white, pulled back from the crumpled linen, the furniture pale green wood, a thirties boudoir, inherited with the house, with flowers in cut-glass vases on the dressing table, irises and yellow roses. Her hair was brushed and glowed, framing the unlined face, that chameleon quality that switched from girlishness to maturity and back again.

"Well?" he demanded. He expected to find her troubled, but the eyes were serene, almost shining.

"I have to go back to Alexei, if it is true."

"Crap."

She showed no emotion. "That's not a very nice word."

He put his arms round her body, pressing her to him, kissing the top of her head.

"You don't love him. You told me that. You took me."

"It doesn't matter," she said slowly. "There is a . . . contract."

"Oh Christ, Lila. You made a contract with me. Last night you made love to me."

"I told you once, in Moscow, that people have needs." She gave a smile, half girlish, half courtesan. "It doesn't mean you possess me."

"It means I want you."

Her hand came up and stroked his face. "Eddie. You have tried so hard."

"And more."

"Go back to Nikky. And your son."

"I can't help them," he said. "I can help you, and Yuri."

She straightened her skirt and walked bare-legged to rearrange the flowers. "How can you help me now?"

"By taking you to America. Away from him."

She shook her head. "I had believed him dead. Now that he is alive I have to see him." She hesitated. "I left him to die."

"There was nothing you could do. And the marriage was broken."

"I am his wife still."

"Broken, I said, do you understand that, Lila?" She did not answer. He said again, "That union is finished."

"Yuri should have a father."

"He can have me."

A tinkle of laughter played on his nerves. It was not her natural tone but pressurized merriment, nervous bubbles.

"You have had me. Isn't that enough, Ed?"

"You bloody know it's not. I want you all the time."

"What do you want with me? What do you see in me?" She seemed puzzled. "I am skinny, I do not make love so well."

"I know. Small tits, brown skin, rough hands. Oh Christ, Lila, don't be so dumb."

Her eyes were round and wonderful. "What do you mean?"

"You have a choice," he said, "between going back to that drunken, overbearing, self-styled genius, or making it with me in a new place. A new place. Alexei Sergevich will take you back to the hutch."

"I ought to tell you to go. Leave me alone." But she made no move. He watched their faces in the mirror, his own tough visage flushed and frowning, trying to come to terms with Lila's struggle to decide.

The next moment she was crying, and he put his lips on her cheek.

In Moscow the facts were well established by Jubal Martin. The last ten days had been the busiest they could remember in the upstairs rooms of the Commercial Section. Martin had spent two nights there stretched out on a settee in the safe room when the news filtered in of Sherbitsky's fall from grace. Sherbitsky, the smartass who thought he could live off both sides: a muffled voice of protest, a straw in the Western wind. Sherbitsky who had sold out Barsov by letting the Americans know, as they drank in the bar of the Bolshoi, that Barsov was a wreck. Martin closed his tired eyes and felt the growth on his jowls: one of the girls brought him coffee and a doughnut. Antoly Sherbitsky was a fraud, a turd of the first order who had sold out on Barsov because he hated his guts, because he feared him. For

Barsov after all had talent, maybe he even had genius, while all Sherbitsky could muster was a crowd of time-servers. He had thrown Taylor Sheen that line about Barsov's whoring just at the time when Schiller had tried to get him out. It had all gone back to Langley and bitten the Calvinist conscience of Sexton Legros, head of the Soviet desk, who had shot out to Moscow like the jerk of a knee. Been talking in this very same room. Had countermanded the plan for whisking Barsov onside, and then disappeared home.

The result, Martin concluded, had been the kind of shambles you expected never to encounter. A Watergate of confusion, half-messages between two sides who barely understood each other. And that was only the beginning, when Schiller had passed on the message that Barsov wanted out. Jubal Martin chewed his doughnut, and scratched the rolls of his stomach. Events had taken charge of men, as they had a habit of doing. Sherbitsky could not know or guess that it would not be plain sailing: when Legros had ruled out a defection, Martin had dropped the soft touch to the KGB, and the Russians had shot up Heusermann and fucked themselves in the process.

Taylor Sheen came in, nosing around as always, after the old man's job. Martin jerked himself upright, pulled his shirt over his belly.

"Dreaming, Jubal?"

"Meditating." Jubal's hands were sticky from the doughnut; jam trickled from his mouth like blood. Sheen stared him out as if to say, "Too damned old, please take the one-way ticket."

"Barsov's arrived in London," Sheen announced. He ran his hand over his sleek hair, a gesture that said to Martin, "You're bald."

Darleen stalked in behind him in a sleeveless print dress that showed too much of her skin. Maybe she was after Sheen, Martin thought, who didn't take much asking.

"So?"

"So we got to take him off the Brits, get the bastard out to Geneva."

"What the hell for?" Martin asked.

"So's he can screw his wife." Sheen leered at Darleen, who tossed her curls.

"Don't be crude," Martin bleated.

"I mean it. Now that he's gotten out we must see if he's normal. Lila will kind of tell us."

Martin despised him in spite of his Ritzy charm. "You didn't think that way one time. You wanted the guy full of lead."

Sheen gave his silvery laugh. "In this game you try 'em all, as they come up. We got to be opportunists, eh, Darleen?"

Stubbornly, the older man persisted. "What kind of mileage you reckon you can get now out of a washed-up dissident by flying him out to Switzerland—if you persuade the Brits?"

"We'll do a deal. Take him out of their hair—for a rest cure. One of the three will blow: Barsov or Lila or our friend Ed."

"That's boloney."

"No, sir. Eternal triangle."

The usual green bottles of water were perched on a side table and Sheen helped himself. "Good for the complexion," he said.

Martin began to pull out of it. "OK. OK. You play it how you like Taylor, I've had enough." The turn-around had unnerved him, he couldn't read the signals when they came that fast.

Sheen laughed again, sipping the gaseous water. "You sound as if you feel like quitting."

"You bet. I've had enough."

"Don't take it so bad." Sheen raised his glass. "Mayakovsky's got the chop-chop too."

Martin digested slowly the news that he had half expected. In some small way he felt sorry, one professional to another, old men on old games. And at first the old games had worked, when Barsov was spirited away. But they hadn't reckoned on Schiller finding his way to the woman across half mother-fucking Russia. And meanwhile the times were changing, dissent was no longer dirty. "You sure?"

"Authentic, on the hot line."

"How come? The old man was well dug in."

"They've been through Schiller's flat," Sheen said. "He left them his stuff on Sherbitsky. So they hauled the gook in, and we guess Sherbitsky shopped the KGB treatment center, trying to save his own hide. Anyways the bastard's gone."

Martin crossed to the window, looked into the bleak well where paper lodged in the gutters, where it would lie undisturbed for six months until the snow covered it.

Schiller had shopped the KGB: he had to hand it to him. Mayakovsky, who had threatened a poisoned umbrella, the sudden shot in the night. With Barsov released and Mayakovsky on the skids, they need not detain Ed now. A sense of weariness sagged through Jubal Martin's veins. Perhaps he could forget them both soon, Barsov and Schiller, and take that retirement. He said, "You can let Ed go, then."

Once again Sheen smiled. "As soon as we get Barsov out there. Help me to squeeze the Brits, and we'll find out who's the winner, Barsov or Ed Schiller."

"Does he want to see you?" Schiller kept asking.

Irrelevant. She shook her head. "I must see him. You can't deny me that."

"For Christ's sake, what is he to you? I love you, Lila."

"I know. I know. But I have lived with him for ten years."

"Ten years of other women."

"It doesn't matter."

"It does to me. Do you love him?"

Very slowly she said, "No," as if it did not concern her. "But I must see him."

They had talked and argued and walked and fought for two days now since the news, and Schiller was unable to stop her. The barrier was between them again, the invisible shadow in her eyes, as if she felt her duty was clear.

He asked Yuri which kind of father he wanted. Yuri clung to his side. "You."

MacPherson joined them for meals, never letting them alone, as if they might cut their throats. They even went into Geneva, over the Pont du Mont Blanc and into the smart city streets to buy fresh clothes, with MacPherson as escort.

"Do you think I'm going to run, Gus?"

"That's not the point, Ed," MacPherson said. "We want your mouth shut." At the time Schiller did not understand.

The weather turned sharp, a bright blustery wind that matched Schiller's mood. He tried putting pressure on Lila through Yuri, who wanted to go away, demanding action, but Lila seemed to recede into the anonymous villa.

"Don't go back to him," he pleaded. "For God's sake don't go back."

They had driven out again, MacPherson at the wheel, to watch the lake in the evening, as if it could tell them something, the moon rising above the silver lines on the water. All journeys were exploration, any movement was better than sitting facing each other, waiting for Barsov in the interminable guest-house. Ed saw that they had joined together physically before they were mentally prepared, and he could not claw her back except by inarticulate warnings.

"I must give him the chance," she said.

Her feelings were unfathomable. What was it she had that he swam towards? Feelings for family, maternal or naïve, that he had never known? Loyalty or pride? She touched and turned and kissed and moved her head away.

MacPherson told him he was free to go when he wanted. There had been changes in Russia.

They watched the boats on the lake, seemingly going nowhere, glowing like circuses. Schiller said he would wait, if Barsov was coming.

"Alexei Sergevich must be allowed to see me," Lila insisted, "or I shall go to see him."

"I guess that's not necessary. The Brits have offered to ferry him out, provided we pay. He says he wants to talk to the boy as well. The guy's confused at the moment, but that figures."

"What will he do for money?"

The psychiatrist shrugged. "He'll get some advances, could be a slice of pension." He grinned at Schiller. "No worse off than you, Ed."

Schiller was equally trapped in this game of cat-and-mouse, but he would not give up. "I'll wait," he said. "It's him or me."

The moon raced in and out of fast, high, scudding clouds like a man seeking a fortune.

37

That night she locked her door. "Oh, for God's sake," he called as he tried the handle and heard her whisper, "No."

Schiller was angry. Now she had humiliated him, and he didn't care who heard, Helman, MacPherson, or any of the other shrinks, as he rattled the door.

"Lila. You must listen to me."

"No."

He stood in the passage cursing, swearing at women in general, at all cunts, furious, impotent. And he walked away to get drunk. MacPherson came and commiserated, supplying a bottle of whisky.

"You'd better let her go. Otherwise there'll be a crack-up."

"No way."

"We-ell—" MacPherson struggled with his spectacles "—don't push your luck. Look, you've got a big story. You need a job. For Christ's sake go away and write a sanitized version."

"Sanitized?"

"You know what I mean. No CIA, no Berlin. Just that you fell in love, obsessed by a beautiful chick married to a Russian nut. That's what they buy. The rest will follow. We will take care of her, I promise you. How's that: a bargain?"

"No," Schiller said.

Next morning Yuri walked in in jeans and a new blue shirt looking lost and lonely.

"Mama is crying all the time."

"She won't see me."

"I know. I tell her." His bright eyes were like a bird's.

"You know your father's coming?"

"That is why."

Yuri was already stateless. His pale hair was longer, flopping, making him almost girlish; apart from the obstinate streak he bore no resemblance to Barsov. Schiller wondered at the chemistry: Charlie was his own, and yet he knew Yuri better, and through him Lila. In their ways each needed the other, Yuri never more than now. He found that the boy had not eaten and they went down together to the breakfast room by the conservatory, where one of their minders, Helman or MacPherson or Carlisle, always seemed to be waiting. This morning it was Helman, tall and neat, his fingernails carefully pruned, reading the London *Times*. There was a picture of Barsov and he joked with Yuri.

"Your pa's had quite a reception. Quite a party."

The little boy's eyes flickered sharply from Helman to Schiller and back. His fists clenched and his face puckered while Helman stared.

"I hate him, hate him, hate him," he shouted as the tears came.

Helman was disconcerted. "Oh, come on, Yuri."

"He used to hit my mother."

Schiller caught Helman's eye, and he shook his head. "I asked her. Lila won't talk about it."

The measure of Schiller's disquiet was getting through, and Helman rose.

"Come on, kid. We've got some work to do." He hauled the boy off, leaving Schiller to wait.

Lila came into the room, still in the black dress, and kissed him briefly, but refused to discuss the night before. Each episode of her past was closed off from him, buried in lead-lined caskets.

He took her for a walk, down to the gates and out on to the main road. There was still a guard but nobody stopped him now, provided, as Helman said, he promised to bring her back. It was a sunny morning; the official climate was changing, the Russians were friendly again, Barsov was out and free. The tarmac shone as if washed. A side road led down to the water, about three-quarters of a mile, villa country, prosperous behind front gardens, their shutters opening. Walking with Lila reminded him again of those first strolls in Moscow, wrapped up like bears. At the time he'd not realized that he was falling in love.

The side road turned into a drive along the lake. They saw the complacent houses of Eaux Vives on the opposite bank: smug and neutral Switzers. He could ape them if he wanted, give her up, leave her to sort things out with Barsov, the boy no worse off than Charlie. And yet he could not. Thinking over the past he began to reproach himself about Charlie and Nikky, but Nikky seemed blurred against the woman beside him, flesh and blood, her hair the color of chestnuts.

"Please understand me. I have crossed Russia for you." It sounded so crazy and yet it was true. She had almost betrayed him, it had so nearly gone wrong, and yet had come through. Until the last twist of the knife, as Barsov re-emerged.

"I dare not," she said, standing beside him.

Now he was a true exile.

There was a small garden, neat as a pot plant, with public benches on which they sat together. He tried to mention their past, in Moscow, in Siberia, even that dreadful shack where the militia boy had died, but she denied him. Her eyes looked at the lake, hands resting in her lap, as if to say "no good."

Her solitariness, her fatalism, seemed to enhance her beauty. He pitied her but could not break through.

"If you go back to him," he asked, finally admitting defeat, "what will you do?"

"Whatever he wants."

"What guarantee do you have that he will stay faithful?"

She watched a pleasure steamer, heading towards Lausanne, white as a swan. "I do not know."

"How will you live?" he persisted.

"God will provide."

"I wonder."

He tried to kiss her. She did not refuse but she might have been a casual friend. Schiller knew his luck had run out.

Schoolboys ran through the flower-beds and hid in the

bushes behind them. He could hear their catcalls as they played hide-and-seek. He wanted to remind her that they too had played that game, in earnest with the authorities.

"You should not have tried," she said. "You should not have come to me."

"I had to." How thin it seemed.

Lila stood up, as fragile as a widow, in invisible mourning, her face like a stone angel.

"You must help me now," he said desperately.

And she would not believe him. "Ever since you appeared it has gone wrong."

"It was wrong long before."

Still she did not believe. "It was a fatal conjunction."

"Come in and hunker down," MacPherson said. "Drink?" He thrust a Jack Daniel's into Schiller's hand in the chintzy room they called a lounge. It had a pile carpet and unnecessary sideboards, with a big TV in the corner. Dr. Carlisle was there too, off-duty in a summer dress.

"Look, Ed. We got the Barsov video. BBC news interview."

Schiller accepted the drink as MacPherson pulled the curtains. Lila had asked him to leave her so that she could talk to Yuri, and he had complied. "I do not wish to see Alexei Sergevich's public statements."

They waited while MacPherson grappled with the VCR. Green lights flickered in the dark, and then the screen lit up.

It was Barsov all right, a strangely muted original. His large head seemed balder, greyish, the skull bones more prominent. He had also lost weight; hardly surprising, Schiller thought, in view of what Lila had told him. His big shoulders filled the tube, but his shirt collar was loose, and the great face seemed to sway on a stalk. They could see the hairs on his chest.

The studio was hard blue plastic, against which his head seemed to float. There was a woman interpreter and an academic from Oxford, who claimed to know his work. Chillingly Barsov said, in halting English, that he did not know why he was there.

The anchorman stroked his chin. He had a ceaseless smile and an irritatingly ragged moustache. "But surely you

wanted to come? You were trying to leave Russia when you
were abducted in Berlin.''

Barsov looked at him hungrily, visibly sweating. "So? I
thought I would be welcome. An artist wants space, freedom to write. Instead I was victimized.''

"Victimized?''

"I was kidnapped and then released.''

Schiller was watching the talking heads, finding it all
unreal that Barsov should be there, alive.

"Does Lila know what he's saying?''

Helman nodded. "She's got a transcript. She told us she
won't look. Not until he's here in person.''

It made Schiller gulp at the whisky and Helman refilled
his glass. Was there hope in that refusal after all?

The camera flickered back to the interviewer who asked
whether there would now be a sequel of *The Great Patriotic
Shambles*, and quoted the famous extract of the panic in
Moscow in the winter of '41: "The pestilence of authority,
caught in the shit-house with their trousers down.''

The look in Barsov's eyes was puzzled, wild, as if the
drugs were still churning inside that Neanderthal skull.
Schiller put himself in the KGB's shoes: the alternative of
killing him off was to let him rot in the West, away from his
cultural roots. And yet . . . and yet Barsov was still strong:
they watched him strike a clenched fist against the side of
his head, and growl, "Did I write that?''

"You did,'' the young don said smoothly.

"Running away, their balls were frozen.'' The old high-
pitched cackling roar that Schiller remembered. "I might
say that again. About the West,'' Barsov retorted.

"Are we running away?''

A pause, then the great head nodded. "You ran away with
my wife.''

Deep in the chairs behind them, Ruth Carlisle chuckled.
"The old boy's off his trolley.''

Schiller sat upright, tingling, hit by an electric shock.

In the studio in London, the anchorman knew that he had
touched the wound. "Who ran away . . . ?''

"Damn you. Cuckolded. My wife has been seduced.''

"What do you mean, Mr. Barsov?''

"God almighty, what do you think? Some obscene Yan-
kee was sent to lure her away."

"I thought you said that you wanted your family outside
Russia."

Another roar. "Of course I do. On my terms."

"Do you know where she is?" The interviewer seemed
uncertain, but Barsov was cruelly cunning.

"I'm not going to tell you," he said with glittering eyes,
some Ancient Mariner.

"All right. Then let's pass on. Why have you now been
allowed to leave the Soviet Union?"

"Because I was half-dead. And it suits them to make a
gesture. Human rights."

"Would you say you were maltreated?"

"I've told you they tried to kill me. My enemies there."
His chest seemed to swell as he rubbed a hand across it.
"But I was too tough for them. I hung on until they realized
my death would make a martyr." He had switched to
Russian now, and the interpreter translated.

"Why did they stop the treatment?"

"Who knows?" Barsov shrugged. "In a society where
fools preside, the orders can change each day. Maybe they
shot the idiots who were giving them."

"And then your wife escaped?"

"Escaped, no. Ran away, yes."

"And you think you will find her?"

The cold eyes in the timber of his face were staring at
them. "I know I will."

The camera held his head. "And then?"

Barsov swore, slowly, untranslatably. "And then I'll have
her," he said.

Helman leaned forward and clicked off the set. In the
silence as the picture faded Schiller was conscious that the
door had opened. As quietly as a ghost, Lila had come in
behind them and was watching. Somewhere a telephone
rang and Ruth Carlisle moved to answer it. Schiller held out
his hand and Lila sat wordless beside him.

Helman yawned. "Jesus. Nice guy. Have another one,
Ed?"

ˈ When Carlisle returned she seemed embarrassed. "That

was the Brits," she announced. "From Sackville Street someplace. They're bringing him over tomorrow."

They were solicitous, concerned, American, a powerful medical team, Helman, Carlisle and MacPherson. Schiller watched them in action with a kind of detachment, half understanding but no longer a part of that do-gooder naîvety. Like softball and ice-cream sodas it was something past and apart, a philosophy he had outgrown. He knew she would reject their help, just as she had gone from him.

"He may threaten you," they said to Lila.

"He won't hurt me, Alexei Sergevich . . ."

"You don't have to see him."

"I shall see him."

"But not alone."

"Alone."

"He may not be right in the head. You saw his eyes."

"I saw nothing," she said, "that I can't handle."

Schiller did not take part: he had come, he felt, to the end of the road. He sat on with MacPherson, long after Lila had gone, and drank more than he should. The moon was a piece of silver through the window.

Yet when he went upstairs to the shadowy corridor he found her there as if she were watching it too. Or waiting in the dream-space between their rooms, the no man's land, it seemed, that she had chosen for goodbye. For now that Barsov was coming, Schiller had no questions to ask.

"I'm leaving in the morning, Lila."

For a moment she made no reply. Then she held out her arms. In the half-light her face was lost but her cheeks were streaked with tears. He heard the short excitement of her breath as she opened the door to her room. "Don't talk to me," she said. "Don't speak."

She took him into her bed for the second time, but this was a different woman, not the soft embraces of their previous loving but a woman charged with a demon. He watched, stunned, as she stripped before him, tense but flaunting. The moonlight played like water on the shadows and valleys of her breasts as she came crawling. Desire overwhelmed him, then she began to undress him with practiced hands, pushing and pulling until he too was naked and her body was on his, dark hair cushioning the mount of her pubis as she rode him. He savored the sweat, the triumph, the tongue probing, the salt of lust in her mouth.

A crazy, creature, a woman released, wanting something he gave, taking it as if for the last time, as if time was limited in the darkened room.

They were on the white coverlet, moving, always her body on his, and always he felt the bones beneath the skin. He could not control or correct her, this was the way she asked, taking him, grinding her flesh. It was a long time before she cried but when she did the howl went up to the moon, the same strangled, soul-cry he had heard only once before in all their time together. The cry that was wrenched from her when she heard Barsov was living. She slipped away from him then, exhausted and wet with effort.

Lila lay like a corpse on the bed as he began to study her. A young girl's body, too thin, brown where the limbs had been exposed, the torso as white as wax and as satiny. Legs open, eyes closed, the lunatic coupling over. For a moment one hand grasped his, then she withdrew. He sat up and felt cold. Shaking, he pulled the coverlet over her nudity, and kissed her once. She did not open her eyes, the girl who had manacled him. He groped for his clothes and dressed.

His last vision of Lila was the tumbled, streaked hair on the bed, the cotton quilt tucked around her, sleeping the sleep of exhaustion. What would she dream, he wondered. Into the past, or the future? Would his face even feature?

He switched off the shaded lights and left her in the heat of the room. His body felt unstable as he came into the corridor and groped his way. The time was ten minutes to midnight.

Lila did not know it either, but another figure crept to her bed as she lay sleeping. Through the connecting door, the noises had disturbed Yuri, animals in the night, thrashing and chasing through a great wood where he ran. He woke up sweating and listened to them: the sounds showed that his mother was there, but he waited instinctively until he heard Schiller leave.

The house was a frightening place to a small boy after the

communal warmth of their tiny flat in Moscow, or even the
wooden bed by the stove in Madeniyet. He thought about
those places and the rough nights on the journey, hungry and
hunted; thought about the strange American who had been
so much a friend, and who had came and left in the night,
Ed whom he loved. At first, while the noises continued, he
went not to his mother's room but to the American's.

But Schiller was not there. So when the noises stopped he
opened the other door and crept back to his mother's bed.
He found her strangely heavy: still sleeping she pulled him
to her as if she could not remember him.

"Mama," he whispered, "he's gone."

38

MacPherson said, "Take the Peugeot. The firm will pay.
We've fucked you around enough. The least that we can
do." He seemed somehow tireless, still dressed and waiting
as Schiller came downstairs, and Schiller neither knew nor
cared whether he had heard their frenzy in the room above.

"OK."

"Know where you're going, Ed?"

"Anywhere until I'm sane."

The other man nodded. "Listen. Check in through Paris
first. You can get a flight from there." He handed over an
envelope containing an address and money, all ready and
waiting.

"We've got a place booked," he said. "You leave now
and you can make it midday tomorrow. There are maps in
the car, which you can sign off when you get there. Just take
it steady."

Schiller had slung a suitcase in the back, accepted a flask
of coffee and driven into the night. The amber headlights
picked out the bars of the gate when the duty man let him

through as if he was coming out of prison. Ivy glistened on the high walls and moths zoomed self-destructively in the beams. Then he was through, shutting the villa behind him, turning to find the frontier at St. Julien.

He crossed it in the dead hours, the sleepy customs post half-awake, and drummed the 405 towards Bourg. It was high country, twisting, close-shaved, and he concentrated on driving. The steamy weather threatened thunder and sheet lightning danced on the skyline, but the rain did not come. There was almost no traffic, only eyes in the road, frozen in terror.

At first light he came through a tunnel of leaves and reached the outskirts of Mâcon. The verges were yellow with drought. He breakfasted on fresh rolls in a roadside café with truckers and early-bird salesmen. After the despair of his last stand with Lila the outside world seemed relaxed, almost on holiday, and the coffee washed away his tiredness. By seven o'clock he hit the road again, and afterwards picked up the autoroute heading north for Tournus and Chalon-sur-Saône.

As the sun rose his exhaustion returned, the sense of a life ended, tasting like sand. The slash-slash of trees, cars, bridges played like a wearying tune. He was forced to give up and pull in, parking off the road and drinking the last of the dregs in MacPherson's flask. Only then did he realize how spun out he really was: his legs unsure of themselves, his whole body aching and old. In the heat of the day he stopped for a lunch of melon and omelette before pulling under the shade of an avenue of plane trees. In the beanfields beyond, men, climbed down from their tractors and curled up for a siesta. Schiller wished that his mind could die like the splutter of their machinery but the savageness of Lila's farewell left him no hope. Had he just been a fool, the means to an end, ultimately the passport to get her out of Russia? But he also remembered how they had begun. Try as he might he could not believe she had used him: he had offered her an impossible choice. All he knew was he was heading north, on MacPherson's instructions, where someone would see him home.

* * *

If he had waited he would have been staked out, for the villa on the Lausanne road had been discovered and by that same morning the world's press was at its door. The road outside the barred gates was littered with abandoned hire cars, and armed police from the canton had arrived to control them. For the secret was out: somewhere along the line Barsov's address had been leaked. The story had been put about that he was meeting his wife, brought out by the American agent who had wanted to marry her. Sex and spies were hot news for the London tabloids.

Helman phoned for reinforcements from the Marine Corps, airlifted in raincoats from Frankfurt. He walked down to the gates and spoke to the press tribe through the padlocked ironwork.

"No story here, boys."

"What is this place?"

"Nothing. Private residence."

"Who's it belong to?"

"A holding company."

He stood there in the sunlight, wrinkling his nose, trying to look less like a colonel in slacks and sweater.

"A U.S. company?"

"You could say so."

"Then why are they bringing this Barsov guy here?"

Louche young men with cameras, photographing through the bars the long view up to the house with Helman in the foreground looking annoyed. Good copy for the Sundays.

"You ask the Brits," he snapped. The bastards who leaked like a sieve. He was already enquiring how the address had got out, but that would be history now. There was a case on his hands and Golgotha rabble outside, trailing cables and cameras. Another one sauntered up, sardonically blowing smoke in his face.

"What's your name?"

"That's no business of yours, bud."

"We can find out through the Swiss authorities."

Helman muttered, "You do that."

They had the villa surveyed, and he doubled the guards in the grounds as soon as the reliefs arrived: the last thing wanted was some mother-fucker over the wall, caught by his balls in the ivy. Somehow they twisted things once they were on to a story, and the rest house was painted as a nest of intrigue. He cursed the unknown Sheen who had given it away.

"This Barsov bloke, why's he coming out here?"

"Who says he is?"

"We got the message in London. Private sources. He been deported or something?"

Helman snapped, "I've nothing more to say. This is a private residence," and turned his back on them, a back with a knife in it.

But the rabble at the gates camped out, awaiting the flight from London, building up the pressure. It could be a neat story, with the woman and boy inside: the first meeting since Moscow. A man called Hafizullah claimed to have brought them across with the American: an Afghan guerrilla in a hospital in Peshawar, care of the Paki army. The man was Ed Schiller, the Moscow hack for the *Washington Post*, and all the *Post* said was "no comment."

A telephoto through the gate took a long drop on the woman, small and straight, holding the little boy's hand.

"Where's the guy who came out with her?" one of the newshounds asked.

"What guy?"

"Don't bullshit. She had a male with her, came out through Pakistan. They got clean out of Russia through the mountains, with half the fucking Soviet army on the alert. Don't say you didn't know?"

"Not my business to answer questions, bud," the young Marine sergeant said.

"Then fetch the boss back."

He shook his head. "No way."

"What are you waiting for?" the local Swiss asked.

A grin like a comedian working up laughs. "Floodlights," the reporter said. "In case something goes bump in the night."

One night too late, as far as Schiller was concerned. Refreshed by a two-hour catnap under the trees, he pushed on steadily north through thickening traffic on long hot roads where each peel-off was an escape route he could not take.

Tired of the autoroute he turned off for a while and took the old road through Auxerre to Fontainbleau, slower, cooler and less used. It gave him a last chance to think.

Had Lila been nothing but a bad dream, arriving in a nightmare? Why had he first gone to Russia: because it had seemed an escape from his mistakes, Nicola and the marriage. His guilt about that relationship was as great as Lila's over Barsov. He had tried to answer a call, set up by Barsov, who had wanted his family free. Set up? Was that the truth, he wondered, as the trees drummed by. There was a pain in his mind, pain for what might have been. He could have got Barsov out, via Heusermann, if someone hadn't spoilt the act and caused three deaths in Berlin; if the CIA had wanted it, remembering Martin and Sheen and Sexton Legros.

He ran the Peugeot into a gas station and refilled, recalling the empty tank in the pig-swill pick-up. That had been the second mistake: going back. It never paid to retrack.

The attendant soaped his windshield, opaque with squashed insects. Families were going on holiday in the other direction, loaded with beach balls and camping gear, their back windows piled high with the detritus of living, and brats in the back seats licking ice-creams. Maybe that was his third mistake. He had not wanted Nicola to repair the family bridge, so he set off in the other direction—for a woman who had let him down. Lila had fallen from a pedestal of his own making, romantic, obsessional love. And left him without an excuse. She had fucked him like a tart.

The cars pulled out and left him alone on the forecourt. He realized the attendant was waiting and paid him with the French money so kindly supplied by MacPherson. Who the hell was paying him? Was he on a CIA payroll, or was it just to push him off? The last mistake, when he found Lila and came through, was letting them take care of the future, the Agency. But he had had little choice, coming across the war zone into Pakistan. At that point they had needed help, and the CIA had fed and watered: for their own ends. At the time it hardly mattered, but then had come the debriefing, days in the shuttered safe house outside Geneva. What had

begun as a rest, a time to make it with Lila and settle their
future, became a prison where even Yuri had asked why
they had to stay there. For his own safety, they said, or to
stop him telling a story. And then it had all changed. Barsov
was free to go. Barsov was on his way, and Lila had curled
up and died with that news. He savored her last goodbye,
exhausted on the bed, her hair damp from their loving.

39

The Hôtel de la Chasse was in the Rue Sèvres on the Rive
Gauche, a small street with one-way traffic. He noted its
name and wondered if MacPherson had a sense of humor. It
was a street of bistros and Chinese and Algerian restaurants
with aromas wafting from basements, reminding him that he
was hungry.

"*Oui, Monsieur, la chambre est toujours reservée.*"

It was all very neat; even a parking space in a courtyard.
He wasn't sure what he expected: an envelope, perhaps,
with more money and explanations, or a raincoated figure
with clearance papers to go home. In fact there was nothing,
except the weight off his mind at leaving Lila. Yet someone
was still taking trouble, and he felt a sense of surveillance,
examining the pre-booked room. No one should start a
game without knowing the rules.

He checked the furnishings over as best he could. Single
bed in the corner, table with its pot of flowers, freshly
picked, the old-fashioned wooden doors opening to the little
balcony. There was a desk and three chairs, a built-in
cupboard and bathroom. The carpet was new and fluffy in
ridges of brown and cream, the curtains were washed and
tied back to give a view of the street. Below him they were
getting ready, putting out menus and pot plants. He was
back in that reassuring country of normal lives, where dogs

watered the shrubs and families sauntered on corners. Paris in the early evening had an air of expectation: hard choices between *plats du jour*, the confident smell of fresh baking, students pining for affairs, comfortable Western values.

The long journey back had conditioned his mind: he no longer thought of a future, only of the next day. He had never persuaded Lila that he had a survival plan. He closed the windows to shut out the noises but they kept creeping through.

Not even sleep would come, only the churning of memories, and after a couple of hours he gave up and went downstairs. The narrow stairwell led on to a cluttered foyer where new guests were arriving. A tour party's suitcases almost filled up the space and he would hardly have noticed the newspaper in one of the window-seats if it hadn't been the *Washington Post*. Then he found himself staring at another face from the past that he preferred to forget: the groomed and scrubbed and pampered features of Taylor Sheen.

"Hi, there, Ed," he said. "I didn't want to disturb you, but it's great to see you."

He led the way with the old self-confident swagger that had put Schiller's back up when they first met. Across the little squares and corners where street-sellers called to each other, ducking across the traffic in the Boul' Mich to find a table in a brasserie, carefully selected. Everything about Sheen, from the lines in his hair to the cut of his new gray suit supported that impression of order, as if he had organized life itself. But Schiller felt the old alarms of rivalry and suspicion.

They sat and observed each other. Schiller didn't care what he ate, but Sheen took his time with his choices. Much of the meal was consumed in silence.

"What do you want?" Schiller asked.

That flashing, orthodontic grin. "Co-operation, in a word."

He ordered another bottle of Médoc, and made sure they were drinking before he enlarged. Then, waving his hand around, "I mean we don't want trouble."

Schiller's old truculence returned: Sheen could have guaranteed that.

"What about?"

The smooth face pressed forward, across the table. "We don't want a lot of stories about Berlin and the firm. You follow me?"

"It's dead. Old news."

"That's right, Ed. Or about Barsov, the snatch and the treatment."

So that was it. They were scared he would talk about Barsov, about the escape with Lila. He hesitated. In fact he could write a book, and now that Lila had gone, it might be the only way. But could love be exorcised?

Sheen refilled the glasses, sensing Schiller's unease. "It wouldn't be good for business if you wrote it up."

"Whose business?"

The eyes didn't match the mouth. "Let's say the new era. Glasnost and non-proliferation treaties. We're onside with the Kremlin. These days it's different."

"I don't see why I'm affected . . ."

"You should do, Ed. You're not that stupid." Even in the restaurant's privacy he lowered his voice.

"We helped send Barsov back. You follow me? We helped put him away, Ed. Then you went mad about Lila and saw the worst. They were hunting you, Ed, because we told 'em."

Schiller saw that Sheen had over-reached; but people would never believe him, never accept that the CIA and the KGB were brothers under the skin.

"You shit." He felt that the face in front of him, confident, shallow and self-centered, was everything that he hated about governments and affairs of state.

Sheen grinned. "Don't take it so hard. We helped to get you out when the game plan changed. They could have pulled you in Kabul, did you know that?"

"Changed?"

"Sure. These days you find good and bad guys in all systems."

"And I could name some of the bad guys."

"You bet."

"So?"

"So there was a change of heart inside the Kremlin and

Barsov was dusted down. And we had a change too, and let him come.''

''But Legros vetoed it.'' That man with the Indian face who had been at the second meeting in Kutuzovsky Street, straight from Langley, Virginia.

Taylor Sheen grinned. ''He was the big white chief.''

''Was?''

''Have some more wine? It's on the firm. Legros has stepped down.''

Legros gone too. Legros who had ballsed up the Berlin crossing and told them to sort out Schiller with the KGB. Legros and Martin and Mayakovsky, the old guard gone, the weather changing, Sheen said. He did not add that he was the real survivor, career prospects much improved.

Disgust filled Schiller's face. Disgust and a sense that he wanted to hit out, to sick it up. But to do that would mean admitting his love for Lila, and that was a passage so harrowing that he drew back.

Sheen pressed his case. ''So we don't want you to rock the boat now. There's a new climate, Ed. New hope. Perestroika and glasnost. Your kind of story don't help us, Ed, one little bit.''

''What do you want me to do?''

Sheen wiped his hands and ordered cognac. ''Do nothing, Ed. Do nothing. Go home and we will help you. Forget it ever happened, Ed.''

Stubbornly, Schiller said, ''I can't do that.'' Lila burnt too big a hole.

''We'll pay you, Ed.''

Schiller stood up. Sheen's arrogant face, flushed with the wine and food, was something he wanted to hit, to hammer those teeth through his mouth. Instead he simply walked out.

Sheen watched him go, still smiling.

Schiller strode back to his room. The meal had taken a long time and the lights were coming on in the summer twilight, normality returning in the busy streets. The foyer had emptied, the hotel seemed quiet and shut down.

But the room itself had changed. As he opened the door,

before he reached for the light, he sensed that change, a hint of perfume. The curtains were drawn, the vase of flowers rearranged, and there was a head on the pillow. She turned her face to meet him as he switched on the light. A small familiar face, paler and more worried than he imagined, her fair hair disarranged.

Nicola.

She put her finger to her lips. "Darling. Don't make a noise. I've got Charlie next door."

As she sat up he saw her shoulders and breasts under the wisp of nightdress.

"Charlie!"

"He's fast asleep."

Somehow nothing surprised him any more. He might have known from meeting Sheen that they would try all the tricks. What he had not expected was to find her so vulnerable.

"Please don't be angry."

"I'm not," he said. "Just weary."

"I know. And so am I,"

This was a more fragile woman than he had known. He sat on the edge of the bed and looked at her, asking the same questions that Lila had.

"Why had you come? Did they pay you?"

She was crying. There was a rapport between them that made him stroke her shoulders and pull up the sheets.

"They wanted to, but I refused. They gave me this address. And told me when you arrived."

"A guy called Sheen?"

She nodded.

So it had all been planned, down to the day of his departure, one woman to the other. It suddenly struck him as funny that they could be so serious, so concerned, about their stupid little policies, intrigues that kept them in business.

"What are you laughing at?"

"Nothing."

"Ed. Tell me?" There was a note of anguish, fear almost, in that question.

"Nikky. Not you. Why in god's name did you come?"

"You know why." She shivered and said, "Get into bed."

"You tell me."

The answer was short and simple, and yet it cut more than he expected.

"Because I still love you. And Charlie needs you. When I read the story about you getting out of Russia with that woman, I had to come."

The room had gone very still. He cried out for noise, distraction, the sound of a radio, anything to stop him thinking. If life were as simple as that marriages would stay in the water instead of hitting the rocks. But there had been Carlo and others, he had seen them there in the bed.

"How is Carlo?" he asked.

She was crying again. "It'll all over with Carlo. Long ago. You got to understand that. Carlo was just a mistake."

"Mistake. I caught you screwing him."

"Ed, forgive me. Forgive me. My past and yours are gone."

Silence.

"For my sake. For Charlie's," she pleaded. "Carlo was a shit. An aberration. I thought I was getting old."

He smiled. "Honey, you're not getting old. But you shouldn't have come."

She put out her hand. "I needed you."

He could have responded then, in spite of the accusations building up, he could have responded because he was tired, because she talked about Charlie, or even because she was pretty and wanted him. A sense of a tide returning, beginning to come back, from one coast to another. He could have climbed into bed and held her tight, forgetting at least for a while how far they had drifted apart, losing himself again in the closeness of flesh and blood, Nicola and Charlie, remembering the good times, the Christmases and Thanksgivings, the holidays in Virginia, sailing and swimming together. He could have put it all behind him in those hours that she offered, from one woman to another, East to West, and he wanted to and would have tried, until he understood the interruption.

The telephone was ringing on the desk.

He waited for it to stop but it kept on ringing. He would have left it for ever, but Nicole climbed out of bed and picked it up. He watched her silhouette, her figure as trim as when they had first met.

She knew she had made a mistake as she held the receiver towards him. "It's somebody in Geneva," she said slowly.

The fates shut in, and he felt then that they trapped him. At the other end of the line, MacPherson snapped, "Ed. We need you. Barsov's back and raging like a bull. He's tried to strangle Lila."

Nicola was holding him, begging him. "Ed. Don't go. Don't go."

"For Christ's sake. Get back here and sort these Slavs out. He wants to talk to you and so does she."

"Oh God, Ed. Stay with me. Me and Charlie."

It was Sheen again, he was sure, up to his dirty tricks.

"No way, Ed. This is for real. Who the hell is Sheen, anyway?"

"Listen, Ed," Nicola begged. She was shivering from cold and fear, and he still wanted to hold her, smaller, more uncertain than he imagined. "I want you back. Haven't I shown that?"

"Ed, you listening? If you don't come back, Lila will blow her mind. She has to see you, Ed," MacPherson urged on the end of the wire.

For the first time, Lila wanted to see him.

But Nicole was screaming at him. "Ed, you must not go. Eddie, no. It's a trap."

MacPherson must have heard that too. "Ed, don't play around. This is for real. She's sick. Lila's sick, do you hear?"

"I hear." He knew he had one more choice.

MacPherson shouted, "Listen, Ed. This is a serious request. If you wait you will hear her crying. She's begging you to come back."

Nicola's whole body was shaking. "No. No."

But Lila's hold was too strong.

"Tell her, I'm coming," Schiller said.

He put the receiver down and pulled his former wife back to the bed. She looked like a twenty-year-old as he tucked her up and kissed her. The first time that they had kissed for nearly three years, and he found that it moved him. But there was one last mission.

"I have to go," he said. "Stay here until I know."

40

The Villa Panama was stained with floodlights which transformed the ivied walls into stage backdrops. Cables littered the road and a gaggle of newsmen gathered outside the gates as he returned. In spite of the hour they seemed to be waiting for something as the police cleared a path. Schiller had come directly on the night plane from Charles de Gaulle and found one of Helman's people waiting at Geneva airport. He had been whisked away as soon as the aircraft touched down.

"What the hell has been happening?"

The driver was Swiss and surly. He shrugged his shoulders and drove like a bullet through the darkened streets, closer and less well-lit than the Paris that Schiller had left. The moon raced through fleecy clouds and the city had switched off. It was a warm night, but no one was sleeping in doorways.

They sped along the Rue des Alpes and into the Quai du Mont-Blanc, past the silent gardens and hotels. It would have been easy to think that the world had died but long before they reached the safe house he could see the glow of lights, and the swarming gendarmerie.

Then they were there, turning into the gates opened just enough to let them squeeze through. The plain-clothes men on duty looked mean and they were armed.

Under their headlights the trees were a paper presence as they skidded up to the front steps. He had never realized before how elegant the villa was: a large, correct, formal house, four windows on either side, balanced by dark blue louvres. Floodlights had been set in the road and pointed towards the façade, which was cream and cool against the night, classically composed.

MacPherson was waiting for him just inside the doors. He came across the black and white checker-board floor of the front hall with hands outstretched.

"Ed. I'm grateful." He put his arm round Schiller's shoulders and led him into the office, full of filing cabinets and unit desks. "Help us straighten this guy out."

"Where is Lila?" It was all that Schiller could say.

MacPherson smiled. "Sleeping, I hope. You can see her in the morning."

"In the morning? You asked me to come at once."

"Yes, because of Barsov."

They went to the big dining-room where he had sat with Lila, but the table was empty and the room seemed cold. One of the nurses served coffee, strong and sweet. Helman and Ruth Carlisle came in as if he had never left. Helman all stiff and silent.

"What has Alexei Sergevich done?" Schiller asked.

MacPherson said, "The press had come over from London because they wanted a story. When Barsov saw them he went down to the gates and asked them in."

"It's a free country."

MacPherson pulled his glasses down his nose and shook his head. "Not this bit of it. This is—was—a safe house. We don't invite people inside unless we want 'em.

"But Barsov did."

MacPherson nodded in an abstracted way. "I guess so. He went down to the gate and made a statement, roaring like a lion. And that crowd of newshawks lapped it up. He said . . . he said that he hated the world, that he was washed up, shot so full of drugs he couldn't think straight."

"Is that right?" Schiller asked.

"He's a pretty sick man. The Reds pumped him up good to pass him over and he's pretty damaged. His mind's gone wild."

"Maybe that's losing Lila."

MacPherson ignored him, intent on his own version.

"Said that we betrayed his trust. When he tried to defect, on his own terms, the CIA gave him away. He labelled you, Ed."

Schiller remembered the floodlights and the flash bulbs as he came through the gate, the shouts of "who are you?" They were being given a story.

"No way," he told MacPherson. "It wasn't my business."

"Well, maybe yes, maybe no. But he staggered down there and invited them in, Ed. Roaring and screaming at them that he'd been set up, that you sent him back to the cage by helping the KGB."

"It's not true."

MacPherson looked angry. "We can't have it said. It won't wash in public, Ed. Collusion's bad. Politically."

Schiller was tired of them. Tired of their glosses on history, and their intrigues. He didn't care a damn for Barsov; the early commitment had gone, replaced by a sense of guilt that was lapsing too.

"I only came because you said Lila asked . . . what the hell are you playing at?"

"Sure. Sure, Ed. As soon as she wakes. But come and see the old man first."

He led the way along an ill-lit passage to the back of the villa, a room that had once been a kitchen. A young man sat on a chair outside the door, which was locked.

Inside, the room was stripped. Again one wall the old black-leaded range was dusty with soot and debris. There was a plain deal table and Barsov sitting on a wooden chair, staring at nothing. It was the face that Schiller had seen, but not the eyes. They were like empty spaces in the great skull with its matted grey hair; enlarged vacant, doll's eyes in the alarming head. A growth of silver stubble, climbing high on his cheeks, was like an early frost, and the wide mouth was slack with dribble. But he knew Schiller without coming out of his trance.

MacPherson said simply, "He's come."

Schiller found another chair on the other side of the table Barsov's hands were dirty and smelt of excrement.

"I know." The voice was the same strange piping from the deep chest. He was dressed in a high-necked sweater grey-flecked, frayed at the sleeves, and creased, voluminous corduroys. One hand clawed and unclawed at invisible objects. The color of his face was beige.

"You took Lila," he said. It was hard for Schiller, a displaced person himself. Hard to look at this wreck, harder still to talk about her.

"I tried to help you."

"Help!" The old fury swept Alexei Sergevich's face, the bleak eyes turned to confront him. "Help!" It was almost a scream.

Schiller could not go on. Together they were lost, apart they might somehow survive. He shrugged.

"She doesn't want me." He heard himself saying the bitter words.

And Barsov charged. He lunged across the table, heaving it on to its side, his hands coming for Schiller's throat. The weight of that top-heavy body knocked the American backwards, his head hit the floor and he lay for a moment stunned. A great vision loomed in front of him, Barsov's face against his own, as fingers tore at Schiller's windpipe, a bloated obscene head, eyes glaring out of the skull, hot and sour breath of decay.

"Want you? You? You rat. I tell you something, I tell you this. I will kill her. She will come back to me, and mother me. She mothers me, do you hear . . . and she is like ice."

Schiller fought to tear away those iron hands, and he saw MacPherson running, jumping on Barsov's back, hammering the dome of his skull. Barsov's grip slackened, and the attack dropped off as suddenly as it had begun.

Gasping, Schiller swayed to his feet, leaving Barsov on the floor, squatting peasant-like and introspective. He growled in the back of his throat.

"Ah . . . ah . . . ah. What fools we are." The great hands pummelled his sides, tore at the strands of his hair.

MacPherson said, "I'll give him another shot," Schiller was conscious that the room had filled up. There was a medical orderly, then Helman, and another doctor. This place too was a treatment center.

"Ah . . . ah . . ." Barsov wailed. "She wants me. And those jackals at the gate, they want a love story. The whole world wants it." He shot a glance at Schiller, rational and suddenly cunning. "Except you, eh?"

For Schiller had lost Lila. He shook his head. More lights came on in the room. Somebody helped Barsov up; they righted the overturned table.

"She won't come with me." The words were bitten from him.

"Ha." Barsov's laugh was surreal, a grating devilish noise. He swung his arms round. "Fools. Fools."

"Come on." Helman muttered.

"You think I want her? Maybe I deserve her, eh? When she comes, I will take her, and we shall see who wins." He cursed at Schiller, sobbing and raving. "She stifles me."

They took Barsov one way and Schiller the other, and gave him breakfast. It was five in the morning, the clouds lifting over the mountains. It would be a day for picnics and summer outings, but inside the Villa Panama, darker than the *izba* in Russia, Schiller saw none of it.

No journey ends as expected, but this one had stretched his powers, shown what he could accomplish, and drained his mind. The CIA, monitoring everything, crowded him with bad advice.

"Too bad," Helman confided. "People just eat each other."

"What will you do with Barsov?"

"Christ knows. What good is he to us? Otherwise why let him go?"

"Will he recover?"

"Physically, it's possible. He's a strong guy. Mentally, I doubt it. Too much scarred. What will he write about, outside the system? Only what shits we are."

Hammering in Schiller's mind was the one reason he had returned. "I must see Lila now. If only to warn her."

Gus MacPherson said, "I've told you. Wait a bit, Ed. She's exhausted." He wanted to put it off.

Softly, almost to himself, Schiller added, "I do not understand her."

MacPherson was ruthless.

"Too bad, Ed. People like you and her are fated. You must know that. Better apart." He offered fresh coffee, along with a form of condolence. "You'd never make it with her. Not for a life, Ed. Do us a favor now. A big one, Ed."

Schiller waited.

"Help us with Yuri, Ed, and . . ."

"And?"

Even MacPherson seemed embarrassed. "If you want my advice . . . hit the sack with Nikky again. You got a son there, Ed. One of your own."

But there was also Yuri.

"Sure, there's Yuri too." MacPherson was defensive. "You want to see him now?" he asked.

It would be rough going. Schiller had come to love the boy as his own son and he too would be taken away, might even be at risk.

"OK." His mouth was dry.

Ruth Carlisle went away and returned in a few moments. Yuri was small and sad. His hair had grown and his round face seemed older, more mature.

He ran across to Schiller. "Daddy, Daddy. Take me away."

Yuri was a tough one, who had come with him all the way after threatening to shoot him. Now he was lost.

"Don't cry," Schiller pleaded.

But Yuri buried his head in Schiller's arms, and the American began to talk fast about all the things he could see in the some sort of life in the West: the football games, Disney World, real cowboys in the Dakotas, a long trip across the States to some new home. The trail could begin again, maybe he'd come and stay, and they would talk, the three of them.

There was a chill. A silence. He saw MacPherson freeze and felt the little boy shudder.

"My mother's dead," Yuri whispered.

MacPherson told him later. That was why they had waited. That was why the press had stayed. That was why they had decoyed him back, not to see Lila, but to take care of Yuri. Alexei Sergevich had been left alone with her, and those great hands had circled her throat. MacPherson said she hadn't screamed. It was almost as if she had willed it. Otherwise they would have heard.

Schiller had gone to see her. Her body was on the bed, in the room where they had made love, covered by a white sheet. Fragile, but also young, and at some sort of peace. The coppery hair had not dulled; the bruises round her throat might have been painted on.

He kissed her, and replaced the sheet. She was as clouded as alabaster, not real to him any more. He said goodbye.

The sun came out in the garden and he walked there, holding Yuri by the hand, trying to make up his mind when to telephone Nicola. It would not be easy. It would never be simple. They would live on the tops and the bottoms. They would love and hate each other, bound by the ties of experience. They would love and despair but they would never look back. They had two sons.